2084

Discovering Amblytopia

Paul Davies

2084

Discovering Amblytopia

Paul Davies

Cover by

Dean Stockton

Published by Bite-Sized Books Limited 2024

16 High Holborn, London, WC1V 6BX England

Registered in the UK. Company Registration
No: 9395379

ISBN: 978-1-7395253-8-5

Post neo-liberalism, post sado-populism, the unimaginably wealthy and powerful have created a global neo-age where need has been all but eliminated – so where is the human spirit now?

Contents

The Pulley

When God at first made man,
Having a glass of blessings standing by,
"Let us," said he, "pour on him all we can.
Let the world's riches, which dispersèd lie,
Contract into a span."

So strength first made a way;
Then beauty flowed, then wisdom, honour, pleasure.
When almost all was out, God made a stay,
Perceiving that, alone of all his treasure,
Rest in the bottom lay.

"For if I should," said he,
"Bestow this jewel also on my creature,
He would adore my gifts instead of me,
And rest in Nature, not the God of Nature;
So both should losers be.

"Yet let him keep the rest,
But keep them with repining restlessness;
Let him be rich and weary, that at least,
If goodness lead him not, yet weariness
May toss him to my breast."

George Herbert

Chapter 1

The noise in the pub was pleasingly raucous, despite the normal use of socio, though it was hardly full.

What was that phrase she'd read in that twentieth novel? *Was she on the pull?* She laughed at herself.

Emma Bartel experienced the time. She had nowhere she had to go and it felt good. It was getting on for nine. The night was young – and she only had to do what she wanted – no pressure It hadn't been a hard day – they rarely were. Perhaps it would be better if there were a few more difficulties.

So what should she do?

She looked around, not at all expectantly. It was just another Tuesday night. Over in the corner talking to some mates, laughing and in general rather careless, she saw a tallish man that she half recognised. She had seen him before and never really taken much notice of him. As she engaged with him fairly subliminally and studied him on her eyescreen, she suddenly felt rather alone.

And a little anxious. Why was that? She couldn't think of any particular reason. Back to the man.

Information about him flashed up. Not much older than her at 41. A writer – it said. Had been married and now in some sort of relationship, so perhaps now wasn't the time to learn any more.

He recognised that she was probing his details and he engaged her back. Bartel didn't feel at all embarrassed, though she was aware that she might have been – and she wondered to herself why that was. Neotiquette was difficult to keep up with. But in any case, if he objected, it really wasn't her fault. He hadn't turned his socio to lock for people he didn't know.

She sensed his message. "Do I know you?"

"I don't think so," she thought back. "Perhaps you should."

"Why?"

"You never know," Bartel t-replied. She daringly stroked his cheek through the socio. He looked surprised and then puzzled and then pleased. She turned her socio to bland, thought better of it and turned it to acquaintance and found his gentle probing something warm and unthreatening. That was a skill that not everyone mastered even with the recently updated neotiquette.

"But you know my situation," he t-said.

"Yes – you left your socio on acquaintance universally. Mistake?"

"I guess so," he t-said. "Not really. Serendipity."

"If you think so," Bartel t-replied. She felt his hand stroke her face, rather gently and rather enticingly.

"Perhaps I do," the man t-replied. He t-said his name, which was charming even if it wasn't actually necessary. "David." "David Worrell. How are you Emma?"

"I was just relaxing," she t-replied, "after a pleasant day. I saw you and thought I'd like to flirt."

"Yes – always good after a pleasant day," and his laugh rippled into her mind.

"And your current partner?"

"She's fine with flirting," he t-replied. He had sat down now, slightly away from his crowd. That was nice. "So you're an imagineer?"

"Yes," Bartel thought back.

"What do you especially imagine?"

"Experiences."

"I should just have probed that," Worrell t-responded. "But I always think it's good to ask. I know it's old-fashioned of me, but I find probes can be deceptive. It's good to exchange information sometimes. Do you agree?"

"I suppose it's a bit more romantic not finding everything out about someone immediately," Bartel t-replied. His virtual hand caressed her shoulder. "That feels nice. That's one of the aspects of the latest neotiquette that is still grey, I think, but it's ok."

"Not invasive?"

4

"Yes – invasive but not threatening," she t-replied.

"I agree," Worrell t-said. "I thought it was all right as you had touched my cheek."

"Was that invasive?" As she had t-said, the neotiquette was still obscure.

"Yes – it was. But not threatening," Worrell replied. "It brightened up a Tuesday evening for me."

"Can I encounter you?"

"That might be awkward," Worrell thought back. "I'm with my friends. Then I have to go back to Cheryl."

"Of course."

"But flirting is ok," Worrell t-said. "Ten minutes?"

"That's good." She wondered precisely what he had meant by that thought – but he was back with his friends and he had switched his socio to lock. She nursed her drink – and answered a voice call from Savery. That was unusual – but in the noisy pub easy to deal with.

"How are you getting on, Emma?" Savery v-asked.

"I'm fine Jonas – probably a little busy at the moment," Bartel v-replied. It was good to use her voice after the intense thoughts of the last few minutes but very unusual when it was so much easier to use thoughts. "Can I help?"

"I just wondered what time you were thinking of starting tomorrow," he v-replied. "I've got an idea and I thought it would be good to share it with you."

"Delighted, Jonas," Bartel v-said. "Quite early – I suggest. Say 10."

"Sounds good," Savery v-replied. "Encounter or engage?"

"As you wish," Bartel v-replied. "I guess we haven't met for a while and it would be good to have a bit of real contact."

"So encounter it is. Where?"

"You say," Bartel v-said.

"The Sensual?"

"I'd prefer something less intrusive," Bartel v-replied. "How about the Ascetic?"

"Suits me," Savery v-replied. "Thanks for talking, Emma."

"Makes a great change now and again."

She rather liked Savery for his enthusiasm and desperation to learn and to do. He wanted to achieve and in some ways he reminded her of herself some twelve years ago. She'd never been a Hedo, nor a Spartan – even loosely. Finding that right balance had been difficult and she knew Savery was having quite a hard time for some reason. Some of that insight that she had came from unguarded socio moments when Savery had not set his personal levels right or just not bothered. Some of it came from watching him and transposing her ideas on to him.

Another call and still no presence of Worrell and no thoughts either. It had been more than ten minutes – but Bartel was relaxed. It had been a fun exchange. She answered another v-call. Twice within minutes with voice was quite off-putting. "Hello, Andrew – can we switch to thoughts?"

"Sure, Emma," Pennington v-replied and then stopped. He t-said: "I haven't seen you for a week or two – wanted to catch up."

"I've been dealing with quite a lot," Bartel t-said, unconvincingly – to herself at least. She checked her socio. Set to Bland for Pennington. Thank goodness. It was still too easy to let one's thoughts spill over and unwittingly convey real thoughts. It must have been hell before those controls came in. "When were you thinking of encountering, Andrew?"

"No thoughts on that," Pennington t-replied. Bartel checked Pennington's socio and saw that his thoughts were set to Bland too. Should she read anything into that? Perhaps it was just being careful. "Be good to get together."

"Engagement? Encounter?"

"I think encounter," Pennington t-said.

"Ok – you can see my agenda," Bartel t-replied. "I'll give you clarity for my persono – fix a time."

"Sure, Emma," Pennington t-said. "Just remember. We have such good times together."

"Yes, we do have good times – but why do you say that? It sounds like you're not quite yourself saying that."

"Re-assuring myself," Pennington t-responded. "I'll check out the day and time for us to encounter. As soon as I can find a time that's convenient for both of us."

The engagement stopped.

Still no sign of Worrell – and then suddenly he was there in her socio. "Sorry about that Emma – took longer than I expected. Can we encounter or is that best left?" Worrell t-said.

"We can," Emma t-projected. "Why don't you come to me?" The engagement stopped and Emma watched as Worrell came over to her – turning back to dismiss what must have been some ribald comments from his chums – and then he was sitting next to her.

"Shall we ignore the socios and the personos and talk?" he t-asked.

"Good idea," Bartel v-said out loud. "I think it's fun sometimes to do without the *oh-so-valuable* Kaleidoscope products."

"You use their tag line with more than a touch of sarcasm," Worrell v-said. "I don't know what we'd do without either."

"In the old days they were apparently one – as I remember from history, the persono was a phone – you know a proper handset – and the socio was the social medium that ran on the phone."

"I don't know why we're discussing history," Worrell v-said, and laughed. "And you got the names wrong. It was social *media* they called it then. Not sure what the handset was called – but I've seen several in the Kalo gallery." He looked at her. "Maybe we should turn on the socio and get to know each other quickly?"

"I don't think so," Bartel v-said. "I think I've got enough information from your socio when we were introducing ourselves. Best to leave some secrets, I like to think."

And suddenly like sunshine coming through the clouds, they both laughed. "I don't think I've got that many secrets," Worrell v-said, ruminating and obviously taking the comment rather more seriously than it was meant. "Certainly none from Kalo."

"Who has?"

"Good point," Worrell v-said. "So why did you intrude on me?"

"I guess I was feeling tired and happy – and I wondered what sort of person you were," Bartel v-said. It was so good, as Worrell had suggested, to use words and not just probe.

"And now?"

"You know I'm not really a hedo," Bartel v-said.

"Spartan?"

"Not that either," Bartel t-replied. Worrell looked puzzled. "You don't have to be just either. At times I can be one or the other. Mostly I'm in between. What's the word?"

"It's a new category – I think," Worrell v-said. "is it serene? It's difficult sometimes to keep up with neotiquette and the constant changes that seem to occur."

"Yes, serene, that's it," Bartel v-said. "Though I don't feel that yet. Not that I ever will. Quite an odd name for that category."

"And now what?"

"I guess I ask you why you agreed to an encounter." Bartel was enjoying this meaningless exchange, because there was a light in his eyes that undermined his serious, rather bleak way of talking.

"That's easy. I liked the feel of you as we exchanged probes and I always think it's good to follow up anyone's probe. You never know where it might lead."

"Isn't that dangerous at times?" Bartel v-asked. It was always difficult switching from thoughts to actual voice, not only having to vocalise but you also had fewer clues as to how the other person was reacting. It nevertheless made it more fun sometimes.

"Not really in my experience," Worrell v-said. "It's knowing the limits and what you want."

"That sounds easy."

"I know what you mean," Worrell v-replied. Their conversation was becoming less forced and strange. "But we have to have an edge to our lives – do you agree?"

"I guess so," Bartel v-responded, "as everything is so much easier now we have socio and persono, and so many worries have been removed from our lives."

"We do have to thank the Trills for some things."

"I never see it like that," Bartel v-said. "I don't think about them that much. Do you?"

"More than you by the sound of it."

"Why?"

"I guess when I was growing up I felt so much that they were the good guys," Worrell v-said, thoughtfully. "Then in my twenties I began to think that they were taking away all purpose from our lives."

"I can see that."

"Then I started to think what that meant," Worrell v- said. "I mean – I think when that Trill – I forget which one – said that we make our own purpose, I realised that she was right. Do you remember who that was?"

"Elora Ghose."

"Of course – Kaleidoscope," Worrell v-replied. "Do you agree with the idea she was putting forward?"

"Sometimes," Bartel v-said. "That's me all over, and I try not to come to definite conclusions. I don't know about the Trills. They seem benign but there's always a lingering doubt."

"They encourage that too," Worrell v-said. "*Never take anything on trust.* Isn't that one of their sayings?"

"But I don't think they are just one group with one mind," Bartel v-said. "You know they disagree on lots. Mind you that could just be the usual gossipy stuff that they put out on the weeds to deflect from thinking about what they're really like. I guess none of us would know what was even the slightest bit true."

"That's right," Worrell v-said.

"But I'd like to think that there are tensions between them," Bartel v-said.

"So would I, but hey – we're getting a long way from the point, don't you think." It wasn't a question – more an instruction. "Could we turn on our socios?"

"Why? I was enjoying this."

"You'll see," Worrell v-said. That was, as always, an exciting phrase. Bartel had loved when that came in as a shorthand in neotiquette.

"Ok." They thought their socios on – and had that initial warm glow that Kalo had built into the system as part of their marketing. *Turn on, tune in, take pleasure.*

Bartel remained passive and let Worrell probe and she let him wander through a few more of her inner thoughts and feelings by relaxing her control to friend. Then he relaxed his level too and she probed, thinking through his relationship with Cheryl, while he thought through her break up with Joe. At this level of course there was nothing really embarrassing on either side. As usual she was fascinated by what was not apparently thought on his side. There was no mention of how he and Cheryl had met and how long they had been together. Their feelings about each other weren't there either. On Bartel's side she was well aware of what wasn't there in a readily accessible form to anyone else. Especially that the trigger for the collapse of her relationship was nothing to do with fidelity, honesty or lack of mutual interests – just a persistent awareness of each other as irritating and annoying and somehow not relevant to what the future might hold.

As Kalo – Kaleidoscope – made clear this was so very late-21st century – with human responses no longer constrained by 20th century issues.

Kalo's tag line always made her wince – *think don't act.* It really meant nothing as most of Kalo's slogans did too, but it was touted as a new way of looking at relationships. It was useful sometimes.

She felt his virtual hand on her shoulder and she thought her hand on to his cheek. It was a delicious moment – and quite unexpected. Not blocking his hand-thought was conscious and she loved the fact that he didn't block her hand-thought either.

"Shall we go outside to the pub garden?" he t-said.

They got up and remained locked together through their socios – not exchanging thoughts but sensations of excitement. They moved to the far end of the garden, through several couples and several groups to stand in the warm glow of the mild light. Bartel took his hand properly and pulled him to her and they looked into each other's eyes, feeling the other's subdued but undoubted excitement. Bartel probed and he had been correct – Cheryl didn't have any objection to flirting and the limit of that was defined carefully. He put his arms around her and slowly and gently pulled her body against his, while she did the same to him. His lips moved closer to hers – and then they were gently, very gently, kissing, and while it was the simplest of actions, it felt exciting and lovely.

"Wow, Emma," Worrell t-said. He looked deep into her eyes. She could feel the strength of his physical and mental reaction and he could feel hers.

"Yes. Yes," she t-said. "That might convert me to a Hedo."

They kissed, again with the softest touching on lips while intensely feeling the physical and their thoughts. "What on earth had it been like before socio?" Bartel thought to herself. *It was now such a different world.* Then another thought: *What would Cheryl make of the thoughts about this encounter? It was obviously still within Cheryl's set limits and Cheryl would be able to detect the excitement and the pleasure.* This latest tweak to socio, where you could have side thoughts that were invisible to others, was so liberating. Almost a return to pre-socio.

"Is this still ok?" Bartel t-asked with a probe.

"I think so." Worrell thought deeply back. "In theory yes. In practice because it was so amazing – I don't know. I'll have to ask as she'll probe when I get back."

"Yes. That sounds right."

"Will we encounter again?"

"I think that depends on Cheryl rather than you and me," Bartel t-replied.

"I guess you're right," Worrell t-said. "Do you want to feel more about Cheryl and our relationship?"

"Not at this moment," Bartel t-replied, letting her thoughts run away with her. "Let's see what she makes of this – and then if we encounter again, I'll let you know."

"Fair enough." Worrell t-said to Bartel, rather deliberately. Then he t-added: "How are you getting home?"

"An autonom." Bartel thought back, then added, "As usual."

"We'll be in thought then."

"We will," Bartel said. As he left she physically touched his face again and he stopped and looked back into her eyes and held her hand. The two of them lingered, with apparently empty thoughts. But happy.

Chapter 2

Gentle thoughts massaged Bartel into wakefulness. She had set the alarm for 8.30 – and she came into her thoughts in the most subtle way.

Kalo thought of everything and had transformed waking into a lovely experience, even early in the morning. Her socio had slowly at first infiltrated her experience of that kiss last night into her dream state and gradually made it more physical and real so she woke to feel that excitement that had rather taken over her mind and body last night.

It was beyond doubt the best way to wake up. She sat up and held her right wrist over the R button on her bedside table. No doubt Kalo would fix this small inconvenience in time – but the ten seconds to recharge her persono and get her socio fully capable was hardly a problem. Her eye-screen told her it was all fully charged up, and she sat on the side of the bed, briefly gathering her thoughts and letting the persono know what she wanted to focus on today.

One thought kept coming back to her and she locked down her socio so she could think it through, *as privately as possible.* That was a good Kalo phrase. Pretty meaningless but it felt important to have that level. She remembered that Worrell had touched on creating meaning in life – something that Bartel rarely thought about but which had been very strong as a thought when breaking up with Thornton.

At that last encounter with Thornton – no shouting, no anger, no recriminations – there had been a feeling of emptiness in her and when he had finally left she seemed purposeless and meaningless even though he had never brought much purpose or meaning into her life. Even focusing on her work had not felt right – though she was privileged to have that role. It was not something she had to do any more than anyone else had to do anything, but it felt creative and full of satisfaction especially when she had imagined a new type of experience for a particular person.

But for the first time for years – the last time immediately post Thornton – s e had felt really disturbed last night and strangely uncomfortable and unable to concentrate and relax.

She removed the lock from her socio levels, re-instating the different levels for different people. She probed from her socio to her children. They were very close to her and never far from her socio even at 18 and 19.

Kalo had been so right that having children young, especially now that everyone had socio, was the right answer. With work being what it was anyway, getting the balance between it and caring for a family had been so easy from the moment that socio was shared with each of them. Roseanne and Alice had their own lives but they were intertwined with hers in a way that pre-Kalo was unimaginable. Roseanne came back with her thoughts almost immediately and yet her level was set to Bland, so there was something going on in her life. That was a relief as she was so often such a solitary person, rather like her father. She got one thought back from Alice: *fine.* She was with her at Relaxed in her socio, so Bartel wasn't going to probe deeper. She shared more feelings with her than with Roseanne and always had done, and since she shared more thoughts it meant that when Roseanne was not communicating there was a reason.

She probed for Thornton and he came back immediately and, as usual, quietly and amiably. He thought that Alice was having a bit of a hard time for some reason. He wasn't sure why, but he said he was in thought with her. Funny how Thornton, even though they had had those years as husband and wife, was usually still very formal with her. It turned out that Roseanne was in a new relationship – but she was being locked down about it. Thornton said he was comfortable with it and as he was closer to Roseanne than Bartel she let her mind relax. They exchanged a few pleasant thoughts and Bartel was glad that he was the father of her children and that they could still have thoughts in common. They didn't share their lives and they both kept the other at a low level, usually Bland but sometimes Acquaintance and even occasionally Friend, yet there was a fellow feeling in all they did and thought.

Bartel wasn't one, she had realised early, for longer term meaningful relationships.

She stopped that train of thought – *meaningful* again.

Bartel shook herself. Time was marching on. What time was she due to encounter Jonas Savery – and instantaneously she knew. How long would it take her to get to the Ascetic? Five minutes by autonom and fifteen minutes walking. That was best.

She probed Jonas. He was going to be early he said. She responded that she'd leave for the Ascetic now and got herself together. She briefly consulted her persono and there was little outstanding to be done. Just creating an experience for a couple who had said that they had started living together and were finding it difficult to adjust. That was Bartel's favourite type of task where the experience had a purpose, but there was something that didn't quite fit this picture when she had actually met the Tomlinsons.

At this moment she had no idea what the experience would be and she left it in her subconscious to come up with the right answer.

She walked briskly to the local Ascetic – a rather bare and stripped down place as the name suggested and difficult to define. It reminded Bartel of places she had seen in films taking place in twentieth high streets, but because you could get a whole range of drinks and substances it was similar and yet very different. The ambience was always minimal and it helped to meet there when it was important to concentrate.

Some people preferred using one of the Sensuals but for Bartel the softness and relaxed atmosphere were counterproductive.

"What'll you have?" Savery v-asked as she sat down opposite him in a well-chosen corner.

"I'll get them," Bartel v-replied. Savery was very proper with her and it was a kind of sensitivity in him that Bartel liked. It was more normal to use t-comms but it could feel too personal and invasive to start like that in a business meeting. "What do you want?"

"I'll have some space and a coffee – Columbian and milk," Savery said.

"Not too early for space? Or something stronger if you need it?" Bartel asked, smiling to make sure it didn't appear censorious. Making overt judgments either in v-comms or t-comms had become the height of rudeness over the last year, and it was still recent enough in the neotiquette for it to be tricky to navigate through. Bartel was certainly quite nervous about using the right tone.

"No," Savery v-responded.

"Shall we switch to t-comms?"

"Yes – this place isn't conducive to v–comms with its echoing sounds," Savery t-replied. He relaxed.

Bartel ordered the right gSynth output for Savery and got for herself a strong coffee from the gSynth. The andro was pretty curt with her and she wondered who had imagineered this experience. It was worth thinking about because though it was annoying it was also re-assuring and reminded her that most of what happened these days was more carefully thought through than it could ever have been in the past.

Some people still declared they could tell the difference between whatever was meant by real and gSynth, but since it was all at a molecular level these days, it couldn't be true.

She brought it back to Savery and just waited for him to think towards her. He seemed reluctant to start for some reason, so she t-enquired: "What's this idea you had?"

"I don't suppose it's that good," Savery t-replied. He'd set his socio to Acquaintance, which interested Bartel. Perhaps he was hiding something.

"Never mind. Just think it."

"Yesterday when we were brainsharing, I wondered whether we could be a little more adventurous in the type of experiences we were imagining."

"What do you mean?"

"We seem to have got a little stuck in a rut," Savery t-responded. "I'm not sure how fulfilling that is."

"Explain."

"I'll try," Savery t-said. Perhaps the cold light of day had turned his golden idea into rust. "Now we don't need to go anywhere in particular to be somewhere, it seems to me that we're missing part of the experience. I think we should focus more on the journey."

"But we don't have to as VR does all that."

"But we don't pay enough attention recently to that," Savery t-declared. "You know that bowling alley experience, where it's possible to score strike after strike?"

"Yes."

"What if we added the journey in, so we have anticipation, and then add a randomising factor into the scoring?"

"I'm sure we've tried that," Bartel t-said firmly. Then within her socio blocking, she thought about where this was going. His thoughts were hardly earth shattering or that novel. This wasn't the point, obviously. There was actually something other than this on his mind – even if his socio level blocked her from finding out. "What are you trying to achieve, Jonas?"

"That's the point," Savery t-said. "What is the point? I don't know what we are trying to achieve."

"So it's not an issue with what we were doing yesterday?"

"No – you're right," Savery t-responded. He seemed really upset. "I don't think I understand anything at the moment."

"About yourself or us or what?"

"All of the above," Savery admitted to them both.

"No wonder you wanted space," Bartel t-said, and realising that this thought was too unkind, added: "this is a bit of a cross-roads I think."

"Between what?"

"Between nothing – but it is a sort of dangerous realisation – potentially," Bartel thought to him. "How deep is this problem?"

"Not so deep. I just got lost yesterday and I've been lost ever since and I thought you might be able to help me."

"In what way?"

"I don't really know what I'm doing – I mean I don't really know where I am going or whether I would know when I got there."

"This is hugely philosophical, Jonas," Bartel t-replied, really struggling to know what he wanted. "Are you sure you want to discuss this now?" It was unusual to have two encounters so close together apparently wondering about meaningfulness. When she thought about it, however, she knew it was becoming more common.

"I honestly don't know, Emma," Savery t-said. "Let me change my socio level to Friend – if that's not too invasive – I mean revealing. Now feel this, Emma. Can you see the problem?"

"I can, Jonas," Bartel t-said. His socio was a mass of conflicting ideas that he wasn't bothering to control. "I think I have to say calm down. I know that's the last thing you say to someone who is agitated. It just feels too much. I think you should take me back down to Acquaintance before we both get swamped in feelings."

"I have." The cacophony – everyone knew it wasn't the right word but it fitted the bill so was still used – was quieted, which Bartel found a relief.

"Would it be better to do this with v-comms?"

"Why?"

"There is more chance to consider what you are really wanting to say – I know that you don't actually know what that is, but it has to be different from these contradictory feelings." Bartel was worried, not by Savery but for Savery. She remembered she had had a similar sense of emptiness when she was perhaps a little younger than Savery, shortly after the beginning of her relationship with Thornton. It's what Kalo in its wisdom labelled a surfeit.

That feeling of having so much you don't know where to start which is then followed by a questioning of where there was a point in life.

Knowing Kalo it was a wonder they didn't call it a *surfei*to.

"Good idea." Savery switched to v-comms. "Have you ever felt like this?"

"I don't really know how you are feeling," Bartel v-said, avoiding the subject, for reasons that she didn't quite understand herself. Then she came to the point: "We can have all sorts of emotional responses to how we live now. It's difficult to identify any particular one from what you've said."

"I just feel that I enjoy what I do – actually what we do together – but I don't know where it's heading and what's the point."

"Right," Bartel v-said. Voice was better for this – something that Kalo would deny vehemently. "And, yes, I have felt similar things. You know when there are few pressures on you except those that you create yourself for yourself, it's very easy to lose sight of who you are and what you are achieving. So I have felt what you're feeling now – only too well. If that's close to what you are feeling."

"That's very much it. And now?"

"Not at the moment," Bartel v-said. "but it's not a one off sort of feeling. I know it's no comfort but this feeling will pass. Once you have less time to think."

"Is that all it is? I don't think so."

"I think it is." Bartel sounded as sure as anything because she was sure. "But that doesn't stop it being a real feeling at the time."

"How did you get out of feeling the hopelessness – sorry, I mean, meaninglessness – of our lives?"

"It's not easy." Bartel tried to look thoughtful as well as sound it. She knew how serious a quandary Savery was in. "I'd usually say – throw yourself into the present. But that's not really the answer."

"I think I am too much in the present in any case," Savery v-replied. "Look none of us has to worry about much nowadays, because the Trills have got it sorted. Their trillions have provided the answers. We have gSynth for food, we have places to live. We have resources that we need and usually that we want. We always have socio and persono. All good things. It goes beyond what was called a *welfare* society. But am I right to feel smothered?"

"No – that's not a good feeling." Bartel thought deeply and was so glad that they had switched to v. "Perhaps think of it like this. You've been freed from what has held humanity back for so long." Hell – she was parroting Kalo's latest advertising. "It's inevitable that once the struggle for existence had been removed as an issue, people lost and lose direction," she added.

"I do know that, Emma. I just felt despair."

"Yes," Bartel v-said. "That's perfectly normal. But has anything else triggered this?" Bartel really felt uncomfortable giving any sort of advice and doing any sort of probing but as it was v-comms she could relax as Savery would only tell her what he wanted to divulge. Socio was rather more revealing even when set to lock, because brains inadvertently went off subject. She really didn't want to know too much about Savery.

"Incidentals, I guess," Savery v-said after a few moments.

"Incidentals?"

"I've been having some relationship issues," Savery v-said. "I guess that hasn't helped." That was Bartel's signal to back off. She said nothing. "I guess that's not a subject we can or perhaps should discuss."

"No," Bartel agreed. The protocols which followed early scandals around socio information meant that anyone in a work or quasi-work relationship didn't touch on such matters.

"I wish we could, Emma."

"Why?"

"I've no one else to have v-discussions with." It was a bleak answer.

"Yes – but explicitly not wise," Bartel v-said.

"But not forbidden."

"Nothing is forbidden, Jonas," Bartel v-said. Hell – she was just repeating Kalo's messaging.

"I know." Silence. "Do you know why we shouldn't discuss this type of thing. I feel desperate."

"I guess it's because of what it could lead to."

"But that is up to us. I suppose we ought to address the opportunity we've got."

"I don't think I'm much help, Jonas."

"I guess not," Savery v-said, "but just being able to encounter you about it has sort of helped. It's given me a perspective. Can we switch to socio now?"

"Ok," Bartel v-said. "But why?"

"I want to feel a bit closer to you," Savery v-said, with the sort of honesty that Kalo encouraged.

They switched to socio – and Bartel set her level at friend and immediately Savery did the same. She could feel the intensity of his thoughts as a surge of feeling, without actually getting them in any sense clearly. He was in turmoil. "You really are in a state, Jonas. Aren't you?"

"Yes – words can't convey that confusion I feel."

"Would it help if I touched your face?"

"I think so," Savery t-said. And he could feel the t-touch of her hand on his cheek. It was comforting and he asked back if he could touch her face.

"Sure." He felt her feelings as he t-caressed her cheek. It never surprised him that, as usual, while they were doing this, their eyes were open and they were looking at each other. What did Kalo call it? *Consensual Sensuality*. It was an amazing experience, sharing not only one's own sensations but to whatever degree, the other person's.

Bartel could feel him calming down and she relaxed into his thought caress. "It's strange, is it not, that this doesn't go against our neotiquette?" Savery t-asked.

"I think it is different – but not sure why," Bartel t-said. "No. I can't work that out. But I understand why you wanted that t-caress."

They sat opposite each other with their minds in some sort of sync, enjoying a moment of calm together.

"Shall we leave the Imagineering today?" Bartel t-asked.

"Is the client pressing for an experience?"

"No," Bartel t-said. "She – or really they – are very relaxed about it. I think, despite what they overtly requested, they want to have something out of the ordinary to impress their friends – and there isn't any hurry."

Silence and, in that word taken over and given a new meaning by Kalo, thoughtlessness.

"Can we stay like this for a bit longer?" Savery t-asked.

"Yes – that's fine."

"Is it odd how the physical takes over and we lose the mental?"

"That's very Kalo," Bartel t-said. "Would you believe that before socio the physical was frowned on and was really the subject of censure?"

"I remember that – but only just," Savery t-said. "I think that's right. With socio, feelings and thoughts have become potentially more available, so of course they are more important." He was really thinking to himself but it was shared. "Do you want any more stimulus?"

"No. I was just thinking whether to have some coke but I don't need it – and when I don't need something, I don't want it. Do you?"

"I had the space," Savery t-replied. "I think I am where I want to be. No. I still feel that edge of pointlessness. Of course I do. But I think I have it in perspective now. Thanks to you, Emma."

"Why don't we walk a bit?"

"I'd like that," Savery t-replied. "And perhaps think through some ideas?"

"If you like," Bartel t-said. The Kalo response of choice, she thought wryly.

They left and started walking firmly but rather aimlessly. That was all right – and there was a background socio chatter between them which was just random thoughts.

Then something odd. For a moment Bartel was affronted and didn't know immediately why. Then she did: "What are you doing?" Savery was probing areas of her socio that were off-limits.

"Oh – I am really sorry," he t-said. "I just relaxed and wondered what you were thinking and the socio took over."

"Just be careful," Bartel t-said back. "Look – I know it's easy to do what you just did, but don't. If I want my socio to be more open, I will let it. Probing aggressively like that is just not on in this circumstance."

"I'm so sorry – really I am." Savery looked at the floor. "I know the neotiquette. I won't let myself do that again."

"Ok."

"You sure?"

"Yes, I am sure, Jonas," Bartel t-replied. "It's particularly an invasion if you use our encounter and virtual touching as a pretext for a probe."

"I wasn't doing that – I was really not taking care," Savery t-responded. He was mortified. T-touching was fine and had become part of the normal, but probing at any level of socio was something to announce and not just let happen.

They lapsed into thought silence.

Then Savery posed a thought: "If you have forgiven that probe – what did you make of last week's political statements?"

"On what?"

"On the new rules about use of gSynth," Savery t-said.

"I didn't take much notice," Bartel t-replied honestly.

"I thought it was very interesting," Savery t-said.

"I don't pay much attention, as I said," Bartel t-replied. "I find all politics pretty meaningless now."

"I know. I just thought that putting the concept of waste at the heart of the new approach was good."

"I guess so."

"It's so easy to imagine that gSynth is limitless," Savery t-mused.

"Yes," Bartel replied.

"And it is as finite as anything else," Savery t-said.

"You're sounding religious on me now," Bartel t-replied. "I can't keep up with the new religions."

"It's nothing to do with that. Just a call to be more conscious of everything."

"That's never a bad thing. But I can't always see where politics ends these days and religion takes over. Remember the last winning slogan – *have faith*? That struck me as really close to the mark."

"Emma." Savery t-said, interrupting her. "Thank you."

"That's ok, Jonas. I've often been where you were earlier. Remember that Kalo tagline – *Just Enjoy*? I know we all make fun of Kalo – but sometimes there's a real message that's worth taking."

"You seem to take everything you say from Kalo – do you value them above Gyroscope?" Savery t-enquired.

"Not really," Bartel responded, "I just think that Kalo has a way of encapsulating thoughts so much better than Gyro. They're both clever and the Trills behind them have something obviously. I guess Gyro is the more important for its products like gSynth – because without it we'd still be farming like they used to. But for marketing it's Kalo every time."

"Good points."

"Look let me give you a t-hug now – and I'll have a t-stroke of your face," Bartel t-said. "Let's engage tomorrow or perhaps encounter. We can then work out that novel stuff for the client. Does that make sense?"

A positive thought came back immediately.

"In that case look after yourself and keep safe." Bartel knew this was a fairly meaningless idea to convey but it felt necessary.

It had been a wasted encounter in some ways – but it had given her a real insight into Savery in a way that almost two years of working together had not. Strange how the neotiquette had kept them further apart than if there were no socio and persono.

Chapter 3

The day stretched out in front of Bartel as she waited to get an autonom. Savery was like an open book to her where he reminded her of herself, and yet his lack of social awareness and the general understanding of what was and wasn't allowed – well, accepted, as that word *allowed* had overtones of control and power – did throw her sometimes, as today.

In the autonom she had an engagement request from Pennington – and typically of him, it was in complete contrast to Savery's approach. His level was set at lock – and it brushed into Bartel's socio almost without a disturbance of her frame of mind. "Hi – Andrew." She waited for him to engage and changed her level to bland.

"Hello, Emma," Pennington t-said. "Is it all right to engage at this time?"

"I'm not doing anything else." He had changed his socio to bland too. He would wait to see what she did next before he would do anything or probe.

"I'd like to say this is a social call," Pennington t-said. That sounded ominous. "And it is in many ways." Even worse.

"And how isn't it?"

"I'll get to that Emma," Pennington t-said back. "How are you?"

"I'm fine – but deeply suspicious," Bartel t-replied. "You don't normally engage me randomly and whenever you do – there's a reason that's not necessarily focused on me."

"You're too cynical, Emma. With good reason. And that's not necessarily exactly true. You do know what I mean."

"I do know what you mean, Andrew. And yes – we've had great times. I also know I've got good reason to be cynical about you." Despite the coldness of the words, Bartel felt softer now. She actually felt comforted whenever Pennington engaged her – he was a warm person and generous. And they'd had a lot of fun together, especially during the time when socio was coming into its own. "So to what do I owe the privilege of this engagement?"

"Finding out how you are, Emma," he t-said back. "And wanting to know if things are all right with you."

"We both know that's not true, Andrew. You always want to change me and, more importantly, change the world. I think you have to accept that you can't do either. I'm not interested. Look we have a great time. We have gSynth and we have time and we don't have people threatening us. We have socio – and can turn it on and off and control its level. We have persono. Can you tell me when it was ever as good as this? Why should I or anyone change?"

"No reason, Emma." Pennington t-replied, in that calm way that always suggested there was a smile lurking behind the thought. "But I can hope."

"No you can't." But she knew he could feel her smile. "You know I really love making love with you – it's the best no-strings-attached physical relationship in my life? Why can't you leave it at that?"

"That's not all you can do, Emma." He paused in his t. "I know this might sound patronising."

"Well – don't say it then."

"Ok," he t-said. One of his charms for Bartel was the fact that he was always very reasonable – sometimes infuriatingly reasonable. And while she knew that was part of his way of convincing people of his point of view and it was very effective, it was also very attractive. "Can we encounter soon?"

"Of course," Bartel t-replied. "When?"

"I was thinking today – if you've nothing pressing," Pennington t-said and then imagined them making love. It was a measure of the sophistication of socio now that thoughts could be part of an imagined scenario. It was quite delicious to be tantalised by him, not actually making her feel him touching her but conveying an image or a sensation of potential physicality.

"One condition."

"Yes?"

"No propaganda," she t-said.

"Some?"

"No – none."

"All right," he t-conceded. "What sort of gSynth were you thinking of?"

"I wasn't until you mentioned it." He was playing with her sensations now, and she could feel the tingling that he thought to her.

"Italian, I think," Pennington thought back. "Romantic."

"Hell no, Andrew," Bartel t-replied immediately. "I don't want romance with you – you know that."

"I do know that." He paused in his mind waves, deliberately cutting her out and making it all the more fun. "But think what *I* may want."

"I do know what you want – and that's what I want too."

"But you know I've always wanted more with you," Pennington t-added.

"I do know that," Bartel t-said. "I think that added tension has been good for me."

"How's the imagineering?"

"That's an abrupt change of thought," Bartel t-laughed back. "It's fun still. I'd stop it of course if it weren't. I've had some flights of fancy – fantasy even – and making it real has been challenging."

"In the sense of making the unreal real," Pennington t-said.

"Exactly." Bartel stopped her line of thoughts. "Do you want to encounter now?"

"Yes – sure," he t-said. "My place?"

"I'll be there in twenty," Bartel t-said. This was a real change in her day and a contrast with the encounter with Savery. Such a contrast. And rather welcome even though there was always that tension with Pennington between the personal and the political.

She redirected the autonom which didn't interpret her thought at first. It wasn't unknown for the odd glitch and it was probably down to some complex interaction between her persono and her socio and the insighto in the autonom. She focused her mind and the autonom corrected itself and headed off to Pennington's. The feedback she got was a little confused but that was usual as the insighto re-adjusted itself. She checked what was happening. It was fine.

She loved the feeling of anticipation of physicality – and double checked that she had changed her socio back to locked before letting herself luxuriate in that pure feeling.

She idled her mind deliberately letting the controlled pace of the autonom lull her into passivity. She checked her persono and realised that there was nothing pressing for the rest of the week once she'd got the current experience nailed down. That was both a relief and a worry – she hated having too much time rather more than having too little.

She had suffered occasionally from depression that she had hinted at several times with Savery which even the combined ministrations of her persono and socio weren't able to entirely remove. It was funny that she had suffered similar feelings to Savery but that hadn't ever made him depressed – as far as she knew. She let her mind wander down the familiar patterns, trying to find the trigger.

For most people it was a feeling of pointlessness, however irrational it was, that was the key to becoming depressed. That's why she took Savery's discussion so seriously. Although in all but the most casual way hierarchies had been found to be unproductive, Bartel was still nominally in charge of him.

She needed to catch that feeling early and deflect it.

For Bartel it was rather different – or so she told herself. She had point to her life – for a start she had her daughters, even though they were old enough to be themselves and completely independently run their own socios. She had her role as a highly respected imagineer. Her ability to put things into perspective – which is what people told her was her number one capability.

She had an inkling where the issue was – it wasn't a problem as no mental health issues were a problem any more. She could feel a sharpness like needle teeth in her brain at times, going back to her insecurity over initial relationships when she had acquired her own persono and then socio. Other people could apparently live with the fact that even the most unpolished user of their own persono or socio would make mistakes sometimes, and unwittingly – and, worse, unknowingly – let slip an intimate or highly personal thought. This was especially true when persono and socio were in their infancy, so to speak, and were rather like having a sledgehammer crashing between two people.

Two completely contrasting occasions when she was learning to live with her socio in particular were always at the forefront of her mind – and often at the forefront of her persono. One that she tried never to bring to mind with the inevitable result it was often there, was with a first boyfriend and she had let him into her reactions as they first kissed. Both of them had been embarrassed. The other was even more difficult and possibly the cause of her insecurity and then depression. At a party she had managed to probe a man's mind and seen into his loathing of another of her friends, whom he was dating.

It was a dark and twisted moment and it had undermined any sense that she understood other people.

Yes – it had been largely his fault that he had not set his level properly. It was still capable of eating away at her.

"We're here, Ms Bartel," the autonom t-voiced. She was experimenting with how she wanted aides such as an autonom to address her – and this made her giggle. It was interesting how important neotiquette was becoming in all lives now. It had replaced most of the issues, like sex, religion and politics, in the weeds as the topic of choice.

Chapter 4

It was always difficult for Bartel not to feel excited when she encountered Pennington – his height, his bearing, his elegance were all fixed in her mind as some sort of ideal. Yet they could argue and trash each other relentlessly – which is why the relationship rarely moved beyond the physical and the comfort that that brought both of them for any length of time. Yet both knew there was a deep affection there and a meeting of minds beyond what socio facilitated. For Bartel it was always an enigma that they didn't make more sense together.

With socio it was always more tricky to think that someone knew you better than you knew yourself, even though it was probably true, because it implied so much that was beyond real understanding. On the other hand, there was always more than the physical with Pennington. He touched something deep inside her consciousness – and she knew in a way that transcended socio that she did the same to him. That twentieth song had it right – *they couldn't live together, they couldn't live apart.*

She thought her way past his lobby door and the lift simply took her to Pennington's floor and he was there to welcome her, having engaged with her rather effortlessly as soon as his socio and persono picked up the presence of Bartel's socio and persono. "So good to see you, Emma."

"And I was really excited to see you too," Bartel t-replied. "We haven't encountered for a while." It had been unusually more than a week, but she couldn't quite place how long it had been.

"Yes," Pennington t-said. "You're often in my thoughts."

"And you in mine." For neither of them was this quite as true as it sounded, but it also wasn't entirely false.

"To what do I owe this – or is it just keeping in touch?"

"You engaged me." Bartel looked at him quizzically. "Don't you remember? Losing your memory Andrew?"

"Not at all," Pennington thought back. "But I'm never quite certain that you will accept. That's what I really meant. No matter. Shall we use voice?"

"Why?"

"I always think that with you the moment when we transition back to socio is such an overwhelming rush of experience. Don't you feel that?"

"Of course I do." Bartel t-said and switched to voice. "Why specifically did you contact me?"

"As I said," Pennington v-replied, with his deep, rather melodious voice that had always spoken directly to her emotions, and which he always used to a devastating effect on her. Switching to v-comms was never just to change the nature of how they were communicating but also the quality of their relationship. "How are you? But first – let me take your coat – anything to drink?"

"No. I'm fine."

"Something stronger? Something different?"

"You know I never need any stimulants when I am with you, Andrew," Bartel t-replied. They had of course used heightened consciousness as it was now called. But they had found that they usually didn't need it.

"May I hug you?"

"Please."

It was odd that even after the depths of the physical relationship that they had enjoyed with each other, they sometimes reverted to this high level of formality.

They embraced, and with his arm around her, they sat on the sofa. His hand stroked her hair and touched her face. She looked at him and enjoyed the anticipation. "Slowly," she v-said.

"Yes."

He kissed her forehead, and she touched his shoulder to bring him more round to her. His lips touched hers gently. They both knew so well – and perhaps would have known even without socio – how important this was to Emma. She wondered whether Dave Worrell had instinctively known that last night. It was good that socio was locked down with Pennington but of course it hadn't been with Worrell. Did that make it artificial? Did that matter? She moved her fingers to undo the buttons on his shirt and, experienced as he was with how she always wanted to make

31

love, Pennington just held his lips lightly against hers. She touched his bare chest and his skin reacted with a little tremor. Her hands moved to his belt and slowly she undid it, undid his zip and opened his trousers and so lightly traced her fingers across his underpants – touching him gently and slowly. She could feel him holding his breath and breathing deeply.

Her persono reported back that Pennington's physical health was fine with no issues that should stop them making love.

"Now you." she v-breathed this rather than said it.

He undid the buttons on her blouse and traced the line of her bra across the top of her breasts. His hand went down to her jeans and undid them and she echoed her hand on him, through the layer of cloth too. "Socio?" she asked.

"Not yet – if that's all right."

"Of course," she v-said.

Even though they had made love so many times, in so many places and in so many ways, this still felt like that new experience – and not having socio in play both isolated each of them from the other but also made them concentrate more on what they could think the other was feeling.

"Why is this so good, Emma?"

"I don't question it," she v-replied, savouring the words and the sensation. He was right to keep socio out of this for the moment as she could concentrate on what she was feeling and not be distracted by their joint thoughts. "Do you ever wonder how something that we've done so often can always been new and fresh?"

"Sometimes, I do," he v-replied. "but, Emma, mostly I don't as I am too wrapped up in what we're doing together. I guess I think about it afterwards." She fell silent. "Oh – I'm sorry how that came out. If it sounded as though I was being critical of you, I wasn't – just trying to be absolutely truthful."

"That's fine, Andrew," Bartel v-replied. They were now lying skin to skin and she could feel his breath on her forehead as they gently, oh so gently, came together.

"Socio now?" Pennington v-asked.

"Yes."

The sudden flood of thoughts was quite overwhelming, and then complete as they both went to the relaxed level and as their bodies moved into and against each other, their thoughts and feelings multiplied. Bartel could sense Pennington's excitement matching hers and her need to share with him her feelings became a primal thought. It felt all consuming.

When they separated and lay next to each other, with her head on his chest and his hands stroking her breasts, it felt so peaceful for both of them.

"As I normally say, can you imagine now how it was before socio?" Pennington v-asked.

"Yes. If I try hard enough. I occasionally try to make love without socio even now – but it is such a different experience. That's why I always want to switch to socio."

"I don't ever make love like that, now, without socio. Maybe I should try. That's a thought, Emma. It is good that we started without it. I think I – we – are always peaceful when we've made love – and with socio there is such a contrast between the floods of thoughts and the wonderful passivity afterwards."

They lay there together – old friends, old lovers, feeling young and fresh and real and re-invigorated.

"Tea?" Pennington t-asked.

"Mmm."

Pennington brought the tea up to his bedroom and they sat up and said nothing and exchanged no thoughts. "We should do this more often."

"I know we say that every time, Andrew. But we should. We're so good together."

"Even though we drive each other mad if we are together."

"But we do have things in common," Bartel t-said. "Why do you think we drive each other mad if we're together any length of time?"

"That's a good question," Pennington t-said back, "and I don't know the answer. I wonder sometimes if it isn't because you are too passive, Emma"

"Too passive?"

"Yes," Pennington t-replied, "I don't really understand how you can be intelligent and not get angry with how things are."

"Why should I be angry? Look – I'm sure the Trills abuse their position, but not like before in history. I'm not oppressed – I don't have to be anything that I don't want to be. No-one tells me what to think or what to do. It's all down to personal choice. We have a democracy that works – everyone cannot only vote but they are required to vote. There's no limit on who can be a candidate apart from normal safeguards. You know that I'm not a hedo and I'm not a spartan – and no-one gets at me about that. I have work if I want it. I don't have to work if I don't want to. What's not to like?"

"We shouldn't talk about this now."

"Why not?" Bartel felt suddenly angry, and felt manipulated. She knew Pennington always wanted to discuss this – and what he called her passivity and she always told him she was content and didn't need to have any discussion. And now she was asking him to discuss it.

"Because. Well – I know you don't want to discuss this – and let's not ruin our magical moment with any irritation or conflict."

"We should – I mean not ruin it, but discuss it," Bartel t-said. "It's like a running sore between us, Andrew. Perhaps it is why we just couldn't live together – we're too different and too much the same. You're always trying to convert me to something I'm not. If you could stop that, then we'd do this more often and we'd be much more together."

"True enough. I won't say any more."

"But I want you to say more now." Bartel felt so irritated.

"All right," Pennington t-continued, "I just think what's happened to us as a nation and a world – perhaps as a human race. We're too content."

"I don't think that's possible at all."

"I said we shouldn't talk about it."

"I won't say anything. Just tell me and perhaps we can get rid of this once and for all."

"Not now, Emma," Pennington t-said. "You and I disagree. Where I see oppression you see contentment. Where I see exploitation, you see security and even pleasure. Where I see control, you see freedom. Where I see coercion, you see freedom to vote. It's true that no-one insists on much now – the GLEAKES have got that right. No such thing as illegal drugs – why would there be? No such thing as fraud – why would there be? But where I see pointlessness, you see fulfilment. I know you won't join us. I'm not trying to convert you. Honestly. I've given up on that. I just want you to know there's a different perspective."

"Who's *us*?"

"Nothing formal," Pennington t-replied, but he seemed evasive, which was unlike him. It was, as far as she could remember the first time he had said *us*. "It's like a debating club. I'm sure I mentioned it to you before."

"Never. I knew that you had several fellow thinkers. I didn't know it was organised."

"I said it was informal," Pennington t-said. "It is just that. But I guess it's becoming more important now."

"Why?"

"We think it's becoming more insidious," Pennington t-replied.

"You always say that."

"But it really is – and there's a development that I don't think anyone is aware of much outside those of us who share this interest."

"And that is?"

"There is a developing rift between the Trills. And before you ask, I don't know much about it or how serious it is. But it threatens the stability of what we've got."

"So that must please you," Bartel t-said, without much thought.

"Not at all," Pennington t-said, very slowly. "It makes it more difficult. If this current order under the Trills and this neo-age, as they call it, alongside the dominance of their companies that make up the GLEAKES, were to collapse with no counter organisation able to step in, it might prove really difficult. As I've said to you before, there is a fine balance here."

"I don't think you've said that to me before."

"Well – now I have and now you know," Pennington t-replied.

"So what do you believe?" Bartel t-asked, almost despite herself, as if poking her tongue at a painful tooth. "That the threat of a break up of the Trills is bad? I thought that the Trills in your opinion are in some way malign. So this seems a bit difficult to take."

"You are simplifying things too much, Emma," Pennington t-said. "It's not what I said. I can believe that the rule of the Trills and by extension, the GLEAKES, is fundamentally malign – and that is, before you say it again, in spite of all the good that this neo-age, as they call, has brought mankind – and at the same time believe that a collapse in the current order, without something solid to replace it, would be very dangerous."

"I can understand that, Andrew. Of course I can. I know enough history to know that the riots and the chaos of the twenties wasn't good for anyone. But I know that you want this neo-age to be brought to a close and I find that self-defeating."

"We shouldn't try to discuss this, Emma. Some other time, when I don't feel so relaxed and happy with you. I don't want to lose this amazing feeling. Do you?"

"No. But that's not the point. Do the Trills interfere with us? Do they concern themselves with us? They have their little scandals and I'm sure people enjoy reading about whether Elora Ghose is breaking up with Jerry Fernandes if she and he are an item to start with, and that obviously sells news and web feeds – sorry weeds as they are now called. But largely there is nothing that bad."

"You don't believe any of that tittle tattle and all that juicy scandal do you?"

"Why shouldn't I?" Bartel was surprised that Pennington had this in mind at all.

"You should know that all those stories about the Trills are just that. Stories. They have a team of people who make them up. I know in your role that you make up experiences and scenarios for people – you imagine them. There are people like you who do the same but about the Trills, although there isn't necessarily a shred of truth in any of them."

"So you're saying that all those scandals are fantasy? Why would they bother?"

"Because it takes people's minds off what is really going on. Do you remember from history what a soap was?"

"Yes."

"It's like a long running soap that they manufacture – partly to say that the Trills are just like us, partly to show how different they are – how they don't have any qualms about doing anything."

"So why is that so bad?"

"Do you know anything about the Trills? I mean – do you actually know anything about them?"

"I think I do."

"Well – that's the point about these stories and story lines. You think you know and you think you understand. If they are prepared to behave like this with their trillions – indulging in multiple extra marital relationships and swapping partners as though there is no other focus in their lives – it means that they can keep their wealth, power and position because that has become a secondary matter. Can you see that in these stories they have become like a pantheon – a classical world of stories about gods. It's all very well, but it is a deflection."

"That's no different from how we are," Bartel t-replied. Pennington was making her angry again. Why this fixation on the Trills? "I mean that even using that term *extra marital* is so lunatic and old fashioned. Why don't you just forget all about them? They mean nothing to us – except they've created a sort of utopia for most people."

"Because that's not how it is, Emma," Pennington t-said. "You've got to wake up to that. You might remember from the twentieth that there was a novel that predicted a dystopia where Big Brother, apparently both a threatening and a comforting figure depending upon where you stood, was always watching you? No? Well – it was a powerful work. We know that the Trills are always watching everything we do. They are like a twenty first Big Brother or the seven Big Siblings, as I suppose we have to call them as they aren't all male. And you can see that the seven Big Siblings – the Trills – can be both comforting and ultimately threatening? Well – we do."

"I don't have to wake up to anything, Andrew – you're wrong. I have a great life. I know what I am doing and I know enough. Why should I wake up to anything? There's no-one telling me what to believe, no instruction that I have to be one religion or another or none at all. I am part of an active democracy. Just stop it Andrew. Kiss me now." Bartel was, as she had been getting sometimes for no reason, very angry. Perhaps it was age? Perhaps it was some other frustration coming out that she was barely aware of – if at all.

"Can we turn socio off?" Pennington t-asked. He had completely changed his tone and he relaxed.

"Why?"

Instead of replying, Pennington brought himself up to look down at her, and stroked her face, and traced his fingers down from her chin, over her breast and between her legs. "No. I actually want socio on come to think of it. I want to know what you are feeling."

"I'm sure that's obvious."

"Not to me," Pennington t-said. "You're always a mystery to me – I can't imagine what knowing you would have been like without socio."

"The same as making love to anyone."

"But making love to you, Emma, is never like making love to anyone." And Bartel knew that he wasn't just being gallant or polite or flattering her.

"Less talking, even t-talking," she t-said, and reached for him. He made her so angry – and yet they had so much more than she had experienced with almost anyone. "Let me hold you."

"Of course – but just one thing," Pennington t-said, "please don't forget what I said about the real rift in the Trills. That is important and it could be life-changing – epoch-changing even."

"Yes, I'm sure – but enough of that. Make love to me now."

Chapter 5

As she took an autonom back to her flat, Bartel was in two minds. Pennington was extremely annoying. He was always actually undermining her confidence in her life which made her feel wretched and they usually argued bitterly over that. Why did he usually always want to make her feel uncomfortable? But this time he had really disturbed her by not focusing on their disagreement – although it wasn't really a disagreement. He wanted to focus her on things that didn't matter to her at all.

Bartel just didn't need to think about such things. And now she had a nagging feeling that she was getting things wrong. And all because he wouldn't argue with her.

The most irritating man on the planet at times. And yet as usual their love-making had been exquisite. And she knew that she was angry partly because she knew that Pennington was right – that she should take a greater interest in what he was talking about. But if things were perfectly fine in her life, why should she not just accept that?

She engaged her eldest daughter, Roseanne: "How are you darling? Ok to engage?"

"Sure, Mum." A pause. "Just need to sort something. Can I engage you back in a moment?"

Roseanne was available almost all the time. At 20 she reminded Bartel more of herself than her other daughter, Alice – who at nearly 19 was already planning her pregnancies. There was an independence in Roseanne that she always felt – and it separated her from her daughter probably because they were so alike, whereas with Alice it was always a meeting of minds. The expression, with its pre-2062 connotations, always made her smile. The arrival of socio had transformed relationships and thoughts even more than persono, almost five years previously. Bartel couldn't remember a world without persono but had what she thought of as a clear understanding of the world without socio.

"Hi, Mum," Roseanne engaged back. "Everything all right?"

"I think so," Bartel t-said. "I've just been with Andrew." A short moment of no thoughts. "That man always disturbs me."

"I don't know why you still see him – or I suppose do but there must be other lovers," Roseanne t-responded. "He always leaves you unsettled or angry or both."

"I know, darling. But he's like a drug. I've never known anyone else like him for how we are together – when we're not arguing. Yes – he is a drug."

"Not one you need every day apparently."

"No – but only because I forget how good he can be for me."

"To what do I owe you engaging?" Roseanne t-asked.

"Just catching up."

"It must be more than that. Just so you know, I am with Claude."

"Serious?"

"Oh – you know," Roseanne t-replied. "I can feel time going on and he's a good genetic investment."

"You old romantic."

"Don't criticise me, Mum," Roseanne t-said, with a laugh. "You had had me by this time – and were expecting Alice. Things haven't changed since your day."

"But I thought you weren't going to conform to these norms," Bartel t-responded. The short catch-up engagement had suddenly taken on another meaning and was serious. Bartel welcomed it as she rarely got the chance to engage with Roseanne on anything but the most superficial level. "Alice was always going to. Aren't you a free spirit?"

"I think that's the point, Mum."

"So you realise that freedom for a woman is rather important?"

"Not that," Roseanne t-said. "I hadn't realised what freedom actually was. I thought it was having fun while I was young and delaying. Claude has shown me otherwise."

"That's good to hear," Bartel said. "Have you spoken to Alice about this?"

"Not yet."

"I suppose there's no need," Bartel t-replied. "But she'll be interested."

"I don't think so." No thoughts for a second. "She's too wrapped up in her own fertility plans."

"Is there any chance we could encounter, Roseanne?"

"I don't know – obviously that would be good," Roseanne t-said. "Can I let you know?"

"Of course darling."

"I think I'd better get back to my plans with Claude."

"Is he with you at the moment?"

"Yes."

"Good of you to take the encounter." They both t-giggled. "Bye."

Now what should she do?

It didn't matter much – there was never any pressure except the pressure she put on herself and she was too relaxed after being with Pennington to even think about putting pressure on herself. For a moment she idly wondered what it would be like to live with Pennington. Then she thought *pure hell* – and laughed to herself.

Almost without thinking she thought through her persono presence and checked her El-balance which was positive – and she could afford to spend money on some indulgence or other. It was funny how that didn't actually make her want to indulge in anything.

Her 5.00pm physio check, or media-stat, completed and told her all functions were fine. No worries.

She thought about engaging Alice and perhaps she should, but Alice was always so single minded. That could wait.

There was something unsettling her and it was gnawing away. Bartel couldn't think what it was. She rummaged through her persono asking questions and it was elusive. No – she couldn't think what it was. Had it been Savery and his disquiet this morning? Had it been Pennington – something he'd said?

The autonom stopped outside her house and she paid automatically and went upstairs to her flat. She had a quick shower and ordered her gSynth and set the time for 6.30. It was early but she wanted an early meal so she could use the evening for imagining. In one way she liked to think of it as work because that gave a sense of purpose but really it was relaxation.

While she was idly waiting for the food, she realised what had unsettled her – and, of course, it was Pennington. It wasn't the sex or the disagreement, which had been much slighter than they usually experienced. Then she had it.

It was his mention of *us*. Who were *us*?

Of course dissent was always allowed – in fact encouraged. There were strict rules on free speech now – nothing that could be interpreted as unthinkingly wounding to another person was tolerated and there was absolutely zero tolerance for that – but other than that, it was really fair game. The government liked as much dissent as possible from as many quarters as possible. For the first time in human history, it was expected and welcomed by the people who might be expected to suffer if dissent got out of hand. *You can always throw the rascals out* was the watch word of all the GLEAKES and therefore of all the political parties. So what was the purpose of having a group to apparently take on the foundations of the society – the whole essence of the neo-age? That might mean that the whole of society would be changed – and after all the struggles of the early twenty first, after which all the advances in human comfort and relationships had been achieved, Bartel was not alone in resisting any attack on the status quo.

Nevertheless this use of *us* sounded serious to Bartel and she next thought that perhaps Pennington was winding her up. That was more likely the more she thought about it. Pennington would have no interest in upsetting the current way of life. It had been more liberating for women than men because women had been far less liberated and tied to obligations and expectations. Now they were free to be women as women. And some men had been threatened by that – but she knew that wasn't what disturbed Pennington. He had even told her how liberating it was for men to know that women were properly liberated.

She couldn't fix it and so she put it out of her mind. She didn't want the almost intimate experience of the eye-screen, so she thought the images onto the wall and caught up with the news. There was a debate in parliament whether the absolute licence to use any drugs should be curtailed more than it was – the government always called it an *absolute licence* – but in reality there were restrictions. Where that line was drawn was always a fascinating discussion. There had been an outbreak of selfishness in Croydon and there had been several examples of religious intolerance – but these had been defused, as they would be. It was hardly news. There were several scandals involving different Trills – funny that with all their wealth and power they didn't more tightly control the publicity around them. Or perhaps they did, as Pennington suggested. Bartel wasn't much interested in any shenanigans involving Trills – but it was quite diverting and fun that with all their wealth and power and remoteness they weren't immune to human failings.

It was difficult to believe Pennington when he said that this was all made up – though Bartel had no doubt it was embellished.

Most news reports finished with some examples of double dealing or jockeying for power by one or more of the Trills. Of course scandal didn't involve sex or drugs or exploitation fraud or corruption any more – though the history of the first half of the 21st century had been pretty well dominated by such scandals, but not amongst the Trills. They had remained above and beyond – it was the politicians that they employed and probably controlled who succumbed to any of that.

The liberation that persono brought, enhanced in due course by socio, had meant that who was sleeping with whom or who had embezzled anything was very difficult to keep secret – and so it became accepted that this would go on – whatever that *this* was.

"Hi, Emma – Alice." This was unusual. For Alice to engage her meant only one thing. Agitation.

"Yes, Alice?"

"Can we engage?"

"Sure." This wasn't like Alice to be so formal. Bartel felt disturbed for the second time. "Can I help?"

"I think so," Alice t-replied. "I don't know if I've done the right thing."

"Meaning?"

"I've decided to get pregnant with Rakesh," Alice t-replied, in a rush of thoughts.

"Marvellous."

"Is it?"

"I think so," Bartel t-replied. "You're 19. No worries. You want children. what's the issue?"

"It seems like a big step," Alice t-said.

"It is," Bartel t-responded. "But think of how your life will pan out. Child-bearing out of the way by the time you are say 23. All the pleasure of children while you're young enough. Then all the pleasures of adult life without a problem. I can't see the downside."

"I think it's a big step."

"And?"

"So you are pleased?" Alice t-asked. "I thought you would be. I was just in two minds."

"Think nothing more about it – just get on and enjoy your making the baby with Rakesh."

They engaged for a little bit more with Bartel catching up on Alice's studies and other thoughts.

With Roseanne their mutual socio was set at Friend. It was never appropriate for parent and child to be at Relaxed. It was re-assuringly close and warm.

With Alice their mutual socio was rarely set at anything higher than Acquaintance – and usually at Bland. Interesting, as Bartel thought about it, that Alice had engaged at Friend level for some of the engagement. It was a level of intimacy that was almost worrying – as it suggested that Alice was relying on her. Natural between mother and daughter but unusual for Alice to the point where Bartel couldn't remember the last time that had happened.

It felt rather good to be that important to Alice.

The gSynth announced her meal was ready. She thought a burgundy white would be appropriate and the gSynth produced it as the temperature she preferred.

Bartel idly wondered whether to engage with Dave Worrell from last night. After the afternoon with Pennington that was hardly appropriate anyway. She could leave that for now. After eating and sitting back in the sofa, letting the wall gently flow with some chat between various politicians, she thought back to that afternoon with Pennington and replayed their love making with her persono. She loved his firmness and gentleness and single-minded focus on her and her pleasure, and she experienced their love making almost as intensely as it had been a few hours earlier.

Chapter 6

Bartel had set her persono to wake her with Pennington making love with her, just for a change. It wasn't so much erotic as comforting – and it provoked her usual thoughts about why they just couldn't get on. They had so much in common and so much real affection but also a block somehow that prevented them from ever being properly close.

What did she have on today?

She tried to think without using persono – but her mind was blank. The days of the week were largely irrelevant to everyone's life now. For a moment she didn't know what day it was at all.

What did she want to eat? Persono had already analysed what she'd eaten the day before and had made suggestions for her meals – and it never failed to amaze her how such a simple question had baffled people for aeons and now it was not a matter of thought beyond wondering. Porridge for breakfast and gSynth now made that so appetising. The latest updates to INsighto had made its capabilities so integrated with persono that Sapiens was rapidly assuming the provider of core technology. Bartel loved the strap line *move on from artificial ignorance* – and knew that it marked a step forward in the widely reported so-called commercial wars between the Trills.

But Pennington had suggested the rift wasn't some sort of commercial war which had been largely eliminated any way as the Trills had carved out separate areas for each of them in TCentral at one of the historic meetings that had produced the so-called Treaty of Delphi. Bartel wondered what possible advantage it could give the Trills if they broke that treaty and created a real schism between them. That was Pennington talk or his concern – she put it out of her head as irrelevant to her life.

The gSynth produced the porridge and kept it at the right temperature as she showered and readied herself for the day. As she was eating, an engagement came into her socio from Savery. That was good. "How are you?" she t-responded.

"Better than yesterday." That was good. "I've been thinking about what I said. It was how I felt – absolutely how I felt. It was re-assuring,

Emma, that you had felt that too at times. I know it's talked about and the agony programs cover it extensively, but that feeling of pointlessness is hard to deal with."

"You just need to think less deeply about that and throw yourself into something – our work, relationships, recreation – anything," Bartel t-responded.

"I know that. But when you don't have any needs only wants, then everything becomes rather impossible to put into perspective."

"Where did you get that phrase from?"

"It's something I was reading," Savery t-replied. "Some historian, I think. It's a good expression, I think. Sums me up at times."

"I can understand that."

"So what do we have to do today, Emma?"

"Nothing we have to do – I love that rather old-fashioned expression, though," Bartel t-replied. "I was thinking we ought to spend some time brain dumping around that latest experience for those people who want to add a different perspective to their lives."

"I'm fine with that. It sort of fits into my way of thinking and my focus and even my fears at the moment. I didn't and don't know where to start. Do you?"

"I do have some ideas," Bartel t-said. "Look – don't let's start from here. Why don't you spend half an hour or so letting your mind go where it wants to – and we'll see what we can come up with."

"Good idea," Savery t-said. "I need a starting point though. Is this real or virtual?"

"Virtual."

"So the boundaries are pretty wide?"

"As wide as you can imagine," Bartel t-replied. "Remember it's a couple. They've been together for a long time – ten years. They need something special – which is why I took on this imagining."

"Will do."

This was a challenge that Bartel relished and if it was good it could be a spring board to more interesting imaginings or even a more general experience that might go viral. Savery turned off his engagement.

There was a holy grail in imagineering – and that was exploding an experience into people's lives in such a way that it went viral because of their reaction. The recent enhancements to socio, which could t-broadcast a rush of enthusiasm or pleasure had transformed most people's experience and changed imagineering for ever. And there was one enhancement that Latitude had recently introduced to its main product called Sofari, that had transformed the commercial or at least the viral spread of products developed in Latitude – selective memory erasure. It didn't appear to have a name yet, but it was, Bartel knew, controversial for reasons that she didn't yet understand.

Savery came back and engaged: "This is only brief, Emma. Where are you starting from? Sex? Drugs? Music?"

"No – they'll have to be part of it – but that's pretty old hat. We have to move beyond that. Look, Jonas, don't use those as building blocks – they're additions now. Our job is to use those but not focus on them. I know most imagineers don't go much beyond the staples, especially if they're older and these stock items still seem a novelty. I know I'm a good deal older than you but I think I keep up with new possibilities. I see that as one of the reasons we work together so well. I bring the experience and you bring s sharper awareness of new possibilities."

"Challenging."

"Exactly."

But Savery's need to engage had stimulated Bartel's thoughts – and she knew where she would be going.

She needed to turn her mind off and let her persono rerun a bit more of her love making yesterday – again not so much for the erotic charge, but more for the relaxation which was always a stimulus for her best imaginings. She t-changed the perspective and made the focus of everything her own body – and luxuriated in the touch of his hands, her unusual passivity yesterday and his sensuousness.

She was brought back from this experience by an engagement from someone she didn't recognise. "Dave here."

"Dave?"

"From the night before last," and then she realised it was Dave Worrell. "Remember?"

"Of course," Bartel t-replied, rather pleased. "And?"

"I was wondering if you might be free this afternoon?"

"I could be," Bartel t-said, rather coquettishly she hoped. "Did you explore this with your partner?"

"Cheryl?"

"Yes."

"She's fine with it – of course," Worrell t-said.

"You didn't answer my question."

"Yes – I have. Would that make a difference?"

"I don't know," Bartel t-replied. "Yes – it would, now I think about it."

"I will then," Worrell t-replied.

That was significant – and made Bartel wary – the new setiquette – recently renamed neotiquette as it applied to more than just socio – was quite precise and while it wasn't a command or rule because very little could be any more, it did provide a framework for assessing how trustworthy a person is. Socio was such a powerful environment that people had to know how and where and when to use it, especially as it was still developing and notwithstanding that it was already highly sophisticated. Not diffusing with someone who was in any way significant to an individual was seen as an important indicator.

"That's not good, Dave," Bartel t-said. "That makes me wary of you."

"Of course. It wasn't good of me. I find it hard to adapt to the new setiquette. Neotiquette, I mean. I hope that's honest enough for you."

"That's better." Bartel t-responded. "I won't encounter you unless you have. And that's not setiquette or neotiquette – that's me."

"I like that. I do. So when I've diffused with her – we can meet?"

"Sure."

He disengaged.

Bartel went back to the basics for the scenario she had to imagine. A couple getting bored with each other – not what they'd t-said or even v-said, as Bartel usually needed some time with voice if it was a couple. She felt voice allowed people more distance, not so much from her but from each other in the relationship, and as they v-spoke, it was Bartel's underlying feeling that they had reached a stale part in their relationship. Sex was part of it – they were rather jaded in that part of their relationship. Drugs had of course come up – but they didn't want psychedelia as they'd gone through a phase using that. What they wanted was stimulus. Music hadn't been on their agenda, but probably because they didn't understand how to use it as part of a scenario. Drama had been – so they wanted a situation, probably soapy. It was also a twelve hour scenario. They were willing to go twenty four hours – but felt that the first time it should be shorter. That had opened up the possibility for Bartel that they would be ideal as they could develop this together – well, she could develop it and they would contribute.

Involving Savery had been questionable. There was always the feeling that imagineering with someone else could limit rather than expand the possibilities, but Bartel felt this time that she needed a younger perspective and one that was untroubled by the recent developments in neotiquette and socio and persono. Older people like herself tended to be somewhat nostalgic or unable to quite grasp the full significance of what they could now imagine.

Savery wanted to engage again – and Bartel raised her level to Acquaintance. "Shouldn't we use Friend?" Savery t-asked.

"Not yet." Bartel hadn't finished thinking through what she wanted and she didn't need the distraction of too many of Savery's thoughts. "We can move there once we've got the bones of the experience in place."

"That makes sense," Savery t-responded. Not that he had any choice but to accept what she thought was the right level.

Bartel ran through the building blocks that she had identified. "Do you have any others?"

"Do you mean ideas?"

"Not at this stage. Just I want to make sure I've not missed anything in the initial brief."

"I think you've got it all," Savery t-responded. "But I don't honestly know where to go now."

"That's all right," Bartel t-responded. "I'm not sure where we will get to. But I often start with random words. I know you and I haven't done that before – but we've not had anything as challenging as this as a scenario."

"What do you mean – random words?"

"Just tell me the first word that comes into your head – just this minute," Bartel t-said. "No. Don't think." She probed at him but it was clear he was at a complete loss. "Can't you just let your mind wander?"

"From where?"

"From the building blocks I went through with you just now."

"Oh," Savery t-responded. "So just the first word? *Aphrodisiac*."

"Good."

"Then let me choose another word – starting with b," Savery said. "Beauty."

"Yes - ok. More."

"C – well catapult. D – dreadful. E – eclectic. F – fear . . ."

"Yes - good." Bartel paused. "Not sure about the other words and I don't think you have to be alphabetical although it seems to be useful – but fear is a great word – unusual in imagining a scenario. Though I guess it shouldn't be. Say some more."

"G – goatskin. H – heirloom. I – icon. Do I need to go on?"

"No," Bartel t-replied. "Let's see what we can do with these, shall we?"

"I'm not sure." Savery was genuinely puzzled. This was out of his comfort zone. Normally – and it had been his introduction to working with Bartel – there was a pretty standard formula to scenarios. There was some sort of quest and then it was sexual or at least sensual and then there was a feeling of achievement as the participants made some sort of progress. "Are you sure these people are worth it?"

"Not at all," Bartel t-responded. "This is not about them really – it's about what we can achieve ourselves. Surely that must chime with you in your current mood – wanting to achieve something."

"Yes."

"Right then," Bartel t-continued, "think of this as an exploration of something that will be really out of the ordinary. Do you see what I mean?" Bartel could feel some excitement now in herself and was relishing what was happening.

"I think I do," Savery t-said, but he was at the same time sounding much more doubtful than that suggested. "I guess fear is something we haven't used much – if at all.

"True. I am more comfortable with that as a starting point," Bartel t-said. "We need to put it into some sort of context. So let's use *fear*. First question – do we leave them in fear at the end?"

"That's a really good question, Emma. What do you think?"

"I don't know," Bartel t-replied. "Perhaps, or perhaps not. No. Fear's a great idea Jonas. Do you think we could just drop them into a situation and let there be real fear?"

"I guess so."

"Actually I was rather talking to myself." Bartel t-said and laughed at herself. "So we need to create fear and we need to make it comforting in some way so they're not actually terrified."

"I don't agree," Savery t-responded. "You said you wanted this to be ground-breaking. Has anyone done this before?"

"No – not to my knowledge as imagineers want to be liked and for people to come back to them because they've had such a good sensation and good experience. Fear has figured in some scenarios, but it's never been mainstream and serious. This could be the key differentiator for what we're going to produce."

"So is it a good idea?"

"I think it is," Bartel t-replied. "Just imagine that you're not expecting something and suddenly you are thrust into a dangerous or threatening situation. That could be so cool. No-one could ever say it wasn't a great experience."

"Are you thinking that's why people watch horror series?" Bartel t-nodded. "Then – this is something that could be immense. If we don't kill the client with a heart attack."

"I think we need to encounter shortly," Bartel was thinking deeply and t-said this haltingly.

"Why?"

"Because we need to work on this separately now – and then meet to put real flesh on the bones, so to speak," Bartel t-replied. "Socio is great for this initial planning – or generating ideas. I find voice so much more focused. Don't you find that?"

"Not really." Savery paused. "But I'm cool with that. When? Where?"

"Tomorrow. Same as yesterday for place – let's make it mid-day," Bartel t-replied. "Good?"

"Yes," Savery t-replied, "that's good. No. Actually I think we need a bit of physical space for this. Let's use the office. Can you book it?"

"Actually – I'd prefer it if you could do that for us. Can you?"

"Yes."

"Between now and then, Jonas, I'll need some ideas focused on how to construct the fear – and what type of fear."

"What do you mean?"

"Are they frightened out of their lives?" Bartel t-said. "Are they really terrified with no way out? Are they in any sense re-assured as they go through the experience?"

"All good questions, Emma," Savery t-said. "Till tomorrow – and I'll be thinking deeply."

They disengaged and it was as much a relief as it always was to stem the flow of another person's socio, no matter how useful it was while it was going on.

As she let herself ruminate about the opportunities this scenario presented, Bartel worried that someone else might be able to beat them to it. She tried INsighto – and found that there were examples of fear running through a scenario but no-one had had enough courage to make it a thoroughly terrifying experience. Could she get away with it?

She thought about the clients – and the more she thought about them the more it seemed perfectly possible and perfectly matched to what they wanted the outcome to be. They'd have to cling to each other and perhaps that would show each of them how much they did depend on each other. It definitely had legs. And if she was clever, the disclaimer could be adapted to give them an inkling of what was to come, and that might be enough comfort.

Yes. One word had made all the difference. Funny that. And unexpected.   Really   unexpected.   *Fear.*

Chapter 7

After a long time contemplating the possibilities for the new scenario, there was an urgent engagement message – Worrell. Setting socio to Bland, Bartel allowed the engagement.

"I've had the t-discussion with Cheryl." He sounded wary of Bartel and at the same time excited.

"And?"

"We agreed that it's fine," Worrell t-replied.

"What is?"

"If you and I meet and if you and I take it further," Worrell t-said.

"Ok."

"What does that mean, Emma?"

"It means just that. Ok,"

"So shall we encounter again or do you want to keep it like this – an engagement?"

"Quite frankly, Dave, I don't know." The problem was that she didn't want this engagement at this moment. Her mind was too far away focused on the scenario and the conversation with Savery. "What conditions did Cheryl put on this – did she want any quid pro quo?"

"A good question," Worrell t-responded. "Can we raise the socio level one point?"

"Why?"

"It's just this seems quite an intimate t-discussion and it's very hard to feel the right things and how you are responding at Bland. It ought to be Acquaintance at least," Worrell t-said, thoughtfully.

"My issue, Dave, is that my head isn't quite in the t-discussion at the moment and it's not that I'm holding you at arm's length, so much as trying to control it so I concentrate on what you're saying." Bartel was rather hesitant thinking this through and she was feeling her way to what she wanted to convey.

"Is this not a good time?"

"Actually – if you can give me five minutes I'll engage with you properly at Acquaintance level. I just need to get my mind in order," Bartel t-said.

"Fine."

He disengaged. Bartel pushed her thoughts about the scenario down further into her subconscious, and questioned herself whether she needed this engagement with Worrell at this point. If she had been a real spartan, she would have dropped the opportunity immediately. If she were a full hedo, she'd have dropped the scenario immediately.

What did she want to do?

They had been on a similar wavelength almost immediately the night before last. Ever since persono had come to the market and started to be generally adopted, it had changed how relationships worked. That compendium of all the information about the individual with its initially crude ways of protecting personal data had meant that almost immediately you could know as much about the other person as he or she wanted to let you know. That direct persono to persono communication had been scary and exciting and fun and almost dangerous all at the same time. But what it did more than anything was give a real immediate understanding of the other person – even to the point of knowing those areas that the other person wasn't sharing. Any danger signals were immediate – but also it meant that you knew almost instantly whether you had any real connection to the other person.

With all of that, wasted dates and encounters were not unknown but were really reduced. Then when socio came along with its ability to interpret thoughts and use persono to communicate them, personal relations became so much less complicated at the initial level of meeting whether that was an engagement or an encounter because you could probe and really see the other person.

Once that initial meeting of minds had happened, socio had naturally complicated any relationship – so that paradox became the subject of immense academic research and study.

To have engaged with someone and to have been mutually excited and have a mutual understanding with a real connection had become so much easier because it was based on real feelings and thoughts, but also harder because almost immediately you knew the downsides of the other person for you.

Thinking this through again calmed Bartel and took her mind from the scenario creation. Yes. She had felt that real connection and shouldn't waste it.

She engaged with Worrell again. "Hi Emma." He felt pleased. "Shall we go to Acquaintance?"

"Sure."

"I thought there was an immediate connection, Emma – not just thought but felt that," Worrell t-said.

"I felt that too," Bartel t-replied.

"What's the issue then?"

"I don't want to risk another relationship just now," Bartel t-said. "I mean I'm wary of intensity."

"That's rather jumping the gun," Worrell t-said. "Is that what you think this is?"

"I don't know – and in terms of relationships and everything, I am in a bit of a muddle," Bartel t-responded. She could sense Worrell probing her persono and she let him slide through some of the relationships there "Do you see what I mean?"

"I do," Worrell t-responded. "I know you're letting me see rather more than you are necessarily comfortable with, but it does help. Was the split with your husband – Albert isn't it? – was that amicable."

"Entirely." Bartel paused. "We grew apart as you do especially now with the enhanced way that socio works."

"How is that?"

"I guess our relationship was based on quite a lot of distance which is how I think pre-persono relationships must have worked," Bartel t-said. "Then when socio came along and we had all that sharing – and the way that people were sort of shamed into always being open and letting your partner see how and what you were thinking and feeling, we became more distant. That sounds a paradox but I know it happens a lot. It's different now that Kalo have got the levels working so much better and introduced those guidelines about not sharing too much, but it was too late for Albert and me. We were effectively set on Relaxed the whole time."

"The whole time?" Worrell was really surprised. "No wonder you fell apart."

"Neither of us wanted to suggest that we needed more separate mental space – it seemed like a cop out from a full relationship," Bartel t-continued. "I know that sounds daft now – but remember we were very passionate about each other, very much in love – we'd had two girls together, then suddenly we couldn't bear being mentally on top of one another all the time."

"I know – it happened to a lot of couples – well maybe not the falling apart, but the stresses and strains."

"It happened to us," Bartel t-said, thoughtfully. "But there was a good side to the persono and socio combination that helped us immensely. We couldn't stay as a couple but we never lost that feeling for each other and we've always been close. He will or I will engage quite regularly."

"And sex?"

"And sex," Bartel t-said. "That doesn't seem important to either of us – one way or another. Which seems strange for me to admit especially to a stranger. Of course that new idea – well it was new when we were the right age – of having children as early as possible if and when you felt comfortable with someone – has benefited us – I mean I'm 39, my girls are 21 and 19 – they're grown up and independent and I'm young enough to find myself properly. Imagine waiting till your late thirties to have children. That becomes a life sentence." They both t-laughed. "Is Cheryl jealous?"

"Like anyone," Worrell t-replied, "she has her feelings – we all do. Socio didn't get rid of feelings of insecurity. But she knows how I feel about her. And so do you."

"I haven't probed."

"Do," Worrell t-replied. "We've nothing to hide."

As socio allowed Bartel to open up Worrell's persono, he guided her to his feelings about Cheryl and what they shared. It was incredibly warm and comforting, but there was an edge of sadness. She tried to probe that but the control level prevented her from finding out what that was. "What's the sadness?" she t-asked.

"I knew you'd ask, Emma," Worrell t-replied slowly and with difficulty. "Most people don't go anywhere near that. I knew you were special."

"I don't know about that," Bartel t-replied.

"I do. Cheryl has two children, like you, and the man she had the children with – like you she started in her late teens – was the love of her life. He died of an aneurism that even Medi-Assist didn't pick up until it happened. She'll never get over that – and although we have a great relationship – as you've felt, it's almost complete – I can never be totally what she needs."

"I didn't know that still happened," Bartel t-responded both saddened and rather shocked. It was so twentieth.

"You mean because of persono and socio?"

"Yes."

"I don't think even the most intimate use of socio in particular is ever going to change fundamental feelings," Worrell t-replied. "It won't change hers – so there's the sadness."

"Is that why you didn't tell her about our engage?"

"No. Yes. Partly. Look – you know that socio has changed all our understanding about physicality and fidelity and really elevated the mental intimacy – a bit like you said actually drove you apart from Albert because it can have the opposite effect too – and neither Cheryl nor I find that a problem. We honestly don't. But what made me reticent with her, is that I knew she'd immediately know that you and I had connected and it wasn't just physical. That felt like a threat – not to her. But to me. I hate – well too strong a word – I really am nervous about letting her see that she's not everything mentally to me. It seems like a threat – not to her, but to me."

"So when you engaged with her about this – how honest were you?"

"Socio level Relaxed."

"So she knew entirely what you were feeling?"

"Almost entirely."

"I know what you mean," Bartel t-replied. "It's funny, I mean odd, how we can train our minds so that even socio is unaware of what we are thinking at the very deepest level."

"I'm sure you know that twentieth statement that we have voices so we can hide our thoughts."

"It was even earlier, I think. Not that that matters."

"Well – sometimes I think that socio has perfected that because now we have thought-trans so we can hide our thoughts even from ourselves."

"That's pretty deep," Bartel t-replied. "I'm not sure I fully understand. But it does make sense now why you didn't immediately engage with Cheryl and explain about our meeting."

"I never want to give her a reason to cut off from me."

"Understood."

"But I'd like to encounter you again."

"You've weighed up all the risks?"

"I have," Worrell t-responded. "I think there's no real risk – just my paranoia. Do you want to encounter me? Again?"

"I need to think about that." Bartel t-replied. "It feels to me that there are many levels to this. And I don't want to make things difficult for you – or really me. Do you have children?"

"No," Worrell t-said. He was controlling his responses very well and Bartel didn't want to probe too much as that would perhaps give him false messages. It felt very difficult. It was good that they were still at Acquaintance. "Do you want to encounter – I mean do you really want that?"

"Actually I really do – but I'm not sure it's wise," Bartel t-replied, "not for Cheryl's sake, but for your sake. I don't think you can be entirely present."

"I know why you say that. Probably true – but I'd like to encounter. That paradox again about socio. It means you know so quickly whether you have any connection and nine times out of ten – maybe even more, definitely more – you don't. So when you do – you always want to capitalise on it. At least I do."

"Ok. Tonight?"

"Sounds good."

"Same place we encountered?"

"Sounds good. Time?"

"Let's make it 8.30," Bartel t-replied.

"Good idea. One more thing, Emma."

"Yes?"

"You t-said that you don't want too much intensity at the moment."

"Yes."

"I'd like to echo that," Worrell t-said. He was more or less repeating himself. That didn't matter at all.

After they finished the engagement, Bartel sat still and ensured that socio was at Lock. She needed time in her own head. This felt quite dangerous and also quite exciting. Yes – those were the two words she needed, both for tonight and for the scenario.

Chapter 8

The autonom dropped Bartel off at 11.55 just outside the office complex that Savery had engaged her to say he had booked. She registered with the Indi-Assist and was directed to the right floor and she found the room – and she thought Savery had done the right thing because the space had an air of calm that wouldn't have been there with other people.

As a corporation Eclectic was the most soulless of the globals. It had cornered the market in making things, providing services, getting raw materials and looking after needs and wants. It was ruthlessly efficient – like the rest of the GLEAKES – and it always provided a re-assuring, comforting environment, but in a way that you always knew was the result of brainstorming, focus groups and calculation. Eclectic completely reflected the personality – or lack of personality – of the completely vanilla Derek Smith who was probably not its founder but was very definitely in charge. Bartel doubted whether his name was in fact Derek Smith because it was so magnolia and that he had chosen it to be quite empty and ahuman.

Of course he figured in the scandal weeds as did all the Trills, but always with much less fun associated with him.

She had formulated some more ideas for the scenario she wanted to produce in the interval between engaging with Worrell and arriving at the office area. She felt a level of excitement that she rarely felt and she knew this was why she bothered with actually doing something – even though it wasn't an obligation. Savery was late – something that was not good. All the autonoms could compensate for traffic and roadworks and unexpected issues – and would pick someone up knowing the time they had to be at any particular place. It was rare for that to be an issue. So where was he?

"You're five minutes late." Bartel v-said when he arrived, and she was cross and wasn't prepared for any excuse. And this needed voice. "Why?"

"I wanted to check out a physical," Savery v-replied. He was quite defiant.

"What do you mean?"

"Just before I set out for here it occurred to me that although this is a virtual scenario, we should make it as close to reality as possible otherwise it might lose the full force of terror that I think you want," Savery replied. He had a pleasant voice, and rather melodious. He had also introduced a new word – *terror*. That was interesting. "So I wanted to check out exactly what a physical was properly like."

"And you couldn't do that virtually?"

"Of course I could. That's not the point. Sometimes there's a lag between the physical and the virtual – I know there shouldn't be, but you know there is sometimes. And when I was there I compared the virtual with the physical – and I had been right. And the autonom didn't have a chance of catching up with our time scale because I didn't think of it till too late."

"And you couldn't engage me?"

"I should have," Savery v-said. "I got too wrapped up in the idea."

"So what physical?"

"The tomb of the unknown soldier," Savery v-replied, with an air of triumph. "I thought we could use that."

"And what was the difference?"

"In one corner of the inscription, and despite all the monitoring and the control, there was some – well I thought it was graffiti but it was, well, I suppose it was graffiti, but very sad. And I thought that we could use this as part of the softening up."

"Softening up?"

"I'd thought about how to make the fear most effective and I think it's by using the old twentieth techniques," Savery v-said, obviously pleased with himself. "If you make the scene as ordinary as possible – no, I don't mean that quite like that. I mean as normal as possible in the circumstances because the tomb wouldn't be part of usual experience. Then you lull someone into being more at ease and so when you hit them with the cause of fear, it's a bigger disruption. Does that work for you?"

"Yes – it's good." Bartel wondered whether to stay annoyed at his time-keeping but decided that it wasn't worth it because the reasoning was so good. "What did the graffiti – I think that should be graffito – say?"

"That's the point," Savery v-replied. "It was graffiti – because there was a first message then a second. The first said – *how long did you wait for this person not to return?* That seemed to me to capture the reality of that tomb."

"And the second?"

"*Till I could cry no more.*"

"And you found that so very sad?"

"Actually, Emma, I did," Savery v-said. "It felt as though both graffito – see I do know – were absolutely encapsulating the feelings of grief of what – 175 years ago. And I felt transported back to the twentieth, and yet, because the words had apparently appeared quite lately otherwise they'd have already been removed, it seemed someone had really got inside the feelings that had existed then."

"I see that. Of course I do. What I don't see is how this helps us."

"That slight variation in the physical – it may already have gone by now – means that we can place the scenario in a particular time and place – and I suggest we build the whole imagining around this particular moment," Savery v-said, obviously excited by the idea.

"Yes. If you put it like that, I really get it."

"That's great Emma. When I have an idea I'm never sure whether it's good or just that I think it's good."

"This is really good thinking," Bartel v-said. "I hope it makes you feel a little more worthwhile."

"It does. And what had you been thinking?"

"I hadn't got to details like you have. Well – some. My focus was on making the experience as terrifying as we can without making it gratuitously and viciously unpleasant – and then to bring the people out of it by their own efforts. I was looking at the fear as a stimulus for giving them some meaning – you can see I was affected by our conversation the day before yesterday."

"I like that."

"So I think – and I'm vamping now and I've picked up that new word that you used *terror* – it has to be a pleasant June day and the couple are on a sight-seeing trip. I know. I know." Bartel waved aside Savery's objection. "Just listen to me. This is a physical experience that we are imagineering. I know there's a paradox, but go with it for the moment. I'm sure there are any number of people who would probably like to have an actual physical experience – which might not be as good as the experience from Sofari – I mean Latitude has really taken virtual travel to the limit – but might have a desire for a retro experience. Anyway – it doesn't matter. I think we can blur the line between virtual and actual – certainly Sofari does."

"Sorry – I was being too literal." Savery was obviously really wrapped up in this experience.

"Forgiven." Bartel was picking up Savery's excitement and she smiled. "So they are sightseeing – and I think this is where we lull them into a false sense of comfort. That's why they are in Westminster Abbey – and they come across the tomb of the unknown soldier. That's a great detail, Jonas. There's a scene of a few minutes, taking in the enormity of what the tomb represents – and we can use the environment around the tomb that Latitude created, with its echoes – I think that's what Latitude calls them – of the conflicts."

"I've had that virtual experience," Savery v-said. "It is amazing – and you can really experience any of the conflicts that you want. First World War, Second World War, even the events that looked like leading to the Third when the fighting broke out. It is frightening in itself."

"Yes – but that's the point. Everyone knows that you can have that experience of the trenches in a safe way. Think what it would be like if the whole Abbey collapsed around the couple, having been shelled – and the coffin and the unknown warrior are exposed – and they see that graffiti. The couple fall into the grave itself. How am I doing?"

"You're frightening me." Savery looked really frightened too.

"But we've got to take this one stage further – so what can we do? Can we make the experience really on the edge so they feel totally abandoned?"

"That's the real idea – well done, Emma, I couldn't have got here. How about as they climb out of the exposed grave they can see the total devastation of London – so it's not just the Abbey that's destroyed?"

"Yes. That's it. So we've got the opening sequence and the set up for the whole experience. How do we go forward?"

"We've got to give them an escape route – a way back that is down to their ingenuity – then the fear and terror become valid and legitimate and not just gratuitous." Savery v-said all this slowly, working it out as they went forward.

"Yes – let's work on that. They've got to see something that gives them hope."

"Well," Savery v-said, "we could perhaps give them a glimpse of something that hasn't been destroyed. Not sure how. But they could see something – I know some place they love – which is still intact but they have to find a way of getting there. Do you know anything about a place that could do that for them?"

"How about the Lake District – I know that they love that type of experience?" Bartel was racking her brains for what they had talked through at the briefing.

"I think that's too far away," Savery v-said. "Is there anywhere closer or more accessible?"

"Curiously enough – there's Whitstable," Bartel v-said.

"Whitstable? Why?"

"One of them grew up there and it's a sort of nostalgic thing," Bartel v-replied. "Yes – that's good. What's more, although we can make it actually Whitstable, we can make it generic enough so that if anyone else has this experience, it will mean something to them. We now need to flesh this out and get Sofari to make it as real as possible. Have you got time?"

"Not only time – but I want to work on this."

"Do you think this gives you a sense of purpose?"

"Yes," Savery v-said, "It makes me forget everything else and then we can – I mean I can – just focus and feel some sort of achievement as I do at this moment. I know Latitude's strap line is pretty cheesy – but actually it does make sense to me at the moment."

"*Creativity, experience and Sofari – pure meaning*? Does that really do that for you?"

"At this particular instant – yes," Savery v-said.

"I think we need to use socio now – for the detailed work and the interface into Sofari works better through socio. Is that ok?"

"Of course," Savery v-replied. "What level?"

"Shall we try Acquaintance – and if that doesn't work we can always go to Friend?"

"Yes let's." Savery thought socio on – then Bartel did the same and they engaged.

"We need this closeness of thought," Bartel t-said.

"Yes."

They went through the whole scenario, and Sofari built the scenario as they thought to each other – and after a couple of hours they believed they had the finished scenario.

"Can we present this to the clients, do you think?" Savery t-asked.

"Yes. Of course. Why not?"

"I'm just concerned that the terror at the beginning will stay with them till the end," Savery t-said.

"It's got to, hasn't it?"

"I think we ought to leave them with more of a sense of achievement than we have done at this point," Savery t-said. "I don't think it's enough that they have got through a whole range of difficulties. They could get that from one of the twentieth games – if it is properly updated of course."

"You might have a point. I think you do. We need them to have a more than a fuzzy warm sense of getting through. Yes – we said that at the beginning, more or less. They have to have succeeded – no triumphed – against these odds. How do we give them that?"

"Let's think," Savery t-said, ruminating.

"I know." Bartel was alive. "We create a sort of show reel of their various triumphs – you know when they manage to get through the minefield by working out what pattern the mines are in. we celebrate that and the other achievements as a continuing record that they can engage to all their friends and relatives if they want. It's that sharing of the experience afterwards that will make this memorable, strangely enough."

"Great."

"One issue with that, come to think of it," Bartel t-said. "We want this to be a repeatable scenario – because it if is as good as it appears to me at this moment, we could have a winner here, something that will really go viral. That means we'd want to use the selective memory wiping that's just coming in so that they can't tell anyone else and prepare them for the experience. So how do we deal with that?"

"Not sure we can."

"Then may be the show reel is something that has to be unlocked only when someone else has been through it? Bartel t-said.

"I think it's easier to drop the idea," Savery t-said. "It becomes too complicated. For example, what if someone wants to experience it again? We can possibly think of something else."

"OK. We also have to make sure that the warning at the beginning makes them aware of the scale of what they will be doing – without actually letting them know what that is. Does that make sense?"

"Yes. I'll devise that," Savery t-replied. "What are you doing this evening Emma?"

"Why?"

"I thought," Savery t-said, "we might have some time together."

"I can't today. I'm not ruling it out entirely. But let's not get carried away because we have shared so much today. Actually I do have something else more or less planned." It was curious to Bartel that she wasn't admitting to herself that in fact she had got something definite planned. "But I do think we should at some point get together. Perhaps when this is successful?"

68

Chapter 9

Bartel took the autonom home, feeling pleasantly exhausted. She looked at the time. Food. Shower. Perhaps engage with Roseanne and Alice. Then out to meet Worrell. She went through persono. Yes. 8.30.

What was this about? She had shared more with him than she had with anyone for a long time – a couple of years perhaps. What did she want from the encounter?

She didn't need anything from him.

What did she want?

Once in her flat, she engaged with gSynth and thought what she wanted to eat. Time? Make it 7 she thought. No. 6.30. She was hungry. She had given herself a treat – her favourite carbonara. It was expensive but her El-balance was fine.

Washed, fed and as she saw it primped, Bartel thought ordered an autonom to get to the pub at 8.30. It would be with her in fifteen minutes. She idled her mind through the scenario they had been developing through the day and got an update from Sofari about where the implementation of the scenario had got to. Even though Sofari was really powerful – actually because it was so powerful and was backed by the latest in bio-quantum processing – it would take a while to get the full immersive experience right. It had been quite a breakthrough when Sofari allowed two people through their socios to share an experience completely, but it had almost doubled the processing power required – and also doubled the intellectual effort required to create the scenarios that were now possible.

There was something, however, nagging away in her mind over what she and Savery had devised and were implementing through Sofari. There was something missing. Was it a prize or recognition of some kind? Was it too old hat to create rewards and achievements?

What could she do better? What was their solution so far? Some sort of togetherness?

It didn't quite match her vision of something ground-breaking.

She tried to put the idea out of her head. She could come up with a better answer later and Sofari could make the changes relatively easily once the major computational stuff was put to bed.

In Bartel's eyes it was no wonder that the greatest imagineers were really celebrities in their own right and had immense followings through their personos. The importance of Sofari and, for that matter, its creator, Latitude, was increasing all the time. It had seemed that latitude was the least important of the GLEAKES, but almost overnight that perception had changed. It had been a real breakthrough when the first 3D and dual imagineer was given an award – and recognised as someone who had achieved some sort of greatness.

The autonom engaged her and she went down from her flat and took her seat and the autonom immediately cocooned her as they always did. Bartel was excited even though she had no clear idea why she was actually meeting Worrell and what it would lead to or not. She couldn't help it.

As she got out of the autonom, she realised that Worrell was also getting out of his – and they saw each other in that split second. It was curious because Bartel could have engaged him or he could have engaged her while they were on their way, but it was as if they were keeping radio silence. Bartel deliberately put her socio on to Lock. She didn't want in any way to be overwhelmed by her own feelings and thoughts – and certainly didn't want to be overwhelmed by his. This was a moment for voice.

He came up to her and kissed her on the cheek – and they went side by side into the bar. It was noisy like the night before last. It was always remarkable if it was. Socio had largely removed the need for voice – but there was still something about voice, and the way that could hide what people were really thinking that made it attractive in relaxed social settings.

Worrell acknowledged a few people as they made their way through into a quieter spot towards the back of the bar. "Socio?" he asked. "It's so noisy I think it would be best."

"Ok."

"What level?"

"Let's start with Bland," Bartel responded. She could sense Worrell's immediate probe but it was gentle and unassuming. That was good.

"Why did you agree to see me – or even want to see me?" Worrell t-asked.

"I think *I* ought to ask that," Bartel t-said. She immediately realised that as far as she knew he didn't know any details about whether she was in any particular relationship at the moment – so it was a fair question. "But to answer your question, as I think you and I know, there was a connection. That's not too common. Socio sort of strips out any pretence that you can get away with if you're using voice in a bar. So to have that connection seems really important. Now you?"

"Well. I think we've already said it – didn't we?

"All right, but why did Cheryl see this as good?"

"I don't want to speak for her," Worrell t-replied. "Let's get away from this navel gazing shall we? I want to move to Acquaintance."

"I think you're going too fast for me," Bartel t-responded. "I need to hold on to my thoughts a bit longer – and I also don't want to be swamped by your thoughts and feelings, which you know happens or can happen."

"It does. But I'm rather impatient to get to see whether that connection we had is soundly based."

"Does that mean we sleep together tonight?"

"It might do," Worrell t-responded. "I don't think that's the important issue here at all."

"Why not?"

"Because, Emma, what is valuable to me is that human connection," Worrell t-replied. "All the modern aids and attitudes, enabled by persono and socio – and, for example, Medi-stat – mean that sex is still important. That's obvious. But for me – it's the human connection. It's possible to focus on that because the sex issues are largely taken care of, or, I mean, understood."

"I don't think I believe you."

"Is that because secretly at heart you are a hedo?" Worrell t-asked.

71

"I don't think so. I think there's too much propaganda that downplays how important sex is to relationships – and it is a sort of deflection."

"From what?"

"I don't know," Bartel t-said, rather surprised herself at what she had thought. "Actually – that's not entirely true. I do know some of it – but not in a really joined-up thinking way. Look – it's really not what I thought we'd think about."

"But worth thinking about?"

"I guess so," Bartel t-said. "I'm all muddled Dave. Don't take any notice. It was just – well, you know that feeling of pointlessness that we all get because it's hard to find purpose once all your needs and some of your wants have been taken care of? The person I imagine with had a bad sense of that yesterday or the day before and it reminded me of when I had that. It just made me think that somehow or other we're getting something wrong?"

"I take it that your *we* isn't just you and me, but the neo-age." It wasn't a question. "So you're taking a political activist approach?"

"Not at all – I'm not political," Bartel t-said, quite sharply. "In fact that is why I really don't get on with the person that I'm closest to at the moment. He feels that I'm sticking my head in the sand – whereas I think he's looking for problems."

"Are you looking for problems yourself? I could make a case for that, Emma."

"I expect you could. Perhaps I am. But I think I've got more important things to do."

"Do you? What are they?"

"You're just being argumentative," Bartel t-said. "Today I did some important stuff. Well – important to me. I had purpose. I don't need to take on the Trills or whatever the current political cry is. Let them do what they want. They don't impinge on our lives."

"They do."

"Not really," Bartel t-replied. "We can have any drugs we like – or none. Socio has virtually eliminated crime – I mean when was the last time you heard of anyone being raped? We can have any religion we like

– and start a new one if we want. Daft as that sounds. There are no restrictions on political parties or political movements. Voting is free – and compulsory so we all have to be part of this democracy, even if we vote to abstain."

"So what were you saying about sex – we seem to have lost that?"

"Yes. You're right. I don't know I'm a bit muddled now. Can we talk about something else?"

"Of course. I just thought you were saying something really important for – well – us."

"I doubt it," Bartel t-said. "I don't do important speeches." They both t-laughed. "All right. I guess I was saying that for the first time in history – as I understand it – the availability of sex . . . No the attitudes towards sex is what I mean. Mean that it's *just one of those things.* Like you were suggesting. It wasn't important if you and I ended sleeping together this evening. Or if we didn't. And, of course, on one level you're right. I'm enough of a hedo to be able to have a connection with you – I don't sleep with people where there's no connection, and I think that's common now. I don't just enjoy the physical because I know it's safe because of Medi-stat, so no disease is transmitted, and we've sorted out contraception, and now it's a male responsibility as well. All those things. Just I think sex is more important than that."

"Do you mean jealousy is an entirely human reaction?"

"I wasn't thinking of that. I don't know about that. Yes. I've felt jealousy and it's a destructive feeling. And sometimes I don't trust acquiescence by the other partner. I guess that's what I mean."

"I'm glad we're having this thought, Emma."

"But?"

"There is a but," Worrell t-agreed. "I didn't expect this type of t-conversation. I was anticipating seeing whether there was a strong connection between us."

"Can you say what that is?"

"Yes," Worrell t-replied, "it's that moment when socio shows you something about the other person that makes you think about yourself in a different way."

"That's a great chat up line."

"I didn't mean to be so sententious or pompous," Worrell t-replied. "I honestly do think that's right. Look just one more question – the one I asked earlier. What is it that you think is a deflection, because I'm not sure I understand that, and what would it be deflecting us from?"

"If I knew that, Dave, I'd be a politician." Bartel t-laughed at herself. "Or I'd become some sort of preacher."

"Fair point, Emma. I really want to change our socio level to Friend. I know that that is a misnomer – I think Kalo was having a laugh when they gave these names to the socio levels – but I want to be able to probe you more, and I want to let you probe me more."

"Ok." Bartel was surprised because the t-conversation hadn't been going in that direction. She thought the change and felt the warmth of his feelings and thoughts as Worrell did the same. Sometimes a probe could be invasive and most people changed the level down again quickly. With Worrell it felt quite natural. And as though they were giving to each other. "I'm glad we did that," she t-said to him. "I do feel different now."

"I don't want you to forget what we were conversing about."

"I won't." Bartel t-said. Then she gave herself up to her thoughts and feelings, and in a quite crowded room, she felt alone with him. That was a wonderful part of socio sometimes.

She t-felt him put his arm round her, and felt the gentle pressure of his hand on her shoulder, and she just relaxed and luxuriated in a warm feeling of closeness. Without socio this would have been impossible. Thank you Kalo. Thank you Elora Ghose for creating Kalo and persono and socio. She t-placed her hand on his thigh and felt him relax and tense at the same time. His hands were t-stroking her breast and she moved her hand upwards to touch him – slowly, sensuously – feeling her own sensations and his, while he shared hers and felt his own. He t-kissed her and it was so gentle and so tantalising and so intense, as he probed her feelings while letting his feelings become entirely open to her. It was at moments like these that she felt she could become a hedo – and give up entirely any sense of balance. It always made sense to be serene, but sometimes being sensible wasn't that important. She could never be a spartan.

"Autonom?" he t-asked.

"Yes."

They walked, physically holding hands outside and waited briefly for the autonom. Bartel t-instructed it to take them to her flat, and as they sat in the machine silently taking them through the night, they t-fondled each other and were so relaxed. Worrell insisted on using his El-pay.

In her flat they sat opposite each other – the gSynth had produced some coffee to his precise instructions. They drank and t-caressed each other tantalisingly, knowing that they would soon be physically making love and enjoying the anticipation. Bartel was, unlike how she often was, relaxed and enjoyed the feeling as he first t-undressed her, using her own knowledge of her body to feed his thoughts. When she was t-naked, she t-undressed him. It was almost too much to bear – but it was so like the actual that it meant that it was doubling the pleasure.

They moved to her bed and she let him undress her, and then she undressed him, before they lay gently down on top of the bed and let their bodies and their minds mingle and excite and satisfy.

"Let's change to Relaxed for the socio," she t-suggested.

"Good for me."

Their thoughts were overwhelming for a moment or two as the socio adjusted and filtered the feelings. The physical excitement was tantalisingly slow for both of them – as both the physical and t-caresses were almost too much to bear. They were totally connected and both lost themselves in, and focused on, each other's feelings and their own. At Relaxed socio allowed them to sense the feelings and thoughts that were barely conscious to the other person. And the feel of skin on skin, the sheer pleasure of his finger tips touching her breasts while she held him was all consuming.

"The extreme pleasure that I have," Worrell v-said, "if you don't mind me talking at this moment, is knowing that even before we made love that it would feel fulfilling and total afterwards. Is that strange?"

"I like you talking."

"Do you know what I mean?"

"Yes." Bartel was so completely overwhelmed with him now, lying with her leg across his body, and just feeling his complete calmness, that she could hardly bring herself to v-talk, but wanted to have that extra dimension even while socio was at its highest level.

They lay quietly, with his right hand around her body, tracing small circles on her back.

"That was complete, Emma."

"It was for me," she v-said. "Can we put socio to Lock?"

"Why?"

"I want to lose my consciousness of everything and focus on the here and now," Bartel v-said. It was lovely to hear her voice, quiet and clear.

"Sure," Worrell v-said.

Bartel didn't want the distraction of his thoughts and feelings and sharing her thoughts and feelings, but wanted to savour the physical completeness in her own way and time. And as they thought socio down to Lock, the silence and the rapport were both entirely present to her and the two of them drifted off to sleep.

Bartel woke first and her movement woke Worrell. They both sat up and looked at each other.

"Were you expecting that?" he v-asked.

"No."

"Nor was I. Socio makes a huge difference to making love, even casual encounters, and I often wonder how previous generations found sex before socio, but sometimes it goes beyond and takes my breath away." He was voicing this for her and for himself.

"For me too." Bartel was very nervous about this conversation, because she had been overwhelmed too. She had had an inkling strangely enough that she would be when she first engaged with him. But she didn't want complications at the moment and relationships always became complicated. The end of her marriage to Thornton, the tortuous and almost labyrinthine quality of her relationship with Albert, which had ended in bewilderment rather than acrimony and pain, meant that she was happy to engage with men, to encounter men, and to sleep with them, and not ignore the emotional elements in any of it, but she didn't want entanglement any more. She needed her space. Perhaps that was one of the reasons that she kept Pennington at a metaphorical arm's length.

She could feel a painful edge to this moment, and wanted to ignore it, but her mind kept going back to touch the painful tooth. She didn't want to spoil the moment, but she was frightened, partly of herself.

"Is there a problem?" he v-asked. Thank goodness socio was on Lock. She v-murmured something. "That's all right, Emma – what is it? I could feel you change – even without socio."

"I'd rather not talk about it at this moment."

"That's fine." He said nothing, and she could sense, even with socio at Lock that he was puzzled and now not relaxed.

"How will Cheryl feel about this?"

She's part of it," Worrell v-said. "I don't have any important secrets from her."

"What does that mean?"

"We'll share this experience," he v-said, "as you might expect."

"I'm not sure I expect that," she v-said. "I do know that some people do and some people would rather not experience it like that."

"How do you feel about that?"

"It varies," she v-said, truthfully and slowly. "It depends how I feel about the man I'm in a relationship with and also about the man I am engaging and encountering."

"How do you feel about me?"

"That's the issue," she v-said. "I feel that you and I have a real connection – I don't know what to call it. It feels like more than sex. More than an emotional attachment. And I am frightened. Are you happy with Cheryl?"

"Yes, of course," he v-said. But he wasn't at some level. They lay in silence. "Perhaps I don't know if I am or not."

"Oh, no, Dave," Bartel v-said. Without socio she was less inclined to control her thoughts and emotions.

"Why – 'Oh no'?"

"I'm not ready for a relationship," Bartel v-said. "That is – not ready to live with anyone or focused on one person. It's not about fidelity – I know that's redefined now we have socio – and it's not about sex, but I just can't take any complications."

"I can understand that. That wasn't the implication of not being that happy with Cheryl. I'm not the sort of person to bounce from one relationship to another. I need that space too."

"But . . ."

"No – that's true," Worrell v-said.

"But don't you feel that you are not being fair to Cheryl?"

"That's something I'll have to think about – because I think you're right. These new ways of having relationships – I don't think it is a new way just a new perspective on such relationships – is at times very confusing. Do you agree?"

"Yes – that's why I am very wary. What we've just shared is amazing – and probably unforgettable and out of the blue. Because of Medi-stat and socio there is no anxiety about such an encounter – but that doesn't take away the psychological effects and the way I sometimes get bewildered. I mean – how could we have had such a perfect experience? In one way it doesn't make sense."

"I think it does."

"How?"

"Perhaps you're right," Worrell v-said. "I'll know better when I've seen Cheryl. She is actually the only person I've been able to share with – till today. I mean fully share and not hold back. In the past I've always been able to control my feelings and not share them fully. Be in my head. Yes." He paused. "I do feel destabilised. That's not a bad thing. It may bring a different intensity to my relationship with Cheryl – if that makes sense."

"Do you think things were this complicated before we had socio and persono?" Bartel v-asked.

"Do you?"

"I think they must have been – but in so many different ways. Imagine being in your own head and only in your own head when you're making love. Do you remember that question people used to laugh about – 'How was it for you?'"

"Yes."

"So I expect the physical was much more important, and because you could know so little about the other person, it was all conjecture and faith or belief," Worrell v-said. "Can you imagine how complicated that could become? Imagine if you felt insecure and you thought sex was the most important element in a relationship and you just didn't know if the other person was faithful?"

"I guess – and I probably know – that that must have been more complex than this. At least more room to destabilise someone. Are you ok though with what I said about Cheryl?"

"Perfectly." She reached for him. "Set socio to Relaxed?"

He looked deeply into her eyes and traced the shape of her face and v-said: "With pleasure."

Chapter 10

Bartel woke from really not much sleep. Worrell had left around 3 am. She felt tired and warm in a way she hadn't since the early days with Thornton. She set socio to Lock as she didn't want to be disturbed. There was quite a lot to do before 11 when she and Savery were to report back to the clients. She checked Sofari – and the scenario was complete in outline form. It would be only another few hours and the experience would be finished.

She looked through the thumbnails – and it was really almost perfect – the way that Sofari interpreted ideas and brought them to virtual life was astonishing and the physical environment it created using the Exo-sim 3D physical environment was still impressive to Bartel. She thought Sofari into making a few tweaks and engaged with Savery.

At the back of her mind was that nagging question about the scenario. What had she missed? She thought about the details of the scenario – but then realised that wouldn't help. Her mentor when she started out in imagineering had always said *go back to the client*. What was it about them that she had to build on? Suddenly she knew how to address the weakness in the experience that had been troubling her. She engaged with Sofari and created the outline of the changes – and left Sofari to fill in the spaces.

"Are you still all right for 11?"

"Yes – and raring to go," Savery t-replied. "I've been through the Sofari scenario and it looks ground breaking to me."

"Why do you say that? I actually agree with you, but what in particular?"

"I think it's the way that fear and terror is generated by the ordinary – or the changes in the ordinary – that do that. I can't seem to express it. I know what I mean but it's difficult. It's also the way that even in the depth of the terror there is a real sense of – I thought *comfort* initially – but that's not the word. I know. *Re-assurance*. Even in the depth of terror, we've given just enough of a hook to reality to make it bearable."

"I think that's right." Savery had t-expressed something she had been grasping very badly. She t-added: "I'm not sure how we did that."

"I don't think it was so much *we* as you, Emma."

"That's kind of you, Jonas," Bartel t-replied. "I couldn't have got here without you. I've changed one or two things though."

"What?"

"Let me not answer that question. I'm really pleased with the idea at the moment – but I might feel differently about the change when I am going through it again."

"Ok. See you at 11." Savery disengaged.

Bartel wondered if this might be a good day and perhaps a few good days. There was always Pennington and how he discomposed her and really threatened her equanimity. Why did he always have to question the status quo which worked well? She went through some of the tired old thoughts she always had at this point. Need had been eliminated through the efforts of the Trills. They weren't dictatorial unlike powerful people in the past – and they allowed people to flourish with no sense of need – and that global revolution had been so significant. It was a highly individualised culture now and Aristotle's idea that people were social beings had been subverted if not replaced by the way that individuality was now so prized.

Was it curious, she thought to herself and not for the first time, that the very existence of socio, which created contact between people had really emphasised how important being an individual was to everyone?

She thought the time for the autonom to pick her up and it responded that she'd need rather longer than she anticipated to get to the clients' house. That was fine.

She had time enough to prepare the presentation of the scenario – and wondered what to call it. That could be important in this world of brands and associated ideas. Bartel liked to call her scenarios by type – using words prominently like *fun, exciting,* and even, once, *tedious* and then add a word that was unusual. She leafed through the INsighto dictionary. *Demotic* sounded right – unattached in meaning to the experience she had created. *Fear-demotic* or *Demotic-Fear*. She engaged with Savery. "What do you think?"

"I like the odd word you've chosen, Emma. I don't think *fear* is right though. How about making it alliterative and using *dread* – *Dread-Demotic*?" he t-suggested.

"Perfect."

Then there were a few little odds and ends to clear up. What sort of compensation should she ask? It wasn't that important but to make the clients feel they were involved in something significant it required a certain sum. Four times or three times the weekly stipend for entertainment? Try three she thought. This could be important in establishing the value of Dread-Demotic and at the same time she didn't want to put them off.

The autonom took her to the clients' house out in the country. When she had first seen it at the time when the clients briefed her about the type of experience they wanted – and that had been only a skeleton which was just as she preferred – she had been rather overwhelmed. The couple, the Tomlinsons, Reginald and Jeannette, in their late thirties were obviously successful – and there was a hint that they were rather better connected than might be expected but what that might mean was opaque as far as Bartel was concerned. The couple had said that although they were really in a positive position socially and hierarchically, in terms of their personal relationship they needed something, as they felt jaded.

One thing that puzzled Bartel for the moment was how they had been introduced to her and what she did. No light was shed on that even searching socio. It was a nagging feeling of concern, but she didn't know why.

The Tomlinsons had insisted on an encounter and not just a socio engagement. That had been unusual for a first meeting but also interesting. They had only a few things they didn't want but they were very important issues and once again it seemed to Bartel that it was quite odd but it also made the encounter all the more interesting.

The Tomlinsons stipulated that it wasn't to be a sexual experience – that was too easy and wouldn't require an imagineer, let alone a team of two. It shouldn't be ordinary – though they couldn't define that. Not religious. Not political. No psychedelic elements, despite the obvious use of Sofari. It shouldn't be off the shelf and it should task Sofari to its limits.

Sitting talking to them had been quite disconcerting. They t-explained that they had been incredibly intense with each other for a few years, but while the physical remained at a high level their engagement on a socio level had been waning. So what could she do?

Savery was waiting for her outside the house – he'd got there a minute before her and had let her know. They engaged with the clients' socio and they came to the door and they were shown into the same room – more a studio than a living room – as before. Bartel engaged them and asked what level of socio they wanted to use. "Can we use voice?"

"Of course," Bartel t-replied. "We'll lose some of the subtlety and some of the insights – but that's fine. It may make *Dread-Demotic* more powerful. It might."

"That's good," they both v-said together

"So – let me outline what we intend you to experience," Bartel v-said. It had been a good idea to use voice. She could control the way she communicated with less effort and focus more on the actual message she wanted to give.

"Please do. But first – does the name of the experience tell us anything about it?" Reginald v-asked.

"It may do." Savery came in quickly – with what was a good answer.

"And you followed the brief? Not focused on sex, politics, religion, or the ordinary?" Jeannette v-asked. She was evidently quite excited.

"To the letter." Savery v-said.

"Now let me outline what this experience is," Bartel v-said. "I'm not going to give away anything. This is an experience that shouldn't be anticipated. You do have a panic button. Think *red* twice at any time and the experience will end. I don't want to say much more than that."

"Is it real time?" Reginald v-asked.

"Almost." Bartel thought about this. "It's a twelve hour experience which is condensed. I won't tell you by how much – not least because that depends on you."

"Are you two pleased with it?" Jeannette v-asked.

"Without being smug – yes." Bartel v-answered slowly and with a smile on her face. "The only question we have is when do you want to experience it?"

"Could we start it today – more or less now?" Jeannette had some impatience – Bartel was glad that socio was at Lock and not being used because she felt irritated by the question for some reason. She had been planning for them to go straight into it. She asked herself why was she irritated? Perhaps she was just tired after the night with Worrell.

"That's the plan, actually," Savery v-said, seeing that Bartel for some reason wasn't comfortable. "So – don your Exo-Sims and we can start Sofari and engage."

"Please set socio to Friend," Bartel v-said. "We need to monitor this experience and how you are. We won't invade or probe – but we would like to be aware."

"Should we eat first if this is going to be extended?" Reginald v-asked.

"You can – but I'd suggest not. We build all of that into the experience – so comfort breaks, food and drink are all in the environment and time is allocated depending upon how you feel." Bartel looked quizzically at them: "Ok?"

"Yes great," Jeannette v-said. The two of them went off to put on their filmy Exo-Sims and returned. "Should we set socio to Friend now?"

"Yes."

"Right then – I think we're ready," Reginald v-said.

"Do you want to use the Exo-Sim 3D or a different eye display?" Savery v-asked.

"I think we're happy with the in-built – it's usually simpler and there are no connection issues," Jeannette v-said.

"That's good," Bartel v-said, "and I think you should go to your bedroom or some other comfortable place. This is a long experience. OK?"

The two of them left and Bartel and Savery settled down in the studio-like room. They set their mutual socio to Relaxed so they could share the probe into the Tomlinsons' socio as they went through the experience, and at the same time set their mutual socio to Friend with the Tomlinsons, and were pleased to feel that they were taking this experience without mutualising their socio. It would be a much more raw experience like that.

Sofari started and the Tomlinsons found themselves happily in a sight-seeing group and they were puzzled but very relaxed as they entered Westminster Abbey. Bartel and Savery could feel their underlying tension but were pleased at the way the tension was gradually being reduced and reduced till the Tomlinsons had apparently forgotten they were in a scenario. Because this was exactly as they had hoped and planned, Bartel and Savery exchanged congratulatory thoughts – perhaps too soon. The Tomlinsons didn't even notice that they were not with anyone else as they approached the tomb of the unknown warrior.

Then absolute terror gripped them both as the slab of black marble started to move towards them and stopped just in front of them, and they could see human bones of clearly more than just one person. And they moved backwards and found themselves against a wall which pushed them more and more towards where the slab of marble had been, as the earth under the bones started to fall away. At that moment Westminster Abbey started to shake, and the whole edifice started to crumble around them, and as falling masonry, statues, roof beams and dust enveloped them but didn't touch them, Bartel and Savery felt just the touch of security in the Tomlinsons' minds that Bartel had been so intent on creating in the scenario. The intensity of the fear was palpable even so.

Through the next four hours, the four minds, Bartel and Savery's vicariously, went through emotion after emotion as they dealt with a scorched earth landscape where London had disappeared and the Tomlinsons had to find their way to gain the key to returning from the scenario. They also had to understand what the nature of that key was.

As the time went on it became clear that the Tomlinsons were learning to be resourceful, particularly as they realised the predicament they were in – and were apparently unable to tell themselves this was just a scenario. Bartel felt most pleased at that moment by this, perhaps unwilling, suspension of disbelief. As it was real time, the Tomlinsons had to find food, find toilets, rest a little and get somewhere.

That had actually been the weak element, she had thought, in their scenario – turning the experience into a quest and that would echo so many stories and even the video games that had ushered in virtual reality. Making that more complex or perhaps simpler – she couldn't work that out even to herself what she had done – had been a master stroke as far as she could think.

As she had realised in time, the weakness had been the idea of rewards.

She had therefore got rid of the idea that achieving certain goals would get rewards such as food or rest or new tools or new insights which had been a staple of most of the experiences she had created on her own or with Savery. She had made it so that there was nothing incremental about the quest for something. At any moment post the initial traumatic terror, there were to be no more actually terrifying events, but the clients wouldn't know that and would always be on edge. At no point were they to feel that they had reached a better place. At no point were they to anticipate what was happening. So for hours they would be on the edge of their consciousness unable to think about anything else but getting through the next five minutes. And yet she had built in a confidence that they could get through and that what they were doing was worthwhile. Bartel had achieved this by getting Sofari to create a sense of heightened togetherness which was injected into their socios, individually and as a couple. That had been the initial stimulus for the experience and what they had wanted had made this the centre of the experience, although the real terror would be the most immediate element. There was to be no artificial sense of achievement, only a heightened sense of their relationship.

Perhaps that was the paradigm of life in 2084.

At the end of the first four hours, the Tomlinsons were really flagging but had passed several points where their socios were really complementing each other's. "Is this what you meant, Emma?" Savery t-asked.

"By what?"

"When you said that you'd been worried about a weakness in the experience and you'd found a way to strengthen it," Savery t-said, looking at her intently.

"Yes – I guess it is." She t-explained her reasoning and how she had come to the solution that the Tomlinsons were experiencing.

"Did that come from my melt down two days ago?"

"Partly." Bartel felt obliged to give Savery some credit and make him feel better as he was probably still fragile. "It was partly through going back and understanding what the clients had focused on when they briefed us."

"What in particular?"

"It was when they said that their relationship was jaded – or some such idea – so I thought that if we could find a way to reinforce their togetherness that could provide the motivation for them to keep going rather than some sort of incremental reward."

"I see. That's either brilliantly clever, Emma, or too trite for words."

"Let's see. By the way, do you feel as tired as I do? I didn't realise that we would live this experience with them, and we would have to be with them in real time."

"I surely do, Emma. Normally we can just set them off with Sofari and get reports as Sofari monitors them," Savery t-ruminated. "I hadn't realised that it was so important that we went through the experience with them, but of course that was short sighted of me. This is so novel, I'd have wanted to do this. Wasn't that moment when the slab moved impressive?"

"Yes – Sofari did a great job with that," Bartel t-replied.

"I didn't mean that. I meant their reactions and that sense of blind terror."

The Tomlinsons needed a rest too – and Sofari had built in ten minutes of peace which was undercut by the sense of foreboding in the whole experience. It was fascinating monitoring the way they were asking each other and probing each other to know what to do next.

"Do you know what the best thing is about this so far, Emma?" Savery t-asked. She looked at him quizzically. "As far as I understand it, the idea of terror and focusing on their togetherness seems to be working. I was worried that terror would mean they would push the metaphorical escape button. That hasn't occurred to them."

"You're right," Bartel t-replied. "That is working. Even better than I had hoped. Why, I wonder?"

"I think you were right about giving them confidence in each other," Savery t-said. "Now what have they got to do?"

"The experience is telling them to move on somehow and find something that they don't know is what they are looking for. They've coped with that well so far. I'm hoping that they will recognise that stretch of green in the far distance as some sort of goal through the contrast with the destruction in the landscape around them. I guess it doesn't matter if they don't. They will still be metaphorically and probably physically clinging to each other."

"I guess that perhaps your focus on their relationship will mean that they could make love." Savery was very thoughtful as he t-said this. "I think that that might be my reaction."

"They might. I doubt it. Let's see. Especially as they were very insistent that there should be no sex."

The next hours were fascinating to Savery and Bartel as they realised the strength of their scenario and the depth of the experience the Tomlinsons were having. The Tomlinsons were exhausted at the end of that time and the experience came to an end quite naturally although it might have gone on for another few hours. As they emerged from their bedroom, there was an air of relief.

"Can we use voice?" Bartel t-asked.

"Why? I guess so as we've been engaged on socio all this time. Let's do that." Reginald was worn out and his t-response was almost a faint whisper. They all set their socios to Lock.

"So?" Bartel v-asked.

"Absolutely amazing and a crazy experience and beyond what I could have imagined, and exhausting and exciting – I don't know what to say," Jeannette v-said.

"Terrifying?" Savery v-asked.

"For a purpose," Reginald v-responded. "I don't think I've ever been that terrified. I hated that at first."

"And then?" Bartel v-asked.

"And then – well it didn't go away, that terror, for the whole experience, but we learned to cope with it," Reginald v-said.

"We?" Savery v-asked.

"Yes – *we*," Jeannette v-said. "And we didn't just cope with it. We used it in a funny – I mean, strange – way."

The debrief went on for another half hour as the Tomlinsons recounted their feelings and how they had developed a sense of purposefulness – much to their surprise, they v-said – in their relationship. They were overwhelmed and amazed and engaged and would have gone on talking with Bartel and Savery for hours despite their tiredness. "The best experience of our lives." Jeannette had v-said.

"How are you using that word *experience*? Do you mean just virtual or do you mean all experiences."

"For me – the best experience bar none," Reginald v-said.

"I agree." Jeannette v-said.

"Anything in particular?" Bartel v-asked.

"I think it was the totality of the whole experience – like nothing I've experienced and nothing I expected," Reginald v-said.

"More than that," Jeannette v-said, "I can't forget the outcome. You really understood the brief we gave you and you actually produced an experience absolutely tailored to our needs – wants even."

"Yes – that's right and I hadn't thought of it like that," Reginald v-said. "It was finally very life affirming and also gave us a new edge to our relationship. Yes. That's really important."

"That's great to hear," Savery v-said. "Just some thoughts. As the content is so important and we think ground breaking, please don't spoil the surprise for other people by ever mentioning what happens, if you actually manage to remember anything, once the selective memory erasure happens. Is that ok?" They both agreed. "Secondly, it would be very helpful if you could use all the usual places for a review."

"I'd be delighted to do that," Reginald v-said. "Jeannette?"

"Absolutely."

Chapter 11

Bartel and Savery shared an autonom back to Savery's place. They were on a real high. Neither had experienced something so wearying, exciting, challenging and rewarding in their professional lives. They had immediately switched to socio and Friend in the autonom and the rush of ideas and excitement was overwhelming. As the autonom pulled up outside his place he invited her in to wash up and relax after the excitement.

With some misgivings, Bartel t-agreed.

Inside Savery offered the usual choices of beverages and Bartel decided that alcohol was the best drug at the moment. They waited the few minutes for the gSynth to create the Burgundy that Savery was especially fond of – and sipped the wine. "What do you think could be better?" Bartel t-asked.

"I think there is one thing that we need to address if this becomes at all popular," Savery t-began, "and that is how we monitor it or how Sofari monitors the experience. We shouldn't forget that there is a terrifying experience here and not everyone may be able to take that."

"A really good point, Jonas," Bartel t-said. "We wouldn't be able to monitor the experience in real time like we did today. And there are real issues as you say. Let's engage now with Sofari and see whether there are any ways to make that a reality."

They engaged with Sofari and probed through the Sapiens element of the program and found a thread that they needed. There was a health and safety element in the artificial intelligence that could be brought into action properly with a bit of thought, and Savery and Bartel could tailor that to the experience.

"One further question that came out of our discussions with the Tomlinsons was around the memory issues," Savery t-said.

"Yes – I hadn't actually thought those through," Bartel t-replied. "There's a real difficulty in getting people to recommend or even talk about the experience if we've wiped the memory of the experience from their minds."

"Just my point," Savery t-said.

"Do you know how partial the memory wiping can be?"

"I don't," Savery t-said, thoughtfully.

"Perhaps you could look into that for us, and see whether we can leave some vestigial memories that people can use?" Bartel t-asked.

"I'd be delighted to do that – it could be important and as this is a new facility, might add to the ground-breaking nature of Dread-Demotic," Savery t-replied.

"Can I get you some food?" Savery t-asked.

"No – I'm all right. I probably need to get back."

"For any particular reason?"

"No – I suppose not," Bartel t-replied.

"Can we spend a bit of time together?" Savery t-asked.

"I don't think that's good at the moment," Bartel t-replied. "Too many moving parts in my life for the moment. As I said, I'm not ruling it out. I know what you are feeling at this moment – of course I do know that as we have set socio at Friend – and I share some of that feeling. This is not the right time. I need space."

"Understood."

They t-talked some more and Bartel got up to go. Savery escorted her to the front door and rather clumsily hugged her to say goodbye. "No problem." Bartel t-said to him as she felt his body against hers. "See you tomorrow, I hope – or in all likelihood."

She left and t-called an autonom. Standing outside Savery's building, she turned her socio with him to Lock and wondered whether she was encouraging him or discouraging him or what signals she was giving. Sometimes socio and persono together made life more complicated not less.

The autonom dropped her off and as she was entering her flat, Pennington engaged her. "Are you free?"

"Not really, Andrew," she t-replied. "Why?"

"I just want to see you and make sure that there's no ill feeling between us," Pennington t-said.

"Can we do this via socio?"

"I'd rather we encountered," Pennington t-responded.

"I'm very tired, Andrew."

"I won't take long and I will let you rest, I promise." Pennington made a presumptive close. It wasn't too much of an imposition, but Bartel didn't want any aggravation and too often that was the result of being with him. She was also not clear in her mind how she felt about Worrell so this was a complication she could do without.

"When?"

"Ten minutes – I'm not far from you, Emma," Pennington t-responded, and disengaged.

Bartel went in and relaxed in her favourite chair. Probably she ought to freshen up and prepare for Pennington's visit, but she couldn't be bothered. It had been a great day – now how to follow it up. She thought hard about that and wasn't too clear what she could do.

Pennington arrived and engaged to tell her that he was coming up. She opened the door for him and gave him a glass of red wine as he came through the door. "Voice?" Pennington t-asked.

"Why not," Bartel v-said, and ensured that socio was on Lock. With Pennington it was always so easy to let thoughts leak unwittingly, as he got below her threshold. "So why the urgency?"

"It's not sex – well not just sex," Pennington v-said. She loved his voice – and he knew it which is why he often wanted to talk rather than have a t-discussion.

"You are incorrigible, Andrew."

"I know," he v-said. "I had a message which I thought was strange from the Tomlinsons. They were so excited I wanted to find out from you what that was all about."

"How do you know the Tomlinsons? Oh. Of course. You introduced me to them. I'd totally forgotten that. What did they say?"

"Nothing much," Pennington said. He sat opposite Bartel and looked very intense. "But what little they did was really amazing."

"So what did they tell you?"

"They said that you had imagineered a brilliant experience and the scenario had been out of this world – ground breaking, exciting, challenging and fulfilling."

"Was that all?"

"Yes, actually no – they couldn't go into details and they said you'd asked them to keep anything they remembered from the experience and the scenario to themselves and not let on," Pennington replied. "So what have you been up to, Emma?"

"Not to be too immodest, I'd worked with Jonas Savery – not sure you've met him – oh you have – on creating an experience. They had some specific qualities they needed to have in it and I think we met the brief brilliantly," Bartel replied. "Are you interested?"

"Of course, I am Emma. Anything you do is interesting to me and I'm glad my recommendation worked out so well for both of you, I mean the Tomlinsons and you and Jonas. Would it work for me?"

"I don't think so, Andrew," Bartel v-said, without explanation.

"Don't be coy, Emma, why not?"

"It's quite simple – it's a couple experience," Bartel v-said. "I don't think you are in a relationship that would make it suitable for you."

"Why?"

"The Tomlinsons were drifting apart," Bartel v-said. "Besides the depth and the extent of the scenario, which is probably ground-breaking – a phrase I've used an awful lot today as it does go straight to the point – and in doing so it went by a route that was unexpected to them."

"What's it called?"

"Dread-Demotic," Bartel v-said. She looked at him.

"So you use fear?"

"Yes," she v-said. "But that's not the clever part at all. And I don't want to tell you what that is."

"You're making this sound more and more intriguing – and good for you. I really didn't see you as a great sales person, Emma, but it's working on me. Can I do anything to help?"

"What do you mean?"

"Do you want me to spread the word, for example?"

"That would be great, Andrew," Bartel v-said. "So pleased the Tomlinsons liked it – loved it perhaps."

"They said it had changed their life."

"That's good to hear. I'd forgotten you'd introduced us – not sure how I did manage to do that – but how do you know them?" Bartel v-asked.

"Let me ask you a question first?"

"Sure."

"Well," Pennington v-said, "you know that I am quite aware of some of the networks that lead to the Trills?"

"Yes. It's all part of your conspiracy issues and the way that the society is run – in your opinion – solely for the benefit of the Trills," Bartel v-replied.

"Hardly a balanced way to report what I do, Emma, is it?"

"How would you describe it then, Andrew?" Bartel t-asked.

"It's true that I see the Trills as a malign influence on our lives – notwithstanding some of the great things that have been achieved in this neo-age – but I don't deal in conspiracies. I do try to keep abreast of coming people – like the Tomlinsons – because I need to understand how all of this works so I can somehow subvert it."

"Ok – let's not go down that route," Bartel t-replied.

"I didn't intend to – but just know that the Tomlinsons are coming people – and before you ask I do not really know what that actually means in practice – only they are people to keep an eye on."

"Yes – that's enough. And I appreciate the introduction," Bartel v-said. "You could have done this over socio, Andrew. Let me tell you – I don't want to sleep with you at the moment."

"That's fine," Pennington v-said. "Let me, then, just say this – you're an intelligent person, and yet you close your eyes to what is going on.

Why is that? I mean why won't you even let me talk to you about our situation?"

"I'm not interested," Bartel v-said. "I'm just not interested at all. I know that you think our lives are terrible, that we're in some sort of slavery to the Trills, and that they are an oligarchy that's beyond accountability. But look at it from a different perspective. Honestly I don't know how many times I have to tell you this. If it is an oligarchy, it's the first time in history that it is a benevolent one that doesn't rely on repression and violence. What's not to like in a world – a world, Andrew – where everyone's basic needs are met, there is disease control and possibly at some point disease elimination, where we have more or less done away with crime because that can't exist where socio and persono are in use. Even sexual assault is very difficult nowadays. I think it's never been easier to be a woman."

"I didn't mean to raise this really," Pennington v-said. "I really can't stand being at odds with you Emma. I think we have such a lot to share – and that's not just sex. We love the same things. When we're engaged on socio there is really not a finer feeling."

"So please leave it at that."

"Ok, Emma. I know – let's just have this to think on. You are totally aware of what you've got – and yes, you're right. Those are positive things from the first apparently non-repressive oligarchy in world history. All I ever want you to do is be aware of what you haven't got." He paused and came back before Bartel could respond. "End of. End of."

"I know that you think you're doing this for my own good, Andrew," Bartel v-replied, "and I think you probably are. But it's not up to you to define what my own good is. That's for me. And I don't feel what I haven't got. Look I don't want to part with you again on bad terms – we do enough of that. Set socio to Relaxed – yes Relaxed – and let us exchange our thoughts."

They both did – and each could feel the other open up – and it was lovely for Bartel to feel the pure emotion that Pennington felt for her. As with Worrell this was a two edged sword. It was lovely but it was also a threat to her peace of mind and her independence and the way she wanted to live her life.

"This is so lovely, Emma," Pennington t-said.

"I know – I feel it too. But if I probe, you know what I see in you – that frustration and that anger – and I don't need that in my life."

"Don't go there, then," Pennington t-replied. "Come with me a little bit in our memories – do you remember when we first met and we first made love – and how we were both unused to socio – as I suppose everyone was – and it was overwhelming and wonderful."

"I remember, Andrew."

"We have that always, Emma," Pennington t-said, wistfully.

They stayed like that for more minutes, echoing thoughts back and forth and feeling very close, but always with that undercut of what Bartel saw as his disappointment in her and he saw as her failure to grasp the world properly.

"I'll go, Emma," Pennington eventually t-said. He stood up and she followed and hugged him close. Near her door, she turned him back to her. "How can I be still in love with you, Andrew? When I don't really like you. When you irritate me beyond reason. How?"

"You do the same to me, Emma," Pennington t-said. He brushed her lips in thought and walked through the door.

Bartel turned socio back to Lock and didn't know what to say to herself. She was hardly in control and Pennington had really, unwittingly, destroyed her triumphant moment. She sat back down where she had been, with the light fading. Pennington engaged her from his autonom. "Have a look on some of the weeds, Emma."

"Why?"

"Dread-Demotic has caused a ripple or two."

"How could it?" She was genuinely puzzled.

"The Tomlinsons are perhaps more influential than you think or know," Pennington t-said. "You don't have a house like theirs or a lifestyle like theirs without access to one or more of the Trills. They've obviously been singing your praises."

"Thank you, Andrew. I will. But, honestly now, how do you know them? You know them well enough to introduce me – so it's not some idle research project or some political necessity."

"Curiously enough from my agitating." Pennington wondered whether to continue, but decided he would. "You know how the Trills don't actively encourage activism against them but think that it's best out in the open?."

"I didn't know it was quite like that."

"It is, Emma," Pennington t-said. "Well, the Tomlinsons picked up on some articles I'd written and the persono trail I created and they asked to see me. I was suspicious."

"I bet."

"I was." Pennington paused and then t-added: "They asked to encounter and that's when I went to their house. I didn't know why – but they didn't pretend that they were likely to be converts, only that they were interested in what motivated me."

"How did you answer that?"

"I said," Pennington t-replied, "that I felt that as humans – as a race that is – we are being reduced to little more than pleasure seekers and that is finally a dead end."

"What did they say to that?"

"They weren't talking to me to argue – you should understand that this was all voice – no socio involved so I wasn't given much of an insight into what they were thinking, either. They said they genuinely wanted to know. I didn't believe them because I presume the Trills have their secret police – no authoritarian regime in history, even one that appears as inchoate as this one, has dispensed with secret intelligence services. They questioned me a bit about why I thought the Trills represented an authoritarian regime – and I pointed to all the things I've tried to interest you in over the months, Emma. You know the shadowy nature of what they are and how they operate, what rewards they get and how they exercise control."

"Don't go through all of that Andrew. You know it just upsets me."

"It shouldn't – it really shouldn't," Pennington t-replied, sounding exasperated.

"Well it does."

"Ok, let's leave that there, Emma. The important point was that we had a civilised conversation and I guess I was quite pleased that someone, well, the Tomlinsons, who were evidently in some way engaged with the Trills – and how many people do you know who can say that? – were taking me seriously."

"So how did you get on to the subject of me?"

"That was quite easy, in fact, Emma. Part of my problem with them was that I really liked them as people. I guess in my demonology anyone associated with the Trills, and I've never knowingly encountered any before, was bound to be difficult and completely alien to me and our way of thinking." Bartel noted the change from first person singular to first person plural in Pennington's statement. "In fact I found them both charming, thoughtful and accommodating. They didn't argue with me – I think that's a general Trill position – but they did want to understand. And also they had a sense of humour."

"In what way?"

"I'm not sure I can tell you. I think Reginald made some sort of remark and Jeannette made fun of him. It was that sort of lightness. Then I was racking my brains to see how I could maintain the contact with them. I know I was providing them with insights but they were also making me think in different ways about the Trills and what their end game is – or rationale."

"So I was just a convenience to you?" Bartel didn't know why she was thinking so angrily and why it was coming out like this. Then she realised it was because Pennington always made her feel uncomfortable once they left aside the sex and the generalities of life and talked what Pennington described as politics and Bartel described in her head as deflection.

"You mean because I introduced you to them? I guess that would be a view – but I think an uncharitable one. Yes – it was to my advantage. I justify it in my head as it was also to your advantage. You know I've always valued your imagineering, Emma. This might give you a wider audience and more exposure."

"And also keep you in touch with them?"

"Yes," Pennington t-said.

"If I had known that I'm not sure I would have taken on the commission." Even Bartel was a bit surprised at the vehemence of her reaction. Pennington had helped her – but she felt betrayed because it hadn't been what she originally thought. On the other hand Pennington hadn't told her about the Tomlinsons' connection with the Trills and that was probably a good thing. If she had known, it might have made it more difficult to have confidence in her ideas. But not letting her know about the connection with the Trills was a sort of deceit.

"Are you really angry with me, then, Emma?"

"At this moment I am – but I am confused, Andrew," Bartel t-admitted. "I'm not sure this is logical, but I feel betrayed in some way – I'm not even sure I can justify that, even to myself. I think using me as a pawn without telling me was unconscionable and underhand."

"If I had told you, would you have taken on the assignment?"

"I don't know," Bartel t-added, "I'd like to think I'd have turned you down. I am too confused. You always have this effect on me, Andrew. I'm so comfortable with you in so many ways – and you get under my skin in a really bad way. At this moment I want to tell you to piss off and I want to say I never want to engage or encounter with you again."

"Why don't you?"

"I'm," Bartel t-searched for the right response, "I'm not sure."

"I hate upsetting you and I know it's patronising to say I was doing it for your own good. And not entirely true. But let's leave it here – unresolved – angry though you are. We've had plenty of these conversations. I'm not saying you will forgive me, but I hope you do and it works out for you and me."

"What does that mean?" Bartel felt betrayed and was unable to just let it pass.

"You know that I always want to have a relationship with you," Pennington t-said. "I know we have difficulties but I always want to be with you – whether we engage or encounter, you know it makes us both feel good. Well, usually it does."

"Well – I don't honestly know what to think at this moment. I've told you and told you I don't want to be part of what you call politics. I'm happy. I don't only have what I need, I largely have what I want. Why would I sacrifice that?"

"I know, Emma. Can we have a t-kiss – and I'll leave you to work it out as you want?"

Bartel relaxed and t-felt his arms around her and she put her arms t-round him – and they t-kissed gently and quietly.

"That's always good, Emma. Let's stop there. But do look at what's happening on your persono. I think you will be surprised."

Pennington disengaged. Bartel felt a very lonely, disturbed feeling immediately. What should she make of this? It had been such a great day up till Pennington had ruined it. If that was what he had done. It had felt before the engagement with Pennington as though it was all on her skill and experience and imagination. It felt sullied.

And then she calmed down enough to wonder what on earth Pennington was doing on the edges of the Trills' world – and how that seemed to put a different perspective on his antagonism to the Trills. And although it had been self-interest on Pennington's part, it was also, as he had said and although she hated to admit it, to her advantage. It had introduced her to a commission that she would hardly have had any other way, and it had stimulated her beyond what she was normally capable of.

She flicked through the headlines on persono, and there appeared to be nothing at that level, so she searched for *Dread-Demotic*, and instantly up came a few thousand references – most asking what it was about and where to obtain it. That was flattering but hardly based on good business practice. It would quickly blow over as these immediate shooting stars usually did.

Turning away from any such thoughts, and wanting to see if she could engage Worrell – she found Savery engaging with her. "Yes?"

"I wondered if you'd seen that Dread-Demotic is buzzing," he t-asked.

"I was just having a look. It wasn't in the headlines."

"No – but it was going to places you'd never reach normally," Savery t-said. "Don't think about the quantity of references. Think who is making the references."

"And who is that?"

"The people asking about Dread-Demotic are nearly all A listers – they aren't Trills, obviously, but they're the sort of people who move a bit within their orbit according to the weeds," Savery t-replied. "That's pretty special, Emma."

"I guess it is," Bartel t-said. This felt interesting and strange.

"You guess it is? Most imagineers would give their eye teeth to have comments from any of these people. Did you know that the Tomlinsons were so well connected?"

"No. Did you?"

"Hadn't a clue," Savery t-said. "Not surprisingly actually as I've traced them on Sapiens, and they keep a very low profile. But they do have a profile – and they seem to be connected with the Trills quite closely."

"Which one – or ones?"

"I'm not sure," Savery t-responded. "My guess – and it is only a guess – is that it is Kalo and Elora Ghose. I just know for certain that if they post something, it gets a wide coverage. It seems it's quite important. I think we should congratulate ourselves."

"Great." Bartel was absorbing what Savery was saying rather than reacting to the actual meaning of his words.

"You don't seem very pleased about this, Emma – I'm over the moon. Why not?"

"Oh – I'm just being irritable, Jonas. I didn't realise how we got the assignment, and it's all going too fast."

"My advice is just enjoy it."

Chapter 12

Bartel was really agitated when she was finally going to bed. She wondered whether to use any of the drugs that would help her brain get over this feeling of disturbance. That seemed too easy which was weird. The drugs, whether recreational, therapeutic or psychedelic were designed to make it easier to live – so there was something rather deeply disturbing her if she was reluctant to use them, as she recognised.

She knew it wasn't the right thing to let herself stew in the present moment without doing something about it, and had more than one reason in her head why it wasn't right, but she couldn't persuade herself what she should do.

She engaged with Worrell. He was in Lock and didn't change his setting so she knew that she had been wrong to do so. Still she was glad that she had tried. He'd know that she had probed. The expression of being *under someone's skin* had in a way become both more real and had become more accurate with socio.

And she could really feel that he was under her skin.

Why didn't she want to have a good night's sleep and just take the right drugs? She was too disturbed and didn't want to smooth over what was going on in her head. And she was annoyed, really quite angry with Pennington. She knew it was irrational to be this cross, but she felt violated, and yet it had worked to her advantage. That actually made it worse.

She agonised about it lying in bed. Then Alice probed her. "Well, daughter, what do you want?"

"Have you seen what's happening about you on persono? And on Sapiens? It's all a bit overwhelming to know it's my mother. Can we include Roseanne?"

"Sure." Alice engaged Roseanne and they all engaged together. Alice and Roseanne were overwhelmed by what was happening on persono – and were amazed at the celebrity that their mother had achieved.

"I had no idea it would be like this." Bartel felt she had to keep putting disclaimers in.

"Does it upset you," Alice t-asked.

"No," Bartel t-replied, "But it does disturb me."

"What does?" Roseanne t-asked.

"Oh," Bartel t-explained, "it's not the celebrity – such as it is because it is only a very small ripple, but how it happened. Andrew – you know Andrew – had introduced me to a couple, the Tomlinsons, and it wasn't quite what I thought. He was doing it to help himself."

"Is that a problem?" Roseanne asked.

"I suppose not," Bartel t-replied.

"It obviously is," Alice t-responded.

"Yes – it is," Bartel t-agreed. "Not entirely sure why actually – but I feel Andrew took advantage of me."

"But for your advantage." Roseanne was always blunt.

"I know," Bartel t-replied. "I am too confused at the moment. Yes. I think it is a good thing. Yes. But I felt betrayed."

"How you feel is how you feel," Alice t-said. "But I'd say enjoy it."

"And I would too," Roseanne t-added.

"Yes – you're right," Bartel t-said. "Curiously you're not the only people to say that. But how much stuff is there on persono now? According to Andrew it wasn't a great quantity, but it was the quality of the respondents that was important."

"Exactly right," Roseanne t-said.

They t-talked a bit more with Alice and Roseanne very excited and Bartel really feeling that she was getting everything wrong. It was great that they had engaged – and she was grateful. When the engagement finished, she did feel a bit better.

Why had she been so angry that Pennington had helped her and in doing so in some way had helped himself? That just wasn't sensible, and she felt quite bad about it. Perhaps it was all down to the mixture of emotions and feelings that she had about him. There was always something that held her back from committing herself in any real way to him – and yet she knew that he was really committed to her in all sorts of ways. Even though she wasn't sure quite what those ways were. Introducing her to the Tomlinsons was actually quite a risk for him, she thought.

She was suddenly conscious that she was on her own in the dark. She smiled to herself at this thought. Metaphorically and literally.

Then she had her first media probe – and although this was unexpected, she should have expected it would have been on the cards following the engagement with her daughters. Bartel set her socio to Lock and lay in bed wondering what was going to happen. Dread-Demotic was not mainstream nor was it intended to be a product for general consumption. It was bespoke. It was hugely greedy for resources and it used a lot of Sofari's processing power. It wasn't mass market and would be quite expensive in time and computing power. But perhaps that would make it more desirable.

She was more agitated than she had realised and then she felt guilty again about how she had reacted to Pennington. Should she apologise? There was no way of knowing. She also felt that he had taken her for granted – and so even though she felt guilty and upset about her response, there was a good deal of her which would be damned before she apologised.

She felt trapped a little and added to that was some excitement about what might be happening. In all of her mixed emotions she hadn't really taken that into account. She had been hung up on the affront to her feelings, the encounter with Worrell and not focusing directly on what was happening. It was, she realised every imagineer's dream – something that they had produced was in demand and was highly rated. The fact that the Tomlinsons were so well connected was serendipity – but perhaps more than that when you took what Pennington had done into account.

She toyed with the idea of talking more with Savery – and he would necessarily understand more about what was going on across people's personos. And what this might mean. It made her smile again at the thought that Savery would have stumbled into this because she had needed extra stimulus and she needed a younger person and a younger person's perspective on both the tools at their disposal and the potential scenarios they could develop.

How would they deal with establishing who deserved the greater kudos? Did they need to?

If she engaged Savery at this point he might read that wrongly – and that would be unfair to him – and to her. He was an attractive person and he had sensitivity and some flair, but there was something missing in their connection that meant that they were partners for the imagineering but not for anything else, although he clearly wanted more.

Bartel had had some experience of dealing with partnerships – especially when she was starting out and it was difficult to understand how sometimes, even having spent four hours with someone struggling with a knotty logical problem in whatever scenario, there wasn't ever a deeper connection. As Kalo said on many occasions, socio had seen off exploitation of women or the exploitation by women of their position because socio made everything as transparent as the individuals required. And if someone wasn't prepared to be transparent – to set the level to Relaxed then everybody was aware that they had to be wary. But it was also somewhat brutal in that if there were a lack of connection that was immediately exposed.

Of course the introduction and then the continuous refinement of socio had been carried out over the last twenty years so Bartel had grown up with it, having had enough time before it was a standard to stumble her way through relationships unable to see whether someone was a rogue or well-intentioned. Of course it had transformed the whole of the sexual act, but for most people of Bartel's age, it had been the sudden warmth and feeling that could be experienced when socio became active that stuck in her memory. There was a huge contrast between her first kiss with all its unknowing and novelty and the first time she kissed someone when they had socio engaged, let alone t-kissed.

In those early days, there hadn't been the fine control that levels brought, and it was sometimes hit and miss whether someone was able to tune into the other person's mind without losing his or her own thoughts, and there had been the astonishing moments when unexpected thoughts and ideas were exchanged.

Some of the people just a generation older than Bartel had claimed that socio took all the mystery out of feelings – and to some extent they had a point. If you know what the other person is thinking, and feeling, then it becomes almost impossible to get the wrong end of the stick. In fact, as though to emphasise this, as fast as any rogue figured out a way of fooling socio, Kalo had come in with fixes that blocked off that potential issue.

Bartel was feeling so confused, she needed to engage with someone – but she was at a loose end and there was no-one that she wanted to willingly engage with outside of Pennington and Worrell. She checked persono again and searched for Dread-Demotic and she noticed that there was a great deal of traffic about it, but actually not that many individual people were accessing the subject.

That was interesting. If inexplicable.

She looked closely at the endorsements and the comments – and it was simply amazing. Only the Tomlinsons had actually been on the experience and yet people were talking about it as though it was on general release – although there were, fortunately, precious few details about it, as was obviously likely to be the case. That selective memory wiping was clearly effective although neither she nor Savery had set it up. It must have been completely built into Sofari without them knowing.

Bartel thought about engaging with her ex-husband, Thornton, and then with her long-term lover prior to Pennington, Albert, but decided that the first was too awkward and she wasn't yet able to think about Albert in a balanced way. Their actual break up had been too traumatic and unnecessarily so, because it was quite simply that they had not grown together enough.

She got into bed and decided that she really had to have a drug to take her away from the feelings of agitation, indecision over Pennington and even excitement at what was happening with Dread-Demotic. She engaged with the Ambience environment and was taken through a good series of questions and her Medi-stat was engaged, and then she was directed to Eclectic's Rest-Assist service, which engaged with her socio and gently soothed the issues out of her system by focusing on Bartel's well-being. It was interesting to her that in fact no drug was actually required and she felt better because of that. And she drifted effortlessly into sleep.

Chapter 13

Right on 7.30, which was the time that Bartel had set for her persono to wake her up and accept fresh information, the clamour started. She went through all the strands in her persono and was astonished because over night the discussions and mentions of Dread-Demotic had been transformed from a small number of highly influential people to a general flood of discussion. So many people were actively questioning what on earth Dread-Demotic was and why it was such a phenomenon. The lack of information, thanks to the selective memory wiping which now appeared to be called sswipe, having been given a branding overnight perhaps in response to the interest in Dread-Demotic, clearly stimulated more and more interest.

The Tomlinsons must have been very influential but even that connection couldn't entirely explain what was happening. It was exciting and rather daunting.

The persono traffic was incredibly huge and rather overwhelming. The discussions were fascinating at first – no-one appeared to know what Dread-Demotic was – but there was speculation and discussion. It seemed the world – or at least the world related to the Trills – was hungry for new experiences and scenarios.

Every news weed and every gossip weed had been in touch with her persono and some of them were very insistent.

She engaged with Savery – and he was there immediately. "What do you make of this, Jonas?"

"I don't know – but I think we've got a tiger by the tail," he t-replied. "Is this what celebrity is?"

"I doubt it, Jonas," Bartel t-replied, "but it is overwhelming, I have to say that."

"What do we do about it?" Savery was clearly anxious but not as much at sea as Bartel.

"I've no idea," Bartel t-replied, "as I am out of my comfort zone entirely."

"The advice my parents – my mother actually – gave me – for what it's worth – is that if you don't know what to do, do nothing until you have worked it out. Is there anyone you can ask?" Wise thoughts from Savery, Bartel thought.

"Yes," Bartel t-replied thoughtfully. "Yes. I know someone who is on the fringe of the Trills' circle – and I think this is where all of the fuss is coming from. Should I approach him?"

"How well do you know him?"

"Oh – really well. I just didn't know he had such connections."

"You never do – not you but anyone," Savery t-stated bluntly. "It's partly how they keep themselves apart. It appears to be an unwritten rule – or it might be written somewhere that we don't have access to – that any connection with the Trills – however slight and distant – is to remain almost completely secret."

"That is worrying me, Jonas."

"Why?"

"I just didn't know that this person was that involved or knew any of this in such a way," Bartel t-ruminated. Pennington was rather more interesting than even she had imagined, when he was just a lover and a potential influence on her views.

"Sounds just like the text book," Savery t-said.

"Not sure I understand what you mean?"

"It's just that whoever this person is, he or she is just like I'd expect from what little is written about the people in the Trills' circle – or who is even slightly well-connected to them."

"Does that mean that I won't be able to question him about this or find out more about him?" Bartel was really worried. "I really thought I knew him. How can I know?"

"I don't have the answer to that, Emma." Savery t-responded and added: "I would have thought you would know more about this than me."

"I've never involved myself in politics or public affairs, Jonas," Bartel t-admitted. "I've never had to. Yes. I vote and I do follow the news. But I don't know how any of this works."

"I don't think you need to, actually. All that's required is to be aware."

"Is that your mother speaking again?"

"Yes," Savery t-said, with a smile. "Look – the only thing I can suggest is that you talk to your friend, whoever he or she is."

"Good advice." Bartel had to get to the bottom of Pennington, who was now becoming even more of an enigma to her, the more she thought about it. She disengaged with Savery on a promise that she would share something of whatever she found out with him.

She engaged Pennington who was on Lock. She left a message. She was worried. She was trying to put things into context. Why had Pennington always tried to recruit her to what he on one occasion had called the *resistance*? Was he an agent provocateur testing her out? How was he connected with the Trills – was it close or was it just a passing acquaintance?

"Morning, Emma," Pennington t-responded. "Sorry – I was – well not asleep. I was otherwise engaged." She knew what that was likely to mean. It was no good, but she did feel jealous. It was such a strange effect he had on her. She could contrast that with her feelings for others – even Worrell – where she felt no jealousy. Of course Kalo said that socio and persono had removed all need for jealousy. It always sounded hollow even to Bartel but it did have a rationale of sorts. If you always knew everything, you could make decisions based on that. As so many of the historical novels that were still popular in some circles suggested, it was always not knowing and suspicion that made any feelings of jealousy that much worse. That feeling of betrayal.

Bartel shook herself. "I've a question."

"And what's that, Emma? This isn't like you."

"I think I need to do this face to face. When can we encounter?"

"Shall I come to you – shortly?"

"That would be good – if that's not difficult or embarrassing." Bartel couldn't resist the little, gentle as possible, question about what Pennington was up to.

"Not at all. I'll be with you in about twenty five – subject to what the autonom thinks is possible."

He was taking this seriously then. Perhaps he was hoping that this was her awakening. Perhaps it was some sort of testing of her. And she had thought she had known him – not inside out, as they had always maintained some distance even with socio on Relax, but enough to understand him and hold him at bay.

Bartel busied herself, first t-instructing the Home-Assist andro and then getting herself ready for the day.

All the while her persono was being probed and pushed – which was uncomfortable and so unusual – and her socio was being continually probed by all sorts of organisations and people. It was very disconcerting.

"I'm just outside," Pennington t-said.

"Come up."

She opened the door and he came in and embraced her. She started to t-say something and he looked and shook his head. "Let's use voice." She was about to ask why – but decided that there must be a good reason and clearly socio wasn't appropriate for some reason. "Is socio on Lock?" It was a strange question in a normal context as he would have been able to read that, but obviously he wasn't using socio at all.

"Yes."

"Good," Pennington said. "Can you turn persono off for me?"

"I don't ever do that," Bartel v-said. "What's the need?"

"Just do it," Pennington v-said. Bartel thought it off. "Done?"

Bartel nodded. It was all rather frightening. The clamour that disappeared as she turned off persono was thrown into real perspective when it went. It had been at a fever pitch. "What about socio?"

"That's more difficult," Pennington v-said. "Leave it."

"Thank you for coming so promptly, Andrew."

"You sounded distressed," Pennington v-responded, "and I wondered what the issue was – though I thought I could guess."

"What did you guess?"

"It's all the traffic on persono and your socio," Pennington v-replied. Bartel was desperate to ask him out right what his relationship was with the Trills and the question kept bubbling to her surface. It was so good that socio was properly locked down.

"Yes," Bartel v-agreed, "partly."

"Partly?"

"I just feel all at sea, Andrew," Bartel v-said. There was actually no way she could raise the real issue because she didn't know what would be the right questions at this point. She would have to talk about other things. "I'm not used to anything like the impact that Dread-Demotic has made and is making. Normally I just do my job – create an experience, let Sofari sort it out and that's it. People are pleased or not. I know that Dread-Demotic is something quite new and it is ground-breaking. I didn't expect this reaction. So what do I do?"

"I might not be the best person to answer that," Pennington v-replied. "I'll have a go. I guess my answer is that you should embrace this as a new experience. Just go with the flow. Enjoy it."

"But who are the Tomlinsons?" Bartel realised that this was one way that she could introduce the subject.

"I told you, Emma," Pennington v-said, looking at her quizzically. "They are well connected."

"But how do you know them?" This was the nearest she could get to her real question.

"I thought I told you – they approached me," Pennington v-said. "Actually I did tell you that. Are you trying to test me?" He said it with a smile but he was now suspicious. "What is it, Emma? What is it really?"

"What do you mean by that?"

"You're obviously disturbed and not just by your Sofari experience going viral." Pennington paused. "You find it strange that I've talked to the Tomlinsons – but I explained that. They were trying to understand me and why I was so opposed to the Trills. Do you understand?"

"Not entirely," Bartel v-said. "Why would they approach you? Are you that influential or notorious – at least to the Trills?" She was getting closer to her real questions. "Who are you Andrew?" There she had said it.

"An interesting question after all this time, Emma," Pennington v-said, thoughtfully. "I would have thought that all our time together, in and out of bed, would have told you that."

"Hardly."

"I see what you mean," Pennington v-said. "Let's go get some coffee."

Bartel was about to suggest that she could get the gSynth to prepare the best coffee, but she realised that that wasn't the point – whatever the point was. "Ok."

Pennington used his socio to order an autonom which would be there in a few minutes. "Come. Let's go down and wait for it. So lovely to see you, Emma." What did that mean? "I really think you're going to be in for a fantastic time."

"Why do you think that?"

"This fuss over Dread-Demotic isn't going to be a damp squib – it's already taking off hugely, as you know," Pennington v-replied, as though he was avoiding saying something. "Enjoy that thought."

In the autonom Bartel started to speak and Pennington put his arm round her and kissed her. To keep her quiet? Probably. They sat in a form of silence which seemed full of import to Bartel although she couldn't work out what that was.

They found a booth in the coffee shop and the andro cleared the table and absorbed their order.

"Now what's going on, Andrew?"

"What do you mean?"

"Look – you can't answer all my questions with a question," Bartel v-said. It was good the place wasn't that quiet – most people were using voice to have their conversation. Perhaps they were all on some sort of clandestine mission like Bartel felt she was.

"I know, Emma," Pennington v-agreed. "What I have to say is what you've always objected to me saying – so I'm wary. I don't want to have another row with you. There's a lot at stake. And we haven't much time."

"Why – what's the hurry? Things aren't going to change quickly."

"I didn't mean that, Emma," Pennington v-replied. He was keeping his voice low. "Things won't change quickly. Although they might – because if a change came, it will be sudden and I suspect quite serious. But forget that. You are right in general that there won't be any quick and significant changes. I was talking about the future– as I might call it – actually your future because of Dread-Demotic which means that your time isn't going to be your own."

"Oh – I see. I wasn't thinking about that."

"I know," Pennington v-said. "I imagine that you're suspicious of me because you've apparently seen a connection between me and the Trills and you know that I've been trying to understand them and what they are doing to us as human beings. You're worried that the two things don't go together. I can't re-assure you – and I don't want to use socio as that's too insecure."

"Even if we are on Relax with each other? It's meant to be encrypted, isn't it?"

"It is," Pennington v-said, smoothly. "But someone can always unencrypt anything that's been encrypted. And the Trills do. Not that that's at all important. We aren't hiding – but if we were we would be hiding in plain sight, as there is very little that can be done to keep anything secret from the Trills. That's part of how they operate – and it is so sophisticated."

"That's paranoia isn't it? Imagining that everything is open to the Trills?"

"It could well be," Pennington v-said, disarmingly. "It could also be true."

"Ok. So now what?"

"I guess I just have to open up a little more," Pennington v-said.

"I'm not sure that's necessary."

"It is," Pennington v-added, "if I'm to retain any of your trust."

"So I've got to hear more of your views?"

"Not if you don't want to," Pennington v-replied, looking closely at her. "Do you?"

"Probably not," Bartel v-said. "But I think I have to – or at least I owe you that."

"You owe me nothing, Emma," Pennington v-said. He was talking very quietly and Bartel had to strain to catch his words. "The point is that we're living in what the Trills call a utopia."

"For lots of good reason."

"Yes," Pennington v-agreed. "That's entirely true. You can look at human history – and I'm not being over grandiloquent or too pompous, by saying that in some terms we are in something of a utopia. To some extent – and we might disagree about how much – the Trills have abolished need. Of course no-one could abolish want. But you know that we have made lives around the planet so much more materially better."

"Agreed."

"And we do have as much a semblance of democracy as we have ever had," Pennington v-said. "Perhaps more." He paused as if waiting for Bartel to object. She was prepared for once to listen. He continued: "I thought you'd object to that."

"Why?"

"You would normally," Pennington v-said. "In terms of hegemony – which I know you don't think is worthwhile discussing – we are in the control of the first oligarchy in history that is not only mainly benign but also potentially likely to be benign for the foreseeable future. No guarantee about that and we know – and I use the word know advisedly – that there are different factions within the Trills that might alter that benign quality. No – before you ask, I don't have any inside information on that, except I'm not relying on the weeds for this. Within the opposition to the Trills there are people who are far closer to them than I am. I trust what they say and tell us. But let's be positive and not go down that route because it is unlikely to affect us – that is you and me and most people – very much if at all. There are no restrictions on belief, on personal freedom, including drugs and moral constraints."

"Not entirely true, as you well know, Andrew."

"Oh – you mean that expressions of hate are not allowed? I give you that. But remember that that is always a continuing debate – even now. I won't get into that debate as I'm sure you understand it. The main point is that no-one is telling anyone else what to think or do. The use of persono and socio has virtually eliminated crime. The use of gSynth has more or less eliminated hunger since we can synthesise any food and drink from chemicals."

"That's a good thing – isn't it? I mean eliminating crime and hunger?"

"Of course," Pennington v-said. "The position of women has never been more secure. Abusive relationships are very difficult to hide now. Environmentally the planet has never been safer. Obviously fusion helped but also perfecting carbon capture. All priorities of the Trills, it has to be admitted."

"Disease control?"

"Yes," Pennington v-said. "We haven't actually eliminated disease nor death – but we've addressed the former and for good reason not done much about the latter." Bartel nodded. "Does that nod mean that everything is ok with you so far and that I'm not being controversial?"

"Yes, I'm just waiting for the downside. I think most people in human history would have been delighted to live like this."

"Perhaps there aren't any downsides, Emma. And don't look at me like that. You know that I don't believe that. I've not sold out. I can acknowledge all the benefits while also understanding what's wrong. There's also virtually no restriction on political dissent and political association. At least it appears that that is the case."

"Are you saying that that is not true – and that political dissent is not allowed?"

"Not at all," Pennington v-said. "As you know, that's why I was invited to talk to the Tomlinsons because they knew that I am opposed to the Trills and this way of living. Perhaps to find out how dangerous I am – and of course I am no danger to them on my own – perhaps to find out what the Trills need to do now to prevent unrest. As I said, I really liked them as a couple, and I think they're pretty benign."

"But why didn't you tell me about the connection you had with them?"

"I might have," Pennington v-said, "if you'd asked. As I told you – I didn't want to make you feel additional pressure that you might have experienced if you'd known that they weren't just another couple in better than average circumstances. As you know, there is no objection by the Trills to people becoming better off than the average. They recognise that this means there will be people below the average – and so they don't think about averages but real measures. Did you ever know about poverty definitions?"

"No."

"Not to worry – it's just that the Trills have worked out what a person needs to be comfortable. We might not agree with the measure they use – but it's pretty transparent."

"So why are you against them? This all sounds positive to me. Is it jealousy of their wealth and, I guess, their power?"

"No. What an interesting thought, Emma. You don't have to think of this world now as a dystopia – you know a waste land – to believe, to rationalise I should say, that there is something deeply wrong with how we're living."

"And there is a group of you who think this?"

"Yes," Pennington v-said. "As the Trills well know, in actual fact."

"But you've not really explained the link with the Tomlinsons and through them the Trills. Not that I have to believe that the Tomlinsons are connected with the Trills. I've only your word for that."

"Yes – and you will never get confirmation of that from anyone, although you might see it with your own eyes.."

"I doubt it."

"That's my Emma,"

"All right." Bartel v-said. "Because I was worried about you for all different reasons – that you might be pushing me in a direction to find out if I was really a subversive or could become one – and doing that on behalf of the Tomlinsons and whoever is controlling – perhaps involving – them, I've allowed you to talk more than usual. I think you are utterly wrong – and elitist to think that you want to sacrifice all of the benefits because it doesn't suit your ego."

"That's one way of looking at it, Emma. Not my way. Just one question – then I'll shut up about this and tell you about the roller coaster you're about to get on."

"Ok. But how do you know so much?"

"I've watched a number of people," Pennington v-said. He left it at that. "My question. Don't you ever look more deeply at what is happening? Do you ever think that in order to use persono and socio to eliminate crime, there has to be surveillance – then what that means?"

"That's three questions, Andrew," Bartel v-said. "And, no, I don't. And I don't want to. Right – so I've had all the propaganda, now you can tell me what I'm in for."

"That makes me sound patronising," Pennington v-said.

"If the cap fits."

"You can be an absolute nightmare, Emma, I don't know how I can love you so much and find you absolutely the worst person to be with sometimes. And that's two *absolute lies* in one sentence. Do you want to know what I think will happen?"

"Yes, of course I do. That's why I was desperate to talk to you. But let me tell you first that I think this. Dread-Demotic, is going to be a nine day wonder – if it isn't a two day wonder and is already over."

"It won't be," Pennington v-said. "You very cleverly have created something quite astonishingly new."

"Not on my own. Jonas helped. And I'm not sure it's all that new. I'm sure there have been horror experiences before."

"Of course there have." Pennington paused. "Look – don't be so obstructive, Emma. I don't want to persuade you about anything. If you don't see it as I see it, that's fine. But let me tell you how I see it."

"Ok."

"First of all – it wasn't the horror or not just the horror. You're so right about that. It was the combination of absolute horror – there's that word again – and somehow that sense of re-assurance you built into the experience."

"That was deliberate."

"And it worked too. I think it was the fact that this was a two person experience that helped that – but let's not analyse it too much. If you think of our culture – the whole culture not just the Trills – you know that one of the worst feelings is a form of, well, disaffection."

"Pointlessness."

"Yes, pointlessness, if you want. You took the Tomlinsons out of that entirely – and focused their minds entirely on survival and working through something, but at no point did you leave them completely bereft,"

"Sofari had a lot to do with that."

"Of course it did and no-one could construct these experiences without Sofari," Pennington said. "It's like what were called at the end of the twentieth century a video game producer with built in artificial intelligence but it is a complete experience using as many of the senses in as many ways as possible. That's why Sofari is so brilliant – although it is still just a tool."

"But that's to downplay all its real breakthrough qualities."

"Of course," Pennington v-agreed. "Prior to Sofari, you didn't have actual total physical sensations, smells, three dimensions indistinguishable from real all combined. And total immersion – which was the real breakthrough Latitude made. Anyway – to get back to what will happen. You will be feted and I'm not sure how much you will be absorbed into the higher reaches of the Trill circles but you will come pretty close. You have to remember that they are always desperate for new experiences and new understanding of themselves – and, for that matter, they are desperate to have new people in their circle – which, by the way, they call ImCirc – their immediate circle."

"But they can do anything they want at any time, in any way. Isn't that true?"

"Yes. But think how much that excess can be in itself a turn off."

"What?"

"Scarcity makes for pleasure," Pennington v-said. "You won't hear that from any of the Trills but I can assure you that if you have too much of anything, you soon become jaded."

"And then what happens – after I've been absorbed into an inner circle?"

"That, apparently, is up to you," Pennington v-said.

"How?"

"The worst that can happen is that you become a plaything of the gods – of the Trills – and you go through whatever that means. I don't know what the best is. I only know it's going to be difficult to maintain any integrity."

"Integrity? I haven't heard that word used in anger for years."

"True. No call for it when it's almost impossible to lie effectively and get away with it, to defraud someone, or otherwise ruin lives. But remember the word, and stay true to yourself, Emma."

"I honestly don't know what you mean. But you think I will become some sort of celebrity?"

"You are already. And I don't think you can return to normal life again."

"That sounds threatening."

"Only if you let it be threatening," Pennington v-said. "Embrace it – but don't forget me. And what I've told you. Remember that we're living in what I call an amblytopia."

"Meaning?"

"You won't find that word anywhere," Pennington said. "I think the best way of thinking about it is to think it means *dull*."

"Seems a long and difficult word for something so dull in itself," Bartel v-said. "What does it mean in practice?"

"It means a world where there is no striving – is the simplest way of describing it. And at that point, I think that humanity is to all intents and purposes dead."

"It seems to me that there is always a trade off in everything we do – and I think the trade off that the Trills have created is fine with me – and I have no quarrel with the neo-age."

"I know. But keep what I say in mind, Emma. Oh – and one last word of warning."

"What's that?"

"Remember," Pennington v-said, "the news cycle. You'll start off as some sort of magical figure who can do no wrong and who has been living a charmed life that has culminated in this celebrity. Then, however, they will knock you off that perch. It's what they still call a *news cycle*. It's to be expected. Don't allow the former to take your head. Don't allow the latter to depress you. Your real audience isn't the news and the weeds – but the Trills."

"I do know that," Bartel v-replied. "I wasn't born yesterday. Honestly Andrew – at times you think I'm so naïve. Just because I don't agree with you that this is a world that has to be overthrown, it doesn't mean that I'm unaware."

"Point taken – and it's well said." Pennington paused. Then he v-added: "I really care about you, Emma. I wish you'd see this as I – as we – do. But do you think you can give me any insights you might gain from any experience with the Trills?"

"I don't know. But I will keep it in mind."

They switched on socio and with the level set to Relax they probed each other, and Bartel t-suggested that they go back to her place and make love.

"I think we should." Pennington t-said. "There aren't going to be many opportunities for some time."

"I hadn't thought of that," Bartel t-replied. Pennington t-summoned an autonom and Bartel t-stroked Pennington's face and let her hands trail down his body, till she was stroking him through his trousers. It was extraordinary and she was sharing a new thought with him. The conversation which would normally have made them poles apart had drawn them together. Bartel told herself not to analyse too much – and Pennington found that amusing, as he t-fondled her in reply and then physically put his arm round her and kissed her tenderly. Bartel let herself melt in his arms.

Chapter 14

Bartel lay in Pennington's arms feeling a mixture of complete relaxation and anticipation, and a certain amount of concern about what was about to happen. She found the contrast between these feelings so confusing, but was happy to let the emotions just flow as they wanted. It was odd that it had been the first time that she had actually listened to him and not just argued that she didn't want to know, although it didn't alter how she was thinking.

And what he had said about what was to come was both exciting and to some extent terrifying.

She also didn't know what to do about Savery – and whether she should involve him or not. The only answer to that was to ask him what he wanted.

It was now midday and Bartel decided she could avoid her future no longer. "Andrew – wake up."

"Of course," Pennington v-said, sleepily. "I don't know why you and I don't just give in to our feelings, Emma."

"I don't think this is the time for that conversation, Andrew."

"You're right."

"I think I'd better deal with the clamour on persono and the probes into my socio," Bartel v-said. They had switched socio off for the whole time while they made love – something they occasionally did.

Why on earth did she have such contradictory feelings about this man? No – she had to concentrate. "Do you mind?"

"Of course I do. But I do realise that there is something going on here that needs to be addressed. All I will say more is that you shouldn't go for every invitation to talk or comment. Be selective."

"How?"

"Well," Pennington v-said, "Try it and see. Don't respond to the first you see – look for a prestigious invitation and address that first."

"Is it going to be big – and not a nine day wonder?"

"It might not even last nine days, Emma," Pennington v-said. "I just happen to think that this is going to be a tsunami. Remember – if it's appropriate I'm always here – but I won't expect to hear from you even on socio for the immediate future. It's going to be so overwhelming."

"How do you know that?"

"I know that this is part of their approach and method," Pennington v-said.

"*Their?*"

"Yes – their. The Trills. At the very least you are a diversion and a deflection of interest from them – and even their manufactured news stories and intrigues aren't entirely satisfactory to them and for them. They like to have what they call *reality* as part of the mix. While people are wondering about you and Dread-Demotic they won't be even thinking about any of the Trills and whatever they may be up to."

"You really do think they are malign – don't you?"

"Not sure that is the right word, Emma," Pennington v-said, thoughtfully. "I think the word is *indifferent*. That's not quite right – but it's a better way of thinking about them."

"You really do know more about them than most people – don't you." It wasn't a question.

"Yes," Pennington v-said, "that's probably fair. I've studied them as much as I can, but there are very few real sources as opposed to the weeds and the sensationalisms that they put out to deflect. I guess even knowing that is something more than most people."

"Worrying?"

"Yes. But do remember that the way the Trills operate is that they have no problem with opposition and they want it out in the open. That's why there are some of us right in the middle of ImCirc – and those sources are very valuable to us, and I suspect valuable to the Trills too."

"I'm actually glad I don't have to think like this, Andrew," Bartel v-said.

Look – get yourself ready. I'd suggest minimal make-up, rather conservative clothes, and try to put on a confident but not arrogant air – you know – surprised by all the fuss works well, but you should have an underlying view that what you've achieved is significant, *although you'd be the last one to make that point.* Ok?"

"Whatever you say, Andrew. You don't think I'll be able to keep in touch?"

"You won't be able to do that. Technically you could but in terms of time and focus, it's extremely unlikely. Just remember I'm here and I'm always here for you."

"I'll be thinking of you," Bartel v-said. Why did he have to be the most annoying man in the world?

Pennington left. Bartel made sure that socio was on receive – and through the noise, she could feel Worrell trying to get in touch. "I'm sorry, Dave. I really can't engage with you at the moment," she t-said.

"I can understand that," Worrell t-said. "I only put two and two together about you and Dread-Demotic just now. I think you're going to be very busy. Just wanted to say that I picked up your probe last night – and let's do our best to stay in touch."

"I'd like that, Dave." Bartel felt very confused suddenly. It made her yearn for the much easier world of the novels and plays and series of the fifties – before socio – when feelings had to be gauged and you couldn't really have conflicting feelings like now. Although she resisted it, she was in love with Pennington but couldn't commit to someone who was so tied up in things she wasn't at all bothered about. At the same time, there had been that almost immediate connection with Worrell – and she didn't want to lose that. "I have to go."

Bartel got herself ready and the Home-Assist andro sorted out her clothes and prompted her as she was trying to follow Pennington's suggestion. She looked at herself in the mirrors and felt a fraud.

What next?

Ah – Savery.

She engaged him and he t-responded immediately. "I wondered when you would engage, Emma."

"I had to prepare myself, Jonas," Bartel t-replied. "I'm told it is going to be quite frantic."

"I've been thinking about that."

"Oh yes. And what did you think, Jonas?"

"I'd obviously like to be part of what's going on, Emma," Savery t-said. "I mean it's not every day that something creates a stir – any stir. There's always too much creativity and excitement – so it's difficult to break through. I've been thinking, though, that I want to wait and see how this works out. Is that cowardly of me, Emma?"

"Probably," Bartel t-replied, "but I think very sensible. I've been listening to some advice – and I think there is going to be a bit of a maelstrom for a while – and you know how the media flips between lionising and denigrating. I don't think it will last – or will have any real effects on my life – on our lives."

"One request, though."

"Yes."

"Don't forget me," Savery t-said. "I guess I'm hedging my bets. But Emma – I believe in you."

"Thank you for that, Jonas. I'm not sure why."

"I think you're a kind person, Emma. That's worth a lot."

"That's a lovely thing to say. But let's see what happens. At the moment I am being bombarded with probes. It's going to be good, I think. For a little while."

"One good thing – and I think this is a really good thing. You know those feelings I was having of pointlessness and lack of direction and all that staring over the edge into nothingness?."

"Yes."

"This has taken all of that away, I think we – you at least – we have done something valuable."

"It's good to think like that. keep thinking that. And you know I'm always here." It was strange to be echoing Pennington.

"I do. Good luck, Emma."

Bartel started to organise herself. It was a relief that she could just worry about herself and only think about Savery if things started to work better or in a different way. She went through her persono seeing if there were any things outstanding in her life that had to be dealt with. Nothing that the House-Assist and the Money-Assist andros wouldn't be able to handle, especially now that INsighto was so powerful. She loved the Sapiens tag line – *from artificial ignorance to Artificial Intelligence.*

She went through the probes to her socio – and made sure that the media ones were organised – in order of how prestigious they were. Then she looked at the probes from friends – even one from Worrell which was rather nice – *just thinking of her.* Then there was one from the Tomlinsons – from Reginald. That would be the first to respond to.

There was nothing new from Pennington which rather disappointed her. Not that she expected him to be able to say or do anything more – but she had realised that there was a depth of feeling about him that she hadn't experienced for so long. She could just remember the feelings in the early days with Thornton and then the different sorts of feelings with Albert. That mad rush of blood to the head with Thornton, confusing huge physical needs with overwhelming amazement that anyone would be this interested in her which had meant her life had been disrupted for almost five years. Then the calmer, more distanced and very much more comfortable feelings with Albert. And how different from either of those it was with Pennington. Even down to not calling him by his first name in her head.

So where did Worrell fit into this? That was almost a too difficult question – but one that she wanted to answer. Just not now.

Reginald first. She probed his socio – leaving hers on Bland.

"Hello, Emma," he t-responded. "I was hoping I could engage with you, especially before things might get out of hand with the media."

"That's good of you, Reginald."

"I think it's going to be a bit of a roller coaster. I didn't know how prepared you would be for that."

"Not at all prepared. I just don't understand it."

"It is difficult to understand how something just breaks through – but what you created, Emma, was just so overwhelming for Jeannette and me and was so innovative and we had such a different, overwhelming experience – I keep using that word with Jeannette too – that we wanted to make sure people were aware of it," Tomlinson t-said. "I guess you realise that we have some influence and know a lot of people – hence the furore. But I make no apology for that."

"It is overwhelming."

"Have you been inundated with probes and requests to engage?"

"Yes," Bartel t-said. A bit at sea as to where this was going.

"I'm not surprised," Tomlinson t-said. "You know our society is built on novelty and the search for the next big innovation."

"Yes. Of course. But what I don't understand is that once you experienced it, it became – well – old hat."

"You've missed something, Emma."

"What?"

"It's quite new, I guess, so no reason why you didn't know about it. You obviously constructed the experience in Sofari?"

"Of course."

"Well, that's the key."

"How?"

"Latitude . . ."

"What?"

"I mean the company, Latitude, Emma, as they are the brains behind Sofari, as you know."

"Of course but it doesn't impinge on my mind much." She rummaged through her memory and INsighto gave her immediate answers, as it always would do. Sapiens was such a great company. Of course she knew that Sofari was the brain child of Jessie Dressus, the CEO of Latitude, who had become a Trill on the back of it. She or he? She. "What relevance is that, Reginald?"

"Well, JD, as she is often known, added a vital element to Sofari and I suppose it's not generally known yet."

"Do you mean sswipe?"

"Exactly. The capability," Tomlinson t-said, with the air of a magician revealing not how the trick was done but the denouement, "of selectively wiping the memory of the experiencer so that the novelty – if there is any – can be maintained. I guess I'm surprised you know about it."

"Well – I guess imagineers are privileged in some ways – or some of us are. So why are you telling me this? Is that what happened to you?"

"Actually no," Tomlinson t-revealed. Pennington was right. The Tomlinsons were privileged then.

"Does it always happen?"

"No," Tomlinson t-replied. "It's controllable. If you've had the best, most agreeable, shall we say, experience you'd want to remember that. The thing that JD worked out was how to make it possible for memories of experiences to be partially wiped. You can see why that would be necessary."

"I knew it was experimental – how was it incorporated in Dread-Demotic?"

"Jeannette and I did that," Tomlinson t-said. So what was his relationship with Latitude and Jessie Dressus – JD?

"Why?"

"To protect your experience," Tomlinson t-said. "Funnily enough it had one really unexpected benefit." He t-paused. "Actually – it was to be expected. You see the idea was to allow the novelty to remain for everyone but it also meant that no-one else could then copy the idea."

"How did you have control over Sofari then?" This was becoming a bit weird in her eyes. As far as Bartel was aware she had total control over Dread-Demotic – apart from Savery's ability to make changes.

"Well – we have influence," Tomlinson t-said. "Not much – but enough that we could ask Latitude to over-ride what you had produced so that it could be protected."

"But you remember it all?"

"Of course. Well – not entirely because we wanted to keep some novelty. But it's in our interest to maintain complete lock down on what's in Dread-Demotic. And you can rely on us."

This was becoming slightly creepy and Bartel was becoming discomforted. Even with her socio set to Bland this was obvious to Tomlinson.

"It's not something to be worried about, Emma," Tomlinson t-said. "It's part of the testing of any new product – well any new element in any product – that it will be open to user testing. That's all that this is. Normally Jeannette and I wouldn't be able to do this."

This sounded too glib. Bartel cursed Pennington a bit for making her so suspicious, as she felt that she would have been re-assured by Tomlinson if Pennington hadn't alerted her to some underlying elements in the world of the Trills that the Tomlinsons were on the edge of.

"That's obviously a good thing, Reginald."

"Yes," Tomlinson t-said, "but that wasn't really the point of my engaging with you."

"Which was?"

"How to deal with the tsunami that is about to overtake you."

"Tsunami?"

"That's the best way of looking at it," Tomlinson t-said. "Best to think of it as destructive rather than positive. It is thoroughly positive and will be life changing. Yet in the short term at least it will be rather destructive – certainly of your peace of mind. You won't know if you are coming or going. So I wanted to give you some suggestions. Not advice, Emma. I can promise you that. You know that free will is pretty much sanctified nowadays and neither Jeannette nor I would want to get in the way of that."

"I appreciate that." Bartel was becoming baffled. Free will? Tsunami? Where was this going?

"My suggestion is that you handle this all on your own, Emma," Tomlinson t-continued. "Look – you know that wealth isn't involved so no-one can defraud you or take advantage of you like that. I don't mean that you won't see a change in your life-style in all probability – that's not what I mean. But what you don't need is financial protection or anything like that."

"Where is this going, Reginald?"

"Nowhere, Emma," Tomlinson t-chuckled. "As I said, just a suggestion. What I mean is you don't need an agent. You don't need protection from anything. Just handle this on your own."

"But what if I feel out of my depth?"

"Jeannette and I are always here," Tomlinson t-said. "Not to interfere, but we can be part of your comfort zone."

"Not to be rude – but if you're sort of advising me that there are all sorts of pitfalls out there, and you are sort of hinting that there might be unscrupulous people, how can I know I can trust you?"

"A good question, Emma," Tomlinson t-said. "Don't trust us – test us. That's all I can say – and you can probe Jeannette and me to any depth if that makes you feel happier."

"It's not that," Bartel t-said. "Perhaps it is. I'm confused now." Bartel found it almost impossible to trust a single word that Tomlinson was t-saying.

"As you will be," Tomlinson t-said. "That's not a problem. So – I've got to go now. Be yourself. Take yourself seriously. Make sure you use socio effectively – you know: always be aware of the level you are on with any individual. Is that all right?"

"Sure." Bartel paused. "Just one thing more. Well, two things really. Just let me confirm that this new facility in Sofari is called sswipe, and then how capable is it – I mean how effective is the selectivity?"

"You know JD is so good at naming her products – and you are right this is called sswipe a double *s*." Tomlinson t-replied. "And as far as I understand it, you can set the selectivity level really quite precisely."

"That is very clever – if it does do that," Bartel t-said. "How do I invoke it normally?"

"I'm not sure," Tomlinson t-said. "I know that I asked for it – and it was immediately applied."

"Does it work after the event then?"

"Yes," Tomlinson t-said.

"Just one thought," Bartel t-said. "If people can't remember it – how do they know it was a brilliant experience?"

"That's where the clever part is – the selective memory wiping," Tomlinson t-said. "I am assured that it can be focused just as I say and it removes any details which are considered important to keep the experience secret. I think that, at the very least, it must leave intact some sense of having had a great experience."

"I'd like to see that."

"And I'll come back to you about invoking it. Though actually I don't think it works quite like that. I think it is inbuilt and the AI is programmed to deal with the selectivity automatically."

Chapter 15

Bartel tentatively relaxed her control over persono. Unlike socio the controls for persono were rather crude or imprecise mainly because it wasn't apparently so personal, despite the brand name, and Kalo obviously thought it wasn't so important. She could use Lock, which she was on overnight, Open, which was the normal mode, and Clarity – which no-one ever did because it meant that everything in persono was just out there. She switched to Open. The flood of messages was amazing, and she applied the filters by trial and error. She tried Closeness, Significance, Appropriateness, Random, and then, what she thought she should have started with – Unknown.

It was easier to deal with like that and she picked her way through the requests until she came to one that absolutely got her attention. Tryptico. Tryptico? That was something. She wondered which aspect of the three elements behind Tryptico was actually trying to engage her. It could be 24 hour news, it could be current affairs – just – and it could be tech developments. Did it matter? Not really. Tryptico wasn't the most important weed in the world. Latitude was the company that had a virtual monopoly of weeds and media organisations, but Kalo had acquired Tryptico somehow or other and broken Latitude's monopoly, then turned it into the astutest media organisation in the world as far as Bartel was concerned. It always found a different angle on everything.

Following Tomlinson's advice, she set socio to Bland and engaged Tryptico. Whoever was managing their interface – or whatever – she was soon put through to what was described as the *executive office*.

"Good afternoon, Emma – so glad you engaged," a dark voice t-said. "I am the executive office andro and I'll shortly be putting you through to a real human being, here at Tryptico." Why did they have this sort of run around? Perhaps it made their executives feel more important. "Putting you through now to Serena Velasquez, Director General, New Initiatives."

There were some interesting noises as connections were made. In more recent times none of that would have been heard but some person in Kalo had worked out that it gave a more human touch if connection wasn't instantaneous – and had a mechanical feel.

"Good morning, Emma," a rather sultry voice t-said. "As Cedric – our executive office andro said – I'm Serena Velasquez and I'm in charge of all new initiatives and we should be talking to you as one of those." It was a mixture of condescension and a patronising attitude – almost as though there was a sneer behind it.

"Glad to meet you, Serena."

"You've obviously responded to one of our engagements to your socio," Velasquez t-said. "Can I ask why you chose us?"

"How do you know I chose you?"

"You will have been inundated with engagements and as this is pretty early in the process, it seems to me that we would be either the first or among the first you engaged," Velasquez t-said. "Would I be right?"

"Yes."

"So what we'd like to do now," Velasquez t-continued as if Bartel had not added anything to the dialogue, "is engage you over socio and see whether we can help you or you can help us understand more about this phenomenon that you called Dread-Demotic."

"Ok."

"Are you quite comfortable using socio for this? We are very happy to encounter, if you'd prefer."

"Actually that would suit me better," Bartel t-replied. "I've never understood how a multi-faceted weed like Tryptico works – and I doubt if I'd be any much wiser seeing you close up but I might."

"Perfectly fine," Velasquez t-said. There was less condescension in her voice now. Perhaps she had already established how important she was.

"I'll t-summon an autonom and if you t-send the address I'll be there as quickly as I can."

"No need for that," Velasquez t-said. "We'll have one of our Kautonoms engage with you and bring you over. How does that sound?"

"I don't know – I thought an autonom was an autonom," Bartel said, not really thinking about who she was talking to.

"That is true in an overwhelming number of cases and of course we at Kalo don't make the exterior of a Kautonom any different for obvious reasons, but I think you'll be pleasantly surprised by the difference between an ordinary autonom and a Kautonom," Velasquez smoothly said. "10 minutes?"

"Make it twenty," Bartel t-said. "But one question. Why are you interested in me?"

"I would have thought that was obvious," Velasquez t-replied. "You are a potential star."

"That's not quite what I meant. I mean which part of Tryptico is interested in me?"

"That's difficult to say," Velasquez t-responded. "You see although we're called Tryptico and we were originally a triple window on the world, once Kalo took us over, we rid ourselves of all that fancy marketing – well it wasn't hype, but it no longer actually fitted what we do. I think you can see that all three of our windows – you would know them as weeds – are engaged with you – news, current affairs and high tech. Why do you ask?"

"I was fascinated to see the answer because I agree with you that Dread-Demotic does exist in all three worlds," Bartel t-said.

"Don't get us wrong, Emma. We are interested in Dread-Demotic obviously, but you will find that Tryptico like all of Kalo's companies is actually a people-focused organisation and it's you we're interested in."

If she believed that, she'd believe anything, she thought. "Ok."

She waited for the Kautonom. This was going to be a new experience. And unexpected. This was the first time she had heard of a Kautonom. Kalo autonom? Probably.

It arrived having announced it would be there in two minutes – and was, of course. It was completely indistinguishable from the normal autonom on the outside. Its door automatically slid up and she entered and sat down and as the door closed with only a slight swish she was suddenly in a world of complete calm, even though the Kautonom immediately set off. The four seats were in a circle and an automatic restraint was placed with precision in front of her – not that there were many, if any, collisions these days. Rather softly her current favourite music was playing and she thought an increase in the volume, and the clarity was astonishing with no external sounds intruding. Yes – the usual autonom was brilliant but the Kautonom was in a different league.

The Kautonom whisked her right into the building and the door was opened in front of an elevator, and the door to that opened and Bartel stepped in. She was fascinated by the little details of this rather inconspicuous wealth. It was all so understated but clearly the result of intense and focused design and construction. At the 15th floor the elevator opened with a satisfying, or rather a satisfied, sigh and Bartel walked into an area flooded with light from floor to ceiling glass.

"Welcome," the andro on the reception desk said. "Please take a seat and Serena will be with you as quickly as she can."

"Thank you, er, Cedric," Bartel said, just remembering the andro's name. It always felt odd using names like this, but it was part of the late twenty first neotiquette.

Bartel took a seat and looked at the art work on the interior walls. As any paintings could be copied in fantastic detail, in three dimensions, and with any degree of aging or cleaning that was required, it was breath taking to see Michelangelo's *Last Supper* not as it is but as it was shortly after it was painted. Although this capability was well known, the computing power it took and the mechanical capabilities that were required meant that such a fantastically astonishing version of the original was very rare, even with all the capabilities of contemporary quantum computing. Looking out through the glass was equally breath taking as the cityscape before her was a recreation in incredible detail, she realised, of how the city had looked just before the Second World War – and by removing all the high rises revealed a different scale of city. Bartel had seen reports of this capability but had no idea that it was so brilliant – and yet it also allowed natural light, or apparently natural light, into the building.

"I can see you are admiring both the art work and the view," that same dark voice t-said. "I'm so pleased to meet you, Emma. As you can guess, I am Serena Velasquez, and Director General, New Initiatives. I do think this environment is stunning – the result of the collaboration between

Eclectic with its manufacturing capability and Sapiens with its intelligence and analytical engines."

"Of course I'd heard about these new developments. As you know there aren't that many examples yet – but they are stunning – as you say."

"Would you like to come this way?" Velasquez t-said. It was just about a question.

As Velasquez guided Bartel along a central walking area, Bartel t-said: "I do know there are collaborations between the Trills but that's not that usual is it?"

"No," Velasquez t-agreed. "and as you know I work for Kaleidoscope. Kalo."

"I guessed that – I didn't know it."

"Well – really it doesn't matter at this point," Velasquez t-replied. "But one of the key misunderstandings in general is that the Trills are always opposed to each other. It is sort of true, I have to say. But I don't think you want a history lesson or an essay on how the Trills became Trills or what they do and how they act – whether together or against each other. One important concept that they do have is interdependence. I realise that that is not might be gleaned from the weeds or what you may see in practice, but it is incredibly important to the stability of the Trills' power and position. "

"So you're saying that as a Kalo environment you're very happy to showcase INsighto from Sapiens and whatever is – what? – built, manufactured? – by Eclectic?"

"Of course."

"I didn't realise that it was like this," Bartel t-replied, thoughtfully.

"I expect you know that there is a certain amount of spin created around the activities of the Trills and quite honestly you can't believe everything that you read in the news weeds. Gyro – you know Gyroscope – actually publishes all of them, even though there are eye-ball wars between its products. I think you know that Veritable is the publishing arm?"

"I wasn't aware of that."

"Well, it is," Velasquez t-continued. "You must remember that Gyro also publishes most of the fiction." Velasquez looked at Bartel and smiled. "You see what I mean? Remember that interdependence although it's not a concept that will be stressed outside of the ImCirc – the immediate circle of the Trills." They came to an area where the lighting had become softer and they then entered a room where the seating was arranged in small booths. "Here, take a seat, Emma." They sat opposite each other.

"One question. Why are you being so open with me?" Bartel t-asked.

"We're always open with everyone. Especially at Kalo. We have nothing to hide, after all. It's really that most people aren't actually interested in the inner workings of this society that we've developed – this neo-age."

"Developed?"

"Well, it wasn't planned, if that's what you mean," Velasquez t-replied. "There is no central planning – that's quite against everything the Trills stand for, as I'm sure you'd understand."

"But – it's co-ordinated?"

"Not even that, really."

"Isn't there a central ethos? Some sort of guiding principle?"

"Yes – and no. At best there are agreed guidelines. We call them the *Guiding Principles* – I'm sure you know about them, as they are part of the common understanding in the neo-age. But I'll come back to that. I think we should talk about why you are here. Don't you?"

"Why am I here?"

"Well – we all know that you've done something absolutely amazing, I'm not sure that you knew about the new capabilities in Sofari that haven't really been announced yet. I understand that you do now – so that's all that is important. These were discussed at TCentral of course."

"TCentral? Is that what I think it is – I sort of remember vaguely about it – being some sort of council operation?"

"Oh – yes. It's the Trills', well, you could say, council or parliament, or really a mediation environment. It's where they iron out any disputes."

"But just a second – before we get on to that. you said that you work for Tryptico or for Kalo that owns Tryptico. But you also said that Latitude has a monopoly on news weeds – through Veritable. How does that work?"

"It's a bit difficult to understand, Emma," Velasquez t-replied, rather conspiratorially, as though she was imparting a deep secret. "You know I said that in general the Trills compete with each other?" Bartel nodded. "They also co-operate. But one of their guiding principles is that there shouldn't be any cartels."

"Guiding principles?"

"I just told you about them – well, maybe, I didn't make it clear – that there are a set of ground rules – we call them *Guiding Principles* – that all the Trills have signed up to," Velasquez t-said. "I guess the nearest idea is like a written constitution – though it doesn't cover everything and isn't really detailed. And there is a conciliation body comprising representatives from each of the Trills – the GLEAKES – who decide everything – on a two thirds majority."

"And that works – even though the Trills are all pretty powerful individually and can do what they like?"

"Yes," Velasquez t-said. "It's a matter of being in their interest. Look – we're getting side-tracked. But the answer to your question is that Latitude owns nearly all the publishing – that's not the right word any more – but you understand the concept. Tryptico is Kalo's answer to that. It's not a direct competitor with Veritable – because it only concentrates on those three areas – news, current affairs and tech – that I think you know. For the moment Tryptico is my baby – it's part of Kalo's innovation strategy and that's my area. I see you as a major celebrity – or you shortly will be – and therefore probably an opportunity for Tryptico to increase its eye-ball, eye-screen and thought share. Now do you see why you are here?"

"It does make some sort of sense – but there's a lot I have to absorb," Bartel t-said. Going through her mind was what Pennington had said to her – and it made her very nervous of trusting anyone.

"Of course. No-one in Kalo is into coercion at any time. As you should know, it's one of the GPs, the Guiding Principles that I mentioned. Another relevant one is *no cartels*. Nothing any of the Trills does can restrict any other Trill's competitive position. And no two or more Trills can agree to do something which excludes anyone else or gives one or more of them a competitive advantage that is unfair."

"I think I've understood enough for the moment. I did know there were Guiding Principles, but I've never taken much notice up to now. They seemed worthy but pretty irrelevant to my life. Now what do you want from me?"

"I want you as a key performer – that's what we call our reporters or our presenters now because that's what they do." Velasquez looked intently at Bartel. "Of course you might get a better offer from Veritable – but actually now that financial incitements aren't an issue. What we compete with Veritable on is really exposure."

"But Veritable, as you said, has the majority of the market sewn up. So wouldn't I get greater exposure working with them?"

"Yes," Velasquez t-agreed. "Immediately you would. But think of it this way. Veritable has a thousand – you might say a million because the actual number doesn't matter – projects on the go at any one time. You've probably heard that celebrity is like a shooting star these days. A moment of extreme brightness then you fade out as the next shooting star takes over. What we can offer you is longevity."

"How do you know I have enough in me to sustain interest other than what you generate?"

"I've looked at your record, Emma," Velasquez t-replied. "What you have – and I'm not mincing my words here – is not just a creative mind, but an innate sense of what will appeal to people. It isn't just Dread-Demotic – but your track record of experiences and scenarios. And the fact that you can exploit the new elements in Sofari like sswipe – even though it's from Latitude and one of the entities that we compete with fiercely – makes you very valuable to us."

"So what do I get in return?"

"Creative freedom," Velasquez t-said, "and a long term celebrity and access to the Trills' world in a way you couldn't imagine. Yes. Any of the others, including Latitude, can offer you some of that – but you'd be one in a million. To us – you'd be so important. I mean – why did you respond to me in the first instance – and didn't take any of the other probes?"

"You have a real point. I don't actually know why I did. I guess I have always rather liked Kalo as a brand."

"You don't have to decide this moment. Go home and discuss it with anyone. I know you have a creative partner – does he want to be part of this? Lots of questions for you to answer. And I know that you're going through quite an emotional turmoil at the moment."

"How do you know that?"

"I do my research – or my people do," Velasquez t-said, completely unfazed. But the answer made Bartel nervous. Velasquez picked that up immediately from Bartel's socio, even though they were still only on Acquaintance. "Don't be concerned, Emma. You know we live in a very open world. You know that we live in a surveillance society. We couldn't operate properly with our Guiding Principles unless a great deal of our personal information is out there to be assessed. You're not going to be treated any differently. If you were in my position, and I were in yours, you'd want to know all the digital trails about me. Wouldn't you?"

"It's still a shock that you know so much," Bartel t-said.

"Not really – if you think about it," Velasquez t-said, soothingly. "You might not like to think about these things, but you do deep down know that it's true. Our digital footprint is pretty indelible."

This was an unsettling development at this point in the t-conversation, even though Bartel was conscious of how much surveillance was possible in the neo-age. Bartel, however, thought about how Pennington would react. He probably was aware of all this all the time and that's why he was rather more worried and engaged than she was – though he couldn't realistically be less.

"What you have to know, Emma," Velasquez t-continued, "is that there is nothing judgmental in what I am saying. Remember the GPs –

those Guiding Principles. We're not here to harm you – and knowing things about you, isn't to your detriment – though there are some people who disagree and who is to say that they are wrong?"

"I need to think."

"You do. Take your time – although actually it shouldn't take you long. You saw the Tomlinsons' home and environment. That would be only scraping the surface of what you can gain. Look at this world here, just here, that we're in now. You live in comfort, Emma. Everyone does – it's another of the GPs. But we're offering you so much more."

Velasquez was opening a world up that she had no idea existed, or, rather, that she had never bothered to think about. Perhaps Pennington did know all of this and that was what was motivating him. On the other hand, he did seem quite relaxed about the progressive elements in the neo-age, so where did he draw the line? It was important to Bartel that she kept going back to thinking what Pennington would make of all this.

Chapter 16

Bartel was in a spin when the Kautonom dropped her off back at her flat. There was so much to absorb – most of what she had learned things that she didn't usually want to think about. Velasquez had been so open – or apparently open. It created a feeling of suspicion.

What else didn't she know?

Every element in her mind resisted the implications of what Velasquez had said – the *Guiding Principles*, TCentral, whatever that was in reality, and the difference between what she had seen for a few brief moments and her own normal life and how she perceived life.

It had been an eye-opener and one that she didn't want to have experienced as it was so unsettling. She was after all really very happy with her life. She was, she knew now, in love with the most irritating man she could think of, who was interested in so many things she didn't care about; she had had that experience with Worrell and that had a delicious edge to it – that wasn't at all just physical. She had worked with Savery to create something really exciting – and discovered new capabilities in Sofari which meant that her work was protected in a way she hadn't imagined possible.

It was all tremendously fulfilling.

Her daughters were independent but attached to her in ways that she hadn't always appreciated. She needed nothing and, better than that, wanted for nothing that she didn't have or could have. She could look back on her marriage to Thornton and her relationship with Albert with equanimity – they had both been positive aspects of her life.

Her persono was screaming with discussions about Dread-Demotic – and the air of mystery around it was fuelling the discussions. Even though the Tomlinsons hadn't invoked sswipe to wipe their memories of it, they were keeping absolutely quiet – but feeding comments into the weeds that were picked up by all of Latitude's weeds: news, comment and chat channels. Her socio was a constant stream of engages and requests. Then a series of photographs were drip fed into the system – clearly by Tryptico as Kalo's answer to Latitude – of Bartel at various points in her encounter with Velasquez. That felt weird, but it was also presented in a way that made her as much of a mystery as Dread-Demotic. In a really curiously pleasing way even Savery was brought into the mix with questions about who was the shadowy partner in the development and deployment of Dread-Demotic.

Bartel could see how cleverly Kalo was manipulating the situation. Velasquez was creating a feeling of something slightly supernatural and this was clearly brilliant marketing. Latitude, on the other hand, in its typically right on, rather aggressive and certainly sensational approach across most of its weeds and channels was playing into the sense of excitement from the point of view of the developer and owner of Sofari. *Why is everyone talking about Dread-Demotic, the latest blockbuster from Sofari* – was a powerful message, and *what is it about Dread-Demotic that has made Bartel and her undisclosed partner the key question today* was not much more subtle but was certainly pitched brilliantly.

Pennington engaged her. She didn't want to respond immediately and just messaged saying he needed to give her half an hour. He t-came straight back with *understood*. Bartel engaged Savery. He had evidently been waiting for her engagement. "And, Emma?"

"It's getting a bit out of control," Bartel t-responded.

"You're telling me! What's this about me being the shadowy added dimension to the mystery?"

"It's marketing," Bartel t-responded. "Look at the difference between the Tryptico inspired messages and those from Latitude. And Latitude is playing catch up."

Bartel explained the encounter with Velasquez and how things were panning out.

"So are you evaluating what Kalo can do as opposed to Latitude?" Savery t-asked.

"Don't think so," Bartel t-replied. "I've got to talk to a person I know who understands this. Do you still want to stay in the background?"

"Yes – more than ever."

"Cowardice?"

"No," Savery t-said, carefully and without any emotion, "I hardly think so. I need to work out what it might mean before I get into the maelstrom you are in, Emma. Call it preserving my sanity. I've read about celebrity and what it can do to you."

"That's probably some sort of propaganda – you know – false information," Bartel t-said.

"I can understand that," Savery t-replied. "But one thing I did learn when I was finding out about imagineering was that it's always best to have a grain of truth in everything you do. I'd point to the tomb of the unknown warrior as something like that. I suspect that it's very easy to become twentieth."

"True. But there wasn't as much bad about the twentieth as we are told. It's the past – yes – but think of the creativity that want and fear created," Bartel t-responded.

"I didn't mean it quite like that, Emma. I was just using shorthand."

"I know. But status quo then Jonas?"

"Please. But bring me in if or when you think it may be safer to do so. I don't want to be a meteorite just flashing across the sky for a few moments. And I think it's also only fair, Emma. I added to what you did and imagined. I was part of what you did, not what you did."

It did feel easier without the complications of Savery's presence because it would give her time to get things straight – and then get back to him.

Bartel t-engaged Pennington. "It's really quite bewildering, Andrew."

"I thought it would be."

"I've seen a world that is just like ours – only more so," Bartel t-said, unable quite to put into words what she wanted to say. "Let me just tell you what happened." Bartel went through the whole experience rather more slowly that she wished but she felt she would give a wrong impression if she left things out.

"So you feel that there are greater depths to what is going on in our society than you originally thought?"

"Yes."

"A sort of epiphany then, Emma?"

"I don't know what that is," Bartel t-responded. "Is it some kind of awakening?" Pennington t-affirmed. "Then it was in one way – but one I don't want. I haven't argued with you all these times and insisted that I don't want to get involved in anything other than just living, to find that I'm forced into doing something I don't want to be involved in."

"So what disturbed you?"

"I don't know where to start," Bartel t-said.

"The luxury?"

"Yes – certainly. I didn't know that so much was possible for the Trills and their immediate entourage. Well – I did. But I didn't really visualise what that meant. But that wasn't disturbing."

"So what was it?"

"I don't think I've worked that out properly," Bartel t-replied. She racked her brains. "Can we encounter? I think I might be able to squeeze it out of my mind if we're actually face to face."

"I can later – not just at the moment. Do think, Emma. There is something that is troubling you otherwise I am the last person on earth that you would engage with over the Trills."

"Well – have you time for this now?"

"Yes," Pennington t-responded. "It's just that I have to be in a t-conference – an important one. So – let's talk until that starts."

"I think I've one question before we get back to what has traumatised me."

"Traumatised?"

"That's too strong a word," Bartel t-said, firmly. "It does feel a bit like a trauma. No. it's more disorientated me. Anyway – the question." Bartel explained what the Kalo offer from Velasquez was and how it was based on Tryptico and what the alternative offer from Latitude might be – and the rationale that Velasquez had given. "Do you think Serena Velasquez was right?"

"Let me think about that," Pennington t-replied. "I'll do that quasi-out loud. Latitude is the bigger weeds organisation and you'll get a greater exposure more immediately. Kalo's Tryptico is far smaller – so it would be at best a slower burn – and might not see the light of day at all.

Somehow I doubt that – now having said it. Kalo is brilliant at marketing and I think from what I've seen on my persono weeds that Kalo is creating the right sense of mystery. I think she's got a lot of sense and her rationale makes a very strong argument. Tryptico appeals to a more thoughtful demographic – and one that isn't so fickle. Inevitably whichever you go with will build you up then knock you down as part of their standard celebrity exploitation as it gets more eye-screens for a longer period. I suspect though that Tryptico would be less extreme. Yes – I know what I'd do, having talked it through. I'd believe Velasquez and take the Kalo offer."

"That really helps, Andrew. Thanks."

"Now what has really disturbed you about the encounter with Velasquez and the Kalo upper echelons?"

"Is she in the upper echelons?"

"I've no idea how the hierarchy works at all – but for her to engage with you and to tell you that she's the global head of innovation seems to me either to be a convenient lie or something that makes her valuable to you and you valuable to her," Pennington t-said, thoughtfully. "And I don't think it's worth her while not telling you the truth. That would soon come out."

"How? We know the Trills control the information weeds absolutely. You tell me that all the time."

"I think you would soon find any misinformation out. Think carefully now – what is it about that encounter that has disturbed you? Try to think."

"I don't know," Bartel t-responded. "Yes I do."

"We're making progress."

"It's," Bartel t-began hesitantly, "how much she knew about me. I knew that we're exposed to video capture all the time and it's easy to monitor persono and socio too, of course, but I began to think that socio especially isn't at all secure."

"It's what I've been telling you, Emma," Pennington t-replied.

"No you haven't," Bartel t-said. "You've been telling me that there are greater depths to what the Trills do than I realise. And you always hinted it wasn't entirely benign – though I could never see that. It did just astonish me."

"You know that this is being monitored too?"

"I hadn't thought like that," Bartel t-said. "Of course. Can we encounter? I need that."

"I can see you in a couple of hours," Pennington t-said soothingly. "My place or yours?"

"Yours, please," Bartel t-said, "as I need to distract myself."

"All right," Pennington t-replied, obviously looking at his persono, "order an autonom to get here for six o'clock this evening."

Pennington offered Bartel some more comfort – it would all work out and it was easy to come to terms with how much was known about anyone. Bartel was unconvinced. Pennington disengaged.

What made the unease she felt worse was that in her head she had really known that this level of surveillance was possible – perhaps probable – but she had never had to face it before. She felt that she had in some way betrayed herself.

That wasn't right in any sense.

She tried to distract herself. She had another interesting scenario which hadn't been a priority but she had been working on it before Dread-Demotic, and she picked up the threads and engaged with Sofari but she couldn't concentrate. Yes the person who commissioned it was an interesting character and the subject was intriguing but it wasn't Dread-Demotic.

She felt desperate. In a mad moment she engaged Worrell. No response. What good would engaging with him do anyway?

"Hi Emma," Worrell suddenly engaged her back. "You felt distracted and uncomfortable. What can I do to help?"

"Could we encounter?"

"Yes, I guess so," Worrell t-replied, a little surprised obviously by the halting way his thoughts came across. "Where?"

"Here," Bartel t-said. "Now?"

"On my way," Worrell said, very unexpectedly.

"Will you let Cheryl know?"

"Of course. Wait a moment." He paused. "I've sorted an autonom for five minutes – be with you in ten or so, it's said."

"That's great, Dave."

Bartel disengaged with Worrell and engaged with her Home-Assist andro. She had time for a very quick shower. That was excessive but she was on tenterhooks and needed distraction.

Bartel let Worrell in and he came up to her apartment. Once through the door he started to say something, but she took him by the hand and led him into her bedroom. She feverishly undid his trousers and pushed them down and pout her hand inside his pants to feel him. He was surprised. He v-asked: "What's up Emma?"

"I can't talk," Bartel t-said. "Socio to Relax. I need this."

She pushed his pants down, and undid his shirt. She pulled it off him. She pushed him back on the bed and lay on top of him and rolled him over on top of her. He took his socks off and she lay holding him, fully dressed. "Undress me now," she v-said. And he started to do so, agonisingly slowly. She need sex and this was excruciating. She felt desperate and then suddenly she felt the flood of intensity as their socios engaged and she understood that he was intensifying her feelings by being so slow.

"I need this now." Bartel t-said. "Now."

He fondled her and she dragged him on top of her again and felt him and she was almost violent as they made love almost in a blind panic on her side – which he shared deeply with her though he was far more calm, and yet responding to her need almost violently. "Yes – yes."

In the aftermath, they lay there entwined. Bartel needed to hold him and let herself calm down. She hadn't realised that she was in such an intense need until she saw him. She always understood how strong her libido was, especially in moments of extreme anxiousness, but this passion had taken even her by surprise.

"What was that, Emma?" Worrell t-asked, feeling so calm after that storm of passion.

"I just needed that, Dave."

"What had happened?"

"Something and nothing," Bartel t-responded. His calmness was flooding her socio and making her calmness more real. "Not at the moment."

"Something to do with Dread-Demotic?"

"Yes," Bartel t-admitted. "Let me kiss you. I need to be – I don't know – just to be."

"Sure."

The lay there and both drifted off to sleep.

When Bartel started to wake, while Worrell was still asleep, she wondered to herself where that passion had come from. She hadn't known it would be like that until he came through the apartment door. As she lay there, with him on his back gently breathing, with her lying against him, one leg between his, she found it impossible to think straight. It had been so intense and so fulfilling and so breath taking.

She couldn't think straight. When had she been like this before? Not for some time. Yes – the early encounters with Thornton – they weren't called encounters in those days before socio had become so sophisticated – had been desperately passionate as they discovered each other's body and were desperate to have every possible experience. There had been times since. Once or twice with Albert, certainly. It had once been really like that with Pennington, but not with any of her other lovers. Why had that happened with Pennington?

Of course. It had been anger. Pennington made her angry, incandescent even, so many times – and yet this occasion hadn't been like that, so it must be something more. Worrell hadn't made her angry – and she hadn't known that she was angry. That couldn't be it.

She puzzled and puzzled. It had been a great experience and it was entirely right that it was with Worrell. She hadn't just wanted sex. Even though it had been pretty crude or almost brutal sex. It was important that she and Worrell had that connection. So it wasn't just anger or sex. What was it?

150

As she lay there, she started to become more self-aware. She'd been angry with herself.

As they had coffee together, Worrell probed her a bit about what had happened and they shared a deep sense of being together. "I don't know why." Bartel t-said. Several times. "You will tell Cheryl – won't you?"

"I told her I was coming to encounter you," Worrell t-replied.

"And?"

"That was all right," he t-said, but there was an edge of doubt – and a trickle of uneasiness as Worrell thought about whether Cheryl would be jealous. Of course she would be.

"Ok." Bartel t-said.

"Why are you so keen that Cheryl knows all?"

"It's just the way I am," Bartel t-said. "I think our new approach to – well – sex is challenging for everyone. I know that socio created a different perspective because now you can know – really know – what the other person is thinking and whether to be concerned, or whatever is a lesser word. But I don't think that secrecy is justified. Of course we can undercut socio – anyone can if they put their mind to it. I just don't want to go there."

"Are you really asking how I feel about you?"

"Perhaps."

"I don't want to go there at this moment." Worrell was thoughtful. "Is that all right?"

"I guess it has to be," Bartel t-replied.

"Not at all," Worrell t-said. "I will go there if you need to. I just would rather have this after glow and talk in a different time when things aren't so simple."

"Simple?"

"I always find after making love that life seems simpler than before," Worrell said. "Actually I must be going. But you surprised me, today, Emma."

"How?"

"The passion and the need. It was as though it wasn't me – but something else driving you."

"I think," Bartel t-said, figuring out what she wanted to convey, "that you're right. I think this situation is pushing me hard."

"How?"

"Just not knowing things about myself," Bartel t-said. "I don't know what I feel. Some of it is anger, I know – but I can't think why. Some of it is just being out of my comfort zone. I needed that raw passion to know who I am."

"I'll think that through," Worrell t-said. "You are a complex person, Emma."

He ordered an autonom and they kissed goodbye.

About five minutes after he left, Pennington engaged her: "Sorry I can't make it to encounter you, Emma. I've time now to engage, if you want to." Just as well, Bartel thought to herself, as she was physically all over the place and encountering Pennington in this state would have been utterly confusing.

"I'd like to – but I am confused," Bartel t-replied. "That meeting with Kalo has rather disturbed me. I feel angry and upset and excited and everything else. I guess it's good to engage if you do have time."

"Why are you angry?"

"I'm angry with myself," Bartel t-responded, not quite answering the question. "Part of me is angry because I didn't take any interest in what you were trying to tell me. I'm also angry with myself for thinking like that. I don't want to change anything. It's good as it is. At least I always thought so. Now I don't know what to believe."

"All from just that one meeting?"

"I guess it's not just the meeting – but it's months – or perhaps years – of feeling some frustration but not wanting to confront it. And I still don't, before you start making me do so," Bartel t-said, firmly.

"You are a bit confused – or more than a bit, aren't you," Pennington t-said, carefully. He didn't want to upset her. "How can I help?"

"I don't think you can."

"I do have one way of helping," Pennington t-said, "and I can't guarantee that it is a help, of course. Put it like this – we all know what we need, but we don't know what we want any more. Does that help?"

"I'm not sure."

"Without starting an argument – and that's the last thing I want to do," Pennington t-said, "I think you've been going along with things. Perhaps for the first time, you've seen behind the curtain a bit. I don't suppose that it was all that revelatory because, deep down, you must have known that there was this other world – the world, if not of the Trills, the world close to them. You just saw a bit – and it made you think that you don't know what you want from life."

"I'm not sure I agree."

"You don't have to, Emma," Pennington t-said, "but I'd just like you to think what it is you really want – because you are actually on the threshold of something that might give you anything you want."

"That's a sobering thought."

"Just try to work that out," Pennington t-said. "I'm always here. But you are going to be in a whirlwind and you have to think that through first."

"Why is this happening? I know that there's Dread-Demotic but is it that important? Is it that world changing? Is it so easy for something to be so different?"

"There's the real question," Pennington t-said. "And the answer is yes. Think of it like this. You're a Trill – there's nothing you could possibly want that you can't have. Fame. Sex. Adventure. Thrills. But imagine if you are desperate for something more. Then the prospect of Dread-Demotic comes up. That's how you have to think."

"Thank you, Andrew," Bartel t-responded, "I will think that through. I had better prepare myself for what's next."

"And shall we encounter some time?"

"I'd like that," Bartel t-said. "I'll engage you to sort out when we can when I know more about what I'm doing. Is that ok?"

"Sure. And I know that it probably won't be immediate but some time will pass. I'm happy with that, Emma."

"And do you want to know what else I've been doing today?" Bartel t-said this in as gentle a way as possible.

"Do you need to tell me?"

"Actually I just don't know – and I don't know myself at this moment."

"Then – let's leave it till you want to tell me."

Chapter 17

Bartel's persono was flooded with new queries and new requests. She applied her normal filters, and there was a message from Thornton – that was rather nice – and from Albert. Good from Thornton – that relationship was well in the past of course, but still amicable and they did have the girls between them. Bartel was more dubious about anything from Albert.

There was an urgent probe into her socio – which seemed to bypass every filter and level.

Velasquez.

So they could over-ride all the levels. Bartel was only really dimly aware that the probe had taken place – as it was almost subliminal. But it had been a real probe – and it made her ask what on earth the probe had been used to discover and why it had been so effective.

The same thought came to her again and more insistently. So the Trills could bypass some of the controls and levels?

Pennington had said as much once – and she hadn't cared enough. Now she felt affronted. How come this was possible? It was the first time ever it had happened to her. It was an invasion of her space, her psyche and her equilibrium. The nearest feeling that she could immediately understand, was that this was a violation of her whole being. It wasn't rape or anything as serious, but she felt violated. Yes. Violated. Perhaps it was the psychological equivalent of rape. This felt dangerous.

Velasquez wanted to know if Bartel had made up her mind – and whether they could start the process of what Velasquez called rather oddly *grooming*. That was a really worrying word. What did it mean? It had awful connotations in history. She used persono and found that it was really straightforward. It was now used as a way of acclimatising people to work with the Trills and was necessary because it was a world with its own etiquette and own standards.

Bartel realised that she had made up her mind – and was going to go with Tryptico and Kalo. Velasquez probably already knew that, she decided, but she engaged her – and gave her the message – adding it to Velasquez's persono. She wondered idly how many such messages Velasquez would have and how long it would take for her to get back to her.

In the meanwhile, she focused on what Pennington had been saying to her. It properly made her think – what did she want? All sorts of things that were simple and concrete. Some opportunities for her girls. No that was too mundane.

Velasquez engaged her. That was quick. A Kautonom would pick her up at 18.00. Very presumptive. Perhaps this was the way the Trills always worked. No wonder people needed to be groomed. Nevertheless Bartel realised that she was excited. Could she ignore the other probes and invitations? Of course. But she idly flipped through one or two. All very persuasive and effective as all direct marketing was.

What was it she really wanted. She had to concentrate on that. something for her girls. Yes. Beyond that it became rather vague and not at all concrete. Some purpose in her life? Well, she had that more than most people. She didn't need politics. Different sexual adventures? She wouldn't say no – and suddenly she was aware that her libido had gone into – if not overdrive – into some sort of high alert. The last few encounters with Worrell had shown her something about herself that she hadn't realised for a time. She couldn't quite put her finger on it. It was being alive to her own body again. She hadn't had a sexual famine but had been relaxed and undemanding of anyone and herself. Now she felt, despite the hour or two in bed with Worrell, that she needed what she called to herself *intimacy*. She was shocked rather by the prissiness of the word. But it was what she felt.

What else?

How would she know whether she had achieved anything if she didn't know what she wanted to achieve?

Her mind felt like mush.

Pennington engaged her. "Can we engage?"

"Yes – of course," she t-responded, not really concentrating. This was a distraction.

"Can we encounter?"

"I'm sorry, Andrew – I just don't have that amount of time," Bartel t-responded, anxious to go on thinking about what she wanted from any involvement with the Trills. "Not today. Not now."

"That's all right, Emma. I understand. But you do have time now to engage?"

"Yes," Bartel was t-responding in a very distracted way.

"Did you get any closer to understanding what you want from any meetings or involvement in the Trills' circles?"

"Funnily enough I was trying to think that through, Andrew. I didn't get very far – but I know you're right to make me ask that question. I just get as far as saying to myself that I want something extra for my girls – and perhaps I want some adventures. Real adventures – though I know it's difficult to tell the difference now that Sofari is so powerful – and I get my satisfaction from creating those adventures. You can see I'm in a muddle."

"That's really understandable, Emma," Pennington t-said soothingly. "I don't think there's any need to decide what you want or to come to any solid conclusions – just keep it in your mind. I did want to suggest one thing. Suggest – not anything stronger."

"Yes?"

"Remember who you are," Pennington t-said.

"That's not very helpful."

"I mean, you might find yourself caught up in things that don't feel comfortable. Remember you can always take a step back."

"Do you think that's likely?"

"I've no idea," Pennington t-said, "but what I do know is that the Trills live a life so different from us – even though there is a fiction that they are just like us except they are trillionaires – that I think it might be baffling and then easy for you to lose sight of yourself."

"Do you know anyone that this has happened to?"

"As it happens," Pennington t-said thoughtfully, "I do. It's what started me on my – what should I call it? Mission? Well, whatever,

Emma, it made me realise that the benign Trills are in fact more dangerous than we might think."

"Don't start all that, Andrew. I don't need that now. Look – they might be evil as you say – but they are the least evil oligarchs in history. We don't have secret police, euthanasia, concentration camps, or people rounded up for their beliefs. We can believe what we like. We really do have freedom of expression. I know you think they are sinister. But they could be a good deal worse."

"I know that, Emma. I'm not sure we should be using the word *evil*. But taking that for the moment, just because they aren't as evil as they could be – and just because they seem to provide for everyone's needs in a way never seen before in history – doesn't mean to say that they are not destroying our humanity."

"No, Andrew. Don't go there at this moment. But tell me – what happened to this friend – acquaintance – who got caught up in the Trills' world – that was so bad."

"We'll only row if I do, Emma."

"I'll try not to. Explain."

"The first thing – well actually there is no first thing," Pennington t-began, "but one thing is that she realised that what she saw as free will and common sense was part of the world the Trills had constructed to preserve their position and remoteness. Secondly you say there is no secret police. No need for that. Persono was the first tool – crude but effective. We're taught to believe that persono is some kind of diary – some kind of to do list with information at our finger tips. It is all of that. But it's also a repository of all the information the Trills need about everyone."

"But they can't keep tabs on all 8 billion people in the world," Bartel t-said.

"True," replied. "They don't need to. The surveillance is really just automatic. You think how powerful INsighto is – and how powerful Trarieux has become since she created Sapiens on the back of it. Don't take my word for it – and let's not get bogged down in that now. Just take it from me that persono was the key to the change in our society and

Sapiens' INsighto – fairly recent I know – was the real enabler. *They* – whoever they are – now had access to everything about the whole world."

"I know that. That doesn't say it's sinister."

"It doesn't, I agree" Pennington t-said. "All right. Just think of the potential. But there is the next step. You know that socio is the key. If you think of persono as what people are, socio is how people are. At least that is the way the Trills think of it."

"But we know they don't all work together. They are deadly business rivals as well."

"They might be, I don't know," Pennington t-replied. He was infuriatingly calm. "As with so much about the Trills there may be truth behind what is said, but it won't be the whole truth. The point is that with socio they now have the key to what people are feeling all the time."

"Not true," Bartel t-said, firmly. "That's why we have levels – I can put my socio on Lock and I'm secure. No-one knows what I am feeling or thinking."

"You know that's not true, Emma. Did anything that woman from Kalo communicated – said or t-said – to you surprise you?"

"No, of course not," Bartel t-said.

"You sure?"

"Have you probed my socio?"

"Actually no. I just know from Agatha . . ."

"Agatha?"

"The person who was encircled by the Trills. Who was disturbed by it. She said that her first awakening or inkling of a deeper truth, was when she felt that the Trills knew things about her that were secret and entirely confidential and never shared with anyone. You know – her deepest feelings. I guess that hasn't happened to you yet, Emma. But I'm told this is a common experience."

"It has happened to me, Andrew." Bartel, in t-saying it to Pennington, was also admitting to herself with some surprise that something she didn't want to disturb her was actually very disturbing.

"What was that?"

"It was – well, I don't know what it was," Bartel t-stumbled through saying. "It wasn't that overt or something I was conscious of – and I don't know what it was intended to discover, but there was a probe – well, I had the sort of aftershock of a probe – into my socio at a very deep level. How did you know I'd be subject to that?"

"According to Agatha that first deep probe – and your consciousness of it because the Trills can completely disguise and cover up any such probe – is done as part of the grooming, as they call it. It's getting you used to a different level of thinking."

"You're making my head hurt, Andrew."

"I'll stop then."

"No – I don't mean that." Bartel paused. "I don't want to think like this. Let me have the comfort of knowing we live in a very comfortable world. What if we overthrow the Trills or whatever it is you want. Will it be better for the vast majority of people? Remember what it was like in the twentieth. Would anyone want to return to that? Over population. Global warming. Hunger. Disease. Starvation. No health controls. Pandemics."

"Let's not go there, Emma. Just be aware that I think this is an amblytopia. And I think that is anti-human."

"Don't go there again, Andrew."

"Ok," Pennington t-said. "Are you sure we can't encounter now?"

"I've got a Kautonom picking me up shortly," Bartel t-said.

"Of course." Pennington paused. "And you were with Dave Worrell earlier."

"How do you know that?"

"I don't have any over-ride powers like the Trills, Emma. But I tried to engage you while you were with him and you had left our level at Friend. So, of course, I knew. It was inadvertent on my part."

"And?"

"And nothing, Emma," Pennington t-said. "I have no ownership of you. I could understand that you needed something after the encounter with Kalo. And for your peace of mind, as soon as I knew that, I set my socio with you to Lock and didn't stay engaged with you."

"Did that do anything to you?"

"Yes," Pennington t-said. "I was jealous, of course. But it wasn't that searing jealousy that we learnt about used to happen. It wasn't nice. But you weren't in any way doing anything I wouldn't have done. I'm not sure I understood why it was so important – I got that immediately from you. but – it's fine, Emma."

"Ok."

"I'm here any time, Emma," Pennington t-said.

"Just one thing – before you go and I have to get ready. I guess this t-exchange is absolutely known to the Trills – to – what do they call it? – TCentral?"

"Yes. It's quite a nice twist on surveillance that they want all opposition out in the open as much as possible. I don't mean that it is publicised, but it is generally available to them if there is an individual or a group that is opposed to what they are doing. But unlike every other oligarchy in history, they don't feel the need to shut any of it down. Perhaps because they have so much power now, they have no need to be concerned about any opposition."

Chapter 18

The Kautonom was there at exactly 18.00. It whisked Bartel to Velasquez's offices and she found herself again in the presence – as she had started to perceive it. She felt very uneasy – but forced her mind to appear calm. Bartel was aware that almost immediately the luxury of the Kautonom and the environment that Velasquez was in had become *normal* – as she put it to herself.

How was that? Was Kalo – Velasquez – controlling her socio so that she felt comfortable. That was worrying.

Or was it just because of Pennington? Had he made her paranoid?

Any regime that made people lose need had to be good. Bartel was hanging on to that as solid fact that she absolutely believed in.

Velasquez welcomed her again. She t-began: "I expect you're wondering what we will do first. It's relatively simple. It's really a rapid orientation, then we prepare you for the world you are about to enter. A world of celebrity. Does that make any sense to you?"

"Of course," Bartel t-replied.

"There's a *but* there, I think," Velasquez t-said.

"No – well, yes," Bartel t-stumbled through. "I think you used the word *groom* – and I know I'm not that familiar with archaic language – well pre-Trill and the GLEAKES and TCentral – but it used to have rather sinister connotations."

"That's true – and it's one of the reasons why we chose it. Now that we have virtually eliminated – because we can't actually, nor would we want to, completely eliminate human nature – we have decided to rehabilitate some of the words that used to have such bad connotations."

"So it's deliberate?"

"Oh yes," Velasquez t-began, "you will find that nearly everything – if not everything – is deliberate. It may not be planned in the old sense, but you will find, as we get closer to the centre of the neo-age – and I don't mean TCentral – that very little is left to chance."

"But isn't that a denial of human nature?"

"I can see we're in for a long discussion," Velasquez t-said and smiled. "And that's all right. Grooming isn't a one-way affair – we orientate you, and of course you have an input and we learn from that. I think you'll actually understand better when we start. Although, of course, we have already started the process."

Bartel looked at Velasquez to see if she could detect anything from the way she was holding herself and her general demeanour, but it wasn't at all clear to her how Velasquez was actually intending this all to come across.

Velasquez t-continued: "The thing most people find difficult, Emma, is that through socio we have a real understanding of people and psyche – and so, for example, fraud has become – if not eliminated – so difficult and so unrewarding that it rarely occurs."

"Why this focus on *fraud*?" Bartel didn't know if she was acting out of line – but she presumed this was the input that Velasquez had mentioned.

"You will understand more about that shortly," Velasquez t-said, "but it's a good question and deserves an answer. You can imagine that in the early days – we privately call them the *billionaire years* although I don't think that phrase occurs much in modern discussions of society and, if anything it's known as the time of the Bills – there were many pretenders to the throne of being a top billionaire. It was a period of genuine innovation and creation of wealth but there were also a few – not that many but they were high profile – people who acquired their wealth illegitimately, through what we now call *Stein* felonies. That's a broad term for – I guess you don't know the word *Ponzi* – systems where essentially for the promise of untold wealth, people were conned out of huge sums in total but not necessarily that much for each individual. It was very clever – and really fraud. The genuine Bills, genuine billionaires – that is those that created wealth out of genuine business – were affronted by this. Obviously they could do nothing about it so when they became able to do so, they eliminated as many chances of fraud as they could because it undermined their legitimacy.

"It became generally seen as *common sense* that every Bill had acquired his or her wealth illegitimately and so it had tarnished their individual reputations. What's more the organised crime gangs – that weren't just the old style drugs cartels and mafias but groups that had taken over political parties and come to power in quite a few of what were called the democracies – were skimming off billions from the public finances, all in plain sight. And this was another fraud that the Trills had to eliminate because it clearly affected the perception of their legitimacy."

"Do I need this detail?"

"Don't be impatient, Emma," Velasquez t-replied, not harshly but firmly. "You may not *want* this detail – but I promise you that you may well need it. And you did ask about fraud – and this is highly significant, especially in understanding how we got to the neo-age."

"Ok, I understand what you're doing and why you're taking this approach, or at least I think I do. But you do know that I've never been one for too much delving into how and why, preferring to accept."

"Unlike your friend Andrew Pennington you mean?"

"Yes – I suppose so," Bartel t-replied, rather startled at the way Velasquez was prepared to be quite open about how much she knew about her. Pennington had been right – only too right. It really discomforted her – but perhaps this was the idea. "All right. So were those the only large scale frauds that the Trills eliminated?"

"Oh," Velasquez t-continued, "it wasn't our current Trills at this stage, but yes. As soon as they could create TCentral they looked at other forms of fraud that were doing their reputations no good."

"For example?"

"So many," Velasquez t-responded with a smile. "For a start, there was a thing called *private equity* which was basically a parasitic way of acquiring wealth. No wealth creation – and I keep talking about that as it is the key to understanding the Trills – just wealth acquisition at other people's expense."

"How?"

"Well – it was presented as a victimless method of streamlining business – making it more efficient not only in production but also in financial terms," Velasquez t-responded. "Look – let's not get bogged down in this. Just take it from me that private equity was essentially a major fraud perpetrated against the whole of society, not just individuals. It is, however, a side issue to what is important for you here and I've a lot more to talk about"

"Now you've started, I'd appreciate understanding more," Bartel t-replied, firmly. "You said I should be an active part of this grooming."

"True enough," Velasquez t-replied. "Ok. What the parasites did was identify a large company with no debt, not necessarily that profitable because that would increase its value or price to them, but with a good cash flow. They'd borrow money – well, they'd call it creating a fund – and buy the company, more or less on spec.. They didn't have to do much due diligence – and were quite prepared for one in three acquisitions not to work out."

"What?"

"You'll see," Velasquez t-said, "because there was no risk. Once they'd bought the company, on the basis of the cash flow and the promise that they'd make the company twice as profitable, or three times or as many times as was needed to convince someone or some corporation, they'd borrow on the company's books as much money as they'd paid for it and pay themselves a special dividend of that amount of money. They'd put a new management in – and if it went well, sell it for no less than three times what they'd paid in the first place, repay the loan, and walk off to do the next one. If it went badly – they'd close the company – perhaps with a pre-pack and no, I won't explain that – and walk away having lost nothing."

"This was allowed?"

"More than allowed," Velasquez t-replied. "The people making money this way were lionised. It was, as you can imagine a real threat to the people who would become the Trills – they might find their own company taken over because of the way the stock market works, but, worse than that, they'd find their reputations besmirched by these very clever pirates hiding in plain sight. It would seem to everyone that all billionaires – as they were then – were of the same cut. The Trills didn't want that – and, in fact they couldn't afford that."

"Who were the victims – you said that it was presented as a victimless sleight of hand?"

"Well – the people who worked for the company, the pension funds who loaned the money, the pensioners relying on those funds, taxpayers – because these scams also had fiscal benefits – and no, don't worry about that. The point, Emma, is that the soon-to-be Trills couldn't afford to have their reputations and business methods associated with these gangsters and manipulators, even though the gangsters and manipulators were working in plain sight, with the active support of politicians on the make."

"So how did they eliminate this if they weren't in political control?"

"Well – it depends how you see political control," Velasquez t-said. "They donated to political parties – sometimes, if not usually, to both sides in any election – and were so important to the elected politicians that they were able to force them to legislate against these practices. Note that they called these donations but it would be very hard to distinguish donations like these from bribes. And what it did was squeeze out the fraudsters."

"So this was a real benefit to society?"

"Yes – oh yes," Velasquez t-said. "I'm glad you have seen that so quickly. So let's get back to the grooming programme."

"I'd be pleased to understand that – and I'm not sure how useful what you've just told me will be," Bartel t-responded.

"It's all local colour and helps you understand the motivation of the Trills – and that's really important in this process," Velasquez t-confirmed. "The first thing I want you to understand is . . ."

"Sorry to interrupt but I think I'd like to understand the process first," Bartel t-replied. "It'll help put this in context, so I know why something's important."

"Good point," Velasquez t-confirmed. "Ok. This grooming explains to you the Trills' world in as much detail as you want or perhaps need. We find that important – and believe me you really don't know that world of the Trills no matter how much you apparently know about it from all the weeds. Secondly there is the process of explaining – or showing you really

– why you are important and where you fit in. Thirdly – how to exploit your celebrity. That is – we manage you to give you the best experience – and we'll introduce you to some of that. The rest you'll learn on the job so to speak."

"What does that mean?"

"For example, Emma, you will have a whole new appreciation of the word *want*. You know that our society is really free from need. The wealth of the Trills has been created and exploited to ensure that's a result."

"Why?"

"That's a deep question," Velasquez t-replied. "Self-interest. If the Trills know that people are not in need, then they know that they won't question deep down too much. One of the main drivers – not the only one – that motivate the Trills is not only survival but continued and continuing position and, to be crude, maintaining their power to organise and run the world."

"Really? Power? But people have free votes and elections and can create governments."

"Power," Velasquez t-confirmed. "You'll find that that is true – though not talked about in those terms anywhere but in TCentral and between the Trills. You are being groomed, Emma, for a position in this new society – and so you need to understand that more than anything. As we always say, the Trills have constructed the first society ever which is benign from top to bottom. But to maintain that, they need power."

Bartel was rather shocked again at the openness of the conversation. Velasquez was stripping away euphemisms and focusing on essentials.

"Ok, Serena." Bartel t-began, "where do I fit into this. Why me?"

"As I think you know," Velasquez t-continued, "you have created something really remarkable – a new experience – well not that new – but a new way of confronting an experience. The Trills love that. They also see you as a really good person to promote. You are very much what they call *neo-age*. You embody all the qualities that they think makes for a good role model."

"Such as?"

"You aren't hung up on sex," Velasquez t-said. "That's important. You have longer relationships, you have one night stands, you engage with people and encounter them. That's really important."

"So is sex the most important thing about me?"

"No."

"So why is it the first thing you mention, Serena?"

"It is very important – and it puts the other things into perspective," Velasquez t-replied. "Look – we haven't eliminated jealousy. Nor have we eliminated heart ache, unrequited love, desperation for someone and all the usual human emotions. We have, however, eliminated *infidelity*. Like you and Dave Worrell. We were really impressed that you insisted on his sharing what you two were doing with Cheryl."

Alarm bells were ringing in Bartel's head. So they knew all of this about her. Of course they did – but having it out in the open was rather more of a shock than she might have imagined. Did it matter?

It did at this moment.

"That's so neo-age. And don't be so shocked that we know all this about you." Velasquez was obviously picking up Bartel's reactions from her socio. That was unnerving. "You also have a – we would have called it a *work ethic* during the age of the Bills or the first Trills – but now we call it *equilibrium*. So many people can't get that balance between doing things to the best of their ability for the joy and satisfaction of doing something as against indolence – you know that feeling of *why bother?*"

"I can understand that. I've seen that and felt that feeling – but also gone through it. Yes. That makes real sense."

"This is all so important to the Trills because the deep and underlying malaise that they haven't yet fixed is about purposelessness. You know – like Jonas Savery felt earlier this week. And we know you've felt it. That purposelessness is a real threat to the stability of the Trills' world. Perhaps the only threat."

"Right. So what else do I have to know – now I understand a bit about where I fit in?"

"Just some basics, Emma. You know about the GLEAKES – everyone does. There is actually no hierarchy amongst them. They are all deemed equal – at least as far as TCentral is concerned – which is, you remember, their equivalent to a parliament – though really it's a mediation and rules enforcement body. Well – that's one and the same thing.

"It's not law – that's still as independent of the Trills as they want it to be. It – TCentral – is what I told you was responsible for the Guiding Principles. I told you about them – and here's an aide memoire that I'm transferring to your persono. And you know each of the GLEAKES *owns* one at least of the GPs. Ok. For example my organisation, Kalo owns the GP that means that there should be no cartels – no way of excluding competition. So far so good. Hence Tryptico is part of Kalo even though Latitude is the owner of the biggest weeds. I know this is new to you, Emma. But you know enough for now. Then there are essentially two types of the GLEAKES. It's not entirely cut and dried.

"On the one hand you have Kalo – Kaleidoscope – responsible for persono and socio and you could say private data. On the other you have Eclectic which is a services company – it produces things that underpin everyday life – you know, andros and the like. There's the dichotomy. Brain or brawn."

"That sounds a really crude distinction, Serena."

"It is," Velasquez t-confirmed. "And not rigid as I say. I don't know quite whether Gyroscope – you know it as Gyro – is brain or brawn or both. It produces drugs, food – you know gSynth – and consumables – from essentially the basic chemicals – many of which come from Eclectic originally. Not exclusively – as there are no cartels. Is this clear?"

"I think so – and while I didn't know the precise distinction, it's not that new to me either," Bartel t-said. "But you also said interdependence between the GLEAKES was important. Is that to prevent one of them becoming too powerful."

"It may not prevent it because we won't know if interdependence does finally have that effect unless one or more of the Trills tries to take over – and as that is a remote possibility, we think interdependence is one of the best safeguards we've got."

"Nothing you have said is that new – I mean, I don't think about these things, but if I did, it wouldn't be too far-fetched to suggest that I would be able to come up with this on my own."

"I rather doubt that, Emma. I think I should just go on with this overview – perhaps redundantly but just in case there are gaps in what you understand. There's Sapiens with what used to be called artificial intelligence – and you can see how that fits in with Kalo," Velasquez t-said. "There's Ambience – really just think health. But don't forget that Eclectic has Medi-Assist which utilises all of Ambience's products – and Ambience utilises all of Eclectic's products and services. They are especially intertwined. Then Elura with the financial systems – what people used to call banks – but they don't have an equivalent in neo-age now that wealth and cash or money are so different."

"How is that?"

"I can explain later," Velasquez t-said. "Finally, there is Latitude – which you know especially well because that is focused on experiences – travel, well v-travel – and creativity of most sorts. Drama for example. You use Sofari as part of your work every day. And most importantly some of the time, it owns the weeds. So Latitude is important to you not just in your new found celebrity but because Jessie Dressus brought Sofari, your major tool, to the market."

"And what do I do with this information?"

"Nothing much, Emma. You just needed to have this information – and for it to be confirmed to you. By the way you can see that Latitude for one doesn't necessarily fit into either category. It's cerebral as it operates on the brain but it's also physical as it interacts with the body. That's the beauty of Sofari of course – as you well know. Happy so far? Any questions?"

"No. I guess I'm not sure why I need this. Am I groomed now?"

"Not quite," Velasquez t-replied. "But probably enough for now. Just one last thing – and it's quite a weird joke – and one thing you'll learn about the Trills is that they have a sense of humour – that you are to look on me as your Mephi."

"Mephi?"

"It's short for Mephistopheles."

"And what's that?"

"It's an old legend about a philosopher who sold his soul to the devil in return for a lifetime of bliss and whatever he wanted," Velasquez t-replied. "Mephistopheles was the devil who was assigned by the devil, Satan, to pander to the philosopher's every want while he was alive and then to cart him off to hell when he died. I'm your Mephi."

"That's really sinister."

"Yes – in some ways," Bartel t-agreed. "It's just a joke really."

"So what's next?"

"I show you your new environment," Velasquez t-said.

"Don't I go home?"

"Sure. If you want. And at any time. Remember we've not abolished free will or whatever you want. But we thought you'd like to experience this environment first. It'll help you in the next steps."

"Which are?"

"Introduction to the real celebrity world – which will initially be a bit of a whirlwind – but you'll soon get used to it. Is that all right, Emma?"

"Yes."

"So what do you want to do? Stay here or come back in the morning?"

"I think you already know the answer to that, Serena, since you have access to my socio."

"True."

"Don't people find that really disturbing?"

"Yes. At first. But think of how safe it makes our neo-age. We all can understand the other person's motivation without having to guess."

"Yes. But you can obviously over-ride my levels. If I set my socio level to Lock – would you still be able to access my thoughts?"

"Does that disturb you?"

"Yes, Serena, it does."

"It won't." Bartel found that really chilling, but drew in a deep breath and just accepted it for the moment. Perhaps something to tell Pennington if she ever had the chance to engage with him.

"One final – for now – question: if I think about how celebrities are created and lionised then knocked down and abused in a sort of never-ending cycle of nonsense. Will that happen to me?"

"It's a possibility. But remember all of that is very trivial, has actually no meaning, and every element of celebrity is just exploited, perhaps to keep people distracted, perhaps to keep them happy with their own lot. I'm being realistic now, Emma."

"And very open."

Velasquez walked with Bartel into an expansively luxurious area where above all else the subtlety of the lighting and its effects were stunning – and said that Bartel should relax and take some time to get used to this new world.

Chapter 19

"Welcome to our neo-age environment and your own special part of it," the andro v-said, as Bartel entered the 18th floor of the same building, having been directed there by Velasquez after about half an hour luxuriating in the beautiful area she had gone into. Velasquez had said that she had to attend to some other things but would catch up later.

The andro v-continued: "I am here to meet your needs – not to replace Serena, your Mephi, but as an adjunct. And you can call me, I suggest, Peter, but your own preferred name is fine with me. And do you wish me to be a total verisimilitude or would you prefer me to be more andro?"

Such a weird question but so twenty first.

"What does that mean?" Bartel asked. It was good that you had to use voice with an andro. She didn't want any socio engagement with Peter. "And by the way, Peter is fine." So he wasn't an andro but a holo. This world in TCentral was very odd. Holos weren't this convincing in Bartel's normal world.

"How you want me to appear to you? As you might not have realised I am a hologram and I can reconstitute myself as anything you prefer. Male or female. You cannot choose to have my appearance as something illegal – for example some men have been known, in the old days admittedly, to ask for school girls. But I can be old, or, as we call it, mature. Younger."

"I'm quite happy with your appearance, Peter." He was about 35, younger than Bartel, and smart casual. And quite a verisimilitude as he had called it. This was a development of a newer technology that Bartel had only learned about recently. Clearly hologram technology had come on quite rapidly. Peter looked substantial.

"The evening is your own to do as you wish – and we start at 9.00 tomorrow – I know that's early for you, but we think it's important to get cracking," Peter v-said, in a friendly but matter of fact way. The programming that had gone into making this andro experience re-assuring and sort of authoritative and yet non-threatening had been very sophisticated. "So – food, I think?"

"Yes."

"And catch up with Andrew and Dave and possibly Jonas? I doubt that you'd want to engage with Thornton or Albert – but I can arrange that." He was well-programmed. No – that was the wrong perspective. Well informed. He clearly had access to her socio.

"Not all three. I'll think about that."

"Engage or encounter?"

"I was rather thinking that it had to be engage," Bartel v-said. "Can I just engage?"

"Of course."

There was something quite different about Peter – Bartel found it difficult to call the andro that because normally andros were called rather mechanical names although, of course, as it was entirely up to an individual what he or she called an andro, this was hardly cut and dried, but he was amazingly lifelike. In fact Bartel realised that he was indistinguishable, at first sight at least, from an andro and virtually indistinguishable from a person. And this is a hologram? So there was nothing substantial actually in her line of sight? It was mind-boggling, even to Bartel who had grown up through many unbelievable technological and psychological changes.

Although the andros she was used to were really quite astonishingly lifelike, there was a subtlety about this Peter that she couldn't quite put her finger on. She slowly realised it wasn't one thing but a combination of all sorts of details. His skin – and she felt she had to say *his* skin – was not only really astonishingly like skin, but was mottled in places, the hair on the back of his hand was almost invisible, but still there; his eyelashes were a bit askew; and he was, she realised, quite round shouldered. Andros weren't usually given any minor defects at all.

That he could read her socio was expected as the latest andros in normal life were quite capable of that. What was quite astonishing and worrying was that the levels in socio didn't seem to make any difference. He could read her socio to any depth and go through her past.

"One question, Peter. Do you know what my programme will be tomorrow?"

"Yes – of course I do," Peter replied. At least because he was an andro, he was using voice. Bartel was becoming a bit paranoid – or so she worried to herself – so she didn't want this to be via socio at all even though it probably couldn't be.

"And?"

"First steps are to orientate you about this world of the Trills in a bit more detail," Peter v-responded. "You might think you already know a great deal about us but you will be surprised at how different reality is." *Us? The andro referred to this world as us? And reality?* Suddenly Bartel was rather frightened – not by any threat, but because this was all so unknown.

"Should I be worried?"

"No," Peter v-replied, soothingly. "Not at all. You are being groomed as a celebrity – and in order to fulfil that role, you will need to understand much more than you do now."

"So I can tell people about it?"

"On the contrary – so you know what you can't tell people," Peter v-said. Pennington would be amazed to hear this. Then – perhaps he wouldn't. "Notice that I said *role*. It is not so much an act as you might expect, but more a presentation of yourself. Dread-Demotic is going to be a very important stimulus to people – and as the imagineer behind it, you will be important. So there will be a bit of *weed* training – what used to be called *media training* – how to conduct yourself in all the weeds. And of course we'd like you to focus on the neo-age aspects of your life and how you can be an exemplar of that. So that will form part of the explanation of your role. Is that enough detail?"

"Thank you, yes, Peter."

"Do you want to engage with anyone now – this minute?"

"Actually no, Peter." It was strange how she had to call the andro by name all the time. "I need time to think and digest what I've got on tomorrow. Then – in say twenty minutes I'd like to engage with Jonas Savery. Is that all right?"

"You have no need to ask permission," Peter v-replied. "You are absolutely in charge of yourself. I don't suppose this needs saying, but just for completeness, you are free to duck out of this role at any time of your choosing – now, tomorrow or at any time. Are you happy with that?"

"I am."

"Ok," Peter v-said. "I'll leave you for twenty minutes."

"Does that mean that I can't just engage Jonas through my socio as normal?"

"Of course not," Peter v-said, rather abruptly, Bartel felt. "You can. Of course you can." Peter was really contradicting himself but was that deliberate to put her off her guard? "Often, though, people find it more helpful if an andro like me arranges it."

Why did that sound threatening? Bartel felt out of her depth.

"So, Emma, I will leave you to your own devices." With that the hologram disappeared.

Bartel felt bewildered and frightened – and also excited. What was she going to learn? What was the difference between her understanding of the world and the *reality* that Peter had mentioned? One thing was certain, however – she didn't want to duck out of the programme – if that was what it was. There was so much that was different already – even having a hologram as an andro was spectacularly new and technologically innovative. Most andros had physical attributes. Clearly Peter didn't need actually to do anything because that had been a limitation of holos up till now at least.

Bartel engaged Savery – but he was at that moment busy. She didn't want to engage Pennington and Worrell was a different kettle of fish. She had to be on top of things to engage him.

"Did you engage, Emma?" Savery t-asked suddenly. He had obviously noticed that she'd tried to engage him and had dropped whatever else he was doing.

"I tried to."

"How's it going?"

"It's interesting – I'll say that for it," Bartel t-replied.

"I'm sure it is – and don't forget me, Emma. I didn't want to be a guinea pig – but I'd like to be part of anything – if that works out."

"I'm not sure it will, Jonas. It's very odd – but I won't forget you."

"Have you seen the stir that Dread-Demotic is making at the moment? It's a whole new industry by the sound of it. No-one knows what it is and what it does – but everyone wants to know. I'm just surprised that the Tomlinsons haven't spilled the beans about it – and told everyone what the experience is and how the scenario works out."

"They can't," Bartel t-began. "I mean – I think *they* can but won't, but anyone else who signs up for it, probably can't let alone won't."

"Why?"

"There's that new feature in Sofari that we didn't know about, Jonas, before we met the Tomlinsons. I think the Tomlinsons experienced it before it was switched on in our scenario – so they can remember it all. Or perhaps it didn't need to apply to them. This new switch, sswipe, erases all memory of the experience – or it can erase selective parts of the memory. This new feature is undocumented. Unknown. But something we desperately needed if Dread-Demotic was going to become more than a one night wonder."

"Do you mean to say that people's memories of Dread-Demotic will be wiped completely clean when they exit Sofari?"

"I think it's more subtle than that." Bartel gathered her thoughts and t-continued: "I think the easiest thing would be to wipe all the memories a person has – but this new switch in Sofari selectively erases memories – so people don't forget who they are and all that stuff, and they hang on somehow to the favourable parts at the close of the experience – you know a warm sort of glow from having got through it, just as we planned. They do, however, forget the central action – the terror and the potential violence."

"That's so cool." Savery was clearly impressed and at the same time thoughtful. "Can we use this all the time?"

"I don't know," Bartel t-replied. "I don't know how it works or when it works. All I know is that it's a great new tool for us – if we're allowed to use it. And that's not all. What appears to be my own personal andro – though I'm not sure if he – I think I say he – is just for me – turns out to be a hologram."

"How the hell do they do that?"

"Obviously," Bartel t-replied, "Peter – he's called Peter – can't actually do anything, like lifting something or cleaning – but that's not his role. He can be configured as anything or anyone – within the rules of taste and decency. It's quite weird. He is the gofer, the do-it-all – well sort-it-all at least. And he looks totally solid and lifelike. You just wouldn't know that Eclectic had advanced andros this much – it's like they are ghosts but they don't look like ghosts."

"You are really at some sort of cutting edge, Emma. Can I ask a simple question knowing the answer won't necessarily be simple? How are they going to market Dread-Demotic?"

"I haven't got to that," Bartel t-responded. "I'm in the sweet shop at the moment surrounded by all the goodies – and I don't think I can take it all in."

"Surely once you know persono and socio are possible – and we have all the other things the GLEAKES have brought us – we can cope with anything new and completely disruptive?"

"I think that's the point," Bartel t-replied. "that we are used to disruptive – what do they call it? – technologies but each time something disruptive comes along, we are still disrupted."

"What else have you learnt?"

"Too much to tell you in an engagement," Bartel t-said. She wanted to tell Savery about the fact that anyone's socio or persono was completely transparent to the Trills' organisation – if that was what it was, that is an organisation – and even thinking it meant that they knew that she was trying to tell someone. But it seemed impossible to tell him in a way that was discreet. "I don't think I can t-say anything more."

"You've already blown my mind – that switch in Sofari and the Peter stuff – wow!" Savery t-said. "Can I change the subject?"

"I think the answer's still no, Jonas," Bartel t-responded.

"You don't know what the question is."

"I do," Bartel t-said. "You were alluding to us becoming intimate. I don't think that's a good idea."

"Have you been let into their surveillance ring? How did you know that was going to be my question?"

"You don't have to be in on any surveillance, Jonas, to know that," Bartel t-said, with a laugh. "And I know you are genuine – and everything else that socio lets us know about someone. I just don't feel like that with you."

"I'm not expecting love."

"I know that," Bartel t-replied. "But ever since we've had socio, there's been something other than lust and love – something between. Obviously sex is a way of becoming closer – but I still have to feel something rather than have a transaction."

"It wouldn't be transactional for me," Savery t-replied.

"I know," Bartel t-responded. "Let's leave it there, if you don't mind. I'm not denying there is chemistry between us. And the reason is not because you are so much younger than me – although by mentioning it, I am showing you it is a factor of some sort. Just my mind is too involved – and I've never been one for mixing professional relationships and personal relationships."

"You can't blame me for trying, Emma. I know there's that chemistry too. And I'm afraid I do have feelings like that – you know personal feelings."

"Ok."

When they finished the t-conversation, Bartel didn't feel cross or annoyed – just a little discomposed. In most senses Savery was her junior – age, ability experience, understanding, imagineering – and weinsteining was always suspect. She knew she could sleep with Savery and not have any regrets and it would be fun – she was sure of that. But it made her uneasy in terms of the neotiquette.

Peter appeared – that was the only word for it. "Are you all right?"

"Yes," Bartel v-replied. It was somehow a little strange that she had used socio to communicate with Savery and was using voice to communicate with Peter.

"Do you want to engage with anyone else?"

"No."

"In that case," Peter v-said, "I'll let you get some rest and I will be with you again tomorrow morning around 8 – if that's ok." He obviously knew – was that the right word for an andro who wasn't actually, in any real sense except the visual, there? – the answer as soon as he asked it, if not before.

Bartel didn't want to engage with anyone else. She needed some time with her thoughts – though the idea that everything she was thinking – even this – was capable of being monitored and presumably was, really inhibited her willingness to think.

But nothing had changed, she realised. It had been like this – it was just that she wasn't aware of the fact that every thought was being monitored. At least she presumed that Sapiens was so powerful that it could monitor everything in real time. It was mind boggling.

She set her socio level to Lock – to ensure that she didn't have to engage with anyone. She wanted her own fantasy and her own time – really to relax and to forget about the suddenly overwhelming environment that she found herself in.

Another Sofari scenario which she had imagineered some time ago perhaps even a year ago came to mind for some reason. It had been ground breaking in using a feature of Sofari that had just become available. Sensuo-Contacta had not caught on – though, in her opinion it had everything to recommend it – but she loved it. She especially liked not only that the scenario was completely configurable to whatever she wanted at the time she was in the experience, but that configuring it wasn't a question of setting up the scenario beforehand, but interacting with it through socio meant that it adapted to any desire or even whim while in the experience.

Bartel prepared herself for bed, and climbed under the duvet and lay on her back. She invoked Sensuo-Contacta and brought Worrell into the scenario. He was fully clothed and she slowly undressed him, touching and kissing and enjoying the sensual experience of giving pleasure while remaining completely untouched. She felt the experience in every sense – visual, tactile, smell, sounds and even taste – as she interacted with Sensuo-Contacta, and gave herself up to the pleasure – completely obliterating her concerns about being monitored. And then she brought

Pennington into the scenario – and he touched her lightly and totally while she continued with Worrell. The experience was completely immersive for her – which was what she had wanted in imagineering the experience – and very satisfying as she shuddered through orgasms, enjoying the deliciousness of being involved in something that she would find too challenging in any real situation.

Why hadn't this gone viral – when Dread-Demotic had?

Chapter 20

Rather blearily, Bartel woke in a gentle sexual haze. Peter was on hand almost immediately to tell her what she had to do and she got herself ready.

Bartel was guided to Velasquez's office – which was more of a sumptuous living room in keeping with how offices were apparently being developed in the latest fashion.

"Did you sleep all right?" Velasquez t-asked. She would obviously know the answer to that and Bartel wondered whether to be at all embarrassed by her adventures with Sensuo-Contacta. It was important not to get too hung up on any of this.

"Fine."

"First of all I want to bring you up to date on Dread-Demotic and its progress," Velasquez t-began. "As you know, we predicted that this would be bubonic in its take up – and we were right. Perhaps I should say *of course*. I'm not sure we at Kalo would admit ever to have got marketing decisions wrong since we brought persono and socio to market. There would be little point. Anyway – Dread-Demotic is currently at number 15 in global experiences – and is only at 15 because we're restricting its take up."

"15 – globally?"

"Yes – with one caveat or perhaps two," Velasquez t-added. "In that this is the figure for new releases which are counted as anything within the last 28 days. And it's not the number of people who have enjoyed – perhaps not the right word as I understand it – the experience of Dread-Demotic to the full. It's based on the number of orders – and we're, as I said, restricting supply."

"I didn't know you could do that."

"There's not much in marketing and sales and distribution that we can't do," Velasquez t-confirmed. It wasn't smug – just matter of fact. "Shortage creates demand. Getting the balance right between those two is one of the key elements in the way that Elora Ghose made Kalo so successful. It wasn't the only thing of course. The quality of the products, persono and socio, were important elements."

"So what does this mean, Serena?"

"It means that you are already a global celebrity. Is that the question you were asking?"

"I suppose it was," Bartel t-replied, doubtfully. "No. I guess it was more what difference does it make to my life as I live it."

"That depends on you, of course," Velasquez t-said, rather soothingly. "You can enjoy your five minutes of fame and leave it at that – or you can build a career out of this one brilliant piece of imagineering."

"Is it that simple?"

"No," Velasquez t-laughed back. "But almost."

"What does it mean practically?"

"It doesn't mean," Velasquez t-said, "increased wealth – that's a twentieth and not really relevant. It does mean a higher standard of living – for example your own dedicated Kautonom – if you want that."

"Is that possible?"

"Certainly," Velasquez t-replied. "You also saw the way the Tomlinsons live – and that is now open to you. Of course there are strict rules about all of this – how much exposure you give, how much you reveal about any privileges that you have earned. All of that is strictly controlled. One of the guiding principles which isn't owned or curated by a single specific one of the GLEAKES but is owned by all of them through a function of TCentral is the fact that we don't ever want to excite jealousy or resentment about the Trills – so there is a code of secrecy about our world which you are required not to reveal. That is you are not to reveal that there is a code of secrecy and then you must not reveal any of the secrets governed by that code. You can actually reveal both of course. Another guiding principle is that there is no coercion nor any such restriction. Nevertheless, there is a sanction for disregarding the limits that we set, as long as you are made aware of them, of course. The ultimate sanction is that you would be excluded from the Trills' circle."

"But I thought," Bartel t-replied, "that I already have a good understanding of the world of the Trills – there is enough about them on the weeds."

"Yes – we like people to think that," Velasquez t-said. "All carefully controlled. You may soon realise that while we don't have any restrictions on beliefs or opinions – within the Guiding Principles – in fact we encourage as diverse a range of beliefs and opinions as possible for obvious reasons . . ."

"Obvious reasons?"

"Yes," Velasquez t-replied. "We don't want any dominant beliefs or opinions – so the more the merrier. But we do have some seminal thinkers or works – though I don't think anyone particularly bothers to read them any more as we've absorbed them into our blood stream so to speak. There are a few academically minded people of course who do research them – again no restrictions or involvement in encouraging or suppressing them.

"This may be difficult for you to absorb – but it is fundamental and will be part of your induction which will happen later this morning. We don't have an equivalent to a bible, of course, but being *gramscian* is very much the key word in all of this."

"What does gramscian mean – I mean does it mean what I've always thought it meant?"

"I think he was an ancient philosopher – perhaps nineteenth, possibly twentieth," Velasquez t-said, thoughtfully. "It doesn't matter really. He was one of the people who bezoed this world."

"Bezoed?"

"Yes – you know actually understood the way the Trills' world should operate and how to manage the world in this new way," Velasquez t-said. "Not sure where that comes from. Anyway, as I understand it, being gramscian was developed as part of that bezoing."

"So what does it mean practically? You are confusing me. Do I need to know this?"

"Possibly not – but we always make sure that people are aware of the terms just in case they come across them. Suffice to say that being gramscian is to use the feeds to stabilise and not exactly control, although I understand that was the original concept, but to guide the way that society functions. It's not enough to explain – but fundamentally the Trills have to convince and the best way to do that is not to do it overtly but to use subtlety. We use all the weeds we can to reinforce our messages and contradict the messages that aren't positive to us."

"Can that be right? And why are you telling me this?"

"You really need to understand our world."

"*Our?*" Bartel was puzzled. "Are you a Trill yourself?"

"No," Velasquez t-replied. "But I am in their world. You have to understand that they can't do everything – so they delegate to a few trusted people and that's been *murdoched*."

"Murdoched? Does that involve killing? Doesn't sound very Trill-like."

"Not at all." Velasquez t-replied. "It's to be – shall we say – close, mean – penny pinching. So there are any number of murdochian sayings – and our Trill, Elora's favourite is: *what I need is a few good people around me – the fewer the better.* So we're a tight band around each of the Trills."

"So – I know I'm sort of repeating the question – why are you telling me this?"

"You need to know," Velasquez t-replied. "You know about *neotiquette* – not really a question of course?"

"Yes."

"Well – that's the normal way of people living in our neo-age. There's much more to it, however, if you are invited into the circle."

"And I am being invited in?"

"That's what this is all about," Velasquez t-said. "I'm sorry this wasn't clear."

"So what happens next?"

"You've heard about accelerated learning?" Bartel nodded. "You have an hour's Accel as we call it."

"Is that enough?"

"Yes – it's long enough to know who the Trills all are, their relationships to each other, how they became Trills, the generations of Bills and Trills, and how they succeeded each generation, and which of the Guiding Principles they particularly own, and insights into where we are going now as a global society," Velasquez t-said. "In addition, you'll find out how we completely eradicated need, how we managed a green, sustainable revolution, how we eliminated work – and it's not only andros and Sapiens, but the simplest of things like synthesising food and preserving recyclability at the molecule level. Quite a lot. You see what you will experience really is Accel."

"Ok. You continue to use *we*."

"Of course. Then I will introduce you to Elora," Velasquez t-said. "You'll find she's very approachable. And actually fun. We don't make that a strength in the weeds because we prefer to present all the Trills as serious-minded, non-frivolous people."

"Ok."

"Then it's interviews by the weeds," Velasquez t-continued. "It's really important that you follow the script we will give you – I mean you are not constrained by it, but don't go into areas that might reveal the secrets of Dread-Demotic, and you must play up the effects it has on people without saying how those effects are created."

"Can I mention the new switch in Sofari which wipes memory selectively?"

"I wouldn't as it would only provoke questioning and you'll find it is an unwritten guiding principle that we discourage creating curiosity. You can imagine how curiosity was the cause of so much misery in ordinary people's lives."

"I've never imagined that," Bartel t-replied, puzzled. "How?"

"If you're curious you want to find out as many facts as possible and we don't believe in facts any more – opinion and belief is so much more potent – and malleable," Velasquez t-said, rather openly Bartel thought. "It also leads to finding out that there are other people better off than you, or having more sex or being more popular – even believing different things and having different opinions from you. That's two of the reasons wars started – not liking someone else believing something different from you as it made you insecure. Then there is jealousy – and that came out of curiosity. So try not to feed anything that will make people wonder why. Ok?"

"I had never thought of it like that," Bartel t-replied.

"So," Velasquez t-said firmly, "now you must be prepared for your Accel."

Bartel walked with Velasquez to a different part of the building on another floor. Peter appeared and took over from Velasquez and settled Bartel into a moulded seat, which folded around Bartel and created a new world for her. She was lulled into sleep and what Velasquez had t-promised unfolded before her. The facts came at her so fast she felt that her brain wouldn't deal with them and yet she found that she had time to wonder at the same time as she was apparently absorbing all this new information.

"She already knew of some of the information but had never bothered with the full list, but suddenly she had the seven Trills and their companies paraded before her – not just the words, but video of them, audio and life history. Elora Ghose, CEO Kalo, Jerry Fernandes, CEO Gyro, Derek Smith, CEO Eclectic, Sarah Trarieux, CEO Sapiens, Uhuru Sousousa, CEO Ambience, Alexandr Dermatov, CEO Elura and Jessie Dressus, CEO Latitude became part of her memory and understanding.

How on earth did Accel work this effectively?

Then they were on to the history lessons, relationships between the successive generations of Bills and Trills, the Guiding Principles, the role of TCentral, and then some things that Velasquez hadn't t-mentioned, about where society was going, how it was kept on track – at no point was *control* – mentioned – and the role of innovation.

Bartel was exhausted at the end of the hour, and was bewildered how she had actually absorbed it all. Clearly a new approach to learning – and one that unsurprisingly worked amazingly.

"Ok," Peter v-said to her, as she left the Accel world, "let's go and meet Elora. You'll like her."

The high speed lift almost made her ears burst it was so fast – unlike anything Bartel had experienced. As the doors opened, she was welcomed by Peter – which was disorientating since he had helped her into the lift and hadn't joined her in it.

"This way, please," Peter v-said. "Ah, here is Serena. I'll let her take over and pick up with you when she decides the time is right." Peter faded from view – clearly he or someone could choose how the hologram disappeared.

"Now," Velasquez t-said, "Don't be shy. Nothing to be shy about. She may be one of the four Trills who are women – and the innovator behind so much of what we take for granted, socio, persono, you name it, but she's just like you and me – perhaps only more so."

Velasquez walked with Bartel to a heavy pair of sliding doors – which parted with a self-satisfied whisper which was one of the psychological tricks the Trills had learnt to build into this new world so that people didn't feel completely unnerved by silence and no feedback.

"So glad you could join us," Ghose t-said, shaking Bartel's hand. "I hope you find all of this a rewarding experience." She was a woman of – it appeared – about thirty, barely with any make-up, dressed in a verisimilitude of casual, ordinary people's t-shirt and skirt. Bartel was astonished. She knew Ghose was at least 50 – and while she understood plastic surgery, she was also more conscious of its dangers and its obviousness. This was different.

"Is this where you normally are?" Bartel t-asked, almost just to break the silence.

"Not exactly," Ghose t-replied. "Do you mind if we use voice?"

"Not at all," Bartel t-replied.

"Good. Socio is all very well – and I should know – but there are times when you want to give people time to adjust and understand and I find voice gives more distance and the opportunity to become more comfortable without worrying what someone else is making of your consciousness."

"That's thoughtful." Bartel was very much at sea.

"I have to say, Emma, that I am very impressed with Dread-Demotic and what you've built into it – and with that new switch in Sofari wiping memory selectively – I think you're really on to something,"

"Is it my scenario and the experience – or the switch?"

"Ah," Ghose v-replied, "a good question. I have to say it's your imagineering that makes the difference, but that switch is what makes it possible to become the number one diversion – you call them *experiences* – on the planet. It would be wrong to say it is a bit of both – ideas, as always, are more important. The point, however, is what my old friend, well, colleague, Jessie, at Latitude has done adding that switch, sswipe, into Sofari so we can wipe memory selectively is a master class in innovation. Do you agree?"

"Most certainly – though it was new to me this week – and I hadn't realised, well known, that it was possible. Will you try yourself?" Bartel wondered if she was being tested by Ghose because whether she thought sswipe was an innovation or not was clearly irrelevant. There was something in what Ghose was saying that led her to believe that sswipe was perhaps not everything that she had thought it would be. But that was a puzzle Bartel had no time to worry about for the moment.

"I might – though it's not really my thing," Ghose v-replied. "We had a discussion in TCentral – you understand what TCentral is? – good – about Dread-Demotic and we really thought it was something some of us ought to try."

"Do you really discuss this type of thing at TCentral?" Bartel was rather astonished.

"You might be surprised what we do discuss," Ghose v-replied. She was hardly a warm person but there were signs of a softening, as though she didn't have to put on so much of an act. "I don't think it's a secret – though it probably could be for all I know – but now that we've established this new global order, what we call the *neo-age*, it takes a lot for us to have much to discuss of any weight. Not that what you've done is without weight, Emma. It is clearly impressive."

"I think we ought to be moving on now, Elora," Velasquez v-said, having chosen her moment well. "Emma has to be prepared for her weeds interviews and she is going to be very busy."

"Of course. I don't want to hold you up. And remember that we all love what you're doing."

Bartel and Velasquez were almost instantly alone – as Ghose seemed to disappear. Bartel wondered to herself whether in fact Ghose had been there and whether this was another hologram like Peter. That was a weird thought.

"So what do you make of Elora?" Velasquez v-asked – still apparently deliberately using voice.

"I found her charming," Bartel v-said, rather at a loss. "Is she always as personable as that?"

"No," Velasquez v-said, "is the short answer. But she thinks what you've done is quite admirable so is prepared to go out of her way to be charming."

"Has anyone else actually experienced Dread-Demotic yet?"

"Oh yes – it's been quite a roaring success," Velasquez v-said. "Look I think we ought to switch to socio. Is that all right?"

"Sure. What level?"

"Why don't we start with Friend," Velasquez t-said, "and see how that goes? I don't think Relax is right yet – and I think Acquaintance is too formal." It was odd to switch so effortlessly to socio.

"Ok."

"And now I think we should just orientate you a bit before you meet the representatives of the weeds," Velasquez t-said. "Let's go to my area and I'll give you the overview."

They went back to where Velasquez had met Bartel last night, and sat down. Velasquez v-said there were areas of Trill life that weren't to be mentioned. It apparently didn't matter if they were because Bartel was at perfect liberty to follow the guidelines or create her own – but it was advisable not to dwell on items such as TCentral and the use of handros. Bartel didn't understand what a handro was. "It's a hologram andro – like – I think you call him Peter?"

190

"Why?"

"They are still really experimental at the moment and not on general release," Velasquez t-replied. "We think also that because they are now so lifelike and apparently solid, people will find them disturbing and not know whether they've been engaged with a handro or a real human. I saw you wondering whether Elora was really there just now."

"Was she?"

"Yes." It felt an unsatisfactory response being just one word, but Bartel dismissed it from her mind.

Velasquez went into more detail and then she v-said that she'd give Bartel a little time practising with a tame weedcaster, who seemed anything but tame to Bartel, rattling off t-questions like an automatic gun and in the process muddling Bartel up.

"How was that?" Velasquez t-asked, when Bartel came up for air.

"Daunting and I'm not sure I said the right things."

"Good practice. You'll find that the real thing is just as daunting. You have to remember that basically these are scandal weeds – they only thrive on eyeballs and eyeballs need scandal. That's why TCentral spends a lot of time and energy in creating appropriate scandals."

"Am I an appropriate scandal?"

"Good heavens no," Velasquez t-said. "At the very worst you are a deflection – but actually not that at all. The Trills actually believe in you and want to promote you as part of the extra value living with the Trills creates."

"Is that important to them?"

"Very," Velasquez t-said. "This neo-age is central to their plans and identity. And ensuring that it is robust and won't just go the way of all previous ways of living is vital to them."

"What does that mean?"

"I'm not sure that you need all this – but in the interests of our neo-age openness, you have to remember that people in power – which doesn't, of course, apply to the Trills as they hardly see themselves in power which is devolved to every citizen – always want to believe that their way of life will be *the* lasting way of life. Presumably the Romans –

you might have heard of them but they don't figure much in our edu-world now – thought that a slave-owning empire would always be the way of life. The people living under feudalism thought that there was no other system, and the capitalists thought that capitalism was *natural.*

"The Trills aren't under any illusions but they see that they have benefited the world so much, it is inconceivable that anyone would want to go back to anything different – so they see this way of life as absolutely necessary to continue indefinitely."

"But what do they feel about the people who call this amblytopia and want to change it?"

"Like your friend Andrew?" Bartel was momentarily shocked by this blatant openness of how much they knew about her and about Pennington, but rationalised that it didn't matter at the moment. She would think about that later.

"Yes."

"They see them as a nuisance," Velasquez t-said.

"That all?"

"Oh yes," Velasquez t-replied. "No-one would want to go back to famine, starvation and want."

"Is that the alternative?"

"We think so."

"And amblytopia? What do they make of that idea?"

"They rather like it," Velasquez t-said. "Rather a grey old world of normality than a world of war, guns, famine and evil. Anyway – that's how they see it."

"I find it hard to get my mind around all of that," Bartel t-replied. "I find it hard to know what is acceptable and what is subversive as far as the Trills are concerned."

"That," Velasquez t-replied, "is because this neo-age is so different. I promise you that if you just accept it as is, it will make sense. Now – to business. The press conference will start in about ten minutes and I need to give you some last minute preparations. We organise them so that they sound and appear like a proper press conference – there's a lot of jostling for position and there's an apparent struggle to be the person asking the questions – so be prepared for that. In actual fact just roll with it – and we will filter to you the questions that you should address. Just be honest – but don't give too much away. Remember that Dread-Demotic is partly powerful because it is an unknown. But I'm sure I don't have to tell you that again."

"You do – you need to remind me."

"And one last thing," Velasquez t-said, in a rather conspiratorial voice, "remember that this is all being videoed for the feeds. Keep your cool. The soundtrack will be the babel of noise – and you looking calm and quietly dealing with it will come across as deeply impressive. Just remember that."

Chapter 21

Just as Velasquez had t-predicted, the cacophony of sounds thrusting through Bartel's socio was amazing as soon the press conference was, in Velasquez's t-word, *unleashed*. It was so astonishing to hear, let alone withstand, the barrage of sound, all asking questions, all t-shouting her name, in a constant repetition.

It was with real difficulty that Bartel withstood the assault on her senses, as the questions kept flying at her: "Are you surprised by the effect of Dread-Demotic on our society?" "Are you pleased with the reaction?" "What is Dread-Demotic all about?" "Why is it so powerful?" "Have you compromised your moral position in developing Dread-Demotic?" "What do your lovers think about Dread-Demotic?" "What regrets do you have in bringing this horrible experience to the world?" "Are you proud of what you've achieved?" "Isn't Dread-Demotic a deflection from reality?" "Do you think you will have more sex as a result of developing Dread-Demotic?" "What have you learnt that you didn't know about the Trills?" "Are you shocked by the behaviour of the Trills?" "Do you think Dread-Demotic is worth all this hullaballoo?"

The raucous noise – presumably the soundtrack of the video – didn't subside, but overlaying that barrage, Bartel was then made aware of one t-question: "How does it feel to be part of a massive global change in experience?" The Trills had obviously created an environment that they could control at even a microscopic level if need be.

Bartel cleared her throat and t-began: "Thank you for coming today and for being so enthusiastic about Dread-Demotic and what is one of the new experiences that I and my colleague, Jonas Savery, have developed." Bartel was rather amazed at the words coming out of her thoughts until she realised that in her eye-display she was being prompted with these very words. She thought she could control what she wanted to t-say – but slowly realised that the insistence that the eye-display brought to her mind was almost too strong to ignore. She knew, somehow, that she could say what she wanted, but she realised how much easier it was to go with the suggestion and prompt right in front of her eyes.

So how does it feel to be part of this massive global change?

"I," Bartel t-began, "find it overwhelming." The eye-display was blank and she was left with her own feelings. The Trills were so clever. "I feel overwhelmed – and delighted – and humbled and rather overawed, actually. It's a great pleasure to give people a totally new experience in a relatively safe way." The eye-display kicked in: "Not that Dread-Demotic is particularly safe in that sense. That is what I think contributes to making it special."

And the men in your life – other than Jonas. How do they feel about this – and what difference will it make to your relationships with them?

Bartel thought this was so clever. It was making Dread-Demotic more mysterious and more exciting by not focusing on it. "I think that they're very happy for me." The eye-display was amazingly hypnotic and insistent.

But we know that Andrew Pennington is disaffected. How do you feel about him in the light of your new celebrity?

The eye-display was blank. "No differently."

So you're happy to continue to have sex with him even though you know he disapproves of what you're doing?

The eye-display same into focus. "That's a really interesting question."

Well – how does Dave Worrell feel about you – and how does Cheryl deal with his encounters with you?

Just when she really needed it, the eye-display was silent. "I don't know how this is relevant to this press conference about Dread-Demotic. What I have to say is that I don't really anticipate how my partners deal with their own relationships outside of their relationship with me." Bartel was thrown back on her real thoughts at this point – and realised as she was speaking that what she had said was in fact exactly what she did feel.

So what is Dread-Demotic really all about?

The eye-display was in full swing at this question: "It's about taking life to an extreme. You know how our lives are sometimes too bland –

what Andrew Pennington calls *amblytopia* – so what I've done is create a scenario that blends that experience with something much more on the edge. To learn more, you will have to experience it."

Are you happy that access to Dread-Demotic is restricted at the moment?

"I didn't know that it was really. I can understand why."

To make it more mysterious and create more hype?

"Not at all," Bartel t-replied. "I think . . ." she was waiting for the eye-display to help and it came to her rescue, "I feel that this is just resource constraints – I know that real efforts are being made to allocate more bandwidth to the experience and it is that and not a marketing issue that is making the experience more restricted than we would wish."

So how do you feel about your personal life being exposed?

"I wasn't aware," Bartel t-began, "that it was." Then suddenly and unexpectedly headlines from the feeds appeared in her eye-display – and it was pretty lurid and only just recognisable as herself. Her relationship breakdown with her husband was depicted as a battle over her daughters with a double-edged or at least contradictory take on someone's interpretations of Thornton's sexual behaviour, This was criticised for being too twentieth – a sanctimonious toned voice suggested that he was a hypocrite for not having moved on into the neotiquette – and in the next headline he was criticised for being too licentious. That was weird as neither was true and it wasn't really possible to hold the two ideas in the same conceptual framework without being aware of the extreme contradiction.

"I see what you mean. It's nothing to me."

So you don't care about your reputation?

"I care passionately about that – and I have nothing to fear from my personal life being exposed." More headlines appeared in front of her – some about Wilfred, some about Pennington and, bizarrely enough, one about Savery. That last suggested professional misconduct – which was just an egregious lie – and Bartel was able to dismiss the attack immediately from her mind. Years of dealing with persono and even her socio had created a thicker skin than those who knew her might have expected.

And it kept flashing through her head, once she understood what was happening in the headlines about Thornton, that the questions reflected a whole range of contradictory impulses – on the one hand that there was a neo-age culture, created by the Trills with their technologies, which people should embrace with both arms and on the other a prurient, atavistic feeling that the old morality could still be invoked while, quite bizarrely everything was exposed in full detail.

The questioning immediately changed tack: *You are a member of the neo-age God religion. What does that mean in your personal life?*

Nothing could be further from the truth – were the questions just to provoke her, as Velasquez had intimated? "I'm not – I'm not a member of any religion."

"Does that mean you are anti-religion and determined to close down religions?"

"Not at all," Bartel t-replied. "I'm at least a true believer in one thing – which is freedom of belief. I think that's enshrined in our neo-age culture."

The questioning went on and some of it was quite ludicrous and some of it was highly personal and some of it was clever and designed to trap the unwary. Bartel felt she manoeuvred her way through it well, and felt pleased with herself, without underestimating the value of the eye-display.

Then it was over and she was left rather shell-shocked by the experience.

Velasquez approached her and they went off to sit quietly apparently alone, although Bartel was beginning to realise that that was hardly a realistic view of how life worked in 2084.

"So how do you think that went?" Velasquez t-asked.

"I've no idea," Bartel t-responded. "I thought you'd be best to let me know."

"I think it was good – you handled the rough questions well and you didn't lose your cool," Velasquez t-said. "That's the first rule – as you know. The headlines are already on the feeds and weeds and you come out well."

"What does that mean?"

"It means, Emma," Velasquez t-replied, "that you will come across as a rather complex character with a colourful background and what is more, Dread-Demotic will be seen as all the more complex, exciting and challenging as a result."

"And that's good?"

"Yes," Velasquez t-said, with a smile. "We want you to be more than a passing meteorite burning up very quickly. Our plans for you are for the longer term." That suddenly felt chilling – and another cause of unease in Bartel's mind. What *plans*?

On the one hand, Bartel knew that there must have been plans – but when it was t-said, it felt threatening and destabilising.

"Look, I know you find that disturbing but we do have your best interests at heart." Velasquez t-said, actually further undermining Bartel's confidence in herself and her position in this Trill world.

Velasquez was monitoring her thoughts in real time and responding to them in a way that left Bartel rather paranoid. She had never felt that before. She had accepted that there was surveillance but had seen that as a force for good. Criminality had all but been eliminated. The prison population was minimal. That had always seemed a great benefit.

She had a phrase that she couldn't quite place running through her head that Pennington had quoted to her. *We had been given tongues to hide our thoughts.* Not being able to hide thoughts was somehow inhuman – no inhumane.

"Look," Velasquez t-continued, "I know this is all new to you and you are seeing greater depth in things than you have ever wanted to, but that is what you are being let into. It's a privilege."

"I'm not sure I understand."

"You will . . ." Velasquez looked at her. "Most people will never be given the opportunities that you have, Emma."

"But," Bartel t-stumbled through her sentence, "I thought that there are no restrictions on anyone except those that impinge on others."

"There aren't."

"Then why is this not common knowledge? How can this be restricted information?"

"It isn't." Velasquez looked straight at Bartel as though daring her to contradict her. This was an impossible conversation because Bartel was aware that her innermost thoughts were being interpreted almost before she knew what they were herself. "As you say, there are no restrictions. Any religion – any religion – is as valid as any other – and there are no restrictions. We have a perfect democracy. Anyone can challenge anything – including the Trills without fear,"

Velasquez was repeating the messages that Bartel had imbibed for at least twenty years, after the Trills had started to establish the neo-age.

"Freedom from need, freedom from work as much as possible unless the individual wants work. You know the benefits. They used to say that people were looked after from cradle to grave. The Trills made that a reality."

"So how come that this information is restricted?" Bartel t-asked.

"It isn't."

"But you said people don't know this – they are not initiated into the inner secrets. And that this was a privilege for me. How can that be consistent?"

"You have to remember, Emma," Velasquez t-continued, not directly answering Bartel, "that we are in the early years of the neo-age and as in all human life from the beginning of time, there will be inconsistencies. The Trills didn't abolish human nature. They made it possible for everyone to become as human as possible."

"But how did they do it?" Bartel was puzzling through ideas and thoughts and questions that she had never wanted to think about before, and it was disturbing her.

"I'm sure you understand the history – so I won't repeat that," Velasquez t-said. "As I am sure you remember, and you know why I am sure, the breakthroughs came when artificial intelligence replaced human ignorance – when artificial intelligence replaced artificial ignorance. Don't you remember the crucial breakthrough?"

"Is that the *turning point* – the dividing line between the paleo-age and neo-age?"

"Yes."

They were both t-silent and Bartel tried to feel whether her socio was being probed. It was undetectable so she thought she might assume that there were no probes.

But that was wrong.

She hadn't detected the probes that Velasquez had demonstrated the day before must have been going on.

"Obviously," Bartel t-said, rather haltingly as it was so disturbing that Velasquez probably knew what she was going to say before she even became conscious of it herself, "I remember that. But I didn't know – I didn't know." Bartel stopped. She really didn't know what she was trying to say or what it meant. Her whole mind was exploding.

"That turning point," Velasquez t-said, "was just that. A turning point. Obviously the Trills didn't have all the answers in one fell swoop. But it was the moment that changed history – and meant that everyone would become – not be at that point – but become more human."

"So what else was needed?"

"Everything, Emma, that you see around you," Velasquez t-said. "We couldn't abolish work if, for example, we still had to grow food. But we had andros and then gSynth was a breakthrough. You know how important Gyro is. If we didn't have andro health care, courtesy of Eclectic – we would need human doctors and nurses – and as you know, we still need some of them – but every day means we can eliminate more of human intervention. I needn't tell you all this – except to say we're not perfectly there yet. But we call them *inconsistencies*. That is where we know what is the ideal and we know there are gaps. But you should know that there is no hierarchy amongst the GLEAKES. Eclectic with its manufacturing isn't less important than Elura with its financial system. It's a synergy between them. Remember at all times interdependence."

"And is that why there is TCentral?"

"Yes."

"So why me? Actually I can see why me from what you say but why is there a need for people *like* me?"

"A good question, Emma," Velasquez t-replied. "And one that I will answer but not in full now. All previous empires – and that's not the right word obviously for what the Trills have created but the nearest we have – have relied on repression and restrictions and control. The Trills don't need any of that. They have created what they see as a benign world. Technology has released the human race from its shackles. Everyone is able to fulfil themselves."

"So what's in it for the Trills?"

"You'll see."

That t-statement felt almost threatening.

"But you haven't answered my question at all. Why people like me?"

"Mistakenly people like your friend, Andrew, believe that the Trills have created a monster," Velasquez t-said. "He knows it isn't a dystopia – a terrible world of threat and coercion. He doesn't *want* to see it as a utopia. He is wary – I think we can say frightened – of the neo-age. He doesn't necessarily know why, but he sees this world as – what does he call it – an amblytopia. A world of greyness, mediocrity, shallowness – though it is difficult to see how he could come to that conclusion. Against that negativity, the Trills know there have to be examples of positive, dynamic, exciting and challenging people. And that one person at this particular moment is you, Emma. That's why not necessarily you, but, as you say, people like you, are so important. You bring excitement, challenge and opportunities to develop beyond greyness to the world. The Trills celebrate that."

"Does that mean that I am like some sort of freak show?"

"Not at all," Velasquez t-said, smoothly. "You are the main show. You know how it seems to most people that there are no things that cannot be obtained – attained some say – and how we are not resource constrained?"

"I don't think like that – but now you say it, I guess you're right," Bartel t-replied.

"Well," Velasquez t-said, "One of the key lessons that the Trills learned early on in their deliberations is that without creating some – we don't call it *shortages* but *aspirations* – we create a form of unrest and a form of dissent. We don't mind dissent – but it isn't positive. We can't create aspirations without people like you, because we won't create aspirations for what people need to live. Does any of this make sense?"

"Yes," Bartel t-replied. "It does. But I don't know how I feel about it."

"Well," Velasquez t-continued "you've come through the news conference test with flying colours. You've asked some intelligent questions. I've started to initiate you in some of the more abstruse elements of life in the Trills' inner world. Now it will soon be time for you to see TCentral at work. This doesn't happen to everyone as you know."

"So there are controls and restrictions?"

"I told you there were inconsistencies, Emma," Velasquez t-said. "Yes – that's one we haven't eliminated."

"And you have a job?"

"We call it *a role*." Velasquez t-spoke almost challenging Bartel to come back at her. "We know that that is another inconsistency. And like all inconsistencies we are working on that – to eliminate it."

"Do you want to eliminate it?" Bartel was puzzled because Velasquez seemed to revel in her position and clearly it gave her some power.

"Yes," Velasquez t-replied. "Why wouldn't we?"

They t-talked some more but Bartel felt there were ever-diminishing circles as Velasquez seemed to skate over anything that was difficult – calling it an *inconsistency*, which seemed to mean that it wasn't worth discussing – as it soon wouldn't be.

"So I am to meet the Trills properly?"

"You are – so to speak. You know that most of what they do is carried out in what the paleo-age used to call a virtual reality. So you will be part of that world – some of it what we still call plastic – that is having form and substance. Some of it being what we call sensitive – which was virtual when it was a crude approximation to reality."

"So I am to be part of the Trills' world?"

"Yes," Velasquez t-said. It was a flat, unemotional statement.

"But isn't that somehow – say – subversive?"

"How?"

"I will then see the Trills as they really are – not as they are presented."

"And what's wrong with that?"

"But I can then tell everyone about it – and that may confuse people," Bartel t-said.

"You won't."

"How?"

"No constraints of course. But," Velasquez t-said, "although you are not sworn to secrecy, it's not in anyone's interest that any of that sort of information is given out."

"But why not?"

"It will only make people uneasy without actually changing anything. Can you see that?"

"Why won't it change anything?"

"These are very deep matters," Velasquez t-said. "You will understand more. Let me just say that the Trills have created the most perfect society for the globe. We have addressed so many issues – need, if not entirely want yet, climate change, crime, quality of life, opportunities. Why would the people of the world want to jeopardise what the Trills have created?"

"But is it as perfect as they suggest?"

"That's a matter of opinion," Bartel t-said. "And we don't obviously interfere with people's opinions . . ."

"But don't you help to form, I mean even create, people's opinions?"

"Broadly yes," Velasquez t-said. "We set the agenda. It is gramscian."

"I understand."

"And of course we understand how people react to what is happening," Velasquez t-continued.

"And do you intervene?"

"Rarely."

Bartel was feeling rather uneasy at this. What did *rarely* mean? She resisted the thought – and put the idea that Pennington would have the same misgivings as she did out of her head.

"Why are you so uneasy?"

"I don't think I am." Bartel momentarily wondered how she could know that she was before she accepted that of course she was indeed uneasy.

"We know," Velasquez t-said. "We know."

Bartel felt the chill go right through her body.

Velasquez t-continued: "And we can, as you know, wipe any memories now."

Chapter 22

Bartel was given no time to think. And she was glad of that. She wondered whether Velasquez would continue to bring her into the Trills' world, when she obviously knew the doubts she was having. There was also something about Velasquez that Bartel couldn't quite put her finger on that disturbed her. She thought that perhaps it was the cold, analytical way she spoke about the Trills as though they weren't that significant to her, although that was clearly not true. Perhaps it was the way that Velasquez used the first person plural – the we – that betrayed something. It was as though Velasquez wanted to keep some sort of distance from what she was describing. There was just something there that wasn't entirely in keeping with what was apparently going on.

It was all very puzzling – there seemed to be an almost total tolerance of opposition to the Trills as long as it didn't actually threaten any of their power, but that seemed a contradiction in itself, although she seemed to remember something of the history of the early twenty first that echoed this in the way politics was conducted then.

Bartel focused her mind on what was happening and she let herself be ushered into a lift and transported up to the roof of the skyscraper. There she stood beside Velasquez not saying anything and trying to keep her mind blank, knowing that Velasquez would know everything that she was thinking.

Including this thought.

An el-icopter landed on its el-ipad, and Velasquez motioned her into it and followed.

Was she physically keeping tabs on her? That seemed weird to Bartel as she wouldn't need to do that as she could monitor her mind and actions remotely.

"How long is the flight?" Bartel t-asked.

"About twenty minutes – then we transfer to our private e-plane," Velasquez t-said. "I expect you have many questions. I can see that you are questioning everything – which we think is good. Do you have any specific questions?"

"Yes – one. Why do we have this dialogue which presupposes that you don't know what I am thinking and feeling through my socio when you actually do?"

"That's a good question, as I'd expect, Emma. We know it can be spooky – I mean in the sense that it can spook people – when you realise the real capabilities we have, especially our ability to over-ride the levels in socio. That makes some people quite paranoid. We don't want that reaction as there is nothing sinister in our use of this over-ride. So we tend to use conventional dialogue – not to hide our capability but to make someone being initiated into our world gradually aware of the depth of our technologies and our understanding of how people and the world work."

"And the purpose?"

"That," Velasquez t-said, "is the real question."

"And the answer?"

"We find that *purpose* is a really strange concept so we don't use it much. What is the purpose of life?" Bartel remained silent. "That's a real question, Emma. What is the purpose of life?"

"Do you mean in a religious, social or political sense?"

"Any way that you want to express it – you know that we're not in the least dictatorial about how we want people to think," Velasquez t-said.

"If you ask me that," Bartel t-replied, "I honestly don't know. As you know, I'm not at all religious – don't believe in any transcendent being or beings, though the ideas behind them are attractive. I'm not political either. I see that there are issues but not ones that I want to be bothered with. So I guess my answer must be a social one."

"I like your way of talking. This is good analytics, Emma."

"I don't know about that," Bartel t-said. "I guess I just want to be happy."

"That's not a bad ambition – or do you think it is?"

"I don't – but I have friends who do," Bartel t-said. "You know that of course."

"We do." The switch to *we* was glaringly noticeable to Bartel in view of her earlier thinking about Velasquez. What did that mean?

"But," Bartel t-said, "that's not me. I guess you're going to ask me what happiness is – and I know the feeling when I have it, but I don't know what it is. So I feel rather lost in your world."

"That's a really good way of putting it," Velasquez t-said.

"Putting what exactly?"

"*Your world*," Velasquez t-replied. "Look – this is getting rather off the point. Why do we have the over-rides in socio? I think that's your question, isn't it?"

"I didn't know that was my question – but now you say it, yes it is. Why do you?"

"I guess that seems sinister to you."

"Yes."

"Think of it a different way," Velasquez t-said. "it's not surveillance for surveillance sake – for control. It's benign. We want to ensure the greatest happiness for all – and our over-rides are there to allow us to *know* that we are achieving that. The Trills didn't over-ride human nature when they put in the over-rides into socio and persono. We just want to make sure that envy, greed, violence and every other undesirable quality are identified. Then everyone is happy – content to know that we are all secure."

"What does this mean for me?"

"It means, Emma," Velasquez t-said, "that because of your celebrity and your position, we are going to give you privileges that are denied – for good reason – to most people."

Bartel was again in a flurry of emotions now. She was frightened. She was excited. She was also appalled and yet fascinated. There was an obvious question. "Do I get all the privileges that the Trills enjoy?"

"No," Velasquez t-replied, in a cordial but matter of fact way, as if this was an absurd thing to ask for.

"And what are the good reasons to deny those privileges to most people?"

"It's our belief that giving too many unearned privileges will undermine the stability of our neo-age society."

"How?" Bartel t-asked.

"Clearly there are not limitless resources – even though it may seem like that on an every day level, and certainly compared with the past – so we restrict access to some of them. They aren't serious – particularly if people don't know what they are."

"So what privileges will I be denied?"

"We're nearly here, Emma," Velasquez t-said, smoothly, deflecting the question. "You have to remember, as the Trills do all the time, that these privileges – such as the ability to over-ride levels in socio – have to be exercised with restraint and only for benign reasons. That is part of the contract that is being created with you by the Trills. If you don't follow that pattern, then there are sanctions."

"Such as?"

"Well – nothing overly punitive – but, for example, withdrawal of certain privileges," Velasquez t-said. "Do you understand?"

"Yes."

There was nothing else to say and with her mind being transparently open to Velasquez and whoever else was monitoring her, Bartel decided not to think too deeply.

"That's good." Velasquez t-complimented her on that decision.

"Would people know when I am over-riding their levels in socio?"

"That depends on you and how transparent you want to be with people," Velasquez t-said. "Remember the guiding principle about free will. You must not interfere with a person's free will and your use of the enhanced probe – as we call it because it is undetectable if you want it to be – has to be as free from personal advantage as possible. It is there to enhance experience – your experience – not to deny someone else's ability to deal with the world. Does that make sense?"

"Yes."

"Look," Velasquez t-said, "you did so well with the weeds conference and we love Dread-Demotic so the future is really bright for you, Emma.

Act responsibly and the whole world of experience is suddenly within your grasp."

"What does that mean?"

"You know that there are no constraints – well very few – on people as it is," Velasquez t-said. "As I said, we've eliminated *need* but not *want*. In our world – the Trills' world – we have almost eliminated *want*. Just imagine what that means. If you *want* anything – it is probably within your grasp."

"Will everyone eventually have this?"

"To be frank," Velasquez t-replied, "I just don't know. It's not impossible of course. In our neo-age, anything is possible. Innovation is one of the guiding principles. All you need to know for now is that largely *want* is within your grasp."

"So if I want anything, I can have it?"

"Within," Velasquez t-said, choosing her words carefully, "reason – yes."

"Such as?"

"I couldn't say," Velasquez t-replied. "We find that each individual's wants are different. For some it is sexual, for some it is purely sensual, for some it is intellectual. For some it is a sense of power. For some it is, in the world that you satisfy with your imagineering, experience. And for the Trills there is virtually nothing that they could want that they can't have."

"Within the guiding principles?"

"Yes," Velasquez t-said. "Exactly."

"But I presume – although I am feeling that I am on shaky ground now – that if a Trill wants a relationship with someone and that person doesn't reciprocate, then that want has to go unsatisfied." Bartel was stumbling over these words, but was pleased to get them in the open.

"Yes – that's right," Velasquez t-said. "On the other hand, if you think about it, there would be very few – if any – who would turn down having a relationship of some or any kind with a Trill. I guess that means that such a *want* would probably be satisfied for the Trill."

"As you know, I'm finding this scary. Should it be?"

"I don't think so. It's just human nature." Velasquez looked squarely at Bartel: "Any other issues?

"So why don't you tell people about all of this? Or am I being naïve?"

"Possibly," Velasquez t-replied. "But you must remember what I said just a few moments ago. We haven't eliminated human nature – yet." That chilled Bartel again. "So envy – which we find to be the most corrosive emotion – is still there, no matter how comfortable or pleased someone is. So we don't make a song and dance about what the Trills can enjoy that others can't. It isn't sinister – but it does help with most people's peace of mind – that they aren't disturbed by thinking that there are things being denied to them."

"I think I understand. But you mentioned intellectual as one of the areas where I can have what I want. What does that mean?"

"You know," Velasquez t-said, "that we value individual expression very highly. In fact we can almost make a fetish about that, celebrating what an individual says. If you think about that for a moment or two, you realise that this means that any individual opinion or statement is just as valuable as any other statement by anyone. We pride ourselves that there is no qualitative analysis – all opinions and statements are of equal value."

"I have sort of grasped that. We were encouraged right through education to come up with our own ideas and thoughts and not pay too much attention to what someone else thinks."

"That's it."

"So what does that mean in intellectual terms?"

"It means, Emma," Velasquez t-said, with a light smile for once on her face, "that we have deliberately abandoned much of the paleo-age thinking. At least for most people. For all people, actually, outside of the Trills' world. But we do know that some people want to understand that almost-pre-history that edu-world doesn't cover. So if they want to, they have access to it."

"But how do they know about it?"

"Exactly," Velasquez t-replied. "Most people aren't bothered by it – and we think that's best for the individual and for society and for our neo-age perspectives."

"So I can explore whatever I want in pre-history?"

"Within reason."

"But I find it disturbing that you claim that all ideas and all opinions are equal," Bartel t-said.

"Why?"

"Because self-evidently that is not true – I might have an opinion about something – say quantum, to pick the most unlikely thing I can think of at the moment – which would have no substance when compared with that of someone who had made quantum a life's study."

"It wouldn't matter if you either didn't express that opinion or, if you did, no-one bothered with it, would it?"

Bartel had scarcely noticed that the el-icopter had landed, and they had to transfer to the e-plane because she was so intensely engaged in the conversation – or explanation.

"Where are we going now?"

"It's a couple of hours flight," Velasquez t-said. "That's all."

This was no answer.

"One last question for now." Bartel felt the e-plane start to move, and realised that this was exciting. So little flying was needed now that if and when flying became a possibility, it felt strange and a real novelty. "Will I be meeting more of the Trills?"

"Of course. All of them probably in one way or another."

Bartel reluctantly settled into her own brain, trying not to think, feeling very exposed and very uneasy. This was exciting.

What would Pennington make of it?

The world was growing larger around her and within her – and she had to stop thinking. That was almost impossible.

"What sort of experience would you like Emma?"

"During the flight?"

"Yes."

"I'm happy to relax, actually," Bartel t-replied, absolutely truthfully. She was overwhelmed.

"You do know that you can use Sofari now if you want? Of course you do. I was forgetting."

Bartel didn't want anything to distract her from what was going on and the new thoughts and sensations that she was trying to suppress. Her mind felt as if it was exploding at times – then a sort of peace and tranquillity descended on her.

Was that the Trills using thought control?

Chapter 23

When the e-plane landed, and Velasquez and Bartel left it, they were exposed to a rather searing heat and the brightest daylight that Bartel had ever experienced in the flesh, although she had naturally been in scenarios where it had been this bright. Air travel had become unnecessary, as the Trills had decided, not least because of the work of the imagineers like Bartel, that it had become nonsensical to go to different and foreign places with all the costs involved. Most people actually couldn't tell the difference between the virtual experiences created in Sofari and being somewhere. It wasn't the first time that Bartel had flown anywhere, but it was some time since she had and she felt strange about it.

As they left the e-plane, Velasquez had said to her just to enjoy what was going to happen. That felt both exciting and intimidating.

"What do you mean?"

"I meant nothing by it in particular," Velasquez t-said. "But I thought it best to suggest that this was going to be a very different environment and that you should relax into it, rather than get hung up about it. Is that ok?"

Bartel couldn't make out what sort of relationship she was supposed to have with Velasquez – was Velasquez a mentor or a guardian – or more likely a minder. The word *Mephi* which is how Velasquez had described herself, had all sorts of overtones and undertones. It was very difficult to keep her mind free of all such thoughts but Bartel rather thought that Velasquez and whoever else was monitoring her would expect all sorts of strange reactions and bewilderment too.

"Can I ask one question?"

"Certainly," Velasquez t-said.

"When I met Elora – Ghose is it? – was that the real Elora or was it a hologram?"

"That's an intelligent question and I'm glad you had the presence of mind to ask it," Velasquez t-said. "As you guessed – it was a hologram."

"But you said it was the real Elora Ghose at the time."

"Not quite, if you remember what I said. I just replied *yes* when you asked me if she was real."

"And when I meet the Trills – or some of them – will that be in the flesh or as holograms?"

"I think I should leave that to you to find out," Velasquez t-replied. "Or is that not fair?"

"I don't think it is really," Bartel t-said.

"Ok – it is difficult to tell if things are just normal – by which I mean that what is before you is a real human or a holo," Velasquez said. Bartel had a quizzical look on her face – though that wasn't necessary for Velasquez to know that she didn't understand. "The trick used to be that a hologram couldn't actually move anything. I'm afraid that simple way of knowing isn't so valuable now. Obviously with holograms like Peter – whom you've met if you remember – there are tech generational issues – it's really only the Trills who can utilise holograms in full. It's an amazing technical achievement that a hologram can move objects – at least I think so."

"That's what I was worried about – not worried, perhaps, concerned."

"And rightly," Velasquez t-said. "I know that it is pretty hard to deal with some of the ways things work nowadays – and in the Trills' world, it is even harder."

"Do the holograms have shadows?"

"Oh," Velasquez t-said, "you're thinking it's like vampires or something. No. It's really not like that. They certainly do have shadows if they want one – and the Trills always want to be as authentic as possible. I mean – well, if not authentic, as realistic as possible."

"So how can I tell?"

"I don't think you can," Velasquez t-said. "I'll see if I can ask them to tell us."

"And if one of the Trills is a hologram – are they actually being controlled and directed by the real Trill, or is that just impossible and the holograms are autonomous?"

"It depends," Velasquez t-replied. "I don't think it would be possible for you to know – and in that case, I'd suggest you don't worry about it."

"That seems hard."

"It isn't," Velasquez t-assured her. "It might seem so now – but you'll find that you will have a very good engagement whether it is a real Trill in the flesh or a hologram, and whether the hologram is autonomous or actually under the immediate control of the relevant Trill."

"I'll just have to accept that," Bartel t-said. She felt rather bleak, but perhaps this was a sort of future shock that she had read about – when people couldn't quite adjust to the way technology had advanced. "So who am I meeting?"

"Well – Elora again, obviously as she's what we would call your sponsor," Velasquez t-said. "Kalo is really important to you, I think. Latitude's CEO is important – I think you'd like to get the latest gen on Sofari as that's close to your heart. I know you don't have the names of all the people quite in your own memory, but remember your persono has been specially and specifically upgraded so you can readily retrieve the names you need. In any case, Jessie Dressus, often known as JD, is important for you to meet, and I think you will be or should be excited by the chance to meet her.

"Jerry – Jerry Fernandes – is probably not that important to you, though he is a clever man and where would we be without gSynth and the rest of the manufacturing that Gyro produces? I'm not sure he'll show. If he does, he isn't the most pleasant person. That's just a small insight to make sure you don't think it's you that's making him unpleasant.

"Derek Smith is a person to look for – where would we be without his – they used to be called robots, I think, but now they're quite rightly known as androids – though there are some who know their ancient languages who think that that is very twentieth. Trouble is *humanoids* doesn't sound as warm, somehow.

"Anyway – you don't need me to go through all of them again – but there is Sarah Trarieux, Uhuru Sousousa and Dermatov – let me find his first name, yes Alexandr. Are you ready?"

"As ready as I will ever be," Bartel t-said, really in total confusion. She didn't know why she was there really, didn't know whether she wanted to meet these people who seemed largely mythical to her, but at the same time was going along with the adventure. "But one question, first."

"Yes?"

"Is all the talk about dissension and arguments – even a schism – between the Trills based on fact, or is this just another of those inventions of the weeds?"

"There's always dissension and arguments between the Trills – that's the nature of the people involved. Remember they are all highly competitive and they are always looking to reinforce their position against the other Trills," Velasquez t-said. "In the spirit of the Guiding Principles, I do have to say that there are greater tensions at the moment between some of them than we have known for some time."

"Which ones?" Bartel was surprised at the openness and the lack of avoidance.

"Naturally it is between Kalo, Gyro and Latitude," Velasquez t-replied.

"Why naturally?"

"As you know, Kalo provides the ideas infrastructure – socio and persono – and Latitude provides the environment that you work in, Sofari, and there are overlaps in that which causes friction between them – where does an individual psyche end and begin and a wider, shall we say group, experience begin and end. So there are arguments continually about stepping on each other's toes between Jessie at Latitude and Elora, my boss. Then Jerry at Gyro – with all his manufacturing and supply and delivery capabilities – feels that he should be the primary Trill, and he is constantly looking at what Jessie and Elora are doing, and feels that they are far less important."

"Is this serious for the Trills – I mean their future?"

"Of course not," Velasquez t-said, reassuringly. "These are just normal commercial and political tensions, that are pretty continuous."

They walked silently into what looked like a rather strangely coloured building – and the cold blast of the air conditioning rather took Bartel's breath away. "This way." Velasquez took the lead. An elevator whisked them up very high and they were suddenly in what seemed like open air, but it clearly wasn't as the temperature control was amazing. The air was still and there were no sounds.

"Take a seat." Velasquez v-said for some reason. The sound of her voice in the utter stillness and almost muffled quiet was quite surprising.

Bartel sat down and let the seat wrap around her and adjust to her body. She had read that this type of furniture was coming, but to feel it – as well as see it – was an amazing experience. "The embrace seats are stunning – aren't they?" Velasquez v-said. Bartel nodded.

"Hello, again, Emma," a voice that she had heard before said. She looked to her side and saw it was Elora. "Sorry to startle you – but I wanted to assure you that this time I am a hologram, but that you met me, in the flesh so to speak, last time."

"I'm not sure what the protocol is and how I should talk to you when you're before me as a hologram."

"Just talk to me normally – and you'll find that I pass turing," Ghose v-said.

"Turing?"

"Oh," Ghose v-said, "I didn't realise – it's a twentieth. It just means that you won't notice the difference."

"But are you – that is the real Elora Ghose – aware of this conversation?"

"You're very good, Emma," Ghose v-said. "And the answer is – not necessarily. I know that's confusing, but you see there are such pressures on my time that now I can be in two places at once. I think it's actually possible in fact to be in more than two places, but I find that too difficult to manage."

"And my question?"

"As I said," Ghose or whoever or whatever v-said, "I'm not necessarily actually present in each encounter. I don't have to be as the hologram is programmed to be me – and I have to tell you that there is a wealth of talent expended over months analysing the actual me so that this me is as real as it can be."

"But still not the real you."

"No," Ghose v-said, "but in moments like these, the real me is monitoring the interchange very closely. So I am present both as the hologram that you see before you and the flesh and blood that I appear to be. Does that answer your question?"

"Confusingly," Bartel v-said. "Why are we using voice?"

"Another good question," Ghose v-said. "Sometimes the use of the holo me – you know how good we are at making everything have a shorter name – spooks people too much and using voice is actually rather more acceptable funnily enough. I say funnily enough because you'd think that the holo me would more naturally use thought and the physical me would more naturally use voice. I am assured psychologically that it is better that the reverse is true."

Ghose paused and looked straight at Bartel. "I also know that because I am not here in person, so to speak, you are disappointed." Bartel went to speak. "No – that's all right, Emma. That's natural. I know it's confusing – as you suggest. But just think we've added an extra dimension to our lives."

"And you can actually move physical things even though you're . . . a holo?"

"You were going to say *just a holo*," Ghose v-said. "That's more than ok. Yes – it's unfortunately still limited but somehow or other, I can."

"Limited?"

"Just to smaller objects – you know pens, paper – that sort of thing," Ghose said. "I think we say that it's WIP – a twentieth as it happens for *work in progress.*"

"Can I be direct – again?"

"Of course," Ghose t-said.

"What have I done really to deserve this special treatment?"

"That's a difficult question – not to answer of course, but difficult to have to ask."

"Not difficult to answer? If you say so. I'm glad to hear that – but it baffles me."

"You've had some explanations of this already, I'm sure." Clearly Ghose knew this for a fact. "But I can see why you'd still be concerned – interested – puzzled, whichever is the right verb."

"Yes."

"Let me answer you personally – and not on behalf of the Trills or TCentral," Ghose v-said. "I loved Dread-Demotic and thought it was a stunning idea. That mixture of pure fear and reassurance was something that has been done before, obviously, but never using Sofari. And, serendipitously, as you didn't know it had this capability, it will be a shock, a surprise and a different experience every time through that new capability that Jessie Dressus has built into Sofari now. That ability to selectively wipe the memory of what has happened to the participants. Actually, Jessie and Latitude are probably in the forefront of what the Trills can do now even though they are in that narrow niche. Is that enough of an answer?"

"Not really," Bartel v-said. "I know we've created something that is quite mind-blowing – you saw the reaction of the Tomlinsons who were the first to experience it – but why is that enough to give me entrance to your world?"

"It's your world as well, Emma. We Trills don't live in a different universe."

"But," Bartel v-said hesitantly, "it isn't the same world. As Serena Velasquez said, the Trills have abolished need, but you have almost eliminated want from your world. That is amazing."

"But we're doing that in stages for everyone – once we can figure out how that is done. But let's not get side tracked. One of the key messages about the Trills is that we share. Every regime that has existed before this neo-age has been kleptocratic, threatening and controlling. We're the first to create a different, benign environment for everyone."

"So why me?"

"Because, Emma," Ghose v-said, "whether you understand it or not, you are special."

Bartel was silent and tried not to have any thoughts.

"I know that your friend, Andrew Pennington calls this neo-age amblytopia," Ghose v-said. "I can understand why – and, as you know, he is entitled to his opinion. We don't see this world, this neo-age – what we have created – as nondescript. He thinks we have actually limited human aspiration and human achievement. Perhaps we have – but we've also liberated people – yes everybody who needs to be liberated from need – to allow them to fulfil their lives properly.

"You – Emma – yes, you, are opening up a whole new area of excitement for the people of the world."

"But what's in it for you?"

"Do you mean me, or we Trills?"

"Either."

"That's a strange way of looking at it," Ghose v-said. "I have everything I could ever need – and almost all the things I could want. You couldn't name a single thing that would be beyond my wealth. Ever since we bezoed this neo-age, and probably before that, we had more than we could ever need – beyond what people could imagine. And as one of the Trills I am responsible for the happiness of the billions on this planet. I need to ensure that no-one can destroy this – but beyond that, I have nothing to gain. Nothing. What can't I have?"

Bartel was again silent. The tone was so off-putting, because the words were like a boast, but it was so matter of fact, and so unconfrontational, it was hard to disagree with it. She thought hard. "I suppose you can't control people's free will. Say you wanted to sleep with a particular man or woman, and he or she didn't want to sleep with you, you wouldn't have what you wanted."

"It's curious," Ghose v-said, "how people always use that idea."

"Isn't it true?"

"Up to a point."

"What do you mean?"

"We," Ghose v replied, "wouldn't use any of the methods that we have at our fingertips, that's the truth. Wiping memory is useful, I should imagine. Do you know the difficulty that Latitude had with that switch in Sofari? How to wipe only the specific bits of memory that we wanted to target? Yes – more importantly – we could, after all, alter minds – not that sophisticatedly yet – but well enough to, say, get someone who is reluctant at first to sleep with any of us to do so. We don't have to do that. We don't control through power or coercion but through persuasion. We just gramsci people."

"Meaning?" Bartel felt a chill go through her.

"We create an entire persuasion and focus it," Ghose v-said. "But enough of this. There's something very exciting for you now."

"Yes?"

"There's a meeting of TCentral – a real meeting," Ghose v-said. "Not a virtual meeting. I'd like to say not a holo in sight, but that wouldn't be quite true, as I'll tell you in a minute. Nevertheless you'll understand a bit more about our world view and how we are working."

"How often does TCentral meet?"

"When required," Ghose v-said. Bartel expected more but she had finished.

"And?"

"Well," Ghose v-said, "you will see that we aren't monolithic. We may all be Trills but it doesn't mean to say that we always see eye to eye. I think there's a lot of conflict at the moment."

"Conflict?"

"Yes – and that's why we have TCentral," Ghose v-said, quite quietly. "It's the place where we iron out issues – change the Guiding Principles because they're not set in stone, because nothing is in the neo-age – and where we bring our complaints against one another."

"And you are willing to put that in front of me? Isn't it washing dirty linen in public?"

"We've nothing to hide." Ghose v-said. "And it's not in your interest really to reveal any of this." Again the chill went through Bartel. "And we do now have the ability to wipe your memory. Dangerous though that might be." Ghose paused and Bartel had an odd premonition that what Ghose had just v-said was rather more significant than she had immediately thought. "So let Serena look after you and you'll see me and some at least of the others in the flesh."

221

"Isn't that difficult to arrange?"

"What?"

"Getting all the Trills together in one place," Bartel v-said.

"Yes," Ghose v-replied. "And we have a way of dealing with that. If a Trill can't actually be there, we have a special holo just for TCentral. The holo – it's called a singularity because someone had a sense of humour, I think, and it's not worth explaining if it's not immediately apparent, but a singularity holo is only able to be there if the actual Trill is 100% focused on that holo."

Ghose then said she had to leave and let the Ghose singularity take over because the TCentral meeting would start in half an hour.

Bartel asked Velasquez whether it actually took place in a council chamber. "Of course." That puzzled her – but she left it at that. Velasquez t-added, "I'll let you freshen up and I'll come for you in about twenty minutes. Is that ok?"

"Sure."

"And by the way – I have one important question for you?"

"It is?"

"Is there anything that you want?" Velasquez left the question hanging for a moment. "You now know how important that question is . . . And it's my job to see if I can satisfy any of your wants."

"That's so tricky – I need time to think that through." Bartel was quite bewildered and her mind was like a bowl of spaghetti with conflicting thoughts and ideas going in different directions but all entangled up. "Let me think. I just don't have any wants right now."

When Bartel got to her room she was in a difficult state. She didn't want to think – as she knew she was being monitored, and then it occurred to her to ask herself did it matter if she thought or not? Some of what she had learnt had chilled her. What did Ghose mean when she had v-said that the Trills could control people's minds but chose not to?

Bartel didn't want to think about Pennington but he kept coming into her mind. Perhaps she should actually have listened to some of the things he had said rather than drowning his words out with not wanting to know.

Then she tried to think about what she would actually want at this moment. She realised that it was entirely sexual, as that was simple and easy to express. But then as she pushed herself, she realised that she didn't actually want to be with Worrell at this moment, but with Pennington. It was rather more than some physical need.

Chapter 24

Bartel accompanied Velasquez along a broad corridor, in silence. Bartel wasn't quite sure why she didn't want to v-say or t-say anything, but the importance of what she was about to experience at first hand – or as near to first hand as technology would allow – rather over-awed her.

Previously she'd seen TCentral on some of the weeds and the council chamber shown on them was light and hugely impressive with its acoustics and visuals – and she couldn't wait to see it properly, as she called it. The debates she'd seen had convinced her that whatever the Trills were up to, it didn't concern her as they were painfully dull and quite excruciating. There had been a hint in what Ghose had been talking about that perhaps the turgid debates seen in the weeds were actually deliberately dull to encourage people not to take notice.

Large, two metre high, double doors opened and Bartel found herself in the council chamber for TCentral. "Of course," Velasquez t-whispered, "there is actually no need for a real council chamber but it was early recognised by the original Trills that they needed somewhere which had gravity and presence. This is the result."

"But if the Trills are not actually here – doesn't that make this all a bit redundant?"

"I can't answer that," Velasquez t-said. "You'll see more when the meeting starts."

They sat not even t-saying anything. Velasquez was apparently engaged in something as she didn't look at Bartel although they were in a sort of mini-cubicle and were half facing each other. Bartel was about to t-say something, when the council chamber was t-called to order.

The seven Trills entered, each from a different doorway. "As usual we're going to conduct this meeting with voice. So let's make sure that we are all focused on that, please."

"Who's that speaking?" Bartel t-asked. Bartel recognised the person but couldn't put a name to her.

"That's Uhuru Sousousa – as you know, she's head of Ambience," Velasquez t-replied. "Chairing is a rotating responsibility – and it's Ambience's turn now." She looked down at the chamber. "It's about to start."

"Right – who is here actually?" Sousousa v-spoke in a calmly conversational tone clearly addressing the other Trills.

"Kalo's Elora is a singularity, Gyro's Jerry in person, Eclectic's Derek singularity, Sapiens' Sarah singularity, Elura's Alexandr in person, Latitude's Jessie singularity and, of course, Uhuru you are a singularity," the person sitting next to Sousousa v-said.

"For the avoidance of doubt, before I call this meeting of TCentral to order, every singularity must be in full control all the time," Sousousa v-said. "The meeting has commenced. We have one item that we have to discuss."

"I don't think that's right, Uhuru," Ghose v-said.

"Why?"

"We have two items – one more pressing than the other," Ghose v-said. "We agreed we would discuss the Guiding Principles. I think we should. I know it's not as important as the dispute between Latitude and Sapiens – which threatens instability – but in order to sort that one out, we need to understand our Principles and what they mean in this case. Agreed?"

"I agree," Sousousa v-said. "Anyone else?"

"I have an issue – it may be more a warning," a slight woman v-said.

Velasquez v-whispered to Bartel that this was Sarah Trarieux, CEO of Ambience.

"And that point or warning is?" Sousousa v-asked.

"I have some concerns about the dissident group who are developing a way of blocking socio and persono," Trarieux v-replied. She was in her forties or fifties by the look of her – but Bartel couldn't be sure. She knew of her, but like most of the Trills photographs, the images were always out of date and portrayed the Trills as much younger than they could be. Bartel could just about see that she was Trarieux once she had been identified.

"I'll add that to the agenda – though I don't think we should spend a lot of time on that," Sousousa v-said. "Anything else to add?"

"Yes," a man v-said.

"And?" Sousousa v-asked.

"There are the continuing tensions between Latitude, Gyro and Kalo – which, at the very least, we ought to mention, and preferably discuss."

"Ok, I'll add that to the agenda, as it is important. Anything else?" Sousousa v-asked.

There was a pause.

"The agenda is now: Guiding Principles, Latitude and Sapiens, Latitude, Gyro and Kalo, and I propose to take the dissident group issue last. Is that acceptable?" Silence was apparently consent. "Now Guiding Principles. Do you have anything to say Elora Ghose?" Sousousa v-asked.

"Yes I certainly do," Ghose v-said. "Let me start."

"Before you do," Sousousa v-said, "is it all the Guiding Principles or one or two?"

"It's mainly one – and as it is the one assigned to Kalo and me, I think we need to discuss it now," Ghose v-said. "It does also involve another Guiding Principle – that assigned to Gyro – but only as an adjunct."

"So," Sousousa v-said, "you are focusing on *No cartels and free competition*. And *As little interference in free will as possible*?"

"Correct," Ghose v-said.

"And?"

"At the moment," Ghose v-began, "the Guiding Principle that Kalo is charged with looking after is severely compromised because we have effectively divided up the whole of commerce and human life between the GLEAKES. We are prevented from moving out of our market segment – and that was for good reason when we were establishing TCentral and everything that we created to ensure stability. Now we have an equilibrium of at least sorts, that segmenting is restricting what we can do."

"It isn't a cartel though," Sousousa v-replied. "For example you have yourself got Tryptico – and that is a weed in opposition to Latitude's weeds. Anyone else?"

"What does Elora actually want to do that has made this so important?" Fernandes, head of Gyro, immediately v-asked.

"That's not important," Ghose v-replied. "If I were to reveal that, it would be a nonsense. No-one can deny that our segmentation means we cannot move forward in competition with each other."

This was so arcane and dull that Bartel felt irritated. Here she was for the first time in her life able to be part of the world of the Trills and it was apparently at the level of a dispute that wasn't trivial – obviously – but one which would have very little impact on her own life, as far as she could see. Perhaps the weeds' reports of the goings on at TCentral weren't a fabrication but a real reflection of what went on and they were really of no particular interest to anyone who wasn't a Trill. A debate of sorts droned on and Bartel couldn't be bothered to listen at all – though she found it interesting to see the Trills in the flesh and the nearest thing to the flesh.

The debate became heated for a moment – and then Sousousa calmed everything down – but it was hardly riveting stuff, especially for Bartel. "What am I supposed to be getting out of this?" Bartel t-whispered to Velasquez.

"I just wanted you to see how seriously the Trills take their responsibilities and their Guiding Principles," Velasquez t-said. "It's fascinating – isn't it?"

"I've had better times," Bartel t-said back.

"Just wait," Velasquez t-said. "There is a live issue between Sapiens and Latitude – and I know that Sofari is important to you – so this may be of more interest."

"So that's the dispute between Latitude and Sapiens that you mentioned?" Bartel t-asked.

"Yes – as I said," Velasquez t-responded. "As you know Sofari is built on the Sapiens artificial intelligence engine – and they are in dispute about who gets what from the commercials."

"Money?"

"Hardly – each of the Trills has far more of that than any person could imagine," Velasquez t-said. "This is about influence and the ability to make policy. You could probably say it's about power. And that's what drives each of the individual Trills."

"That's weird."

"Not really," Velasquez t-said. "What else would they be interested in?"

"I see," Bartel t-said. Though she hardly did.

In fact the discussion or argument as it became for several minutes at a time was no more interesting than the previous discussion – and Bartel was feeling very underwhelmed by this experience.

"Ok," Sousousa v-said, "I think we've aired that enough and we will have a resolution worked out between the Latitude and Sapiens people and that will be presented to all of us when that is ready. Ok. So next the arguments – shall I call them that? – between Latitude, Gyro and Kalo. Who wants to speak first?"

"I do," Ghose v-said.

"But I'd also like to make the point that I'm opposed to Latitude and what JD is doing, so it's not just Kalo and Gyro opposed to Latitude but also Elura," a rather thin man v-said.

"Ok, noted," Sousousa v-said. She turned to Ghose and asked: "And what is your point?"

"I have become increasingly worried about the emergence of what I think is now being called *sswipe* – the selective memory wipe capability that is now built into Sofari," Ghose v-said. "I had thought that we had agreed that it was to be limited in application and we would have an agreement between the GLEAKES before it was implemented fully."

"I don't think we decided that at all," Dressus v-said, immediately. She spoke quietly and effectively, and it felt to Bartel that it would be very difficult to disagree with her.

"That's a matter of record," Ghose v-replied. "Nevertheless, whatever the position was – and whether you, Jessie, or I, Alexandr and Jerry are right – the point is that we all agreed that this was a potentially extremely dangerous new development."

"I'd like to add my voice to that," Fernandes v-said, quickly. He was a very large man, thinning fair hair, and apparently sweating even though the air was so brilliantly temperature-controlled. "I see sswipe – and until Elora mentioned it just now I had no idea that it had that as a brand name – as a threat. Not only to the people but also to us."

"How on earth can you justify that?" Dressus v-asked, without there being much of a question behind it. "I can see you might be able to make a case that selective memory wiping could be a threat to the people, but it is hardly a threat to us. In fact it is a level of security as I see it. If we get to a point where there is a strong revolt against the Trills – for whatever reason – we have a tool that can disarm – well, dis-brain – any opposition to us."

"That's my point," Fernandes v-said. "Although we don't retain power strictly on the basis of consent – I accept that, of course I do, as it is a fact of our lives and control – we do have to ensure that people understand that we are acting in their best interests, otherwise we are likely to face difficulty after difficulty. Obviously any revolt against us is facing extraordinarily stiff odds against succeeding – we control all the weeds and we control the whole agenda and the Overton window with our gramscian understanding – but it is just conceivable that a revolt could get off the ground."

"And so? What is your point," Dressus v-asked. "At that point we could deploy sswipe pretty much universally, and so nip any disaffection in the bud."

"That is precisely why sswipe is so dangerous," Ghose v-responded. "If people learn that we have this capability, they will presume that we can use it in precisely that way – to repress people. All the while we are looked at with suspicion, we will be like the Bills at the beginning of this century. They were apparently impregnable and it was widely felt that they were so big and so powerful they could do anything they wished. And look where that got them."

"So you are saying, you two, Jerry and Elora – and you Alexandr – that sswipe is a danger to us because when people find out about this new capability, they will smell a rat and rise up against us? That seems at best fanciful," Dressus v-replied.

"All right – I don't accept your complacency, Jessie – but what's to stop you using sswipe against your fellow Trills? Think of the power this gives you," Fernandes v-said.

"Just plain scaremongering," Dressus v-replied. "Why would I?"

"We don't know the answer to that question, except it would clear your way to excessive power – and we do know that you are only mildly in favour of the Guiding Principles, let alone TCentral, and all that our neo-age stands for," Ghose v-replied.

"That's just not true – I am as committed as any Trill to the Guiding Principles – although I could wish that they were less demanding," Dressus v-said. Bartel found her pompous and for that reason not at all trustworthy. That was distinctly worrying.

"So what do you propose – Jerry, do you want to answer? Or Elora? Or Alexandr?" Sousousa v-interjected.

"I think we should have a moratorium on the use of sswipe as soon as possible, until we've had reports about its likely effect on each of our positions and the position of Latitude," Ghose v-proposed.

"Not possible," Dressus v-replied. The contempt she managed to inject into her voice was quite startling.

"It is – and it must be," Fernandes v-responded.

"Not possible, I repeat," Dressus v-insisted, "because it is already deployed – and as you well know, it is already being used, particularly for the imagineered world of Dread-Demotic that you are sponsoring, Elora."

"It can be withdrawn," Fernandes v-said, quickly.

"Of course it can," Ghose v-chipped in.

"Let me bring you to order, immediately" Sousousa v-said, firmly. "We're not going to get anywhere if we can't reach a settlement. Is there a compromise?"

"No," Dressus v-stated.

"Yes – not so much a compromise but a holding position," Ghose v-said. "Look, Jessie, do you recognise there is a matter of some importance here – both to you and our fellow Trills. Why don't we ask for an urgent report on this, laying out all the pros and cons so that TCentral can make a ruling based on the facts?"

"How long will this take?" Dressus v-asked.

"No more than a few days, I suggest," Ghose v-responded. "Jerry?"

"That should do it," Fernandes v-responded.

"Alexandr?" Sousousa v-asked.

"I agree with Jerry and Elora," Dermatov v-said.

"And what are the terms of reference?" Dressus v-asked, clearly angry and not prepared to compromise if she could help it.

"What dangers there are to the Trills and TCentral if we deploy sswipe, and what is the scale of the risk to us and to our neo-age. Does that make sense?" Ghose v-stated.

"Ok," Dressus v-responded, quickly.

"Is that a normal response?" Bartel t-asked Velasquez.

"What do you mean?" Velasquez t-replied.

"To give in so quickly, and not to fight her corner as I expected her to do," Bartel v-said.

"That's entirely in keeping with TCentral rules," Velasquez t-affirmed. "But usually there would be more discussion before agreement. Remember there always has to be agreement – universal agreement. And holding out for everything you want is a losing strategy, most of the time. So I'd expect Jessie to accede to the compromise – but it's not really giving in and losing her position. It's just put it on hold for a few days. That's not a loss."

"But the other two – well three – also gave in," Bartel v-retorted. "Why?"

"A few days doesn't matter and there's an important principle of some kind being established," Velasquez t-replied. "Now listen."

"Now I think we need to discuss the one issue that I was aware of. It's also the one that I had thought you would bring up Jerry." Sousousa looked at Fernandes – who took the podium.

"It's an issue for all of us – but mainly for Kalo in the first instance," Ghose v-began. "You are aware of the dissident group which is attempting to undermine our neo-age and the stability we have brought. Of course using socio and persono and some of the other tools we have immediate access to nearly everything they are talking about and developing."

"How strong is this dissident group?" Dermatov v-shouted out, very shrilly.

Bartel was all ears about the dissidents. Was this the shadowy group that Pennington was part of?

"Weak, of course," Ghose v-said firmly. "We have it under control – or at least we thought we did. It appears they are beginning to elude us."

"How?" Dermatov again.

"It appears they have found a way to block socio to outside interference and monitoring," Ghose v-replied.

"How could they do that without us knowing that they were developing it? As soon as they communicated that thought, we'd know – or at least that's what you've always told us, Elora." Dermatov was clearly emotional – although Bartel couldn't tell whether he was angry, just upset or fearful. The latter seemed unlikely knowing the strength of the Trills. Dermatov was a lithe, rather oleaginous character from the look of him.

"Difficult to say," Ghose v-replied. "We think that somehow or other they went off grid."

"But," another voice v-said, "we immediately know if that is the case. Don't we?" This was Dressus again.

"Yes," Ghose v-said. "We don't know who or how or even when. Not strictly true – we know names and potential strategy, I mean – we just don't know if we know everything. I bring it up because this could be a threat to our stability."

"Do you know what their perspective is?" a rather deep male voice said.

"Derek Smith of Eclectic," Velasquez t-said quickly to Bartel.

"Yes and no," Ghose v-said. "We know that they believe that we are destroying human ambition and human achievements. Of course we can do nothing about them believing that if we follow our Guiding Principles."

"Yes we can," Smith v-added immediately. "The Guiding Principle is obviously *freedom of thought* – and we respect that. The more important Principle is *as little interference in free will as possible*. I reiterate – as possible. Anything that is a threat to the stability of the neo-age is not possible. I mean we've just spent some time discussing sswipe in just those terms."

"I concede that, Derek, of course I do," Ghose v-replied. "That's not the point."

"Which is?" Smith again.

"Is this important and is this a real threat to us – or could we use it to our advantage by encouraging them – and exposing them as a threat to everyone else?"

"First of all," Smith v-said, "let us know how sophisticated this group is."

"Quite," Ghose v-said. "Of course we've had groups before who just took out the subcutaneous transceiver from their wrists."

"And we solved that by strengthening the power of every transceiver so they only had to be in proximity to someone else for us to monitor them," Dermatov v-said. "I know that means a group who've removed their transceivers wouldn't be safe from us." That word *safe* made Bartel shiver. Safe? What danger did the Trills pose? In all the feeds they were depicted as completely benign having created the neo-age for everyone's benefit. "The point is – how do we know whether we are safe or not? Are we saying that we are effectively blind to what this group is capable of and who they are?"

"Not quite," Ghose v-said. "Kalo's engineers created the warning system if anyone who was on grid went off grid. We knew who they were and could impose a different surveillance."

"Exactly." Dermatov v-replied.

"But to answer the question of how sophisticated they are," Ghose v-added, "I think I'm just beginning to realise that."

"So it's not just the physical removal of the transceivers?" Dermatov again.

"No," Ghose v-said, rather bleakly. "Look – I think we've all been too complacent. We thought that by encouraging multiple views and then attacking people we didn't want to be influential by every means possible except physical – you know accusing them of being misogynists and racists and antisemites and at the same time of being too ineffectual to stick up for their own race or too in thrall to women – we had mastered social control. And it's true – we have been mightily effective in destroying the credibility of anyone seeking to undermine us and TCentral. I just wonder whether we've become complacent."

"So how sophisticated are they – if it isn't just physical removal of the transceivers?" Velasquez t-whispered that this was Sarah Trarieux – of Sapiens.

"We think they can not only jam socio and persono – we think they've found a way to do that without triggering any adverse signals," Ghose v-said.

"How on earth did they get the insights to do that?" Smith v-asked. Interestingly he was becoming heated. "And why is this the first we've heard of it?"

"Let's not try to answer that," Ghose v-said, calmly.

"Why not?" Smith was upset now and Bartel could recognise the strength of his feeling.

"Because we have to work out whether we neutralise them, incorporate them or ensure that they can go no further," Ghose v-said.

"Ok," Smith v-said, calming down. "I'd take them out of the picture before they become too much of a threat."

"How?" Trarieux v-asked. "Physically? That would undermine everything we've done and believed in."

"I don't care about that," Smith v-replied. "This is a threat to the neo-age – a threat that we've allowed to grow without check. Let's face it we haven't had a threat like this before."

"Yes, we have," Trarieux v-replied, scathingly. "And you are forgetting one of our important Guiding Principles." She looked around. "No coercion. We have to achieve our aim through consent – guided consent of course."

"That's all very well," Smith v-replied. "How do we nip something like this in the bud when the bud has opened?"

"We have to find a way," Trarieux v-replied.

"True," Ghose v-said. "Do we want to decide now – or do we wait for people to come up with great ideas?"

"Now." Smith v-said.

"Ok," Ghose v-replied. "Ideas?"

"It's not that simple," Trarieux v-responded. "If it were simple it wouldn't have got this far to the point where we have to discuss it in TCentral."

Apart from Smith there was general agreement, and the matter was put to a vote and Trarieux's view prevailed, on her promise to table ideas within the week.

It seemed that TCentral was so much based on unanimity that if there was a possibility of it not being achieved, then, as with the sswipe discussion immediately beforehand, something would be considered after a report had been produced. Perhaps it was just a delaying strategy so that the Trills would come to the conclusion that they had to have unanimity above any particular policy.

It was quite arcane and very strange.

Bartel struggled with the idea that the seven Trills – all apparently individually very powerful – were willing to abnegate that power in order to preserve their dominance as the GLEAKES. It seemed to her, without putting much thought into it, that while it might create stability, it would also lead to dissension and disputes. It did also hint at a weakness in their power – although Bartel wasn't at all clear whether it was important or not.

Bartel decided it was too difficult for her to think through – it could wait, even perhaps for a discussion with Pennington.

Chapter 25

At the end of several really inconclusive debates as far as she was concerned, Bartel followed Velasquez out of the chamber with more questions going through her mind. Was Pennington involved in the dissident group that the Trills had identified? She thought the answer was obvious and that he was more important than she realised. Perhaps she should have been more aware of that when he talked about being asked to meet the Tomlinsons. How dangerous was it for him? How dangerous was it for her to know him, especially when her persono and her socio were clearly not at all protected from any third party if the Trills wanted to have access to them?

In fact even thinking like this might well be dangerous.

Bartel was glad that she wasn't political.

"And what did you make of that?" Velasquez t-asked her.

"I'm not at all sure," Bartel t-replied thoughtfully. "On the one hand I thought it was really interesting to see the Trills at work. On the other, I thought how dull the proceedings were."

"That's true," Velasquez agreed. "The point, Emma, is that you saw what few people have the privilege of seeing – the Trills working, and working both together and against each other."

"One question I do have – and that is about sswipe," Bartel t-said.

"Ask it"

"How serious is the disagreement over sswipe – and is it really as dangerous as Elora, for example, said?"

"We think it could be," Velasquez t-replied. "It is pretty destabilising if you think about it."

"Not for something like Dread-Demotic because it is really important that the experience is not shared," Bartel t-said.

"Yes – but for other areas, it could be very disruptive," Velasquez t-said.

"In what way?"

"Say for example, Jessie were to use it surreptitiously on the other Trills – can you see how that could be dangerous and threatening? Say she sswiped out the other Trills' memory of what they had agreed to do, then it would be very difficult for the other Trills to resist what she is doing. Do you see that?"

"I suppose so – but that's not very likely is it?"

"What's likely is never the focus of attention in any contractual or other arrangement. You have to concentrate on what is not likely – and that is what Alexandr, Elora and Jerry are doing," Velasquez t-replied. "This is important, Emma. By the way, you're due an update on the progress up the charts that Dread-Demotic is making."

"I'd almost put that out of my head," Bartel t-responded.

"It's why you're here," Velasquez t-replied, "so I don't think you should."

"So how is Dread-Demotic doing then?"

"Amazingly," Velasquez t-said. "We thought it was a breakthrough for Sofari and with the new sswipe taking away the details of the experience, it has proved a massive hit. We also stimulated demand for it by rationing it so that only a certain amount of people could experience it at any one time. As you can imagine that has made it even more important to most of the target audience."

"That sounds very good."

"And that's why we think you are someone very special, Emma," Velasquez t-said. "We want you to be part of what we're doing and be part of the immediate circle – which we know as ImCirc. So what do you think?"

"What does that mean?"

"Have you never heard of ImCirc? I guess not," Velasquez t-said, ruminatively. "It's the immediate circle around the Trills – who have some special privileges."

"So you're a member of ImCirc?"

"Yes of course." Velasquez looked at Bartel to see what reactions were going on in her mind, though Bartel realised her reactions were being monitored anyway. "How does that strike you?"

"Why isn't this public knowledge?"

"It is," Velasquez t-replied.

"But I don't know about it – and didn't know about it."

"It's not hidden," Velasquez t-said. "We just don't make a song and dance about it. The idea of privilege is very difficult in our neo-age. It's bound to exist – certain people are always going to know more and be able to achieve more and be able to exploit more things. Yet while it doesn't undermine any of the Guiding Principles, which are basically there to protect the interests of all the people, it does make the Trills uncomfortable."

"Why?"

"They have the feeling that in some ways it is anti neo-age," Velasquez t-replied, again watching Bartel very closely. "And it has to be said, it might be. But privilege is part of what we're talking about. Look at the privileges that the Trills have. They have absolutely no constraints on them in terms of money, relationships, resources, and any luxury you might want to mention. So they are highly privileged."

"Isn't that dangerous?"

"It could be," Velasquez t-agreed. "If the character of the Trills was different."

"But they could change their minds."

"Not really," Velasquez t-replied. "That's why we have the Guiding Principles. I think you heard in TCentral that they take them very seriously."

"But why?"

"Because, interestingly enough, it actually protects the position of each of the Trills – and the one area of insecurity that they all have is each worries about the other Trills and so each of them will fight to keep the Guiding Principles sacrosanct. But you haven't answered my question."

"Which was?"

"Do you want to become part of the ImCirc?"

"I guess so – from what you say," Bartel t-replied. "Though there's one thing I'm still not clear about."

"That is?"

"What advantage is it to the Trills to have me as part of the ImCirc."

"You're a celebrity, Emma – or are in the process of becoming one. Just think that Dread-Demotic is a revolutionary piece of imaginative development building on the work of the Trills and that makes it a celebration of their work. It's a win-win of course."

"And is that it?"

"Yes."

"What else do I have to do?"

"Nothing – but you will get great opportunities from being part of ImCirc."

"Such as?"

"Real help with the next project for starters," Velasquez t-said. "Then you will have at least some of the privileges that the Trills have."

"Such as?"

"What do you wish?"

Bartel was silent for a moment. She realised that the question was almost impossible to answer properly – if she said something exotic, then what? If she said something mundane, then what? "I really don't know."

"You're not in a stable relationship," Velasquez t-said. "Is that something you would want to change?"

"No. Not at the moment. I enjoy my freedom – or whatever it is that I have."

"Ok. Then think about it. As part of the ImCirc, you will learn how to wish in a new way. Does that sound bizarre?"

"Yes."

"We find that new members of ImCirc don't really understand the freedom they have," Velasquez t-continued.

"More than I have now?"

"Yes. But it is subtle. And exciting."

"So if I said something like, *can I have some man* that would be an acceptable question?"

"No. That's not. Not what I'm talking about – but it's the usual question. Think of it just about yourself. What is it you want for yourself, by yourself."

"That doesn't sound at all right," Bartel t-said. "And what more do I need? That's the point. I have everything that I need. We all do."

"Most do – true. We haven't made it entirely universal yet – but we're working on it. This conversation isn't about need. It's about *want*. But there are of course constraints. One of the Guiding Principles that you know very well should be upper most in your mind: *As little interference in free will as is possible – where it doesn't impinge on someone else.* In short, just think like this: think of yourself and don't impose on anyone else."

"That sounds religious," Bartel t-said.

"In a way it is," Velasquez t-agreed. "It's more than that, though. Just ask yourself *what do I want.*"

"I don't know," Bartel t-said.

"You will," Velasquez t-replied. "Why don't we start by looking at your life?"

"Am I in the psychiatrist's chair?"

"If that helps – think of it like that," Velasquez t-responded. "Let me ask a question. Do you want a stable relationship?"

"You more or less just asked me that. That seems important to you. It isn't to me."

"Why?"

"I've had that," Bartel t-said, suddenly conscious of herself. "To be honest – and I know you can read me so you probably know all of this already – it's not what I need any more. I have my girls. My Roseanne and my Alice. I've had a stable – or at least a long term – relationship in addition to my marriage. It didn't help me – it held me back."

"From what?"

"From what I wanted to achieve," Bartel t-replied, sharply.

"And that was?"

"To do something that no-one else could do."

"And get recognition for it?"

"Yes," Bartel t-replied. "I do want that recognition. Which is why Dread-Demotic was such a great thing for me. I pushed myself, I pushed the technology and I pushed my creativity. And what was most surprising – is most surprising – about Dread-Demotic is that it built on all my previous imagineering and so, actually, it wasn't that difficult. It's almost that it was easy – no, not the right word. As though it was something else – something like *natural*. I felt really creative – down to my fingertips."

"And that's important to you?"

"Now you say it – yes. It's the most important thing in my life."

"But you didn't know that when we started talking, did you?"

"I think I did," Bartel t-replied, a little hurt, "I just couldn't articulate it or hadn't articulated it."

"I think it wasn't that. I don't think you knew it before we talked."

"That's not entirely right. Deep down I did know that. It was more that I never told myself that in so many words."

"But you can now. That's what being part of the ImCirc is about."

"You'll have to explain that more as it's confusing me."

"The reason I keep asking about a stable relationship is because it is a touchstone – a sort of emotional litmus paper. The best way is to ask yourself the question: if I were never to have a stable relationship again would that matter?"

"I don't know. But where is this going?"

"It's focusing on the benefits of being a member of ImCirc. The one real quality it gives you – so people new to it say – is that you have a new focus on yourself and your time. You get to ask yourself the real questions – like do I need a stable relationship. We can't give you one – I've told you there are things we can't bestow on ImCirc members or at least won't – that's not the point. But we can focus on what you want. So as a broken record, as the twentieth has it, hat is it that you want?"

"I understand now. I'll have to think that through."

"And while you're doing that – what do you think about your relationship with Andrew Pennington?"

"What do you mean?"

"I don't mean anything by that."

"You must have had something in mind," Bartel t-said. "Why Andrew Pennington?"

"I was just asking."

"Ok," Bartel t-said, disbelieving. "You obviously know things about Andrew – things I probably don't know – and never wanted to know. That's true, isn't it?"

"I do. I know things about him that you could know if you had wanted to, but you always shut off that part of your relationship. You were happy with the physical and the general sense of shared pleasure – not only physical but also the mental side of being comfortable with him. That's why I asked."

"So this is a test?" Bartel t-asked.

"In a way." Velasquez was being very enigmatic. And it was worrying Bartel immensely.

"What way?"

"Just to see how you would react," Velasquez t-said. "We don't know everything about everyone despite having the tools that almost allow us to do that – and so we keep our eyes, ears and brains on the alert."

"So there is a worry amongst the Trills that they will be – I was going to say overthrown – but I mean probably superseded?" Bartel was stumbling towards ideas and didn't really know how to react.

"Every ruling group in every society has always had that worry," Velasquez t-said. "It's not just new with the Trills as you may imagine."

"But you're telling me things that are perhaps destabilising."

"Not at all."

"I meant destabilising me," Bartel t-replied. "You're making me very nervous and worried."

"I don't mean to," Velasquez t-said. "The point, Emma, is that whether you know it or not – and I rather take your word and your thoughts at face value that you don't know it – Andrew Pennington is quite a dangerous person to know."

"How?"

"Suspicion is aroused about anyone who is in his circle," Velasquez t-said.

"But I only sleep with him now and again and we never talk about anything – even though he sometimes tries," Bartel t-said. She was slowly becoming aware that things weren't as simple as they might be – and the world seemed to be growing larger around her.

"We know that," Velasquez t-said. "Well – we think we do."

"So is that really why I have been invited to meet the Trills and to be part of the ImCirc – so I can be a spy or an infiltrator?" It all started to make more sense. It was far more cynical than it appeared on the surface. "So all that talk about my celebrity and wanting fresh ideas – was just that: *talk*?"

"You might say that."

"And I do," Bartel t-said.

"But think about it, Emma," Velasquez t-replied. "Think about it properly. Would we need an infiltrator when we've got the perfect spy always working for us."

"Which is?"

"Socio – and, of course, the real tool, persono. As I am sure you've worked out, if you can transfer thoughts to one person, then we – and I say we, Emma – can read those thoughts remotely. How else could we eliminate fraud, crime of any kind, bad and anti-social behaviour as we have done, without that? Think of the blessing that those two tools – what they used to call in their first, crude manifestations *social media* and *smart phones*, if you know any history at all – have bestowed on us and our neo-age society. We've eliminated most if not all attacks by men on women. Can you imagine what a great step forward that is for women? If you can read the mind of the person in front of you, at least if we can, then it takes a far more devious human being than any we know to thwart persono."

"So why are you telling me this, Serena?"

"Work it out."

"I can't," Bartel t-said. "It's all too much for me."

"I – and in this case it is *I* – want you in ImCirc," Velasquez t-said, enigmatically.

Bartel was becoming confused and anxious and unsure of everything she knew.

"Why do you – *you* – want me in ImCirc?"

"I have my reasons."

"And you can't share them with me?"

"Not at the moment, no."

"Let me see if I've got this right," Bartel stumbled though her t-words. "You wanted me to be part of this world – of Trills and ImCirc – for your own reasons. You told me it was because I was successful with Dread-Demotic and the way that that was making me a celebrity."

"It is making you a celebrity – every moment that passes increases your celebrity."

"But that is a cover," Bartel t-said.

"No," Velasquez t-replied. "It's not."

Velasquez stopped t-saying anything. She looked at Bartel and slightly shook her head. Bartel had no idea what that meant – and there were no t-words.

"So the references to Pennington were meaningless?"

"If you want."

Bartel was totally confused.

Slowly Velasquez reached out to her and took both her wrists in her hands. Bartel looked at her. She was unable to t-say anything and she couldn't hear any t-words back. She was beginning to panic. Was Velasquez treating her badly like this for a purpose. Why the mention of Pennington?

"Emma." Velasquez v-spoke. It felt shatteringly loud and abrupt and completely unexpected.

"What have you done?" Bartel v-asked, surprising herself.

"I've blocked socio and persono completely," Velasquez v-said.

"How?"

"No need to ask that," Velasquez v-replied. "Just accept that I have."

"Is this allowed? I thought that in TCentral it was seen as a serious threat to their position – I mean the position of the Trills. So if you are part of ImCirc – what are you doing?" Bartel was rightly suspicious. Was she being tested even further?

"No – you're right, it is strictly against all the rules."

"So why have you done this with me? Is it to see whether I am an insurrectionist and would use a position in ImCirc to undermine the neo-age?"

"If I assure you it's not – then you wouldn't believe me – I hope," Velasquez v-said. "You also can't trust me. I can tell you that. At least I wouldn't if I were in your position. After all – I do know all your inner thoughts – or as much of them as is possible with our current technology."

"If you know my thoughts, then you also know that I have never – never – been interested in what Pennington may or may not be doing."

"Why not?"

"Because," and Bartel paused before v-saying: "I can't think of a good reason to be interested. I have a great life. I love the neo-age norms – for women to have their children young so they can enjoy them and not disrupt their careers. I love the freedom from want, hunger – the virtual elimination of crimes against the person. The eradication of disease or at least the elimination of the transmission of disease – and the removal of the threat of a pandemic. What's not to like?"

"I understand that position." Velasquez v-spoke slowly. "But there's more to life – isn't there?"

"What?"

"Look how achievement is no longer a driving force in the neo-age," Velasquez v-said.

"It doesn't need to be like that for everyone," Bartel v-said. "Look at me. I strive for excellence in what I do."

"But do you achieve as much as you could?"

"Who knows? But should I jeopardise everything that's good so I can have a bit more of ambition or of achievement?"

"That's not putting it correctly at all. It's not about ambition. It's not even about achievement though that is an element of it. It's about fulfilment. What's compelling anyone in this society to achieve anything?"

"I just don't understand – and as I've said to Andrew Pennington many times – why would we want to go back to venereal disease, hunger, want, and fraud – not to say not knowing what the other person in a relationship is actually thinking? You don't forget that between them socio and persono have defeated so many evils. Would we give them up? And for what?"

"I didn't know you could be this passionate, Emma," Velasquez v-said. "Are you trying to convince me that you are strictly clean of any contagion that Pennington and people like him – which is to say his group – might have allowed to contaminate you?"

"No," Bartel v-said. She was baffled. "Why would I want to do that? In what way am I contaminated?"

"Well – you asked me if I was trying to trap you. Perhaps I am. You can never know – absolutely know – even with socio and persono – whether someone is actually hiding something deep down or pretending. You must know that there are still limits to that knowledge?"

"But socio and persono are pretty well fool proof," Bartel v-said. "At least in my experience."

"That is true most of the time. But you are dealing with the Trills now – and you must know that they have over-rides on almost everything. Otherwise – how would they survive?"

"I don't understand what you're trying to tell me. On the one hand I think you're asking me to trust you. On the other, you are telling me that no-one can be trusted. Is that right?"

"Yes."

This was getting too much for Bartel and she didn't want any part of it. Pennington was a good friend, with benefits. He was a good lover. He was always there when she needed him – which wasn't that often. Or hadn't been that often. And they both knew – she thought – where they were with each other. Yes – he had at various times tried to recruit her to

246

whatever scheme he was embarked on. She hadn't taken that seriously – because if it was serious, she didn't want to get involved; if it wasn't serious, she didn't want to look to Pennington as though she believed him.

Even lying in each other's arms after they had made love, she couldn't and wouldn't be drawn. So what was Velasquez up to? Was she trying to trap her? Was she serious?

This was too much for Bartel to bear. "I don't want to know any more – and I am not who you think I am, if you thought that I would. Either you are serious in what you're saying – in which case, I don't want any part of it – or you're not and I needn't say any more. Need I?"

"I know who you are, Emma," Velasquez v-said. "I probably know you better than you know yourself."

"How?"

"I've studied you," Velasquez v-said. "Don't take it from me, but what Andrew Pennington is doing is far more important than you can imagine."

"You're right," Bartel v-said. "And I don't want to imagine that."

"Are you waiting for me to say you've passed the test?"

"Hardly."

"Well," Velasquez v-said, "in one sense you have. I know you are loyal. I know you are to be trusted. I knew that, but our exchange has just confirmed that, as you must know."

"And?"

"And nothing. If you are adamant, then I don't want to persuade you."

"Yes – you do. Otherwise you wouldn't have gone to this trouble. I just can't be persuaded."

"You can. Everyone can be persuaded," Velasquez v-said. "You must know that. The whole power – and I do mean power – of the Trills is because people can be persuaded – even against their better interests, even against their own, personal interests. Over the years that has been the power of the rulers – to convince people to undermine their own interests. The beginning of this century was the archetype of that – when so-called *populism* was re-invented, and people were induced to accept that life was getting worse for them on the basis that however much they were suffering, then there were always people and groups who were much worse off. Hate and division – and gramscian control – meant that they willingly voted against their own interests. Remember that and you will always be ahead of most people."

"And?"

"As I said," Velasquez v-said, "*and* nothing."

"How many people are with Pennington and whoever else is involved in whatever revolt he is planning?"

"I can't tell you that," Velasquez v-said.

"Can't or don't know," Bartel asked.

"Can't."

"And is it a revolt?"

"What do you think?"

"I don't know what to think," Bartel v-said. "Look tell me more about Andrew Pennington. Is he really so high profile that the Trills take notice of him and what he is doing?"

"The Trills take notice of anyone who is apparently unhappy with the way things are."

"Is that it?"

"What more should there be?"

"I don't know," Bartel v-said. "I am confused. I don't know whether you are serious or not, whether I am in trouble or not, whether you want me to be an infiltrator or not, whether I can just be part of the ImCirc as I thought I was going to be – or what?"

"You can be what you want to be, Emma," Velasquez v-said soothingly, which was an abrupt change of tone.

Bartel was left with her brain almost overwhelmed. She felt tired. She felt – what did she feel? Angry. She was completely at sea now. Pennington was dangerous – was he? How could he take on the Trills – and to what end? It was too much.

And what was Velasquez about? It just felt too much.

And, as Bartel could do, when things got out of control in her head, she switched off. "Don't think about it," she t-told herself. She thought about her daughters – and how she missed them being small. That was always an effective way of dealing with any present troubles or disturbance in her life.

Chapter 26

Bartel was left alone to gather her thoughts, or at least that was what Velasquez had v-said. Bartel remained sitting, focusing on her daughters for a while – Bartel had no idea how long.

But reality – or what had happened to her – suddenly came back with a rush. It was too important and too worrying to be held at bay any longer – even for someone like Bartel with her iron strength to focus on what she wanted to focus on.

Bartel was perplexed by Velasquez and her refusal to answer any question except, apparently, with a question. Where did she stand now?

What had been merely – *merely* she thought – a fantastic opportunity and privilege being able to see and even mix with the Trills because of Dread-Demotic had become a challenge and potential trap.

Could she trust Velasquez? And why should she? And what purpose would it serve? Bartel believed that she had a really great life whether Dread-Demotic had happened or not, and was this being threatened?

And was Pennington as serious a threat to the Trills as it appeared?

How on earth could he be – when the Trills had all the power, all the technology, all the weeds and all the levers of power?

The questions just kept coming at her.

It occurred to her that if Pennington was a threat to the Trills, he was also probably a threat to her and her life – and to the established order. And for what?

Or was that stupid thinking? For a person who had avoided really difficult political or social questions all her life, this was so disturbing she just wanted it all to go away.

A part of her wished she'd paid a little more attention to Pennington's views when he'd tried to interest her in them all those times – but she'd dismissed it as irrelevant nonsense that she wanted nothing to do with – and, actually, to be honest with herself, she still didn't want anything to do with them.

And what was Velasquez's role in all this? Was she an agent provocateur – or was she a genuine person who believed in whatever Pennington believed in? How could anyone tell?

Wasn't the combination of socio and persono supposed to eliminate all questions like this?

Bartel puzzled it all out for a bit – and decided she couldn't believe anything Velasquez might hint at, because it would never be in Velasquez's interest to oppose the Trills and, by so doing, remove herself from the privileged position she was in, being a director or an assistant – or whatever – to a Trill and in the Imcirc, which Bartel hadn't even known existed before in the form that Velasquez had indicated.

Even if Velasquez was successful with Pennington or whoever was leading this potential insurrection, if that was what it was, what would the benefit be?

It was all too much.

Bartel realised that Velasquez was actually trying to t-talk to her. The engagement was strangely muted – and that was probably an additional reason to worry. "Yes?"

"I hope I haven't disturbed you too much," Velasquez t-said. "But do think about what I was saying. I also wondered what you'd like to do this evening – if anything."

"What sort of thing had you in mind?"

"Anything, Emma," Velasquez t-said. "As a member of ImCirc now, you have access to virtually anything – anything you want to do."

"Even a quiet evening in?"

"Even that."

"Can you let me think about this for a bit?"

"No hurry," Velasquez t-said. "How long do you want?"

"Give me about 30 minutes," Bartel t-replied.

Bartel realised that the one thing she wanted to do was actually have a conversation, even if she now knew it wouldn't be actually private, with

Pennington. She didn't know what good that would do, but it seemed some sort of answer. Could he really be taking on the Trills?

Obviously not, really.

Not Pennington. Andrew.

She thought about their first engagement – did that have any clues?

It was a standard sort of first engagement – they'd matched up somehow and had t-conversed for about a week, until Bartel was actually rather desperate to meet him. He was so different in his attitudes, though Bartel was at a loss to say exactly how and in what. The best she could come up with to herself was that there was a mystery about him, some sort of hidden depth. And that hidden depth had been the major issue that had continued to make her uncomfortable with him – while at the same time she felt close to him and actually missed him when they didn't meet.

She often asked herself if she was still excited to be going to meet him because she doubted her feelings, especially after her marriage and that longer term relationship with Albert had ended, both of which had left her rather numb but not empty.

They had then arranged to encounter. Pennington had been very formal and stiff, even when setting up the meeting. She had thought he was handsome and really attractive both in holo form and in video, but in the flesh, she found him rather stunning. Perhaps that was why she remembered it so clearly, as she so rarely had such an overwhelming physical reaction to someone. Anyone. Even when she had first met her ex-husband, it had been nothing like that. Her experience then had been of a slow awakening of feelings – but with Pennington it had been different.

It always amazed her that she had retained such a clear memory of that first encounter, especially when she thought of how many people she had met under similar circumstances and then had slept with them, just like she had with Pennington.

He had more or less immediately changed his socio setting to *relaxed* – something that was unusual and unexpected because he was so stiff. Bartel's persono remained at *acquaintance* as she didn't want to overstep whatever was the correct Setiquette as what became Neotiquette was called in those days, and it was best to stay safe. "Are you that worried about Setiquette that you have to be so cautious?" Pennington had t-asked, with a smile on his face, as though he was taunting her, but at the same time showing her that her thoughts were still quite open to him.

"Actually," Bartel t-replied, "I am. I know how much socio and persono have changed how people can act and react, and I know that there are ways of dealing with new situations, but I don't think we've solved the problem about how we should interact with people when we don't know each other in any real sense. I don't count knowing someone's thoughts like we do now with socio as properly knowing someone."

"Put it like this," Pennington t-said, gently and rather diffidently, "I think you have to go back to basics to cope with this. Setiquette is the overall set of guidance for socio in all of this. You know – how you should think and allow people to get close to you or not, and what you want to know about the other person. Setiquette is how we conduct t-conversations. I know you know this, so I'm not trying to be patronising or mansplaining, only to give us a solid base so we can go forward."

"What difference does any of that make to this situation?"

"I think," Pennington said, slowly, "that by setting my socio to the most public setting, I'm saying something about myself – and also what I think about you. In fact it does more than that as it gives you access to what I think about myself, and what my thoughts and feelings are in a way that I hope isn't intrusive but at the same time is welcomed."

"But don't you think that puts an awful lot of pressure on me even though you say you don't want to intrude on my feelings?"

"Yes," Pennington t-said, "if you put it like that, I can see what you mean. It might appear that I am daring you to expose yourself and your inner thoughts. I didn't mean it like that."

"I think you overstepped the mark."

"Do you? Do you really?" Pennington looked puzzled. "I'm not sure why you think that. I was only allowing you access to me – not making a request that you should do the same. I wasn't trying to intrude or force anything on you. I trust you know that."

They were silent for a good few seconds. "Have I made a mountain out of a molehill?" Bartel eventually t-asked.

"I don't know, Emma," Pennington t-replied. "All I know is that I wanted you to know what my inner feelings and thoughts are at this moment and not to disguise them from you."

"I know you want to sleep with me," Bartel t-said.

"I'd not formulated that thought," Pennington t-replied, almost annoyingly. He was getting under her skin in a way that she found difficult, but also intriguing. "Is it that you want to sleep with me?"

How annoying could someone be? "I didn't think that, as you well know," Bartel t-said. "It was only that I found you so physically attractive."

"And I extrapolated." It was surprisingly not a question.

"What do you really know about me?" Bartel t-asked.

"I don't know how to answer that."

"Think of something then."

"I think you're frustrated with your life," Pennington t-said.

"What do you mean?"

"Just that. You think there's more to life than this rather hedonistic, analgesic existence," Pennington t-said.

"You are projecting that on to me," Bartel t-said. This was a first encounter unlike any other she had ever had. No wonder he had made such an impression on her – but had also annoyed her beyond what she thought was her endurance.

"Possibly."

"Is that your only response?"

"You are very different, Emma," Pennington had t-said. "Not different from how you were before we encountered, but very different from so many people I've met."

"You've met so many?" Bartel was deliberately lightening the mood and trying to get it away from the psychological depths she thought the conversation was in.

"We all have."

Bartel touched his arm for the first time – and even through clothes she, and she thought he, felt a small delightful shock, almost of recognition, though Bartel couldn't say of what. They kissed without either really knowing if either had initiated it, and had sensuously and slowly come together and ended up making love in the most relaxed way Bartel had experienced, - she thought ever. While making love, she had stopped him and changed her socio level to *relaxed* too and had been bathed in his warm, focused and absorbed thoughts, while he responded to hers.

So far so normal – but Bartel at least felt it was so different. And she could feel from his thoughts that he felt the same.

They lay in each other's arms afterwards, and Bartel probed his socio – looking for some sort of answer to her questions about him. They had, of course, mutually checked their health status, as the standard Medi-assist automatically carried out the process, and they knew precisely whether sex was, as the paleo-age expression had it, *safe*. This was different.

Bartel met a rather surprising blank, which she couldn't probe. It wasn't hidden, it was in plain thought, but it resisted all probes.

"What are you hiding, Andrew?"

"What do you mean?" Pennington t-asked back, though, of course he knew precisely what she meant.

"There is this area which, despite your level being set to *relaxed,* is withheld from me."

"Don't you have such areas?"

"No."

"Well" Pennington t-began, "it's an area that most people find upsetting so I have found a way of corralling it and stopping access."

"I guess," Bartel t-replied, "I ought to ask you how you do that – but more importantly, what is that area?"

"As I said, it's quite private because people find it upsetting," Pennington t-said, slowly and deliberately. While he did, his left hand's fingers were tracing lines down Bartel's face, along her body and, brushing her breasts, and touching all of her. Bartel responded by hugging him closer, and she enjoyed the physical sensations but at the same time she was determined to find out what this was. To her question, Pennington t-said: "It's what the paleo-age would have called politics – or my political position."

Was this his hidden depth that she had been so conscious of?

"Tell me."

"You won't be interested," Pennington t-said. Bartel thought he was playing hard to get.

"Try me."

"I am completely out of sympathy with the Trills and our new way of life." Pennington looked at her, clearly expecting a response. He got none as Bartel stared back at him. "It seems to me that we are living in a sort of serfdom – yes, we're looked after and we're safe, and there is a sense – and actually a real sense – that the Trills are in some way benevolent. I just don't see it like that."

"You are right," Bartel t-replied, "I am not interested. I can understand your position – just about – but I don't have any sympathy for it. Shall we move on?"

"If you want – but you're an intelligent woman, Emma, and you need to be aware of the dangers. No oligarchy in history has ever stayed away from becoming malignant. I think you should be more conscious of how our actual freedoms are being curtailed by these self-appointed, or at least self-created, and self-sustaining rulers," Pennington t-replied.

"What makes you think that I'm not?"

"There's no need to be aggressive."

"I'm not," Bartel t-said, "but I am assertive. There's never been an age like the neo-age. I am just not interested at all in destroying it."

"Ok."

Pennington had brought up the subject nearly every time they had met – which was never more than once a week, because, despite the immediate physical and mental attraction between them, Bartel was so wary of what she saw as Pennington's extreme and hardly justifiable views that she felt he was like a bad tooth which ached if you touched it – so she held off being with him, until she could bear separation from him no longer.

Bartel wondered every time whether the hidden depth that she had recognised in Pennington had always been this darker political side – and decided that it must be. It did add a sense of danger to being with him, because she knew that dissent from what the Trills stood for, although apparently not censored, was extremely unpopular with the generality of humanity, and liable to cause problems that seemed to emanate from the Trills although it couldn't ever be pinned down to them.

Bartel nevertheless recalled how that first encounter had ended, with a sense of deliciousness that even now she could feel. Whatever else Pennington was, he was a really deeply focused lover – focused on the person he was making love to, revelling in their – yes, her – pleasure, and for all those times together, Bartel had felt the most important person in the world.

Coming out of her reverie, now she was in a quandary. She didn't in any way want to subvert or destroy this neo-age. Yet here was Velasquez openly suggesting that she take Pennington's views seriously – either to encourage her to act or to find out if she was likely to be a traitor to the Trills' cause.

But what was Pennington's aim or understanding?

Bartel couldn't pin it down in her head. And not for the first time she went through her familiar arguments: what could be wrong with a world that had all but banished disease as humanity had known it since the dawn of time, effectively eliminated crime because it was indisputably detected even before it was likely to be committed, abolished hunger, created a world in which work was never a drag, but an opportunity that could be taken or could be turned down. Where for the first time in history women were on an equal footing with men, because motives and desires were immediately detectable – and if they weren't, any person with potentially or actually dangerous ideas or habits could be shunned for not sharing their thoughts, based on the assumption that any attempts to hide thoughts would be taken as threatening or at least suspicious, and make that person a pariah.

There was something else that Pennington always went on about – but Bartel couldn't bring it into sharp focus. Was that because he had kept it largely just hinted at and never fully explained?

It was more likely that she had just decided that it was a waste of time.

Bartel racked her brains – but there was nothing, as she had effectively ruled it out of all thought – then she remembered that he had once asked her a question that she couldn't answer properly and that was the clue to this.

She had it. It was actually innocuous and hardly as important as she was making it now. He had made love with her, and they were lying in each other's arms, so intertwined that the other felt just an extension of themselves, and Pennington had asked her: "What would you change to improve life now?"

She had thought it was such a silly question – and she had said so. She could think of nothing – and she told him it was a stupid question, and he had said: "Don't get this wrong – don't get me wrong, Emma – but one day you'll understand how important that question is." She had immediately accused him of being arrogant, nonsensical, patronising and completely wrong.

He had said nothing more – which was strangely enough the reason why she could recall the exchange. She expected a rebuttal or outrage or something. He just said nothing – and they had become absorbed in each other again.

Why was that such an important question?

Chapter 27

Velasquez engaged with Bartel after giving her thirty minutes she'd asked for, and t-asked her whether she wanted anything – or to do anything that evening. "I guess I'm pretty tired," Bartel t-responded.

"I think it'll do you good," Velasquez t-said, and left it there, hanging.

Bartel thought for a moment. "Ok. I guess you're right. Just I was a little disturbed by our conversation this afternoon."

"Why?"

"I think that's obvious, Serena."

"That," Velasquez t-responded, "as may be. Let's not talk about that now. Could you encounter me in say 30 minutes? It is best if we meet in the Secluded Bar. I think it would be good to relax. Whatever we talked about can wait. No hurry."

"That would be good," Bartel eventually t-said. "I'll be there. But what is the Secluded Bar and where is it."

"I'll ask Peter to meet you and take you there in about 25 minutes," Velasquez t-said. "Ok?"

This left Bartel on her own to think again – and she didn't know what to think. She was in a privileged position and yet it felt like a trap. Either the Trills were testing her – and she was probably failing – or Velasquez was testing her on behalf of something else – and she was failing. It was enough to make her scream but she decided that she would just have to control herself.

How much of what she was thinking was being monitored now?

Bartel was again suddenly scared – of what she wasn't sure, but it felt as though she had ceased to have a private life – that space in her own consciousness. It was good to focus on mechanical things – so she had a shower, found that there were numerous new clothes in her wardrobe – and was almost not surprised at that – and chose a slinky low cut, short dress in what would have been leather and to all intents and purposes and atomic analysis was.

She tried not to ask herself why she had made this choice – those people tuned in to her at this moment would obviously wonder. Bartel wasn't very good at mental games – at least she didn't think she was any good, but realised thinking about thinking was a way of hiding her thoughts as much as she could.

Or she hoped it was a way of doing so.

At his allotted time, Peter appeared – and she wasn't sure whether *appeared* was the right term for the instantaneous way he was suddenly there. There didn't seem to be a better word. And was *he* the right pronoun? Bartel hated herself for even thinking of these things which she would never do normally. What was knocking her so far off balance? On the other hand it was likely that all this internal speculation was hiding her real mind from whoever might be probing it.

It was only a short walk to the Secluded Bar – and it was obviously an ironic name as it shouted its existence, from the chrome exterior to the jazzy lights and the electric colours all around her. Peter knew where Velasquez would be and having made sure that Bartel was comfortable and didn't want for anything, disappeared. It felt quite a trick. Though Bartel was obviously used to holos in as much as they existed in normal life now, Peterc was a different form of holo – somehow more complete and more actually lifelike, which made it all the more disturbing.

"I think you need to have your mind taken off what we were talking about this afternoon. Is that right, Emma?" Velasquez t-asked. Velasquez was dressed in a sparkly outfit which seemed at odds with the conversation that had taken place earlier – but that was an absurd thought.

"That would be good." Even though Velasquez was t-searching her and obviously knew the answer, it was best to make a reply.

"Drink? Sex? Games?" Velasquez t-asked.

"Yes." Bartel felt it best to just let things flow. "But first, let me ask a question. Why is this called the Secluded Bar?"

"A good question. It's actually rather special so despite its raucous and overwhelming décor, it is one of the few places where, experimentally, thoughts are not accessible to people outside the bar."

"Is that possible?" Bartel t-asked incredulously, as she thought that she had earlier just learnt that there were no inaccessible thoughts for the Trills. Velasquez nodded. "But we are t-speaking now. How is that possible if there is a blanking mechanism?"

"That," Velasquez t-said, "is a good question. I'm not sure how exactly it's achieved, which is why it is still said to be experimental. There must be some strong force field – magnetic possibly or electronic in one form or another but highly unlikely to be that simple – which jams thoughts."

"But why would the Trills want to have such a mechanism and such an area, if what you've been talking about today is how they actually think?"

"I don't think they do," Velasquez t-said enigmatically. "What I think is going on here is part of their safety first approach. They always try to anticipate problems with how they remain in ascendancy – they rarely call it *control*. So they have their best brains work out how to stop things that they do from working, and another set of brains to counter that counter effort."

"So there are some chinks in their complete – what did you call it? – control?"

"Yes," Velasquez t-replied. "And no-one knows, by the way, how much the Secluded Bar is actually off-limits to surveillance. But let's assume that it is."

"I thought," Bartel t-said, slowly and deliberately as she was genuinely thinking it through, "that you said we wouldn't talk about what you mentioned this afternoon. But wouldn't this be the ideal place to do that?"

"Not really, Emma. You see one of the things about opposition to the Trills is that it has to be conducted more or less in plain sight, in plain thought really, because there really isn't an alternative, well, at least at the moment. It may be the first time ever that opposition is created so openly, but the Trills think that that is far more secure for them – as they know what the opposition is and where it is coming from. Let's move to voice, Emma." Velasquez switched quickly to voice: "Let's forget about what we were talking about. Let's just have a relaxing evening. What do you want to drink?"

"Try me with some cocktails," Bartel v-replied. There was always that strange moment hearing your own voice after exchanging thoughts and no sounds. "Why voice in this Secluded Bar?"

"Just because it is sometimes more relaxing, curiously enough. I'll do use voice now – and try some cocktails with you," Velasquez v-said. She t-asked the bar holos for a range of cocktails. Then she switched back to voice. "I think you are just straight, Emma?"

"Sexually?" Bartel was puzzled at the way Velasquez was chopping and changing, and ignoring answering the obvious question about using the bar's jamming of thoughts to good advantage. Should this be seen as more evidence that Velasquez was trying to trap her?

"Of course," Velasquez v-said. "If you're interested." It wasn't quite a question.

"I don't know in the abstract," Bartel v-replied. "Can we just let the evening develop?"

"Of course." Velasquez v-said nothing while the waiter put in front of them six glasses and explained what each was. "I said we should just relax. I just didn't really know – you understand *know* – what you would want. I do know, however, it's been a rather interesting, not to say mind-blowing experience coming here, so I haven't probed you much at all to understand you."

"I'm not sure I understand you, Serena."

"What in particular?"

"What you were saying about *knowing* and *understanding*," Bartel v-replied.

"We are all now pretty adept at disguising our thoughts – or masking them might be a better way of describing it. And we do have the filters – you know what I mean, the levels that you can hold people more, or less, at bay with. I didn't want to presume that what I had interpreted in your thoughts was what you would actually say in fact."

"You are confusing me, Emma," Bartel v-replied. "I think – is that the right word? – that . . . I mean I thought that now we had socio and persono, that no-one was a closed book to anyone else. But you're telling me different."

"Not really. You see what I said was that nothing stands still and just like we use voice to hide our true meaning, as we have become used to socio in particular we have developed ways of disguising what we are thinking. Surely you recognise that?"

"I hadn't thought about it," Bartel v-said.

"Think about it now," Velasquez v-replied. "Do you have more control over what is transmitted than you used to have when we first had thought transmission and therefore t-comms?"

"Yes, you are right. I hadn't thought of that."

"It's can't actually, as far as I know, be disguised enough to mean that people with bad intent can't still be picked up and we can still see danger signs – if there are any – in how people are thinking, but when we aren't concentrating that much, what someone is actually thinking can drift past us in a haze. It's like we stop analysing."

"Makes sense." Bartel thought about it as Velasquez was v-talking, and recognised it was true. She was immediately conscious of one time with Pennington – why was he always at the forefront of her thoughts? – when she had been picking up his ideas in general but wasn't sufficiently paying attention and had had to go back and probe him, as his mind switched from talking about the social situation into a more obviously sexual mode again.

"A lot of words and ideas, Emma, that are probably irrelevant at the moment. What do you want to do?"

"Can we, as I said, let the evening develop?"

"In what direction?"

"How about?" Bartel paused. "Why don't we ask some people to join us?"

"Fine by me." Velasquez got up and went across the room to a table with five people sitting round t-speaking and t-asked them to join Bartel and herself – or they'd join them. They got up and came over.

They sat down. Introductions. Then the inevitable question from someone called Susannah who v-asked: "What are you doing her? Not seen you before."

Velasquez said nothing and looked at Bartel. Bartel felt very nervous and decided to answer in the blandest way possible. "I'm an experience designer – imagineer – and my latest experience has started to take off and I was invited here as a result."

"What experience?" the man called Wilfred v-asked.

"Dread-Demotic."

"Ah, yes, I see why you were invited," Wilfred v-replied.

"I think we should use thoughts," Velasquez v-said. "It's too confusing to mix thoughts and speech and as we're all strangers to each other – I mean Emma is a stranger to you five and you barely know me although I know who you five are – we clearly need to have the right insights. And let's use Friend level. Is that ok?"

It was agreed and Wilfred t-said: "Dread-Demotic is a great experience so I've been told, but very difficult to experience it at the moment – so to speak."

"Why?" Bartel t-asked, as if she didn't know.

"I think, to answer the point for Wilfred," Xi t-replied, "You probably know, Emma. It's being rationed, I think partly because this makes it more valuable and seemingly more exclusive. But I understand that it probably doesn't need that level of sophistication in the marketing as it is a world-beater on its own, and it uses the latest memory blanker to ensure that once you've had the experience you can't explain it to others."

"How do they do that?" Susannah t-asked

"The memory blanker is a new product of Latitude – sswipe, with a double s," Velasquez t-said.

"To go back to the original question, Emma," Susannah, who appeared to be some sort of leader, t-asked: "what do you want to get out of coming here and being part of this Trills' environment?"

"I can answer that only to some limited extent as all this is so new to me," Bartel t-said, "but can you explain what you each do and why you are here?"

"Ah," Susannah t-replied, quickly, almost as though she didn't want anyone else to answer, "this is, as you realise, a privileged environment. Part of that privilege is that interesting people are invited – much like you – to experience it and to become aware of the greater depth of feeling that can be had at the level of the Trills."

"Meaning?"

"For example," Susannah paused then t-continued, "while you are obviously already aware of how much you can appreciate and understand what someone else is feeling, at the cutting edge of thought transference, especially but not exclusively making love, it is possible to experience the actual sensations – physical sensations – that someone else is having. This isn't announced yet – and may not be for some time."

"Why?"

"A good question," Susannah t-replied. "The answer is that with every new development in any of the new technologies, there are always social, ethical, moral and etiquette questions raised. Is it all right for example to take advantage of someone else's complete absorption in the moment and really feel exactly what they are actually feeling physically? Is that a form of violation? It isn't rape obviously, but is it akin to that in some ways?"

"I understand that," Bartel t-replied. "Then why are you here?"

"That is the key question," Susannah t-responded. "What has been discovered over the years is that while it is possible to predict appropriate responses to a whole range of these social, ethical, moral and etiquette questions, it is only when you are actually dealing with them in the round, in some form of real life, that you can actually uncover the full depth of such questions. That's where we come in."

"And how are you chosen or perhaps why were you chosen?"

"That's sometimes a mystery," Susannah t-replied. "But there is a clue in this group."

"How a clue?"

"You can see that we are pretty diverse," Susannah t-replied.

"Not as diverse as I might have thought," Bartel t-responded, really puzzled.

"How not?"

"For a start you five are all, I would suggest, about the same age," Bartel t-stated.

"That's true," Susannah t-said. "There are, of course, other groups which do cover the full range of the sort of expected diversity you would imagine. We have found that while each group has diversity within it, age is something that prevents rather than encourages real-life responses – and, of course, in our time off, we do tend to gravitate to people our own age. Hence this group. Wilfred and Xi come from a rural background. Gerhardt and Alessandro are urbanites. I am very much from a suburban environment. Wilfred and Alessandro are arts focused in their interests. Xi and I are science based. Gerhardt is focused on social sciences – psychology and sociology in his case. Does that help?"

"Yes."

"And our job – and it is a job in some ways but really I should call it a role – is to anticipate all those questions and see if we can formulate proper guidance or even legal limits," Susannah t-replied. "You know originally what we do was formulated under the name Setiquette as it was focused on what the responses to socio should be. The scope has broadened and we now cover all the elements of social interactions and personal responses – so that's why it became neotiquette."

"And you are the leader of your group?"

"Not really," Susannah t-replied, "but I do take the lead most often. We have a real diversity within this team in that respect too. Despite my scientific bent, I tend to go with my instincts. Alessandro tends to think things through first. I have to tell you that there is an awful lot of thought applied to creating groups like ours. And that's why we're here."

"Do you grow stale – and go back to ordinary life – if I can call it that?"

"Possibly," Susannah t-said. "But once you are part of the Trills' environment, you are essentially part of that privileged group for ever. But I'm sure that's enough. Why don't we relax and just see what we can share? You seem fascinating to me, Emma. How are you finding this place?"

"To be perfectly frank, as you've probably already discovered from my thoughts, I am rather confused at the moment – and I'm not sure that I could ever fit in here."

"So what are you doing to Emma, Serena?" Susannah t-asked.

"Nothing, I hope," Velasquez t-replied with a laugh. "Tonight we're trying to relax after what must have been a tiring although perhaps important day for Emma."

Velasquez and Susannah started to talk to each other – did they know each other before better than any of the others? – and Bartel started to chat to the others, particularly Wilfred, who was clearly interested in her. After the day she'd had, with its questions and surprises, this was a welcome change and Bartel was happily letting the thoughts flow between them, for the most part uninterrupted by anyone else. This felt strange to Bartel because they were in a tight circle and were all using Friend as their filter level, so in theory, at least as far as Bartel knew, all should have been able to engage at least with everyone else.

Wilfred came to her rescue as he absorbed her thought: "We're using a slightly different filter from the one you're used to, Emma. The Friend filter that's just been developed and is under trial – what used to be called user acceptance testing but is now far more complex – allows much more selectivity even with a group, and what I've done is narrowed down the filter for certain thoughts. You don't have to be aware of that or even have that capability in your socio as I can over-ride your filters. I wanted some of what we were t-discussing to be just between you and me – and I can do that."

"So this is one of the new elements that you are testing and assessing for those serious questions?"

"Well, not quite," Wilfred t-responded. "We've worked on it for a little while, and it wasn't so much the moral and ethical elements, but more the social and the etiquette questions that we found that we had to address. I mean you can understand that when I partially excluded other people I might be perceived as rude, presumptuous or just, say, self-absorbed and unaware. So the question is whether I should have done that."

"Do you mean whether or how you could exclude people who were originally part of the conversation?"

"Yes, exactly that," Wilfred t-said. "You can imagine that there might be a lot of hurt if suddenly you exclude people."

"So how do you cater for that?"

"What we discovered was that there isn't really a nice way to do that but that there are competing interests and if we take account of them, then neotiquette's demands are possibly met. But that what you have to do is make sure that everyone that could be involved in the group at any particular filter level is aware of being excluded, because it's worse to find out afterwards. As you can see this is work in progress. Interesting?" Wilfred looked at her intensely as he t-asked this question.

"Yes – certainly."

"So I was able to let everyone know that we were engaging at a somewhat deeper or personal level and that some of what we might talk about – or, should I say think about? – was going to be limited to you and me. By the way one of the other groups is actively considering what verbs we should use for t-comms and v-comms. For example, is it acceptable to say just *talk* or do we use the current convention of either *t-talk* or *v-talk*. The important point though is on whether it is acceptable – or, rather, when is it acceptable – to use the new filter in the way I am."

"I can see that that can be very useful to know and also how it could be hurtful to find yourself excluded from a general conversation," Bartel t-said, thoughtfully.

"Exactly."

"And what in our conversation did you want to keep between you and me?"

"You see that's one of those ethical or moral questions," Wilfred t-said with a smile.

"Oh, I see." She felt flattered and although she hadn't till then found Wilfred that physically attractive, because that concept was the furthest from her mind, she realised that the intimacy that this implied was really welcome. "I'm glad you did that, Wilfred."

"Shall we leave and go somewhere a bit more private?"

"Wait a minute," Bartel t-said. "Serena. I'd like to spend some time with Wilfred now – if that's all right."

"Of course," Velasquez t-replied. "I'll engage with you before breakfast tomorrow and we can pick up from where we were – if that's all right?"

"Perfect."

They left the group, still t-conversing, and walked out of the bar and into the open air. It was a warm night.

"Can we just walk?" Bartel t-asked.

"Of course," Wilfred t-responded. "I'm sure you must find all of this confusing. This is a different world and I think that most people who live in the Trills' inside world – you will have been introduced to the concept *ImCirc?* – forget how strange it is."

"I imagine that's easy to do."

"I think so," Wilfred t-replied. "You see in the role we have, we have to remain as grounded as possible – to think as anyone not in this immediate world thinks. We find that hard enough."

"And do you ever come across people who are less than enamoured with the world that the Trills have created?"

"I don't think I have personally," Wilfred t-said, "but I do know that the Trills themselves are worried – perhaps concerned would be a better word – about any sense that there is discontent with what they do."

"Do you know why that would be? It seems to me that they are pretty well impregnable." Bartel was so pleased to be able to t-talk like this, with it being kept abstract.

"I think it's a fundamental of human life," Wilfred t-replied. "You know how the Trills came to the position they're in today. Once they had established themselves as the richest people in the world – which was really quite easy for them once they gained momentum – they created a monopoly in each of their areas and that gave them security. On the other hand, the way they had achieved their initial dominance was by either completely disrupting an existing market – think persono and social media, and how persono propelled Kaleidoscope to pre-eminence against an existing market leader created by an original Trill – or by a seismic change in how the world worked – such as gSynth from Gyroscope, where food production became completely independent of the centuries old farmed food production. And what they are paranoid about is that someone new will be able to do what they did. And because they think, looking back, it was simple to do – whether it was or not – they are always looking over their shoulders and trying to snuff out any developments that might threaten their neo-age. Does that explain at least some of it?"

"Yes – thank you. I guess I suspected some of that, but put simply like that it is easy to understand. But I thought that there was no such thing as a monopoly – and you said that they had established a monopoly for each of the Trills."

"That was how they got to their initial positions – and, you are right, that has changed now so that the Trills recognise that it is not fully compliant with the GPs – Guiding Principles – and as they feel so much more confident, they explicitly don't allow a monopoly. In fact it is more sophisticated than that. You've probably heard from Serena that the key word now is interdependence?"

"Yes – and that was new to me."

That's good – and really quite cutting edge now as a corner stone of their sense of stability and secutiry. And well spotted."

"Thank you – good to understand. But, if you don't mind, let's leave that rarefied political world, and bring this down to things I'm interested in. What are you actually working on at the moment? You said it was all this neotiquette which is now commonly understood and discussed generally. What precisely?"

"Actually," Wilfred t-replied, "let me answer that in a roundabout way."

"Why?"

"You'll see," Wilfred t-replied. "Let me tell you one of the things that I worked on for the neotiquette."

"Why not what you are doing now? Is it secret?"

"Not at all. But it is not as interesting – in my opinion – as almost the first thing I did."

"Ok."

"I," Wilfred t-said, quite slowly, obviously choosing his words, "was one of the first people looking at sexual neotiquette."

"I can see that that would be more interesting," Bartel t-replied. "Anything in particular?"

"You are an interrupter, Emma," Wilfred t-replied. "Just let me tell you. You know how in the first days of socio and being able to understand other people's thoughts, then both men and women, but it has to be said mostly men, were in an awkward position because if they really fancied someone, or at the least found them very attractive, it was very difficult to obscure that thought from the other person. And before you say anything, it was mostly men because – oh, I don't know – it just was. Remember it took a lot of adjusting to, and thoughts were not something that in those days we were so used to controlling."

"I don't think you're right about that," Bartel t-replied. "I had tremendous difficulty controlling my thoughts well enough – and I think we all did."

"Yes. I didn't mean to suggest that women didn't have the same problem. Sorry. I've strayed into an area that I read about but I can't speak too knowledgably about. Anyway, the real issue was having, say, a sexual thought about someone and whether this was something like an intrusion or an assault even. I mean pre-socio, if someone had made a pass – I hope you are familiar with that twentieth – and it wasn't welcome, then that was a serious etiquette mistake, at the very least, and probably more serious than that. I mean it could be harassment or perhaps worse."

"I do understand this and was aware of it as an issue."

"It's one thing," Wilfred t-stated, "to know the issue. It's another to know what the correct response should be. And it was my first objective to come up with some sort of guidance about this."

"And did you?"

"Yes, I did," Wilfred t-said. "At least I made a stab at it. And of course it's been through several iterations since, as the thing about neotiquette is that it isn't fixed, it's always evolving."

"So how did you?"

"For a little while I tried to see it from the point of view of the person having the thought," Wilfred t-said, slowly. "This wasn't entirely wrong. It just didn't help much."

"Why?"

"Because in those early days, we still had the idea that thoughts weren't that harmful. So having, say, a lascivious thought about another person to such an extent – or should I say with a certain amount of strength of feeling – was seen as just one of those things. *You can't change human nature* being the mantra. But then we had to think about it from the perspective of the person about whom the thought was being projected or received. And it was all about context.

"As you can imagine, at the end of an evening getting to know someone and feeling very comfortable with them – both ways – is entirely different from being the subject of a lascivious thought when you first see someone, and how off-putting that might be."

"I'm not sure about that – it could be very flattering." Bartel realised as soon as she t-said it that it wasn't really what she felt.

"True," Wilfred t-said. "But in a business encounter? It's not flattering then, but intrusive and not at all polite socially, morally and or ethically. Now I didn't believe the then-mantra about not changing human nature, but it has a value and can't be ignored as I think changing human nature takes time. It might be a short or long time – but it certainly takes time."

"So that was the problem – what was the solution?"

"As I said," Wilfred t-replied, "it was to focus on the reaction of the person who was the object of the thought. We all knew that you couldn't eliminate, and nor would we want to, sexual attraction. So what was necessary was to establish a guidance about how to think such thoughts so that the object of the thoughts would not take it as an assault or an objectification of them or a reduction of them to some sort of sexual object."

"And were you successful?"

"Not at first, no," Wilfred ruefully t-admitted. "We couldn't find a way through. We provided guidance focused on the person who was the object of the thought which said that a quick and unequivocal response was needed. It wasn't fair as it put the onus on the object of the thought not the person who was having it, but I have to tell you it was a step forward."

"But we don't have that problem now?"

"Not in the same way," Wilfred t-said. "The solution was actually to refine socio so that each of us had more control over what we transmitted – and while that took time, it was the only way we could make this work. Nowadays both you and I can hide inappropriate thoughts – I mean thoughts that in any particular context are inappropriate."

"I understand – and it must have been fascinating," Bartel t-said. "But if you can hide thoughts that easily, doesn't that throw up all sorts of other issues?"

"Yes," Wilfred t-replied, "precisely that. Which is why, again, we went on working on this issue – and that's our pattern. We come up with ideas, implement them if they gain acceptance, but we never close a neotiquette issue off."

"But you said you were working on something else now?"

"Compared with that, it's pretty trivial and that's why I wanted to tell you about that really knotty one first. My focus – and it sort of came up tonight with you – was how do you discretely and yet openly as far as necessary decide to exclude a third party from any particular thought exchange when you're in company."

"How did it come up just now?"

"I wanted," Wilfred t-stated, "to engage with you and not have our thoughts shared with the others – but to do that, I had to let them know I was excluding them. And as I've no doubt you know, there's no real answer to that too. If you don't want to hurt someone's feelings, and since we all don't like to be excluded, when we exclude someone it can be upsetting almost inevitably. So my interim answer – and all our answers are interim of course – is that if you want to exclude someone from a t-comms engagement, then you have to announce it and – and this is the important point – give a reason. You might be surprised but that apparently little addendum has made a great deal of difference to the responses to the filter being applied."

"All this discussion," Bartel t-said, firmly, "means that I really don't know how to exchange thoughts with you now – although I am doing so."

"You mean it's like when you talk about having eye-contact with someone, and then you can't actually have eye-contact with them," Wilfred t-said.

"Exactly."

"But you can see why I like my role – even if it's not exactly easy to find the right answer," Wilfred t-said.

"Of course. But did you have another subtext in bringing it up?"

"Yes," Wilfred t-said. "Two things. The easier one first. I am not sure what you want to get out of this involvement in TCentral."

"And the second?"

"Try that one first."

"I don't think I have any idea of wanting to get anything out of being here in TCentral," Bartel t-replied. "Of course I knew about it but it was the furthest idea from my head when I was invited here. I was a bit suspicious of why I should be invited. To be honest, I still am. But it's interesting, I'll give you that."

"Good word *interesting*. Most people find it fascinating – and then a bit disappointing. I guess it depends on how happy you are with your life otherwise." Wilfred looked at her directly. "I guess you're pretty happy. Aren't you?"

"Yes," Bartel t-said. She felt strangely vulnerable again – like she had been when Velasquez had started to ask her questions about whether she wanted to undermine the Trills. It was a strange feeling. "Do I need to say more?"

"No," Wilfred t-said. "It's just that there is an undercurrent in our society – and it is a society and not societies thanks to the Trills – of discontent. I didn't know if you were part of it and that was why the Trills had thought it a good idea to bring you here."

"Don't think so," Bartel t-replied, becoming more wary.

"That's *interesting* – to use your word," Wilfred t-said.

"Are you laughing at me?"

"No, not at all," Wilfred t-said. "I just wanted to know."

"And what was your second point or question?"

"A much more mundane one," Wilfred t-said, looking now quite embarrassed.

"Oh – I see."

"What do you see?"

"You want to know whether I want to sleep with you," Bartel said, quite amused that a person who was charged with understanding how to develop neotiquette was so clumsy and unable to find his way to implement it.

"As it happens – yes," Wilfred t-replied, looking a little sheepish as well as embarrassed.

"To tell you the truth, I just don't know." She looked at him. "I don't mean that in an insulting way. It's just that I feel out of my depth here. Do I find you attractive? Yes. Had I thought about whether we would end the evening in bed together? Yes. Do I want to? Yes. I'm just in a quandary with myself at the moment."

"What does that mean?"

"I am being rather bombarded with ideas and questions and thoughts – some of them out of any context that I understand," Bartel t-said, thoughtfully. "I don't know if Serena is testing me or whether she's asking me real questions. In short – and this is a strange feeling for me – I don't know if I have enough confidence at the moment to know what I am doing, should do – or want to do."

"Serena is a dark one." Wilfred t-said, not directly addressing her concerns. "There are few people who really know what's going on in her mind. Sometimes I think that even includes Serena."

"Is she a trouble maker then?"

"Hardly,"

"So what is her reputation?"

"Serena is one of the oldest of the second generation of people around the Trills," Wilfred t-said.

"What do you mean by that?"

"Simply that – though I now see that I've confused things. You know one of the reasons the Trills are so nervous and insecure about their positions in their own hierarchy is that they each replaced one of the original Trills," Wilfred t-said. "That first generation of Trills were very much self-confident and believed in their own propaganda in a way. They made their trillion – and felt that this produced a shell around them that no-one else could break through. Each of them however – and this was without exception, as you probably know – was superseded by one of the current Trills. It was like a domino effect – once someone had seen that the first generation Trills weren't invincible, despite their money and capabilities, new people came in. Perhaps more ruthless – but I'd say more aware of how to hang on to their position. Hence the paranoia – or just sensible precautions. I guess you know all this?"

"Not really," Bartel t-said. "In general terms I know about the way that the Trills have changed – I mean the actual people who are the Trills have changed, as I don't think they changed in their personality – but put like you have, it is a different perspective. So where does Serena fit in?"

"As I said, she's a dark one. She was working with one of the original Trills and managed to spot what was happening and latched on to one of the newbies. But the reason I say she is a dark one is that I have never quite understood whether she has any particular motivation or just wants to stay in the centre of things."

"Do you think then that she's disaffected?"

"I do doubt that," Wilfred t-said. "If she is, she is good at disguising it and is also even deeper and darker than I thought. I wouldn't even be able to guess what her motivation is for that. She's in the very centre of TCentral and has a great reputation – not just with her patron. What on earth could she gain by being disaffected?"

"I would wonder that myself," Bartel t-replied.

"And just so you know, I do have a lot of sympathy with Serena's beliefs, and this isn't a secret as hardly anything is in ImCirc," Wilfred t-said.

"Do you know anything?"

"Me? Hardly. I don't even know your surname."

"Dunster."

"Ok, Wilfred Dunster." Bartel put a brave face on and blanked her mind as much as she could. She t-added: "But to return to your second question. Why don't we go somewhere and have another drink and see what happens? I know it's not spontaneous – but we can think of it like that."

Chapter 28

Bartel woke up, lazily and sleepily. She was still in Dunster's arms, his right arm across her waist, and still holding her. It felt all right.

They had got back to her room and sat opposite each other for perhaps thirty minutes just talking, neither of them making any move or even discussing what might happen. Bartel had stood up and v-said to Dunster, "Come here." He had stood up and taken her in his arms and Bartel blissfully and rather thankfully melted into him. They kissed and with the extra sensitivity that socio gave them for understanding their thoughts and feelings, they had very unhurriedly and even delicately ended up in bed together – and that slow, almost dreamlike state had continued as they made love. For Bartel it was delicious and a way of blocking out Velasquez, the Trills, Pennington, Worrell and even Dread-Demotic, and she had given herself up to their mutual pleasure in almost complete relaxation.

As nearly always at this moment of waking there was still a slight edge to her thoughts, an edge that she couldn't quite explain to herself, but which kept her from totally being at peace.

She knew this was so unusual. This situation.

And now in the light of day there was no embarrassment or regret. It was amazing how liberating socio could be – alongside all the other advantages of late twenty first life. That freedom from health concerns, freedom from worry about being taken advantage of and freedom to be herself.

She stroked his hair and felt the slow stirring as he began to wake up.

"Are you all right?" Bartel v-asked.

"Yes – really all right," Dunster v-said back. Of course it wasn't the first time Bartel had heard his voice, as they had used their voices when they were making love and in the bar, but it seemed like it, and just the sounds were comforting. Although thoughts were probably more comprehensive as a way of communicating, there was always something about voice that was a whole added depth to any experience. "What do you have to do today?"

"I can't know that until I speak to Serena," Bartel t-said, reverting to thoughts.

"Well – let's have breakfast and I'm sure she will communicate with you – either engaging or an encounter."

They felt remarkably comfortable with each other. Bartel could just remember making love before socio and how isolated it was possible to be in those days in even the most intimate moments. She could remember how disturbing it was waking up with someone new when socio hadn't made communication so effective.

Velasquez engaged with her and said that she'd be with her in about an hour. "Is there anything you'd like to do today?"

"I'd really like," Bartel t-said, "if we could talk some more because I really want to understand more."

"Of course."

Dunster reached out and took her hand when she had finished engaging with Velasquez and v-asked how she was. She replied that she was fine – and hadn't she already said that? They exchanged thoughts for a few minutes – and Dunster t-said that he had to be off, but that perhaps they could meet later in the day,

"Perhaps." They both smiled at this – as it was so neutral – and yet they each could feel something.

Bartel got herself ready and Dunster did too – and just before he was going to the door, Bartel called him back. "Can I ask you a question?"

"Of course." Dunster looked at her quizzically. "What's the question? I can't pretend I can answer any question you ask but I'll try."

"Why are people so opposed to the neo-age?" Bartel looked Dunster in the eye as she t-asked this. She was worried that she wasn't really supposed to ask this type of question.

"There aren't that many who are. You do know that? I don't think there's any one reason for opposition," Dunster t-replied, still looking at her intensely. "But then I've not been into that at all in much detail. Just the normal stuff we get as *our* news source or the normal weeds." That was interesting – ImCirc had its own news feed or feeds.

"Well what sort of reasons are there?" Bartel t-asked. "You won't know this – well, there's no reason why you should but from what I understand you probably do know it – I've always kept out of politics and all discussions about the Trills. I find it hard to imagine what people's reasons are for opposing the Trills as in the neo-age the Trills have largely eliminated crime of all sorts, from violence to fraud. Persono and socio have ensured that. As Serena said, globally they are on their way to eliminating hunger. Racial issues have also largely disappeared as they seem irrelevant especially when you are t-speaking and that has made such a difference to attitudes towards race. Nearly everyone is comfortable, that is, comfortably off in terms of living conditions. They've reached carbon net zero. No-one has to work, but there are roles for anyone who wants or needs one. It seems to me that destroying the first civilisation that has ever achieved that is actually in itself short sighted."

"Those are all the positives," Dunster t-said. "There are negatives of course, but I'm not the fount of all wisdom on this. Why did you ask me this?" He sounded defensive which immediately raised Bartel's suspicions.

"It's because of something Serena Velasquez said." Bartel looked directly at Dunster and added: "Switch to voice?" Bartel was suddenly aware that she had to dissemble a bit.

"Of course. What was it that Serena said?" Dunster v-said.

"Only – well, I'm not quite sure exactly," Bartel v-said, knowing full well what had taken her interest, and could hardly do otherwise. "Just when she was alluding to opposition to the Trills."

"As you know," Dunster v-began, "I'm in a privileged position here. I might not be the best person to ask."

"But isn't Serena too?"

"Yes," Dunster v-said, "she certainly is. But you have to know that she is very ambitious too."

"What does that actually mean?"

"I can't really explain. But she and I have talked about this. She's asked me the same sort of things that she must have asked you. I didn't know whether she was sounding me out or trying to trap me in some way – or, if not trap, at least test me."

"And are you interested in answering her questions in a different way?" Bartel was intrigued and also re-assured that he too thought that she might have been trying to trap or test him.

"You mean by in some way opposing the Trills?"

"Yes."

"Actually – no," Dunster v-said. Bartel really liked his voice and it was interesting how not using voice to talk changed how one felt about someone when you heard their voice. "Are you doing the same thing?"

"Absolutely not," Bartel v-replied. "I'm interested in what any of it might mean – but I'm not interested in going against the Trills. Not one bit."

"But you have a friend, Andrew Pennington, who is interested in that." Dunster v-said.

"How do you know that?"

"We all – well, those of us who might meet you – had a briefing about you," Dunster v-said. "That's completely normal of course. It wasn't special for you."

"But can you continue answering my question?"

"Which one?"

"What are the negatives about the neo-age and the age of the Trills?"

"I don't feel them," Dunster said, rather quickly as if he were uncomfortable. "But there are people who feel that what we have as a life – controlled to the Nth degree by the Trills is an attack on our humanity. That we live in a greyness – what the revolutionaries call *amblytopia*, which I'm sure you've heard of before."

"Is that it?"

"No," Dunster v-continued. "A more serious objection is that in no time in history has a regime that started out as benign become anything but tyrannic. You have to remember that since the mid sixties of this century there's been no change in who the Trills are, that they literally have unfettered power and wealth, and that while there are a few of them, it is possible that one would become dominant, and if he or she did, things could be very different."

"It sounds," Bartel v-said, thinking this over, "that you do have sympathy for the proposition that the Trills should be opposed."

"You mustn't jump to that conclusion," Dunster v-said. "But I do appreciate what has happened and if things did turn ugly, it would be virtually impossible to overturn a determined Trill. But I like my privileges too much to surrender them before I have to."

"Even though it might be dangerous in the, say, medium term?"

"If I think that's the case, then I hope I'd move fast enough to help prevent it," Dunster v-said. It didn't convince Bartel that he was being straight with her. How could he imagine that he would know what was happening far enough in advance to be part of a sort of counter-coup to prevent a tyranny? "But this isn't a profitable line of discussion Emma. You're not judged here by who your friends are – although perhaps there is more surveillance of you because of them. Andrew Pennington is actually well known and monitored very closely."

"Does he know that?"

"I doubt it – the surveillance is so sophisticated, as you might imagine, that it would be impossible to know for sure. But I do know that Pennington does believe he is under constant surveillance. He worries sometimes that he is paranoid too. With some reason – if not good reason. Look, Emma, I've got to go and Serena will soon be here. But before I go – and I include me in what I am about to say – don't trust anyone here. Even with socio and persono, you will probably never know what someone here is really thinking. Remember that there are special tools here that modify both socio and persono in ways that you can imagine but probably don't think about."

Dunster put his arms around her and they kissed, and Bartel felt a bit of insecurity at that moment, mainly because what he had said had taken away much of her confidence. Was Andrew that much of a threat to the

Trills? It didn't seem likely but the Trills obviously thought he was worth monitoring closely, so perhaps he was.

He opened the door to her room and left. They parted as though they had known each other a long time and not just a few hours. *Socio again,* Bartel thought to herself.

She sat and waited and thought about Dunster and then Pennington and had a brief thought about Dave Worrell. Some of her thoughts seemed to her about a different world entirely, as though she was focused on pre-history rather than just a few days ago.

She actually felt really in two minds inside – and while she had lost a little of the worry that had overtaken her yesterday when she couldn't work out what Velasquez meant, what Dunster had said had undermined her confidence.

She asked herself whether she knew more about Velasquez now than she had done – or whether the extra information, that, for example, Velasquez was ambitious, had only added to the mystery about her rather than helping to solve it.

She felt surprised that Pennington was so important that the people round the Trills had been briefed about him in relation to her. Was he a more significant figure in opposition to the Trills than she could possibly imagine?

Velasquez arrived like a whirlwind – and said they had a lot to do – and she needed to brief Bartel about it all. "How was Wilfred?"

"He was fine." Bartel looked at Velasquez quizzically. "Why do you ask?"

"I really like him," Velasquez t-answered. "He's young – just thirty I think." Bartel didn't know whether this was a criticism, a neutral comment, or in some way a warning to her. It was hardly usually a criticism in the neo-age. "He's one of the few people in that group whose role is to look at and define neotiquette that I really respect."

"Why's that?"

"He's very – how shall I put it without seeming to denigrate the others – I was going to say thoughtful but I think ultra-sensitive to nuance,"

Velasquez t-said, quite slowly. "And when I think about it – and I do a lot – it seems to me that his understanding is very valuable."

How did this square with Dunster's description of Velasquez as *dark*?

"I think that's all very sensible," Bartel t-replied.

"I guess what I am saying is that I feel a little protective towards him."

"Meaning?"

"Not that I think you are predatory – of course not – but I do know that you are a very experienced person and I tend to see Dunster as a bit naive," Velasquez t-said. "I think I'm digging myself into a hole here – so perhaps I'd better stop. I think you would know that I wasn't being at all critical of you – and I'm not jealous. I'm sure that's obvious – or I hope it is. Oh – I am making a mess of this."

It was fascinating to see that Velasquez, that calm, assured highly competent person, was in a muddle in her head. Socio and persono couldn't eliminate individual personal failings. Up until this moment Velasquez had seemed cool and collected and totally in control, highly professional and relaxed. Now she seemed very human. Was Velasquez protesting too much? Was she jealous? It didn't really matter. It was probably significant that Velasquez had set her filter to Bland for this conversation – so it wasn't possible to probe very deeply.

"So what have we got to do today?"

"There's nothing we have to do – but there are some things I'd like to do with you if that suits you. Think of this as a time of discovery – in all sorts of ways." Was that a reference to what Velasquez had been suggesting yesterday? Discovering whether Bartel would be an accessory to whatever Pennington and, probably, Velasquez were up to? No way of telling. "I think I'd like to show you the range of things that TCentral does."

"Yes," Bartel t-replied, a bit baffled whether any of this meant anything. "I'd like that."

"Good. My first area of focus is what you might call the museum of the Trills – it's not that, but more a sort of library of what has led to us being here."

"Why?"

"It's probably the area that new comers to TCentral find most surprising because it opens their eyes to things that really they might just have taken for granted," Velasquez t-replied. "And if you need an example, do you ever think about how laws are enforced throughout the world now?"

"Well – I know that there is a lot of surveillance – for our own good, it's always said," Bartel t-said, rather doubtfully. This seemed very technical and hardly of much interest to most people. It just happened, as so much did in the neo-age, and was seen as normal.

"You sound doubtful that it is for our own good," Velasquez t-said, rather sharply. "Don't you believe that?"

"I believe it – but our small discussion yesterday made me think that perhaps I shouldn't. I didn't mean much by it."

"Ok," Velasquez t-said and, surprisingly to Bartel, let it drop. "Let's go."

The kautonom arrived and it must have been planned already by Velasquez as it transported them quickly and effectively to a rather grand building that was low rise and rather sculpted with long flowing curves.

"Beautiful isn't it?" Velasquez t-asked.

"I'm not sure I'd call it beautiful – but it's certainly striking," Bartel t-replied. "Does the shape have a purpose?"

"No. it's purely decorative, as so much of TCentral is. Let's go in."

They entered through whispering sliding doors that shimmered in the morning light. They were met by what was obviously a holo who invited them into a type of viewing gallery. "We have a ten minute video that will set the scene," Velasquez t-said.

"Will you stay and watch it too?"

"Oh yes – it's updated fairly frequently and it's always interesting to see if there are any changes. But watch and listen carefully," Velasquez t-said, before motioning Bartel to a seat and sitting beside her.

A totally immersive experience commenced almost immediately and while it had a burden of information that it had to convey, the dazzling displays and colours and the three dimensionality rather overwhelmed

Bartel who had heard of such environments but never experienced them in such immediacy.

The messages were short and simple. The law was upheld in the neo-age by the use of socio and persono – and surveillance was the key to citizens' security and safety. The key concept was that of guardianship. There were dedicated people who were responsible for ensuring that the right standards were upheld – and these were people who were initially self-selected because they were interested and wanted to spend their lives making this sort of contribution to society. There was no obligation on anyone to become a guardian or stay as a guardian, and so it was only those who were fascinated by being in a position of overseeing that were part of the guardians. Then there was a rigorous, objective selection process that ensured that only those people who could be trusted remained as guardians, and this selection process was continuous – a person was only a member of the guardians while he or she displayed the right attitudes, made the right decisions and kept the world safe.

"Surprised?" Velasquez t-asked.

"Yes. I knew there must be some sort of organisation to uphold the law and standards, but never knew how it worked."

"We find that with most of the people who are initiated here," Velasquez t-said. "So much of our ordinary lives in this neo-age just happens so that after a while no-one seems to want to ask questions about how it happens. This is a direct reminder – that the world requires an organisation even if most people don't think about it. Let's move on."

"To what?"

"I think we ought to look at how work is allocated now."

"Work?"

"Yes," Velasquez t-said, "what we call work. That is anything which is necessary for other people's lives to carry on."

"Such as?"

"Well, for example, you know our food is now all plant based – though with gSynth you'd never know it as it is indistinguishable from what the paleo-age would have eaten as an animal product. There has to be some planning about production that we haven't been able to hand over entirely to AI yet."

"I do know about that," Bartel t-insisted. "I mean it's an obvious part of how this society functions."

"True," Bartel t-said, "but we are at a point of transition where AI is taking over from the people who have been doing the planning. It's cutting edge and very clever. And it's also indicative of how we got to this state, and the direction the neo-age is taking."

"How?"

"Let's go and see."

They walked to another hall, and were greeted by another holo, who was really a very attractive man in Bartel's eyes. That felt a strange response to a holo – but perhaps TCentral was getting to her. "Welcome to the Neo-age frontier," the holo v-said. "I am Pierre and it's my pleasure to take you on part of the journey that we have been on, going from the paleo-age to our neo-age. As you may understand, it's been an exciting and unexpected journey too." Clearly the person creating Pierre had been on a sales course.

"What we need to do, Pierre," Velasquez v-said, "is really understand one aspect of the neo-age which is how we are moving from some human involvement in, for example, developing and providing the raw materials for gSynth, so people can eat what they want, to a totally different system involving our latest artificial intelligence."

"Understood," Pierre v-said. "That's why I usually start a bit further back in the era of the paleo-age where artificial intelligence was really in our terms artificial ignorance."

"That's quite clever, Pierre," Velasquez v-said, rather wearily, "but let's see where we are now and what major change is coming down the line."

Pierre led them to a rather cosy area shaped like a diamond, with two settees forming two arms of the diamond, and he introduced a three dimensional display in the apex of the other two sides. "To be as brief as I think possible to meet your requirements, let me just say that the original work on gSynth was actually conducted by one of the first generation of

Trills. Of course it wasn't called gSynth then – do you want to know the original name? Oh. I see. Let's leave that as it is then.

"What Jerry Fernandes did was to take all the ideas developed by the company, Congo, and actually make them work in a seamless and effective way. No-one thought that Gyro would or could overtake Congo, but what Fernandes did – as you probably already know, is that he engaged with everyone – yes, everyone – who used what he called gSynth. So his technology was better, but far better was his customer engagement and actually his main focus for his – and I'll call it artificial intelligence – AI was using it properly to deal with every single individual who used gSynth in the early days on a one to one basis as individuals, as though they were in contact with Fernandes. There are people who now suggest that this usurpation of Congo – deemed impossible by many people – inspired the rest of the second generation Trills and also created a wariness in them that has kept them both alert to newcomers and actually honest. Remember that Fernandes isn't the only second generation Trill – all of the current Trills came to their positions through disrupting the previous markets that they came to dominate. So their honesty is fundamental and rather more than skin deep. Hence what we now know as *The Guiding Principles* that of course you are so familiar with."

Bartel was amazed at the odd way this had all come out. Pierre had obviously been programmed if that was still an applicable term because he might just have learnt to speak very candidly and also to use something approaching banter where it wasn't just humour. "Excuse me, Pierre. I need to ask Serena a question here. Is that ok?"

"Of course."

"Serena – Pierre seems to be very open and transparent. Is this normal in TCentral?" Bartel t-asked, knowing that Pierre would also pick up the question.

"Yes," Velasquez t-said. "If you think of Latitude's Guiding Principle – *Freedom of thought – religion, political beliefs, methods of association, criticism of any political system or statements* you can see that this is very important to the Trills. To give them their due, they are not only concerned to hang on to their power, but they also want to be able to say that as far as most people and events are concerned, they are ethical. If you remember your history of the paleo-age, it was very common for a person to be elected on the platform of honesty and integrity only to find that within a short period of time, they were as corrupt at the regime they had replaced.

"While the Trills are not willingly going to give up their power and actual privilege, they don't want to have to deal with overt anger against them. They think the best way of avoiding that is to try to be as transparent as possible – unless it actually undermines their position."

Was Velasquez trying to reinforce her questions from yesterday – or were the things she was saying orthodox Trills' attitudes? It certainly seemed very open.

Bartel remained quiet. It was all quite familiar stuff but in an entirely new context – and she was beginning to see the stability that appeared to be embodied in the Trills was not illusory but also not one hundred per cent solid and unassailable.

Not that she wanted to assail it anyway.

"The point I feel I should make," Pierre suddenly v-said, "is that everything is evolving and changing all the time – and that constant change is for the good of everyone."

"Why do you feel you have to say that?" Bartel v-asked.

"Because," Pierre v-responded, "Serena here asked me to show you the frontier of knowledge, technology and our capabilities, and actually gSynth is the best example of the frontier in action. You know that we have eliminated already most of the life-sustaining tasks as jobs for humans – not quite globally, but certainly we're on our way. Food is the most important in the eyes of the Trills. If they can get the provision of the raw materials for food to be self-sustaining – that is totally invisible to any human and requiring no human intervention – then the neo-age will really flourish."

"How close is Gyro to that?" Bartel v-asked.

"Difficult to say – but it's almost completely there," Pierre v-replied. "Do you want further details or to see anything else?"

"No, actually," Bartel v-replied. "It's a lot to take in – I mean it's not that much different from what I thought I knew but it is making my head spin a little. I need time to absorb it. Is that ok, Serena?"

"I need to show you one further aspect of TCentral before we do that." Pierre had clearly been designed to be at the very least assertive, and he – *he* – bordered, in Bartel's eyes at least, on aggressive. "I know you understand how goods and stuff and things are produced now and how we allocate them – and money is still important in that. When you were younger it wasn't like that – well the money was important obviously. But it was different. There was always a sense of *need* and the idea of *want* was a minor element. One big change over the last twenty years has been the importance of *want* as a driving force for the neo-age. I know this is elementary. I just want you to understand how health is guaranteed – as much as it can be – because that is a paradigm for nearly every other activity. Let's go to the Health Environment."

"Certainly," Velasquez v-replied. "I think we need to talk anyway. Let's go to one of the relax areas."

They walked along a few corridors, and arrived at a pleasantly lit area, all blues and light yellow reflections. "Take a seat. Drink? Coffee? I know how you like it."

"Yes – that would be good," Bartel t-said. She waited while Velasquez got her a cup and the right blend of coffee was chosen and dispensed. "Mind-blowing."

"What is?" Velasquez t-asked.

"All of the infrastructure that has been thought through and the way that the future is so rapidly changing what we can and can't do," Bartel eventually t-said.

"I guess you don't really think about it most of the time. But I expect you have wondered about it from time to time."

"True. Wondered but not seriously thought about it."

"So you have a question or two for me, Emma?"

"I do. But you are confusing me. And I don't know where I stand. You asked me about Andrew Pennington and I told you what my attitude towards him is. He is a good lover – actually that is probably an understatement. In the paleo-age I guess we would have been lifelong companions. I feel very comfortable with him. But I find his political position unacceptable."

"Why?"

"Because I can't see why anyone would want to change what is the best civilisation there has ever been. There is little deprivation – if any. There is none that I am aware of, though I know there are frequent discussions about places in the world where there are pockets of it. We've controlled crime to the point that it is virtually impossible. Disease control isn't perfect yet – but we've conquered most transmissible diseases. You can actually only be deceived if you almost actively want to be deceived. The fact that the ultimate power resides with a few key individuals who are unimaginably rich and powerful but who actually exercise that power with restraint and a sense of history – doesn't seem to weigh anything in comparison with the benefits."

"That's a good speech, Emma," Velasquez t-said.

"Am I wrong?"

"Not in so much as you have covered," Velasquez t-said, rather enigmatically.

"What does that mean?"

"You are leaving out so much. So much of what makes us human."

"What does that mean?"

"Did you ever ask Andrew what he meant?"

"He said," Bartel t-said, "that we're living in an amblytopia."

"What did you understand that he meant?"

"He meant," Bartel t-said, "that we are stifled. That we are having all our ambitions crushed by the Trills who want everything to be bland and unthreatening to them. He says they have bought off the world's population and have turned us into an experiment in not living but a sort of living death, where ambition, hope and desire are just withering away. He says we don't know we are alive."

"And how do you feel about things when he says that?"

"I feel at best confused, at worst angry," Bartel t-said, firmly. "I have ambition – you've seen Dread-Demotic. I have hope – a hope for more excitement and better ways of doing things. I'm not bland. I'm an individual."

"Does Andrew say you're not an individual?"

"Yes," Bartel t-said. "And that's patently not true. Because of the neo-age developments, I am free to do so much more than if I were stuck in a relentless striving for existence. You can see why it makes me – me of all people – angry with Andrew. And I don't want to upset the world just so some people can have a little more power or perhaps those few people, the Trills, can have a little less power – I guess."

"What if it's not about power?"

"It must be. Look – admittedly – I don't understand him properly but he wants to have the opportunity to alter things and that requires him to be in power. That's obvious – to me at least."

"Perhaps it's not that. Perhaps it's different from how you're thinking. Can you see that?"

"I'm open to that of course," Bartel t-replied. "But I can't see how. And I wonder if you're just trying to trap me. Wilfred said that I can't trust anyone and I rather imagine that's true – despite the t-comms, despite the ability to know what someone else is really thinking, there must be ways of blocking your true intent from me. I mean. Serena. Are you deliberately trapping me and seeing if I am some sort of revolutionary?"

"No-one is a revolutionary any more," Velasquez t-said, rather coldly. "I could be trying to trap you, true. This could be a conversation with a multiplicity of objectives. Testing you as well as trapping you or instead of trapping you. That's not the point."

"What is the point?"

"The point is that I just want to open your eyes to what things are really like," Velasquez t-said.

"That's a peculiarly arrogant thing to suggest."

"Yes it is. But it is also important to let you know what I am trying to do. I want you to see clearly. That's all."

"Why me? What's special about me that you want to do that. Why don't you want to do that to the population as a whole?"

"I do," Velasquez t-said, quietly. "But I thought I might start with you."

"Why?"

"Because I knew that as an acquaintance – I know it's more than that but let me use it for the moment – of Andrew it seemed to me that this would be a good opportunity," Velasquez t-said.

"For what?"

"To see if I could open your eyes," Velasquez t-replied. "I know Andrew has tried to talk to you about this, so you have an understanding of what I'm talking about. That gives me a head start."

"But do you honestly believe that you can change this neo-age? That you can alter the status quo?"

"That's the point," Velasquez t-said. "If I can't, then we are living in an amblytopia. Think about that Emma."

They walked to the next area, which felt like a pavilion absorbed within the overall structure. "Welcome to the Health Environment," v-said another holo. "I'm Ezekiel and there are two elements to what I can show you – if you're interested."

"And they are?" Bartel t-asked.

"Research and provision," Ezekiel v-replied. "Research is the most interesting because it's how people select themselves or are selected to carry out research. You know, of course that no-one has to do anything – it's not one of the Guiding Principles but perhaps it should be. So people who show an aptitude in their education are – we haven't the right word because it is somewhere between *encouraged* and *expected* – self-selected or selected for research roles. The only reward over and above what is normal for the neo-age is that they have the opportunity to have some celebrity, if they want it. Most don't. Does that surprise you?"

"Not at all, actually." This was commonplace stuff and Bartel was a little confused why so much of a song and dance was being created around it.

"The reason for the song and dance," Ezekiel v-said, smoothly picking up her thoughts, is that this is a major area of review. "The Trills are considering whether or not this is right – and whether or not the outcome of the research is reward enough in itself. Does that explain what I am drawing attention to and why I am doing so?"

"Yes." Bartel t-said doubtfully.

"Leaving that aside – and of course research and development is applicable to most areas of our lives in the neo-age which is why I focused on it first – let's look at provision. In the paleo-age health resources were rationed either with money – what a society was willing to forgo essentially in order to have health care – or with time. Waiting lists. What the Trills are introducing into provision – and this is cutting edge stuff – is focusing on *need* and *want* as drivers for health provision."

"I think I understand." Bartel was actually at sea, but didn't want to prolong this. She wanted to talk with Velasquez. "Can we leave this now, Serena? It's been most interesting Ezekiel."

"My pleasure," Ezekiel t-replied.

"Can we go somewhere and talk?" Bartel t-asked Velasquez.

"Certainly," Velasquez t-replied. "I think we need to talk anyway. Let's go to another of the relax areas.

They walked along a few corridors, and arrived at a pleasantly lit area, all rosy colours and dappled shadows. "Take a seat. Another drink? Coffee?"

"Yes – that would be good," Bartel t-said. She waited while Velasquez got her a cup and the right blend of coffee was chosen and dispensed. "Mind-blowing."

"What is?" Velasquez t-asked. "So you have a question or two for me, Emma?"

"I do. But you are confusing me. And I don't know where I stand. You asked me about Andrew Pennington. Let me ask you where you stand. As far as I can see, you are in a very privileged position, right at the heart of the world of the Trills. You seem to be well respected."

"You can't possibly know that," Velasquez t-replied. "But let that go."

"All right – as they say in those old-fashioned court room dramas, strike that last remark," Bartel t-agreed. "Let me ask my question. What would be in it for you to take on the neo-age – or the Trills if you prefer – because you would probably be in a worse position?"

"Perhaps I'm not thinking of myself, Emma," Velasquez t-replied. "Perhaps – I'm not claiming this yet – there are higher objectives than just my benefit. Would that make sense?"

"Possibly."

"Then," Velasquez t-added, "that might be reason enough."

"I just don't buy that, Serena," Bartel t-interjected. "We have a functioning world. A functioning neo-age which benefits so many people. I never majored in history but I do know enough to know that at the beginning of this century, right up to the riots and wholesale breakdown of order that were triggered by the incredible inequalities that were created by the original Bills and the first generation Trills, the gramscian control was absolute. What these second generation Trills saw was that to survive and keep their wealth, position and power, they had to create a different society, the neo-age. I don't suppose for one moment they have forgotten that – which is why they have the Guiding Principles, why they have these standards and why they preserve their position now, not through repression but through a benign understanding of the needs of people."

"That's all very true, Emma," Velasquez t-agreed. "The point is that you are parroting the weeds. Things aren't as stable as the weeds suggest and the Trills would have you believe. In fact it is an age-old truth that political stability is not something you can take for granted. It has to be fought for every day. If you remember your history – and so far you have shown that you do understand what happened before the current generation of Trills managed to gain their position – you will understand that at the beginning of the century, right until after the riots and the civil disturbance, the rise of neo-fascists was remarkable. People apparently put the holocaust down to the Germans *mucking up* nationalism. The major politicians in the main parties accepted enormous sums of money from foreign organisations and governments to de-stabilise their own democracies – which were hardly that any way, as extremely powerful governments were elected by small minorities – usually less than 30% of the electorate. One or two people at the time who analysed it, wrote that essentially the political parties had become crime syndicates channelling wealth to those rich enough to bribe them."

"I do know all this, Serena," Bartel t-replied. "That's why I was saying I value so highly this neo-age."

"But the flaw in your position is that somehow or other this neo-age represents some sort of perfection," Velasquez t-said. "Can we not do better than this?"

"I don't doubt we can. You still aren't satisfying me with your answer as to why – if you indeed are – you are prepared to take on the Trills."

"I don't think I can say anything else – well, I don't think anything else I say will convince you," Velasquez t-said. "I don't mind that. All I want you to do is think about it. Do you have another question for me?"

"How could a replacement society to this neo-age be guaranteed not to be worse than this one? You've already said that a stable – should I say democratic? – society needs to be fought for continuously. Would there not be a likelihood that it could be worse if we overthrow – if that is the right word – the Trills?"

"No guarantees," Velasquez t-said. "The point is rather that we have to know whether this society – this neo-age – is in fact beneficial overall and through time. To be perfectly frank with you – and you can start to see some of my real colours, though you may not wish to believe that I am being transparent – my view is that there are enough cracks visible already to suggest that on the one hand this society can't last, and on the other that it is not good enough for the future of mankind."

"What cracks? I don't see any."

"But you do know – because Andrew has mentioned this to you – that there are disagreements between the Trills that are rather more than disagreements of the kind we saw at TCentral," Velasquez t-replied.

"But those disagreements are surely why TCentral was created."

"True enough," Velasquez t-agreed. "The issue is whether there are internal fissures that are so strong that individual Trills will take a chance on achieving complete control for themselves."

"Is that possible?"

"It depends who you ask – but looking at the character of the individual Trills – which is not something that is ever analysed, at least officially – you'd have to say there is a strong possibility that one of them might want to do that. After all they achieved their current positions through a mixture of brilliance, timing, a certain amount of duplicity – more than enough duplicity in some people's eyes – and ruthlessness."

"But surely the strength of one Trill would not be enough to defeat the combined weight of the other Trills?" Bartel t-asked.

"Why not?"

"I don't know the answer to that," Bartel t-replied. "How could I? Didn't you mention that interdependence was one of the safeguards?"

"Yes, I did," Velasquez t-said in reply. "We just don't know whether that concept is strong enough to preserve the current stasis – I put it no higher than that – between the Trills."

"Are you saying that it is more than possible that one of the Trills might be able to overthrow the others, despite this interdependence?" Bartel t-asked.

"You don't need to know if it is possible or not. What you need to consider is whether it is possible. And then you have to decide whether you are prepared to take any action."

"I don't think so," Bartel t-replied. "I'm not important. Whether I agree with an attack on the Trills' power or not would make no difference."

"You might be surprised."

"How?"

"Just think about this," Velasquez t-said. "If the Trills know there is opposition to them – and of course nothing is hidden from them – or very little – then the threat to their collective position might be enough to keep them honest and true to the Guiding Principles. If that is the case, then every person who is opposed to their unfettered power and rule means that this neo-age will continue in the relatively benign way it is operating now. With no opposition, there is every reason for individual Trills to fancy taking on the other Trills and gaining complete power."

"So you wouldn't want to overthrow the power of the Trills?"

"I'm not saying that," Velasquez t-said, very quietly and firmly. "But without opposition, there will be an enhanced possibility of the neo-age becoming what every other despotism developed into."

"I really can't understand this. You are asking me to be part of an opposition to something that I don't oppose in order to keep it as it is?"

"That's one way of looking at it, Emma," Velasquez t-agreed. "But really there is more to this than that. I know that the power of the Trills is almost impregnable. I'd be daft not to recognise that. If we can keep them honest – or as honest as possible – that will be a major achievement. But the ultimate aim is to remove the possibility of despotism altogether. In the long term that is the only possibility."

"But from everything you say, all of what you are plotting – if that is the right word – will be known to the Trills so how on earth can you succeed in any way?"

"The answer is like one of those paradoxes I used to love as a child, like the coin which has two sides, one of which says the other side is false and the other says it is true," Velasquez t-said, rather baffling Bartel. "You're looking puzzled. I mean that the very transparency of our plotting – as you call it – is one of the strengths of our position. We need them to know that we are opposed to them. On the other hand we have to work out how to undermine them properly – for long term good. We have to create some sort of democracy."

"A sort of democracy? What do you mean by that? We have a democracy – indeed democracies – now."

"When we have a so-called democratic vote – as the Trills allow us now – they control the weeds and every other form of information, so they have complete gramscian control and the result of the elections is guaranteed as it will be a contest between two – or perhaps more – political parties that are fundamentally in favour or the status quo. It means the Trills inevitably come out on top," Velasquez t-said. "I don't know how it will change. I know it has to. Then we can create a proper democracy where people vote in their own interests and not in the manipulated interests of the Trills. It's not part of the history you were taught or might have learnt on your own, but at the turn of this century the rich and powerful controlled nearly all the means of information, and the so-called democracies were used and manipulated to ensure that people voted against their own interests."

"No," Bartel t-said, "I did know that. It was a very important element of what I did learn. But what are you asking me to do?"

"For the moment – nothing."

Chapter 29

Bartel asked Velasquez whether she could have time on her own. She didn't want to be awakened or put into a position where she would become some sort of sleeper who would be summoned to action. Her life was good and she didn't want to jeopardise it now.

Was she wrong? Was she blind to something? How blind was she? Did it matter? Hardly.

What difference could she make?

Velasquez had been subtle and indirect at first but there was something there that Bartel both couldn't trust and couldn't ignore. Velasquez had shown what might be her true colours – not that Bartel could trust that at all.

She needed to focus on other things. Dread-Demotic was a good distraction.

She looked up its take-up figures and it was clearly stratospheric in its impact. Nearly 25 million individual experiences had been recorded and it was fast becoming a must have experience – especially since, with the new selective memory loss on leaving the environment – sswipe – it could be repeated time and again without becoming stale. That felt good – and she wondered about Savery and whether she was being fair to him in not keeping him with her. Then, of course, that had been his decision.

She let herself drift off even though it was only early afternoon – suddenly very tired. Of course the night with Dunster hadn't meant much sleep but it was more than that. It was a tiredness from trying to adjust to all sorts of new things – not least TCentral. What was this place? Perhaps it would be worth asking where it was too. And slowly she did fall totally asleep.

There was an urgency about the attempt to engage her.

"Where are you, Emma?" Who was that? "It's Andrew, Emma."

"Does it have to be now, Andrew?" Pennington was always so insistent when he wanted something or wanted her.

"Not if you don't want to talk to me."

"It's not that, Andrew. I'm just pretty tired."

"Ok."

"No – you're right," Bartel t-said back. "What is it?"

"I just hadn't heard from you, I don't know where you are and I was worried about you," Pennington t-said.

"Well – you'd never guess where I am and probably won't believe it if I tell you."

"Where are you?"

"TCentral," Bartel t-said.

"What? Really? Why? Perhaps how, as well?"

"I got invited," Bartel t-replied, almost smiling to herself. "As a result of Dread-Demotic – you know, my new experience."

"Yes, Emma," Pennington t-said, reflectively. "And of course that's why you're there."

"Yes," Bartel t-said, and this time there was a definite smile.

"What does it feel like to be there?"

"Surreal."

"Any particular reason?"

"Yes," Bartel t-said, feeling that she had to say something. "You know how you're always trying to get me to be part of whatever it is you're involved in . . .."

"Our resistance to the Trills."

"Yes – that's right," Bartel t-said. "Well, the main person who is my mentor – not sure that's the right word, but the person who's looking after me here – has been testing me out – probably as a result of knowing you."

"That's actually not that surprising," Pennington t-replied, firmly. "You know how their surveillance works. We are under no illusions there."

"At least I thought she was testing me out, but I don't know whether she's doing it to expose me or to recruit me. She was asking whether I supported what you do," Bartel t-said.

"What did you say?"

"What could I say? I told her the truth. Of course not," Bartel t-said.

"I think that's a good answer, Emma," Pennington t-said, "but remember that they're able to trace your thought patterns and they probably would know – they'd definitely know, I mean – if you had any ideas like mine."

"I'm not completely without some knowledge, Andrew. I was non-committal but I did want to talk to you about it. But first – is this conversation open?"

"You mean – can the Trills listen in? The answer is yes – of course. But not what I don't want them to hear."

"How?"

"It's something that our resistance has been working on. It's highly sophisticated because we understand that the Trills will know we're having a conversation, and yet we can substitute other conversations we've had, when I determine we have to. Like now. Obviously this is not *en clair* as spies say but it's also not totally hidden. At best they will know we're engaging. No worries, Emma. Is that a real concern for you?"

"Of course."

"I know that your association with me will be suspicious to them and this call will be too. The point is that as far as they are concerned we're just friends with benefits – and that's the type of conversation that is inserted by our new technology. As I say it's not fool proof and I expect that they will find a way to block this, if they haven't already. It doesn't matter. I wouldn't say we're hiding in plain sight because we're not really hiding. That's virtually impossible in their neo-age. But we like to keep them guessing a bit. But what did you want to say to me?"

"The one thing I wanted to tell you is that they – the Trills that is – seem really quite paranoid about their positions. That was one thing that was surreal to me. I couldn't imagine that they'd be under any threat, what with persono and socio and all the other surveillance tools they've got. And I have to tell you, what they've got is more sophisticated than anything we've got as ordinary citizens."

"Obviously."

"But I found that paranoia really strange," Bartel t-continued. "Do you understand why?"

"I think I do," Pennington t-replied. "Remember all the current Trills are not the first generation of Trills and they all replaced one or two of the originals or the first generation Trills. I'm sure that makes them jumpy – whether or not they've anything to be worried about. Human nature, I think."

"But are you a threat to them?"

"Funny you should start asking that sort of question now – when you're right in the middle of them," Pennington t-said. "I know you weren't at all interested before."

"Well, what you have always been talking about seemed so theoretical," Bartel t-said. "You know – your expression *amblytopia*. That seems so dismissive and really quite patronising to everybody who lives nowadays in the neo-age."

"It isn't, Emma. It isn't just theoretical."

"How?"

"You see – though this is probably the worst possible time to be communicating on this," Pennington t-replied, "It isn't theoretical at all. In fact amblytopia is just so corrosive of the human spirit. The Trills are creating a world that is zombie-like. It suits them because they have all the tools and they can manipulate people and societies farm more effectively even than the late twentieth and early twenty first."

"I don't think that's fair. How do you come to that conclusion? It's not as though they can become any more wealthy, or have greater influence and power."

"You might remember that I tried to talk to you about Gramsci."

"I remember you bringing up the name. And it is commonly spoken about, Andrew. It's not a secret in that sense."

"Well – he really understood how people like the Trills would come to power and hang on to it," Pennington t-said. "He in the paleo-age obviously didn't know how wealthy and powerful they would be and therefore how unassailable. But he said that by controlling not necessarily how people think but what they can think about, very subtly through mass media they – by that he meant the rich and powerful because there were no Trills in those days – will take over completely. And once they can dominate all of the media, then they will create a perfect storm for the rest of us – and most people wouldn't even realise."

"And there's the flaw in your argument – or Gramsci's," Bartel t-said.

"What."

"They don't dominate our media – it's not like the paleo-age when a few rich people owned newspapers and television and radio stations and could direct what news was presented and how it was presented," Bartel t-said. "I can see that in that circumstance, Gramsci might be right. But we don't have these monolithic media channels now. There are thousands of different channels now – thousands of weeds – and no-one can direct the individuals within them to focus on the same area, as if they can just use propaganda.."

"You are so wrong, Emma."

"How?"

"The multiplicity of channels – or the appearance of that – is part of the way control is exercised," Pennington t-said. "But I'm sure you don't need to hear this now."

"Probably not," Bartel t-replied, "but that doesn't mean that you can avoid answering my point by going off at a tangent."

"Ok," Pennington t-replied. "Tell me when you've had enough. Can't you see that the very multiplicity of channels creates – and created – the ideal situation for the Trills? There is a constant noise – a constant tidal wave of conflicting opinions and thoughts and ideas. What the first Trills did was exploit that very fact when they first invented those channels – it was still called *social media* in those days – because they injected into the mix, or at least encouraged and promoted, false statements and news. They'd get people to believe all sorts of things or at least hear all these conflicting ideas and views and facts – and it didn't matter to them, because all these conflicting opinions and ideas just cancelled each other out.

"But what was more subtle was that they also used another philosopher's works. In a rather bitter irony they called it *arendting*. She

304

had written what she did to expose how lies worked in the public discourse. They used what she had worked out to create their way of working. The idea quite simply was that if you promulgate lies and some of them are easily seen as lies, it's not that you want people to believe the lies, it's that you want to discredit all public discourse. So people, in the end, believe nothing that is said publicly – or, usually, just pick and choose what they want to believe, because there is no solid truth any more, so you might as well make up your own reality."

"That sounds too simplistic to me," Bartel t-said quickly. "But I'd heard that last idea before – probably from you – and you called it *arendtian*. Now you're using it as a gerund, I guess, when you say Arendting."

"True enough – Hannah Arendt," Pennington t-said. "And I didn't know you knew what a gerund was – but good for you, Emma. So the Trills just allowed lies and lies and lies and it didn't matter if anyone said they were lies. In fact it worked better if it caused controversy and people objected to lies being uttered. But is that all you have to say in response?"

"No," Bartel t-said. "I mean that all this may be all good and true and what happened, but it doesn't get away from the fact that we live in a world with very little need, with much reduced crime. With a real degree of sexual equality because of the way that socio works. Would you sacrifice that?"

"It's good that you're asking these questions at last, Emma," Pennington t-said. "Being in TCentral is obviously a good stimulus for you."

"Don't be so patronising, Andrew."

"I didn't mean to be," Pennington t-replied. "When I say *amblytopia* I mean a world of greyness and a different sort of uniformity from what we had in the past. The Trills point to the diversity of opinion – but it is all controlled around the ideas that they want people to think about. The paleo-age had two phrases or words for it – gaslighting and dead catting. The dead catting – introducing outrageous ideas that divert people from the real issues – starts it off, and the gaslighting, using lies to confuse people and make them doubt their own experience and be confused about what is reality, finishes it off. You can see how a multitude of different opinions all fighting with each other will fit into such a narrative to the advantage of the Trills."

"I can see that. I just don't see how it affects – say – me."

"But you don't seem worried by what I'm saying. And no – I don't believe we have to sacrifice the really good elements of the neo-age – and there are undoubtedly good elements. But I see the corrosion in the human spirit – and the degradation – and I know you don't."

"I don't know what you mean by that."

"Let me just say," Pennington t-replied, "that I see too many people who won't strive and won't be creative and won't think for themselves."

"I'm sure it was always like that," Bartel t-said. "And not everyone can be creative and innovative and vibrant. Aren't there times when you just want to sit back and let life wash over you?"

"Of course," Pennington t-said. "The problem is that what you see is the surface and you don't see the deeper problems – the deeper threats."

"And," Bartel t-replied, "I'm glad about that."

"Are you really – or is this the same old Emma bravado?"

"You can be so patronising, Andrew," Bartel t-responded. "I'm in the middle of something here and I'm not comfortable."

"What's that, Emma?"

"As I said to you, my mentor is a woman who is in the inner circle, what they call ImCirc, and she is responsible for looking after me. As I said, the difficulty is that she made a sort of overture to me to see whether I'd be part of the resistance – as though she was part of it. Is there any way you can tell me whether she is for real or whether this is, as we said earlier, a test?"

"What's her name?"

"It's Serena Velasquez," Bartel immediately t-replied. "Do you know her?"

"I can find out – probably," Pennington t-said. Was he being evasive? "You know that we don't have lists of people. We work in cells – and know few other people who are involved."

"Is this serious, Andrew?"

"Yes. Why wouldn't it be?"

"You're not just playing at being rebels because you like the idea of taking amblytopia on? That you just like being antagonistic and oppositional?"

"I can assure you, Emma," Pennington t-responded immediately, "that we – and I – have never been more serious about anything."

"You do understand that you're frightening me, Andrew," Bartel t-said.

"How and why?"

"I'm not sure – but I can only say you make me worried – and frightened. I don't really know what and why – only that what is being talked about seems to me to be dangerous."

"Do you mean dangerous to you – or me – or this Velasquez?"

"No," Bartel t-said, slowly, "to everything I understand."

"So what do you want me to do – or say?"

"I don't know," Bartel t-replied. She felt very alone and curiously excited, which surprised her. "I'd like to see you, Andrew."

"Any time. You know that, Emma. Just tell me when."

"I will

They disengaged. She suddenly felt very lonely. Her immediate thought was to engage with Dunster. Would he be free? Was that a ridiculous question because he was presumably under no obligation as was common to everyone now in terms of roles – but perhaps it was different in TCentral.

She engaged with Dunster. "Could you be free, Wilfred?"

"Yes," Dunster t-replied. "When?"

"Now."

"Sure. I'll be about 10 minutes."

Bartel was impatient, partly with herself as she didn't know whether she wanted to see him or not. She was completely at sea with herself. As she was a person who nearly always knew her own mind and had very little self-doubt this was more uncomfortable for her than for most people, especially in the neo-age. What on earth was she doing? Why was she even worrying about Pennington and what he was up to – and whether Velasquez was part of it or was trying to provoke or trap her. It didn't matter.

And what on earth did Pennington want when he engaged her. That wasn't clear now – or did he just want to check up that she was all right. Once Bartel started to think about these things, it seemed like a maelstrom of ideas and conflicting thoughts and emotions.

There was a tap at the door, and she opened it and immediately threw her arms around Dunster. He was rather taken aback but returned the embrace. They went into the room with her arm around his waist, and then she turned to him and started to undo his shirt. Dunster looked at her quizzically. Bartel said nothing but continued to undress him – and then stood there inviting him to do the same to her.

It was a moment of oblivion and they made love passionately and intensely. Dunster was surprised but clearly just abandoned himself to what was happening – while their thoughts were incoherently exchanged, with no control at all. It was her pure lust and need and Dunster responded to that.

They lay in each other's arms, with their bodies intertwined. Bartel engaged with him and t-said that she needed him and needed the physical as she was so confused by things and just needed something that she was sure about and sure of. He didn't respond at first.

"I think," Dunster t-said eventually, "that it doesn't matter if I understand or not. But I don't."

"Nothing really to understand. I needed a certainty – and all I could think of was sex and losing myself in it with you," Bartel t-said. It was good that she didn't feel bad or sad or embarrassed – but with socio and persono that was a rare emotion after sex these days as there was always a mental closeness in the act. "Does that make any sense?"

"Yes."

"You have to see that I don't feel part of anything at the moment – not my work, not TCentral not the Trills or anything. I have always resisted getting involved in things that are peripheral to my life and suddenly, with Serena's questions and words and promptings I just felt that the world was too large and I didn't want to be part of it."

"That's a good instinct," Dunster t-said. "Not sure, however, that it's a good idea to avoid thinking about these things."

"What do you mean?"

"Isn't asking me to come here and make love a way of avoiding thinking about all of this? Sorry," he t-said quickly, "I'm not objecting. That's not what I mean. It's only that these are really serious matters, Emma."

"I know they are. Which is why I am avoiding thinking about them and just needed the certainty that sex can give."

"But you turned down socio so even when we were making love you weren't really with me as much as you could be."

"Do you understand why?"

"Yes," Dunster t-said, "and this isn't a complaint. But you have to sort this out, I think, Emma, rather than burying your head in the sand or just diverting yourself with sex. Don't get me wrong – I'm very happy that you do and you do it with me. That's not the problem."

"What is the problem?"

"Just a bit of a conflict with our neotiquette," Dunster t-replied with a smile. "I think you know what I mean."

"You're the expert on neotiquette – and I don't understand. What do you mean?"

"I mean," Dunster t-said, "that in the neo-age sex isn't private – in the way it was. To withdraw yourself completely from the other person is exploitative – or that's how we think of it. Do you think we are wrong?"

"No – not wrong, but not understanding. I know that in the broadest sense you are right and I do see that you could say it was exploitative with you. But you know why it was as it was."

"I wasn't telling you off."

"It sounded like it."

"Hardly," Dunster t-replied. "But let's not argue because I do understand. More than that, I think I've realised something more profound about you, Emma."

"And that is?"

"You are at a critical point in your understanding."

"That's patronising."

"It may be but not intended. Let me finish. I think you do understand why there are people like Andrew Pennington even though you don't understand quite what their problem is."

"I'm not daft."

"I'd never make that mistake, Emma," Dunster t-said, with a smile. "I think I'm right though – you do understand that there are people like Andrew."

"Yes. There are always going to be people who dislike the current situation, regardless of how good it actually might be, and will plot to change things. That's natural. Andrew falls into that category. He would always be dissatisfied. And – before you say anything more – I do know it is deeper than that – and that Andrew has good reasons, well reasons that he regards as good, for what he believes, so I'm not trivialising his position."

"I think you are – but let's leave that there. The point is that I think you shy away from confronting your own doubts about the world as it is – the neo-age – and just want to let things go on without worrying too much about it."

"And why shouldn't I?" Bartel was quite aggressively staring at Dunster.

"You can – of course you can. Most people do. But people like Andrew Pennington believe in something and that something is about our fundamental human nature."

"Let's not have this type of discussion, Wilfred," Bartel t-replied. "We will just disagree."

"I don't think so. Look there are many great things about the neo-age – I can't deny that. With the Trills – and note I say *with* and not *under* – life has become more fulfilling, easier, better, and they've removed, for example, hunger almost completely, and eliminated most crime, and any sense of poverty for the whole world. I know that you repeat that yourself, so there's no surprise there."

"So what's wrong with any of that?"

"It is," Dunster t-said, "not a question of there being anything wrong with that in itself, but in terms of human life what is the point? We can go on living, having sex without much thought or with as much thought as you'd wish. We can eat drink and be merry – we can even play or participate in experiences like Dread-Demotic. But people like Andrew Pennington believe there is more to life than that – and what we have is . . ."

"Amblytopia. He's told me."

"The point, Emma, is that this amblytopia, this miasma, this greyness, is in the end pointless – and what the Trills have done is subvert human life. They are profoundly anti-human."

"They can't be. They have created a perfect environment."

"Only as long as you don't challenge it."

"But you are challenging it now."

"Yes." This was an admission that felt quite shocking.

"And," Bartel t-continued, "there is nothing stopping you doing that. So the Trills can't be that bad if you are part of TCentral and working here and being in the inner cabal, ImCirc, and yet you can preach what is really insurrection against the Trills."

"You really don't understand, Emma," Dunster t-said. "You know how powerful they are so in one sense there is no point in preaching – as you call it – insurrection. On the other hand – no I think it's too difficult to explain. Or I find it too difficult. It's knowing where to start."

"So?"

"So I propose that we meet with Serena and see if we can explain," Dunster t-said.

"You won't convince me – so it may not be worthwhile."

"We won't try to convince you of anything," Dunster t-responded. "That's not the point. You aren't here to be persuaded of anything. We just want to open your eyes and if you can see, take things from there."

"Why Serena Velasquez? Is she a sort of ring leader?"

"You do use colourful language, Emma. I think the concepts you have are too outmoded. Sorry. Not outmoded, no. Much more at variance with reality for you to understand who we are and what we're trying to do."

"At the moment all I can think is that you want to make people hungry and less comfortable and more prone to crime. And your use of *we* makes me profoundly nervous."

"Let's see if you still believe that when we've talked it through."

Chapter 30

Bartel went with Dunster who led her back to the main building she had spent her first few hours in and asked her to wait in a small room, while he went to find Velasquez. Bartel felt quite at a loss – and was beginning to be impatient and fed up with being inveigled into doing something she was really not interested in doing.

"Hello, Emma," Velasquez t-said as she came into the room, followed by Dunster. "Wilfred tells me you'd like to find out more about what we're doing. Is that true?"

"I don't know. I don't have a clue what is going on at the moment and I suppose I ought to find out a bit more."

"I can understand that," Velasquez t-said. "You see, the point is, Emma, that I don't think you understand as clearly as you might – and might I say, it's not your fault, because it is opaque – what the situation is. And also there is a deliberateness behind the obfuscation and falsities."

"Isn't that rather patronising?" Bartel t-asked. So it wasn't just Pennington who was patronising her wittingly or unwittingly.

"I didn't mean it to be," Velasquez t-replied. "It's just that I know you are nervous of talking to me openly – or to Wilfred for that matter."

"Of course I am." Bartel thought a bit and t-added: "I don't know what your aim is in talking to me – and whether it is a test of my suitability or something more sinister. And I do know that while there may be ways of blocking t-conversations, I would have thought that the very fact that there is a block would excite suspicion and make people – the Trills for example – really aware of what is going on. And you know that Andrew Pennington revealed to me that his – would you call it a group? – possess a thought blocker of some kind. It seems, if not dangerous, foolhardy. And I can't understand why you would bite the hand that does so much more than feed you. I mean – you are in the elite which is what I take ImCirc to be."

"You see," Velasquez t-said, "that is to misunderstand everything about this inner world, this world of TCentral."

"How?"

"Look, you are partly right to be concerned, I don't dispute that," Velasquez t-said. "And I'm sure that most people would be as concerned as you are."

"So are you saying that I don't misunderstand what's going on?"

"You do. For reasons that I think Wilfred will possibly explain in a little while, the Trills are totally committed to the rule of law. I know that they are the ones that make the laws, but they can only control or change those laws within the Guiding Principles. And you know what those Guiding Principles are – every school child is brought up on them.

"One of the Guiding Principles – the one signed up to and managed by all the GLEAKES – is total transparency. This isn't entirely relevant, but worth noting here that there is one proviso that is never mentioned. That one proviso is that, while it is acceptable for all information about the Trills to be available to anyone who has the insight to ask, the Trills actually want to ensure that as little information about the Trills is revealed as possible.

"But taking that proviso as read, what this means is that any group that is actively – or, I guess, passively – opposing the Trills has to be allowed to operate totally without let or hindrance. It might seem completely counter-intuitive because this means that in theory the Trills cannot stop any insurrection that goes against their control. In fact it plays exactly into their hands, because it means that nothing can surprise them and they can take steps to thwart any rebellion."

"But one of the Guiding Principles is that there should be no coercion," Bartel t-replied.

"As we will, I hope, show, there doesn't have to be coercion at all in any of the senses that most people would use," Dunster t-said. "But let Serena finish what she was saying."

"Ok."

"As I was saying, the Trills know that there is always and inevitably unease about the total control that they exercise." Velasquez stopped for

314

a moment and looked to see whether Bartel was taking this all in. "Every other autocracy or oligarchy in the history of the world has had to use a secret police force of some kind to enforce its rule. Thought conversations have eliminated that need – or at least the police aren't secret. So effectively nothing is secret. Yes – there are people who have found a way of blocking access to thoughts, but as you say, Emma, all that does is create suspicion and a bigger focus on whoever is blocking their thoughts. I can also tell you, that nothing that's been invented so far is that successful – although the Trills would not like that piece of information to get out."

"So it's a benevolent – totally benevolent – society that they've created and one that can encompass the opposition to it?" Bartel felt confused. If rebellion was openly allowed, it almost made a mockery of rebellion.

"Not really," Velasquez t-replied. "As you know, there are people who don't believe that it is benevolent. Your Andrew Pennington is one. But you won't listen to him."

"Of course not," Bartel t-replied, rather testily. "Andrew is purely negative about all that we have in the neo-age."

"That's not true," Dunster t-responded. "He does understand what the Trills have done and what is good about it. And he has talked to you about it in those terms."

"So what's his problem?" Velasquez really did know the entirety of the conversations between her and Pennington – or this is how it now appeared.

"From what we understand," Velasquez t-said, "and we do understand a lot, he has two or three issues with the neo-age. On the one hand, he sees that there are all sorts of benefits and it does allow humanity to bring out the best in themselves. And the propensity for evil in some people is effectively removed. No hunger, eradication of much of the violence in the world, control of disease and the opportunity to be yourself as yourself is great. Now, at the risk of repeating what we've already talked about and you know only too well, what Andrew sees is that we are now living in what he calls *amblytopia*. It's grey. It's unfulfilling. It's making the world stagnate. Yes – no-one has to work in the sense that they have to do something that takes away their time and independence and creates pressures on them. There are roles and in that sense jobs – but they are only done by people who actively – really actively – want to take on such a role. It's a society where anyone can do nothing or do more and take an active role. Like you do, Emma. But it's also a world where there is no progress or any kind – no greater understanding of what it is to be human."

It was interesting – if not significant – that Pennington professed to not knowing Velasquez but here Velasquez was only too clearly showing that she knew him. Or perhaps, Bartel reasoned with herself, this wasn't so much of a contradiction. Perfectly possible for Velasquez to know about Pennington without him necessarily knowing about Velasquez. On the other hand it was at best unlikely. Bartel let the idea sink to the back of her mind as she couldn't get to the truth.

"That's just not true no matter how many times you or Andrew repeats the statement. There is human progress," Bartel t-responded. This was making her annoyed. "I think I've learned a lot about myself from what I do. I wouldn't have been able to do most of the things I've accomplished without the structure of the neo-age."

"But where has that got you, Emma?" Velasquez t-questioned Bartel directly.

"It's got me here," Bartel t-replied.

"Ok," Velasquez t-said. "Let me finish what I was going to say about Andrew Pennington. It's not only that he feels that the whole essence of being human is being degraded into greyness, but that there are no checks and balances any more. If we accept, as many do, that the world is all the better for the Trills' neo-age, how fragile is this neo-age? No society has ever lasted as long as it could because the people in control always change into something else. The potential despot who comes to power to clean up corruption inevitably finds that corruption is a useful tool to stay in power. What's to say that the Trills – the current Trills that is – won't succumb to the same temptation. If this neo-age starts to crack as one – or even two – of them creates a putsch and imposes an entirely different age on the world, what then? There is absolutely nothing that can stop that happening."

"Nothing?"

"Nothing."

"Doesn't that prospect chill you, Emma?" Dunster t-asked.

"I'd never thought of any possibility like that – and if you say that they all respect the rule of law, it can't happen," Bartel t-replied.

"Think about it, Emma," Velasquez t-said, firmly. "Just think what they could do and what it would mean."

"So I have to make this neo-age unravel because there is a possibility of a non-benevolent TCentral?" Bartel t-said, rather scornfully.

"Well, that would be one reason," Dunster t-said. "And actually it would be a very strong reason in our view. But it is more than that. Just think what your life is like now, Emma. Think about it."

"In what way?"

"Think about sex, if you want. You called me over to have sex with you. I'm happy with that. So not a complaint. But it wasn't fulfilling for you or me really. Yes we both had orgasms. We both took great pleasure from it – and because of the neo-age, I don't have to imagine that was true for you too. I was with you mentally and physically. So I know about you and about myself come to that in a way that no generation before could know. But it was still just sex. An avoidance. And if you look seriously at your life and your sexual relationships much of it is an avoidance of dealing with yourself as yourself." Dunster stopped t-talking to see whether Bartel was responding. She was looking at him thoughtfully. "Shouldn't it be more than that?"

"Why?"

"I can't answer that for you, Emma," Dunster t-said. "But I know you know that that response isn't true to what you hold dear in your heart. Using sex to hide behind is self-defeating – and I know that you know that."

"You appear to know a lot." Bartel t-replied, but without certainty in her voice.

"Let's leave that for the moment. We can come back to it, if you want. Let's focus on the serious issues. There is one fundamental question that Andrew – and people like Andrew – ask and it's one that I think you should consider."

317

"It is?"

"What gives the current Trills the right to impose their ideas, their approach, on the whole world?" Dunster looked at Bartel and waited. Then he asked: "Is it right?"

"I don't know," Bartel t-replied. "But do I care?"

"Obviously not, Emma," Velasquez t-said, firmly and decisively. "But we do. And Andrew does. And we think you should."

"Isn't that coercion?"

"Not at all," Velasquez t-said. "We are just exposing you to ideas."

"But the neo-age is great for me," Bartel t-said. "I don't want to jeopardise that."

"Ok. We take that on board," Velasquez t-said. "As we said, or should have said, however, there is more to this."

"More?"

"Yes," Dunster t-said. "Much more – and we think this might help you understand why we think it important to talk to you."

"Even though," Bartel t-replied, "the Trills will have a record of this conversation and this will expose you to being removed from the world of TCentral?"

"It won't come to that," Velasquez t-said. "But if it does, then all that that would prove is that we are right to do what we're trying to do."

"So what is this *much more*?" Bartel t-asked, scathingly.

"Really it's the history of how we got here," Velasquez t-said. "Let Wilfred explain."

"I guess you remember the history you had during your education," Dunster t-said, and it wasn't a question. "All of what you were told is true or at least verifiable. It isn't however, the whole truth."

"How so?"

"Well for a start it left a lot of history out of our neo-age history, if that isn't too much of a contradiction," Dunster t-replied. "History in the neo-age starts with the establishment of the world of the Trills and the creation of TCentral. Yes – there are books around that are readily available that go into other subjects prior to TCentral – remember no censorship is permissible as long as it doesn't offend a reasonable person. But why would people read those books? Actually banning them would only make them more significant and encourage people to read them.

"So you can find out about the twentieth century, World Wars, feudalism, classical worlds – anything. You can even find out about the Trills' predecessors. Mere multi-billionaires before the first generation trillionaires. But few people do. And for good reason. Why would they bother? This world – this neo-age – is soporific and bland. No-one needs to find out about discomfort."

"So why should I?"

"Because," Velasquez t-replied, "it's necessary."

"Why?"

"To find out how we actually *are*, how being a human is important, how the struggle to get where we are is important, and because actually the Trills are ultimately not a force for good," Velasquez t-said.

"But you yourselves said that they have eliminated all sorts of evils and the world is being liberated not just from need but also from want," Bartel t-replied. She felt unaccountably angry and couldn't quite be clear to herself whether she was angry with Dunster and Velasquez or perhaps herself.

"But at what cost?" Dunster replied.

"No cost," Bartel t-said, firmly.

"Loss of autonomy, loss of power, loss of the ability to control what goes on in our societies," Velasquez t-said.

"Loss of purpose and even self-respect," Dunster t-added.

"How?" Bartel was still baffled why they were making such a song and dance about all of this.

"Let me go back to the history I was talking about," Dunster t-said. "Before the Trills and the generation of Trills that they usurped and the multi-billionaires before them that they had usurped, were the original billionaires. They were never called *Bills* – that's an anachronism that was only applied to the second generation of billionaires – but they were powerful."

"I know all of that," Bartel t-said. "And they were multi-billionaires too. So there's nothing new – just a difference in scale."

"Not quite and in other ways not true at all," Velasquez t-said. "Let Wilfred go on – and then you can question what we're suggesting from a bit more knowledge. Sorry – I didn't mean to make that sound patronising. You might imagine it's difficult to say all this without being patronising. But I don't mean to be. I respect you deeply. Dread-Demotic is an amazing conceptual leap. But just listen."

"If that's ok, I'll carry on," Dunster t-said. "Those first generation multi-billionaires – because you're right, even the original billionaires had hundreds of billions although we tend to distinguish them from the next generation of billionaires – were a real mixture. Some were pretty benign. Good works focused on poorer people – new medical treatments, new vaccines. Some were downright narcissists – so pretty much a cross-section of any group of people. But let's focus on those – shall I call them *first generation multi-billionaires*? – them, at least. Since it had been so easy for them to get their wealth, they were quite a paranoid lot – believing that they could so easily lose it. I'm not talking about the Russian oligarchs who certainly could. I'm talking about the run of the mill – if that's a phrase I can use – multi-billionaires. They felt that if people throughout the world knew what they did with their money – and then began to suspect that all that money gave them power – then they would face a real reaction and perhaps their ability to evade tax would be curtailed and they would no longer have the influence and power they thought they needed.

"So they bought politicians, the media, journalists, and started their own hidden strategies. I say *strategies* because while there was some co-ordination between them, mostly it was each individual multi-billionaire seeking to protect their own position and if that incidentally protected their peer group, that was a bonus. And when I say *bought* the media – I don't mean they bribed the media, in the same way that they bribed willing politicians. I mean they bought the media outlets – broadcasting, newspapers – and there was a sophisticated method of distributing physical papers in those days – and also what was then known as *social media*. They didn't buy those outlets for any other reason than to protect their wealth and power from scrutiny.

"They had a series of strategies, as I said, but the main element was division and divisiveness – getting everyone outside their circle, and outside the people they were bribing, to focus on hating any other group that was handy. You may know that back then sexual preferences, race, gender and even things like abortion could be used to create division between people who actually had more to gain in being on the same side than in being split into factions. They also used conspiracy theories – so-called stolen elections, malign creators of vaccines, immigrants taking over – very effectively and every society was riven with division. To add insult to injury – at least in my view – they called themselves *populists*. They weren't necessarily popular but they employed division and hate very effectively.

"Look – I'm not entirely ignorant," Bartel t-replied. "I know a lot of this. And that's why the neo-age is so different."

"Is it?" Dunster t-asked. "All right. Say it is. But listen to me or let me continue what I was going to say. There's a social history concept called the *Overton Window*."

"I've heard of that," Bartel t-said. "It's what is socially or politically acceptable to talk about and how it is politically and socially acceptable to talk about things."

"That's right," Dunster t-replied, then continued: "They shifted this further and further away from the personal interests of the people – you know the people outside the bribes of the multi-billionaires. That started in the later twentieth century when the people who were enriching themselves and wanted to hide their corruption, created the first scapegoats and the first divisive issues – ethnic groups. The first – but not the only ones – were the Jews, but the multi-billionaires were inventive and widened their scope of scapegoats to include immigrants, people on what they called benefits, foreigners, foreign governments, vaccines, climate disaster deniers. It didn't matter which group they selected, they just both vilified them and made them into threats. You might think it paradoxical that people with nothing – asylum seekers for example – were characterised as both without anything and liable to take everything away from their target audience and actually a powerful threat, but that was how they used what one twentieth century writer called *doublethink*. Doublethink where you convince people to hold two totally opposed ideas in their head at one time as if they made a coherent whole. And if all else failed, one of the populists' favourites was to exploit a war, which is the time honoured way of deflecting people from their own true interests."

"And this was to fly in the face of the experience in the mid-twentieth," Velasquez t-added. "After that Second World War, particularly in the US, the ruling class were frightened to death of socialism or communism and their response was double edged. I think it's still part of the curriculum in schools' history to concentrate on the witch hunts against communists but the much more subtle and effective way that the ruling class dealt with the threat of losing all their wealth and power was to buy the working class off. In Europe they created the welfare state – socialised medicine in all sorts of forms, for example. In the US, they bought off the working class with consumerism – the idea that each successive generation under capitalism would be better off and indeed there was a transfer of wealth from the richest to the poorer – so dividends for example were held back and relative wage growth was encouraged. They realised that while this might mean they weren't as powerful and rich as they might be, they could still have more wealth and power than any other group. And before you ask, it wasn't a conspiracy in the normal sense. They didn't have to agree this with anyone else. Collectively as a class they saw that this worked."

"And the result?" Dunster t-said, "There was an equilibrium. No rich people suffered – punitive rates of tax were apparently there for some, but the tax rates were evaded – or perhaps avoided. It required restraint by the richer people – but the benefits were that they could enjoy their riches without interference as increasing prosperity for everyone – a trickle up economy if you like – meant that some were even predicting the end of history. Funny how they adopted the Marxist view of history that it was a history of class warfare in order to thwart what they characterised as a Marxist threat.

"Then the more ruthless of the rich, now secure in their wealth and power and their ownership of ideas, decided that it was not going to change anything if they grabbed more power and money – and they did. Since they now controlled politicians, whom they bribed relentlessly, and the media – they were the media – they could create illusions of threats to each less powerful and less rich group, and they did.

"Effectively, having derided the idea of class war if it meant the working class threatened the rich, they declared class war on any minority – and their control was absolute. You know the saying *absolute power corrupts absolutely*, and this is what happened. People noticed but gaslighting – telling people that something insignificant was the problem while hiding the real issues – and deflection was brought to a perfection."

"Actually I do understand all of that – not in any detail but it was always part of our understanding," Bartel t-said. "So what are you trying to tell me?"

"Give me a little leeway here," Dunster t-said.

"Yes – this is too important to let it slip by – unless you've actually no interest, Emma," Velasquez t-said. "If this is totally of no consequence to you – tell us now."

"No," Bartel t-said. "I can see that it's very important to you. I don't think you will change my mind – but let's see."

"Ok," Dunster t-said. "Thank you. So you know about the riots and social unrest and violence that was created as people started to realise that the ruling class had changed from that sort of paternalistic, apparently compassionate lot, to a self-seeking and vicious class. That was really quite traumatic – and at the same time you had the climate catastrophe apparently happening."

"Ok, again," Bartel t-said. "But where is this getting us?"

"Against that sort of macro-economic and macro-political world, you had the first real multi-billionaires," Velasquez t-added. "In large part they funded all of this deflection and gaslighting – but appeared to be standing above the political fray. Of course they had bought the media and the political parties and in terms of being taxed were absolutely stateless, and were able to ensure that the Overton window preserved their position, wealth and power, and at the same time they bribed the politicians as secretly as they could. The open bribes were called *donations* – but that's another matter."

"And why did that become a problem?"

"The first generation multi-billionaires effectively could and did control governments," Dunster t-replied. "This meant that they could then alter the whole basis of society – which they did. Their response to social unrest and potential revolution was the opposite of what had happened after the Second World War when they bought off the working class with a so-called welfare state or with a better standard of living. Now they openly espoused falling living standards for everyone outside their circle. One prescient commentator called it sado-populism which they could get away with by saying that although your standard of living is getting lower, you have to realise there is only a limited amount of money, and we will ensure that you are better off than this other group over here who are really going to suffer. And they cracked down. Protest was essentially banned. As they had taken over the media – although completely below the radar and underneath most people's consciousness, as for example the BBC, where the government completely changed the governance and appointed its own loyalists and directed it – all understanding of what was going on was controlled."

"Not entirely true, from what I understood in school," Bartel t-replied. "People had what they called social media which was like the *samizdat* in Soviet Russia. They used that to undermine the control that the multi-billionaires had on the mainstream media."

"But the first generation multi-billionaires either owned or bought the social media giants and controlled them and in the name of free speech – I kid you not – managed to ban most of the protests – and more importantly, news of the protests," Dunster t-said. He was very unemotional and straightforward, which Bartel found strangely unnerving, because what he was saying was clearly very important to him. "So repression was the response – disguised as *stability* and *responsibility*. At the same time, they completely undermined the welfare state – not by abolishing it but by making it irrelevant. I doubt you know, for example, what happened to the National Health Service."

"I don't. I know it fell into disuse," Bartel t-replied.

"Exactly," Dunster t-said. "It was too popular and couldn't be attacked head on, so what they did was just underfund it slowly at first and then at increasing speed. It had the advantage that they could take over parts of it and make money from it, but provide the worst possible service – and then they claimed that it was just not working, far too expensive to put it right, and it had to be replaced. They did this same trick time and again with the result that the few remaining elements of the welfare society – which they renamed *benefits* to make sure that they were seen as inessential and likely to go to the wrong sort of people – were destroyed."

"Ok – but we know that the overall result wasn't successful. Why not?" Bartel t-added.

"In the short term it was," Dunster t-said. "The first generation multi-billionaires began the process of usurping national governments by using so-called *investment zones*, which were completely independent of any particular national government and set their own legislation, people's rights, taxation, social benefits and law. One of the things in their way was supra-national organisations like the European Union – so that was one of their first targets and they successfully undermined it."

"I think you are extrapolating too much because they weren't a conspiracy – they weren't acting in cahoots. I mean you've already admitted that," Bartel t-said this quite defiantly.

"It didn't need to be a conspiracy," Velasquez t-said. Velasquez's role wasn't clear to Bartel but she seemed now much more than an interested observer or and really was part of something and was somewhat of a driver of this action. "They just recognised and shielded their own personal interests – particularly low, if not non-existent, taxes on themselves, a shrivelled state, toothless protest, laws that allowed them to do anything."

"But you said," Bartel t-interjected, "that – actually you didn't. I mean, we know that they weren't successful but the way you are painting them means that they would be impervious to any threats. What happened?"

"The first generation multi-billionaires were overtaken by the second generation," Dunster

"But I can't see how that could have happened," Bartel t-replied. "They had everything sewn up. It was self-protecting as protest was banned effectively, and no matter what people did, they couldn't get into a position of power to stop them. So what happened?"

"It was called something else originally," Dunster t-said, "and remember that this is my interpretation – which is shared by some of us – but effectively it was *transparency*."

"What was it called originally?"

"Lots of things but do you know the word *blockchain?*"

"No."

"Well – it was a new technology that meant that nothing could be hidden any more," Dunster t-said, very firmly. He clearly didn't want to be challenged on this. "You may recall from school that all financial systems depend on confidence. You remember paper money from your history lessons at school? Obviously a major advance for most societies but it had no intrinsic value and depended upon confidence that it would be accepted as having a value of some kind. Which is why financial systems in the twentieth and early twenty first went through cycles of boom and bust. Clever people could exploit what is essentially gullibility or false confidence and the banks, stuffed full of clever people, developed many different ways of effectively defrauding everyone else. There was a huge financial crash in 2008 . . . "

"I remember that from school," Bartel t-said.

"And that was caused by those clever people manipulating what they called *financial instruments* for their own gain, and when any confidence in these fiendishly clever tricks evaporated, as it was bound to do, the whole system nearly completely crashed." Dunster paused to see whether Bartel was still interested and she nodded, which said she was at least tolerating him.

"That wasn't the real problem of course," Dunster t-said. "The real problem was that the clever people – effectively gangsters in our way of looking at them – didn't suffer at all. Nation states bailed out the banks, none of the gangsters in the banks suffered at all, none of the billionaires suffered any sort of set back, and societies across the world needed to re-create the financial system and create confidence, which they did by making middle income and lower income people in their own countries pay for the massive frauds. The second element was accomplished by exporting most of the pain to what they called the developing countries.

"Having managed this little trick with apparently no issues, the clever people running all of this, then realised that there was no way they could be held accountable for whatever they did – and so it became open season for them and they bribed governments across the world to allow them to carry on without any restraint – and if there were any restraints created, they just circumvented them, and there was no-one to stop them."

"That's not how it's taught in schools," Bartel t-said.

"No, it isn't," Velasquez t-said. "But let's keep going."

"So the first generation multi-billionaires saw all this, and looked set to do whatever they wanted. Now let me get back to the thread of my argument. You see at the same time as they had manipulated themselves into wealth and power beyond measure, and bought off the bankers and politicians with bribes, the first generation multi-billionaires had really destroyed any possible national or even international response to, and regulation or control of, any new technology or threat to themselves.

"Clearly in these terms, block chain wasn't so much a technology as an enabler of the second generation multi-billionaires. The first generation multi-billionaires had pretty much destroyed nation states in their programmes of removing any control on their actions and wealth and power, effectively making sure they paid nominal tax personally and corporately, and they had completely destroyed the relevance of supra-national organisations like the United Nations or even the smaller ones like the European Union.

"The result was, ironically enough, that they had sown the seeds of their own destruction. As a result of their manipulation of the way finance and society worked, there was no-one and nothing to stand in the way of the second generation multi-billionaires who completely wiped out the global financial system and fiat currencies. You don't need to understand the ins and outs of all of this – and in particular you don't have to understand the invention of what were called *non-fungible tokens* – all you have to know is that finance, business and any commercial interactions were superseded by this transparency – everything was out in the open.

"The first generation multi-billionaires just didn't have any tools to resist what was happening even though they completely controlled all social media and publishing, and they were effectively usurped by the second generation multi-billionaires, and consigned to history."

"So that was better for people?" Bartel didn't quite know where this was going.

"Not at all," Dunster t-said. "The first generation multi-billionaires simply were replaced by the second generation multi-billionaires who had learnt repression, mind control, and totalitarianism from the first generation multi-billionaires. At first they could portray themselves as saviours to ordinary people by managing to get rid of any of the existing multi-billionaires who were a threat to themselves and at the same time portray the previous multi-billionaires as vultures – and then, since they now controlled thoughts, ideas and concepts, it looked like a complete victory for them."

"So what happened?" Bartel was a bit impatient and felt she was being patronised, but there was obviously a thread here that Dunster and Velasquez were totally committed to.

"What had been created was completely unstable," Velasquez t-said. "It was partly because they had taken over a world which had no way of regulating or controlling them. So the seeds of their own destruction were sown by the very means they had exploited to gain their positions. It could be seen, as I mentioned, as a delicious irony."

"But surely that meant that they had carte blanche to do anything they wanted," Bartel t-insisted. "They were effectively impregnable."

"That's a good point, but let me finish this line of thought and I'll come back to that," Velasquez t-said. "It was partly because this new world was based on complete transparency."

"But those two things are mutually incompatible," Bartel t-said, working it out for herself. "Complete transparency and dictatorships –

or, I suppose, oligarchies – which both rely on secrecy, repression and lies, must be in conflict."

"Exactly," Velasquez t-said. "But it was more than that."

"Well, one thing," Dunster t-interjected, "was that there was a global crisis developing."

"War or wars?" Bartel t-asked.

"Wars certainly," Dunster t-said. "But not the wars themselves but the cause of the wars."

"Which was?" Bartel t-asked.

"The climate crisis," Velasquez t-said. "Both generations were effectively climate crisis deniers. They more or less said it was just *weather* and nothing to do with human actions."

"You can imagine that with more and more extreme weather battering societies there would be unrest," Velasquez t-said. "It didn't matter at first because the people suffering were generally in poorer countries and while it caused inconvenience and shocks of some sort to the richer countries, there was no way that this would affect the power and control of the second generation multi-billionaires. So they didn't just ignore it – and state that it was nothing to do with what humans were doing – but they became more and more repressive. They'd forgotten that repression solves things in the short term but not in any longer term. The very lesson the rich had learnt during and after the Second World War when they bought off poorer people with things like the welfare state, socialised medicine and higher wages was forgotten. You can see the way this argument is building?

"And the thing about repression is that it has to become more and more repressive, to the point where the threat of being killed in a demonstration or revolution has to be weighed up against the certainty that you are going to die from starvation or lack of water." Velasquez paused, then t-added: "And that's where the people who became the Trills saw their chance. They realised that what had effectively become fascist states – although they still called themselves democracies – coupled with the climate crisis, and the underlying contradiction to what the second generation multi-billionaires were doing that was *transparency*, meant that there was an opportunity – and a necessity even – to overthrow the second generation multi-billionaires before they destroyed all human life."

"So did they form a group and a conspiracy or plot?" Bartel t-asked.

"No," Dunster t-said. "Didn't need to. Not at first. What they needed to do was understand the ways in which they could use the transparency of the new age to completely undermine the second generation multi-billionaires, who were called Bills. At first it was a term of abuse invented by the people opposed to them, but they turned the tables on them and adopted the word as a badge of honour.

"If you think back to what was called *capitalism* – it relied on secrecy – insider knowledge and manipulation of anything that might have a value. At the same time, it also depended on controlling information so that people were misled into believing that their interests were threatened by another person or group. One view – from what were called *socialists* – was that the rich and powerful were the enemy. So what the rich and powerful did was to contradict this and suggest that it was another group of poorer people who were the enemy – the standard fascist approach. What we've already discussed. Identify a scapegoat, whether that was Jews – particularly successful early on – refugees and asylum seekers, black, brown or white people depending upon the ethnicity of the people doing the controlling, religious groups, people with a different sexual orientation, or people who had different views even on social issues like abortion. The rich and powerful were brilliantly successful at this."

"So this was the sado-populism you mentioned earlier?" Bartel t-asked.

"A really clever form of populism," Dunster t-said. "You might have thought that *populism* would rely on being popular – giving people benefits. And it certainly did have that quality post Second World War. That promise that things were going to get better. *You've never had it so good* had the underlying message that things were like that and were going to get better. The trick that the first – and second – generation multi-billionaires pulled off was to make people pleased with being worse off and with the prospect of being worse off."

"How on earth?" Bartel t-asked.

"By saying, as I've already said – supported by the mass media and the governments that the rich and powerful bought and bribed – that yes, you will be worse off, but if you stick with us, you won't be as badly off as those people over there," Dunster t-said. "Quite a trick."

"So what happened?"

"You know that," Velasquez t-said. "The riots and repression of the later 2020s and the early 2030s."

"And that escalated so much globally that the second generation multi-billionaires were forced to use more and more violence till it got to the point that we were looking at global melt down – and potentially nuclear war as the various power groups tried to work out how to stay in power."

"And then?" Bartel t-asked.

"You know what happened," Velasquez t-said. "Because of the total transparency that the second generation multi-billionaires had used to gain power, everyone could see what economic trades were going on, and the people who became the first generation Trills identified how to use that transparency to expose the evil of those two generations of multi-billionaires, and develop a way of doing business that guaranteed them total control of the money in the world."

"That sounds very far-fetched," Bartel t-said. She was actually getting impatient. "How could they do that?"

"Not as a coherent group at first," Dunster t-said. "Remember each of the potential Trills had developed significant ideas and technologies, some of them piggy-backing on what the previous generations of multi-billionaires had created, and mostly creating new ways of thinking. The one key concept the first generation Trills had individually was actually rather different – it was stability. The chaos caused by repression and civil unrest had completely removed any of the veneer of decency and benignity that the propaganda had created, and the appeal of stability was so overwhelming that the second generation multi-billionaires were completely outflanked, ridiculed and actually made partly subject to the rule of law.

"So the potential Trills rethought everything – and looked at history and how successful the rich had been in the mid twentieth, in part by letting the population have a share – small but not miniscule – in part of the wealth. They understood that short term gain wasn't going to help them in the long run and that civil and global unrest was a threat to them. You may not have been taught that some of the first two generations of multi-billionaires were so worried by instability and wars – especially nuclear wars – that they started to develop plans so they could escape the Earth and colonise Mars. Sounds far-fetched but that's an indication of the fears and paranoia they had.

"So the potential Trills appealed to the global population with three promises. Stability was the first, and that was founded on universal benefits so that those people who were losing out to new technologies or newly effective technologies like AI, weren't ignored but looked after and given an adequate standard of living. Secondly they preached an ethical sort of gospel – renouncing the systematic use of lies and propaganda so that people could feel they had some reason to truest them. This culminated in the *Guiding Principles* – that everyone is now taught in school, although they weren't published till much later – by the second generation Trills. Their third action gained them credibility because they addressed the climate crisis and mitigated the effects on the populations that were suffering most. And since false science and lies were abandoned people began to have trust in this new world."

"So where's the problem?" Bartel t-asked. "I guess I didn't understand it even in the limited detail you've just explained, but none of what you said has surprised me."

"Just let me finish – not long now," Dunster t-pleaded. "These first issues were quite easily dealt with and then making the individual efforts a concerted effort led to the creation of TCentral. The second part of their overall strategy was ensuring succession for their families. Make no mistake, the Trills created dynasties. The names of the Trills haven't changed but the actual people bearing those names may or may not have. Then there was the issue of making this global – but because the two previous generations of multi-billionaires had more or less destroyed or made redundant nation states and supra-national organisations, that was easier than it might have seemed. These first Trills, remember, had more wealth amongst them, than any three national economies combined."

"There was one other element that needs to be added to this mixture, however," Velasquez t-added. "And this was crucial. Not so much for the first generation of Trills but for the ones who usurped that first generation – our current leaders of the GLEAKES. I know it's taught in school how artificial intelligence was coming to prominence in the first part of the twenty first, and that's one reason why the first generation of Trills had the technological advantage over the multi-billionaires. It's not that the multi-billionaires neglected AI – as it came to be called – because they realised that this was a major technological advance. What they didn't understand was how to use it to bolster their power. The first generation Trills used it adroitly – but also controlled it. They created laws to govern it. Crude laws admittedly – what the second generation Trills called making it *artificial ignorance* – but rules and procedures that effectively limited what artificial intelligence could do, basically to humans. So it sort of asimoved the development of AI. You understand that concept?"

"Yes – Asimov said that robots had to have what I suppose we'd call now Guiding Principles," Bartel t-replied. "We are all taught that."

"I know," Dunster t-interjected. "The point is that our current Trills – some with the same name as the first Trills – pushed that further and also created the rule that AI had to be used for the benefit of all – hence the development of gSynth, for example. Yes it transformed the position of Jerry Fernandes, but only after he had first created something of real value to the people of the world. They then created the neo-age."

"So," Velasquez t-said, "that's the history. And although this neo-age isn't in any sense totally coherent or *finished* as some people might say, it does provide the world that you have grown up in. It's changed hugely in your lifetime – but what the Trills insist is that there is no change – it is totally stable. And they've achieved that recognition even though the current Trills effectively usurped the first generation of Trills. Quite a trick."

"I can understand all of this – even though some of it is new to me," Bartel t-said, "but my point is that I just don't understand what the problem is."

"I know," Dunster t-said. "Nor do most people. And that's not surprising since the present Trills have created a completely hermetically sealed value system. Look, no one is arguing that they haven't done a lot of good and that as oligarchies go, this is and has been pretty benign. It is cradle to the grave total care, if you want. As we've agreed, they've eliminated much of the crime – financial, fiscal, social, sexual, violent – that has beset people in history because of the way that the individual is no longer able to exist in his or her own mind. There was a poet in the seventeenth century – he was born in the sixteenth as it happens, who was very aware of things and he wrote *No man is an* island. If it wasn't true then – it isn't at all true now.

"As we also agreed, hunger is a thing of the past for almost all the population of the world. Despotic governments were destroyed by the Trills easily enough since no-one could withstand their total control of money and resources throughout the world. The climate crisis was averted in large part – not totally – because the Trills were able to impose real actions and create the zero carbon world the early climate activists dreamed of. No-one is arguing that the so-called democracies, autocracies, despotisms and oligarchies that made up the patchwork of governments around the world would have been able to do that.

"So no-one is denying the benefits," Dunster t-said. "But it isn't the full story. It isn't scaremongering to suggest that we are already aware of the seeds that are being sown that will pose issues for the world and its people."

"And those are?" Bartel t-asked.

"Innumerable in some sense – but we don't need to identify them all here," Velasquez t-said, breaking her silence. "What we do have at the moment is the rule of law – it's a fundamental to the Trills that this should be seen to be there. And to be fair it usually is. It's just that it doesn't apply to the Trills."

"So the Guiding Principles don't mean anything?" Bartel t-asked.

"They do," Velasquez t-replied. "And you can actually pick up on any individual Trill and ask them to justify themselves against the Guiding Principles. But it isn't actually worth doing any of that as you get trapped into a sort of whirlpool of bureaucracy to take anything further. But that isn't the most important thing here. As you know, the Trills literally destroyed what vestiges of nation state governments there were because they, the Trills, existed in a parallel universe that they created which was untouched by those governments. The Trills are the global governing operation. That's why we still have democracies even if in name only, because the Trills are very happy for people to vote for whatever they like, since they know that they control what it is that people can like."

"But if they're benign, what's the problem?" Bartel t-asked. "And you've said that all the benefits have flowed from them usurping the second generation multi-billionaires and the first generation Trills."

"They're benign now," Dunster t-stated. "But for how long?"

"You've no evidence to suggest that they won't continue to be benign and working for the good of the whole planet," Bartel t-said. "After all, you said that they'd learnt that repression is ultimately a threat to their continued world domination. They've obviously learnt that lesson and taken it to heart. I can't see the problem."

"You could be right," Velasquez t-said. "But there is nothing in human history to suggest that your confidence is not misplaced. And that's where we come in."

"You see," Dunster t-added, "look at one of the developments that has helped make Dread-Demotic so successful."

"What's that?"

"The new ability to selectively wipe the memory of anyone that has experienced Dread-Demotic," Dunster t-said. "In the neotiquette team that has caused us enormous issues."

"Why in particular?" Bartel t-asked. "It may be a stupid question but it's the one question that occurs to me."

"We just have no idea how this facility might be used," Dunster t-replied. "Think how dangerous sswipe will be in the wrong hands – and the wrong hands might be the Trills."

"For example," Velasquez t-added, "you wouldn't even know that your memory has been selectively wiped."

"But if I don't know whether it has or hasn't been wiped and I can't remember anything that happened that they don't want me to remember, how would I know, and, more importantly, why would I care?"

"I can't answer that for you," Dunster t-said. "Just know we care. Remember this – while you can, and do forgive my little inappropriate joke – control of memory is really the most dangerous threat to us as humans, as people, as parents, children, lovers, as sports people, as anything."

"Look, Wilfred," Bartel t-said, "I know you are sincere about this. But you are not making me worried about the future – especially if I can't remember my past. It all seems fine to me."

"But let's look at something Wilfred t-said to you almost at the beginning of this," Velasquez t-said. "I saw you nod when he talked about the way you two had had sex. You know that it is usually far more fulfilling than any generation that has had sex before – because you are in tune with each other in a way not possible before. There's no way that you can be having a different sexual fantasy while you are making love nowadays without the other person knowing."

"That's a good thing, in my eyes," Bartel t-said firmly.

"Yes, it can be, I agree," Velasquez t-said. "On the other hand . . ."

"No I can't see an *on the other hand*," Bartel t-interjected, quickly.

"Oh, but there is," Velasquez t-said. "You may not recognise it, but according to the neotiquette team it has changed so much about our attitudes towards other people and about sex."

"How?" Bartel t-asked immediately.

"As a member of the team looking at this," Dunster t-said, "I can answer that. You need to think a little, Emma, about what effect it has had on you."

"I can answer that," Bartel t-said. "I know it's made me more honest with any partner – and more honest with myself."

"Yes," Dunster t-agreed. "I'm sure that's true. But see if you recognise this. What we've discovered is that it has, not completely but enough to be worrying, blunted any actual feelings about the other person. Not the physical feelings nor most of the mental feelings – for example sexual satisfaction. But what it has done is taken away that depth of empathy with the other person, as it's focused everything on the physical and the mental feelings of the individual who is having those feelings. Yes. You are more aware of the other person in one sense. But you are less *with* that other person. Do you think that is true?"

"Not really," Bartel t-said, very quickly. "Look, we all know that we can see what the other person is feeling and thinking absolutely clearly. That says you are off beam, Wilfred."

"I think you said that too quickly," Dunster t-said, gently. "Just give it another thought."

"How can I do that? I know what I feel and think," Bartel t-said, rather resentfully.

"All right, let me try a different perspective," Dunster t-tried. "Is that ok?"

"Sure."

"Think back to this morning," Dunster t-said. "Don't worry about Serena being here. You know that isn't important to any of us."

"Ok."

"Really see us now, lying in bed after we had made love," Dunster t-said.

"I felt great," Bartel t-said. For some reason she did feel embarrassed and answered rather more quickly than she wanted to.

"I know this is embarrassing you," Dunster t-said. "We both know that – and I think I'd know that even if I didn't have access to your thoughts at this moment. But take a bit more time. As it happens you were lying on top of me at the end."

"Yes," Bartel t-said, trying to suggest that she was over her embarrassment.

"And I asked you a question that is probably seldom asked these days," Dunster t-said.

"Yes," Bartel t-replied, "You asked me *how it was for me*."

"And you didn't find that strange?" Dunster t-asked.

"I did," Bartel t-said.

"So why do you think I asked it then?" Dunster t-asked.

"I didn't think about it," Bartel t-replied.

"Think about it now. Why did I ask you that?" Dunster was looking at her intently.

"I don't know," Bartel t-replied. "I was going to say I can't read your mind – but of course I could have done if I had wanted to."

"I asked you," Dunster t-said, "because we had been so intimate and so close – at least apparently – and we had done everything to make the other person enjoy, experience and lose themselves in sex, but I felt a million miles away from you."

"It was some classical poet though," Bartel t-said, not willing to think this through properly, "who said that all animals are sad after intercourse."

"True," Dunster t-said. "Ovid."

"I don't think it was – but I guess it doesn't matter," Bartel t-said. "It's what it means that is important."

"Yes – but it wasn't that," Dunster t-said. "I didn't feel sad because we had temporarily been so close and now we were separate. I felt sad because I didn't know you any better than before we had had sex. In fact it felt as though sex had pushed us apart."

"But that's normal," Bartel t-said. "At least in my experience."

"I think that's true, Emma," Dunster t-said. "That's my point. Have you never had sex – say with your husband – where it was more than that, where you didn't feel alienated after you had both had an orgasm but felt closer?"

"I don't think so – at least I can't remember that," Bartel t-said.

"If I can butt in here," Velasquez t-said. She wasn't really asking a question. "Let me tell you – and it's just my experience – I have felt closer, more at peace after intercourse, after other forms of intimacy too. But I believe – and believe this strongly – we have lost something really precious because your *normal*, Emma, is the normal now for nearly everyone."

"So you're basing your entire revolt on the idea that there used to be something different in sex and we've now lost it?" Bartel t-asked.

"No," Dunster t-said, rather wearily. "It was an example of what we're lost. And even if you can't think like that, and never had that experience, there are so many other ways that our humanity has been altered by this neo-age. But now we are facing an even bigger threat, one that your Andrew Pennington hadn't even thought of until recently because it didn't exist though it was obviously on the cards. This ability to wipe memory selectively from people. Doesn't that worry you?"

"Should it?"

"I think so," Dunster t-said.

Chapter 31

Velasquez had left for what she t-said was an important meeting, and Dunster said he could stay if she wanted, and Bartel had t-said she'd like him to. In a way that was a completely new experience for her, Bartel felt embarrassed and suddenly lonely. Bartel gathered her thoughts – not concentrating on the major issues that Dunster had brought up but thinking about their relationship.

"Can I ask you a question, Wilfred?" she eventually t-asked.

"Sure."

"How serious are you – no, I mean, how convinced that you are right about neo-age sex?" Bartel was still embarrassed in a way that she couldn't remember ever feeling before. And this was a tentative question at best.

"I can only say that all of our research in the neotiquette team has led to this conclusion." Dunster t-replied eventually. "You see this isn't something that we take for granted or just decide or interpret from our own experience. It's quite rigorous."

"Well," Bartel t-said, slowly, "it does chime with my experience – my total experience. My physical relationship with Andrew Pennington has sometimes gone beyond what you are suggesting – and I think that was because of socio and persono or at least massively helped by them, whereas you are suggesting that they get in the way of a truly personal experience."

"Get in the way of but don't eliminate," Dunster t-replied. "Where's this going, Emma?"

"I don't know," Bartel t-admitted. "I think you disturbed me and I have to work it through."

"Why does that make a difference?"

"It makes a difference to me." Bartel paused and looked at Dunster. Where was this going? A good question. "I guess that disturbed me."

"More than all the other stuff I talked about? More than amblytopia? If that is the case, I think I misjudged you, Emma."

"How?"

"I thought you could appreciate the larger picture and why there are some of us – only a few, I agree, but not insignificantly a few – who are so concerned and want to do something, almost anything, to change the situation, if we can."

"Don't misunderstand me, Wilfred," Bartel t-replied. "I think I can appreciate what you were saying even though I don't necessarily share your view of how dangerous this is. But first I have to understand – and by that I mean really feel – that what you are saying about personal relationships, about sex especially, is right. If I get to that understanding then there is a chance that I will appreciate more what you are saying and what you are trying to do."

"I understand," Dunster t-replied. "I didn't mean to patronise or rubbish you. It's just that I see everything now through the perspective of how do we defeat amblytopia and how do we wrest control and power from the Trills. One thing I didn't mention with Serena here is that I don't think the Trills are as stable as we might think. And, no, I don't have any grounds for saying that, except that tensions arise between them that I think are rather more than simple disagreements and are fundamental. And I worry about the idea that one or two of them could seize total control. Unlikely but possible,

"I suppose I've been thinking about this for so long, that's my priority, whereas it's new to you and of course you want to see it through the immediacy of your personal experience."

"That's not entirely fair," Bartel t-said. "You didn't overestimate me. It's not that any of the opposition to amblytopia as you call it is new to me. Remember Andrew Pennington. I am capable of taking on the bigger picture. But I was immediately conscious – and immediately embarrassed – by what you were saying about sex because that's what we had just been doing. I naturally thought you were providing a critique of how we had been."

"That hadn't occurred to me," Dunster t-said, thoughtfully. "I guess I get so used to thinking about these things in a sort of abstract, dehumanised – I mean depersonalised – way, that I don't immediately put it into a more interpersonal context. Can you tell me what disturbed you most, then – so perhaps I can understand more?"

"I'm not sure I can," Bartel t-said. "It's difficult. Up till you spoke about it, I had always assumed that post-socio and post-persono, all forms of intimacy were better – more complete."

"In many ways," Dunster t-replied very quickly, "that's right. But are you sure you're not focusing on a relatively minor area of this neo-age and extrapolating from it as though it is of major significance."

"If you remember, it wasn't me that used sex as the illustration. You – or Serena – brought it up."

"I guess it was me."

"And I have to say," Bartel t-stated firmly, "that I think this is important – and you, or Serena, chose this deliberately because it would speak loudly to me. And it did."

"Ok. I understand. But don't just reject what we've been saying about it – which is easy to do because we're proposing a perspective which is fundamentally against everything the weeds, the Trills and most people would say."

"I'm not doing that," Bartel t-said. "But let me think about it. I still think the benefits of the neo-age outweigh the disbenefits. And I think even you two admitted that. Because you are focused on what might happen – and I'm focused on the here and now."

"All I can say is just think about sswipe and think what that could do to all of us."

"Ok."

"And remember that I am thinking this through at the very cutting edge of our world because I have to think of all new developments in terms of neotiquette."

They sat together, just holding hands, and rather gently probing each other's thoughts, rather tentatively. There was a great deal that Dunster wanted to talk about – mainly how Bartel felt at this moment about Pennington and about Worrell – but he suppressed those thoughts to concentrate on what Bartel was concerned with.

Their intensity and reverie was disturbed by Velasquez returning from wherever looking rather ashen-faced.

"Problem?" Dunster t-asked.

"Yes."

"Can you share it?" Bartel t-asked.

"When I've processed it," Velasquez t-responded. "It's not what any of us had actually anticipated – so this makes it really difficult. What you saw yesterday in TCentral, Emma, was a precursor to something else. I can't quite get my head around it. It must have been brewing for a while – more than days, I think, more than weeks, perhaps more than months."

The three sat in thought silence waiting for Velasquez to gather her ideas. None of them was engaging with the others. Bartel's mind was racing as she knew Dunster's was. What had happened at TCentral that Velasquez was referring to? When it was taking place it hadn't seemed that out of the ordinary apparently to Velasquez, so was there some subtlety that Bartel was unaware of?

The minutes passed, and Bartel felt she ought to ask something or do something, but the thought silence and the actual silence was intimidating.

"Actually," Velasquez eventually t-said, "I'm not entirely sure that I can share anything with you. Let me think about it."

Dunster and Bartel sat still, not trying to engage or to say anything. Bartel felt – what did she feel? Concerned? Frightened? Something of both those feelings but also a sense of detachment – which was curious. Did it matter to her was her first thought? Something in the way Velasquez was stroking her own face almost obsessively made Bartel think that this was more significant than she might have imagined.

"Look," Velasquez eventually t-said, "I'm sorry to be so dramatic. It may be nothing or it may be something – I can't work it out."

"Take your time, Serena," Dunster t-said. "It sounds serious and worrying – but if you can't share that with us, that's fine."

"It's not really," Velasquez t-replied. "After all we are supposed to be transparent. Always transparent. Perhaps you can understand if I say that it's something that I both want Andrew Pennington to know about – and also I don't think I can let him know."

"Serious then?" Bartel t-said, and immediately realised it was such a limp thing to say.

"Very serious," Velasquez t-replied. "I don't know of anything that has happened in the last ten years that is as serious."

"Well," Dunster t-began, "if you can't tell us, I think it's very difficult because you've worried us and yet we have to respect your integrity and, at the same time, your position. But do give us some clues at the very least."

"If I do more than I've said already I might as well tell you everything," Velasquez t-said. "That's the issue I'm dealing with. I'm not sure it's fair to either of you in both your separate positions to say more – but I want to."

"Ok," Dunster t-said. Bartel didn't know what to do – but t-added her acquiescence.

"Good," Velasquez t-said. "That solves the issue of whether I can tell you or not. Best not, I think, and as you are agreeable to that, it's fine."

Bartel wondered what the fuss was about – and sat there thought silent and Dunster was the same.

"I've just had a further thought, unfortunately," Velasquez t-said after a minute of silence.

"And that is?" Dunster t-asked.

"This does actually concern you, Emma," Velasquez t-said. "It's not as straightforward as I thought."

"How can it concern me?" Bartel t-asked. "I have nothing to do with TCentral or any of the infighting – if that is what it is – between the Trills."

"As usual," Velasquez t-added, "it's not as simple as that. The point is that Dread-Demotic actually has been deployed using sswipe – as you know."

"And is that my problem?" Bartel t-asked.

"Yes," Velasquez t-answered. "It is. Do you remember what the dispute about sswipe was at TCentral?"

"It was about whether it was a danger to the Trills – and whether it should be restricted, or not even deployed," Bartel t-responded.

"Correct," Velasquez t-stated, firmly. "The point is that Latitude and Jessie Dressus are now using it and are deploying it more widely than we thought."

"Who is we?" Bartel t-asked.

"Elora, my boss, Jerry Fernandes and Alexandr," Velasquez t-replied.

"So that is Kalo, Gyro and Elura allied against Latitude," Dunster t-said quickly.

"Yes – and it is looking very difficult as it is a real threat to stability – and stability as you remember was the watchword and the slogan of the second generation Trills," Velasquez t-stated. "This is looking like some sort of existential crisis for the Trills and for TCentral."

"Aren't you over-exaggerating – it's surely not that bad, and people will come to their senses?" Dunster t-asked. Bartel felt too far out of it to think anything like that. But once Dunster had said it, it seemed a real possibility.

"I hope so," Velasquez t-said, quietly. "I don't think so. You saw the intransigence that Dressus was showing in TCentral, and I think she sees this as a major opportunity to gain absolute control of TCentral and the whole world."

"Would she really want that?" Bartel t-asked.

"I don't know," Velasquez t-replied. "If it is even a possibility it strikes at the heart of TCentral – and undermines everything that the GLEAKES have collectively done. If there is one person in total charge, then the dangers that I was warning you about come into even more sharp focus."

"So what do you think will happen – and what should we do?" Bartel t-asked. It was interesting that Dunster was very t-quiet and very reserved, just when she thought he might be questioning Velasquez more deeply.

"I've no idea," Velasquez t-said. "I think it might be worse than just a dispute over sswipe too."

"As I saw it," Bartel t-replied, "I thought you were suggesting that the dispute over sswipe would be catastrophic – at least for the Trills – and then perhaps the neo-age. So what could be worse?"

"As far as I am concerned – and remember that you know I am opposed to the Trills and to their control over all society – anything that threatens the stability which underlies their power is much more dangerous for us all," Velasquez t-said. "What we – people like Andrew and me in our separate ways – have argued for is a transition to a world where the ultra-rich and privileged have no more power than any other individual. I'm sorry – I am in a muddle at the moment, so I'm not thinking straight. I have to talk to Elora as soon as I can. I can't say it will be catastrophic – in fact I'm not saying that. What I meant to say is that the causes of the dispute between the Trills are far wider than just over sswipe. Although that is the trigger."

"I can see why you are in a muddle," Dunster t-said. "I'm not criticising – only is there anything we should do? Can we protect ourselves – to be brutally personal? This seems a significant moment. I wonder if we should get Emma out of here and back to her life. Would that be prudent?"

"I honestly don't know," Velasquez t-responded. "Let me think about it. Elora is trying to engage with me."

Velasquez blanked out Dunster and Bartel so they were left there rather puzzled but worried and Bartel felt excited, which surprised her. It was so interesting that just as she was at TCentral this should happen. In the midst of it all, Bartel had enough awareness to wonder how Velasquez was able to segment her thoughts so effectively that whatever was being t-said between Ghose and Velasquez was invisible to her, but at the same time she was aware of Velasquez's t-presence. It must be another of the options and capabilities that were available to ImCirc. She engaged Dunster: "Do you understand what's going on?"

"Not at all – but it is serious," Dunster t-replied, "though I doubt that I had to say that. There's a lot at stake, clearly."

"But where does that leave you and Serena and, for example, Andrew?"

"Your guess is as good as mine," Dunster r-responded. "Curious how our loyalties are being split by this. On the one hand we know we have to oppose the power that the Trills have over society and every single individual. On the other hand, the stability that they provide is also valuable."

"All this is making me think," Bartel t-said, falteringly. "I seem to have moved from suspicion about Serena's motives for talking to me as she did, to acceptance that she is at one with whatever Andrew's trying to do. And at the same time, I've accepted that you and Serena have the same programme. I'm not sure that I shouldn't be worried about that."

"Perfectly natural to be worried," Dunster t-agreed. "But actually it's almost a Pascalian wager. Do you know what that is?"

"Not a clue."

"Pascal said that even if it is, say, one hundred to one against the existence of God, then it's wise to bet on the existence of God – because you have one chance in a hundred of being right, whereas if you don't, you have a one hundred per cent chance of having nothing at the end of your life."

"So how is this a Pascalian wager?"

"It's simple," Dunster t-replied. "If we – Serena and I, as I can't speak for Andrew – are duplicitous, the worst that can happen is that you are tested, found wanting and removed from ImCirc. You've lost nothing of all that you had up until a few days ago. If on the other hand, Serena and I are genuine in our opposition to the power of the Trills and we are in any way successful, you will be aware of probably the most important movement that there can be in the neo-age. I take that as a real bonus."

"But I've already said," Bartel t-replied, "that I want nothing to do with what you – and, or Andrew – are plotting, if that is the right word."

"But you could change your mind, very easily, Emma."

"I don't think so," Bartel t-said, but she knew that she wasn't as sure of herself as she had thought she would be. This was a moment of real tension and perhaps she should try to be on the side of a better neo-age – if that is what Dunster was talking about.

"Good to see you're having some doubts at least."

"I didn't think that," Bartel t-replied, rather testily.

"That was my interpretation," Dunster t-replied.

They were both suddenly aware that Velasquez was trying to engage with them. Had she finished with Ghose?

"Here is a real quandary," Velasquez t-said to both.

"What is?" Bartel t-said.

"Something that I know that Wilfred was t-saying to you while I was engaged with Elora," Velasquez t-replied, rather enigmatically.

"And that is?" Bartel t-asked very quickly.

"Whether our opposition to the Trills is more important at this moment than the stability that existed before Jessie Dressus launched her attack," Velasquez t-said.

"Are you classing it as an attack?" Dunster t-said more quickly than Bartel could manage her thoughts.

"It's definitely that," Velasquez t-said. "Elora was laughing at me in one way."

"Why?" Bartel t-asked without much thought – and then realised that there might be good reason. And then she thought that this rather endorsed her understanding that Velasquez was genuine in her opposition, however weird that might be.

"She was laughing at me – and it was quite a bitter laugh – because she has obviously known of my opposition to TCentral and the neo-age," Velasquez t-began, "and she knows this is a real test of what I believe in."

"But why, knowing that you were opposed to what TCentral stood for – and, by extension, the power of the Trills – did she want you so close to her?" Bartel immediately t-asked.

"You've heard the expression, *keep your friends close and your enemies closer*, well, Elora both believed that and understood that I wasn't exactly a threat to her," Velasquez t-replied.

"Especially as Elora would know everything that Serena was doing, most of what she was thinking, and how limited her power was," Dunster t-said, very quickly. "And you have to understand that Serena is a late convert to what we have come to believe – if you can use the pronoun *we* for who we are, as we aren't that co-ordinated. So it was difficult, well, perhaps not difficult and more like inconvenient, for Elora to do anything else."

"I can't believe that," Bartel t-replied. "This sounds absolutely unbelievable."

"I can only tell you that in the neo-age, this is perfectly understandable," Velasquez t-stated. "And no – before you ask – I have never discussed this with Elora. But she knows that I understand how her organisation works and I truly understand rather better than she does how people are associated with her. Originally she was a details person, but over time she wanted different things and I suppose I became quite valuable to her. But we are talking about trivia compared with what is going on. I want to brief you about the current situation. I don't have to – but as you are here and are at the centre of the whole issue, I think it's only fair to tell you the current situation. And I have Elora's imprimatur to do that."

"But will knowing make us in any way vulnerable?" Dunster t-asked. That hadn't occurred to Bartel as a possibility.

"Yes," Velasquez t-said, "it might. But I don't think you should worry about that. If you become that vulnerable, then we are all in a different world altogether."

"Please can you explain, then?" Bartel t-asked. It was becoming more frightening by the minute.

"As you know," Velasquez t-said, "Latitude – under Jessie Dressus – has developed sswipe. At TCentral you witnessed that this was seen as a real threat to the neo-age, probably to TCentral and certainly to the current stability. Deployed in a ruthless way – or despotic might be a better word – sswipe could be the end of TCentral as who would know what anything was any more. If Dressus could sswipe memory from the Trills and from all the people in ImCirc then nothing we have could be guaranteed to be properly remembered or properly recorded and adhered to."

"I don't see that necessarily," Bartel t-replied, thoughtfully. "There must be documentation and a public record – or at least a record – which would be independent of any individual memory. So people could always refer back to that."

"You haven't remembered your history well enough," Velasquez t-said. It was actually chilling to see how calm and yet worried Velasquez was. "First – Dressus could control that record and that would probably be her first step in taking over TCentral and ImCirc. Secondly remember the gramscian underpinnings of the power of the GLEAKES. The Trills control all the weeds and therefore control the Overton window. If Dressus had all of that under her control, we know that people get to the point where they don't know what to believe and therefore think everything is a lie, including any historical records."

"Why is that something I've forgotten from history?" Bartel t-asked "I don't remember that it was anything that came up at any time."

"I'm just telling you that I'm sure it was taught," Velasquez t-said. "Perhaps I've got that wrong. You remember from the early years of this century – no, do you remember your arendtian quotations?"

"Which ones?" Bartel t-asked, puzzled still where this was going.

"One in particular. Not really what she said but what had been learnt. The thought where the powerful in the twenties and thirties had learnt from the mid-twentieth that lying was not employed to be believed, but to destroy any trust in whatever was said or written," Velasquez t-said. "It reached its peak in the twenties. And it worked. The powerful then became so powerful and so confident that they lied and lied and lied – were backed up by the equivalent of the weeds – and people didn't actually have to believe what was being said. In fact it was better if they didn't. And eventually it became impossible to believe anything that was being said – and so nobody believed anything was true and there were no such things as facts – and it became a post-truth society. A writer in the twentieth had said the ultimate point in hegemonic control was when an individual would be able to believe the exact opposite of what they actually knew and could verify with their eyes and ears.

"He was wrong eventually because the ultimate was ensuring that nothing was believed, there was never to be anything verifiable again and so trust was completely destroyed. It was only the riots in the late twenties and early thirties of the twenty first that changed that. As an aside it was typical that it was the French that forced that change. Philosophy became action. But what Dressus has now is the capability of repeating that experience and making sure that when memory is selectively erased, nobody believes any written record, any evidence or anything. That's what I meant when I said you'd forgotten history."

"I never saw it like that in my history lessons – it was more a sequence of dislocated facts and events," Bartel t-said. "You are putting together things that obviously I was taught, but which were never quite put together in this way. You are frightening me."

"I don't want to do that," Velasquez t-said firmly. "But I do want you to be realistic as we are having to be at this moment."

"But I never wanted anything that Andrew was talking about at any time," Bartel t-replied. "I loved the neo-age really. I was aware of irritations and limitations – but I have to say they didn't bother me. I thought that most people were actually living the good life."

"And you were right – as far as that went," Dunster t-interrupted. "The trouble was that people were like hens in a battery cage – if you remember what they were. They could know nothing of potential."

"But," Bartel t-interjected, "as we've already discussed almost ad infinitum, it was better than that – the neo-age was the best social system that had ever existed for the majority of people in the whole world."

"Let's not rehearse all of that," Velasquez t-said. "The point is that we are now facing a major crisis and I ought to brief you about that."

"Do. Just can you tell us what this action of Dressus is going to do?" Bartel t-asked.

"I've taken this from what Elora shared with me." Velasquez t-replied. "According to Elora, Dressus is out on her own and is aiming to secure total power to herself and Latitude. Remember this isn't about money and a bit about power, which is what the overthrow of the first generation Bills, the second generation Bills and the first generation Trills was all about. This is purely about power."

"So this is really serious?" Dunster t-asked. "I thought it had to be, but this could be the end of TCentral and the GLEAKES as we know them. And, I guess, what we think of as the neo-age."

"Yes," Velasquez t-said, quietly and firmly, "it is serious. Dressus is making a play for total power – and while you wouldn't have thought that possible, with the way she is going about it, Elora, at least is concerned she could succeed."

"So what is happening?" Bartel t-asked.

"I was going to explain a little – I don't know why I am getting side-tracked, but I guess it's the seriousness of the situation," Velasquez t-added. "Let me give just a bit of background and a bit of the thinking behind TCentral."

"Please do – although, of course, Wilfred won't need as much of that as I do," Bartel t-said.

"I'm not sure about that," Dunster t-said, quickly. "All of this is beyond our normal comprehension. As you might expect."

"The starting point is that Jessie Dressus has always been the most difficult of the GLEAKES' CEOs," Velasquez t-said. "She was one of the first – no, actually the first – of this generation of Trills and she rather feels as though she should be in charge of everything. She has never made a secret of that although she has always, up until now, acceded to whatever TCentral has decided. As far as Elora understands, the resolution that Emma saw passed at the latest meeting of TCentral, that there should be a report into the viability of removing sswipe from the social infrastructure of the neo-age, was the flash point for her. She could see that her one chance of becoming number one – if not the only one – in charge lay in being able to deploy sswipe pretty much wherever and whenever she wanted. She sees memory as the most important element in any individual's life and if she has control of how much memory is allowed, it would give her total power."

"Do you think her analysis is right, Serena?" Dunster t-asked. "It seems to me that she is over-valuing the difference that sswipe could make to any of us."

"My view is perhaps not as valuable as that of Elora's – backed up by what Jerry Fernandes, and Alexandr Dermatov believe," Velasquez t-replied. "Those three believe – at least from what Elora has told me – that sswipe is extremely dangerous."

"What does that mean?" Dunster t-asked.

"I guess the meaning is that it is dangerous relative to the current position," Velasquez t-said. "Do you remember from history how many people got wound up by what they called AI – artificial intelligence – and its dangers." Both nodded. "Well – this is at least as dangerous as that was perceived to be."

"But once it was surrounded by the appropriate safeguards, AI had nothing that was dangerous – even in the wrong hands," Dunster t-said.

"That *once* was pretty difficult to achieve," Velasquez t-said.

"Yes but even I know that most new paradigm shifts were identified as existentially dangerous when they were first thought of," Bartel t-responded.

"True," Velasquez t-said, "but that doesn't mean that people were wrong to be concerned about them. The point is that we now have a very new technology which, whether it turns out to be dangerous eventually or not, is perceived as a threat to everything. And we need to do something about it."

"So where do the other Trills sit in this at the moment?" Bartel t-asked.

"An interesting question," Velasquez t-responded. "As far as Elora knows, the other Trills are either unconcerned or not on her side. Her reading is that Sarah Trarieux, Sapiens, is aware of the danger but hasn't really come out on one side or the other. Derek Smith, Eclectic, is also neutral as far as we know but not willing to take on Dressus as he doesn't believe that sswipe is as big a danger as we do. Uhuru Sousousa, Ambience, is unconcerned."

"But they could be right," Dunster t-said.

"Yes," Velasquez t-said, "except that if you examine any of the possible outcomes from the use of sswipe within TCentral it is pretty clear that it could be devastating and certainly could mean the end of TCentral."

"As bad as that?" Bartel t-asked.

"At least Elora thinks so and I would tend to agree with her," Velasquez t-replied. "It's created a crisis that I've never seen before. The future of TCentral is at stake."

"But isn't that what you have been creating opposition to?" Bartel t-asked.

"Yes it is," Velasquez t-agreed. "I must say it is causing us – and whoever us is isn't that important – some difficult questions. On the one hand we want to remove the power of the Trills and create a more balanced and socially just society with real democratic controls. On the other hand, the stability that the neo-age represents is a positive and one that we are desperate – and I put it no lower than that – to preserve."

"I don't think you can do both," Bartel t-replied, thoughtfully.

"You may be right," Velasquez t-said. "But we have to try. Where are you in all this, Wilfred?"

"I'm really not sure yet," Dunster t-said. "I just keep thinking this is a major opportunity because if the Trills are divided amongst themselves, we have a chance – perhaps the only chance ever – of ending their total hegemony. But, as you say, Serena, at what cost?"

"But what is actually happening now?" Bartel t-asked. "It seems to me that if we can talk at length like this, it isn't much of a crisis."

"No – that would be wrong," Velasquez t-stated firmly. "But to answer your question, as far as I understand it from Elora, there is intense lobbying going on against Dressus – and the idea is to isolate her. In addition, the whole apparatus of TCentral is being brought to focus on what she's up to – and the idea is to get Trarieux to take this seriously, to make Smith aware of how dangerous sswipe is in our opinion and to convince Sousousa that this is a battle that must be won."

"Isn't Jessie Dressus intrinsically weak?" Bartel t-asked. "She won't be better off if she destroys TCentral and the stability that it has brought. So at that point, she has to back down?"

"That's not her calculation," Velasquez t-replied. "If Elora and Jerry and Alexandr try to move against her, then TCentral is probably going to be destroyed as a governing force – as all its internal logic around agreement and compromise is lost, and, in fact, her objective of being in total control becomes easier for her to achieve. I know it's a paradox, but to preserve the stability of the Trills and of TCentral is possibly to hasten the demise of the GLEAKES and TCentral. And it would make our struggle against the Trills that much harder."

"But," Dunster t-said, "Latitude is deeply dependent upon the other GLEAKES for its position, and its power. I know that Sofari is important as an experience engine, but it relies on so much from Sapiens for its artificial intelligence capabilities, from Ambience for its welfare and health systems, from Elura for its financial stability, Kalo for all the social and personal elements of our lives, from Gyro for its infrastructure and food, and from Eclectic, perhaps fundamentally, for all the raw materials. Without them, it is only an entertainment provider – isn't it?"

"That *only* is quite a word, Wilfred," Velasquez t-replied. "But you are right – the interdependency of the GLEAKES is important and a significant element in the creation and development of TCentral but the important thing to remember is that it is *inter*dependency – and what Latitude brings is an important social glue. And Dressus believes that she can outmanoeuvre the others and gain total control."

"But from what you say, she has no-one else on her side. Is she that powerful then?" Bartel t-asked.

"On the face of it - no," Velasquez t-stated. "But if you think of the delicate balance that I've been explaining or alluding to, she actually has a lot of power."

"So what will happen?" Bartel t-asked.

Chapter 32

Velasquez was again summoned elsewhere, and left with hardly a word, leaving Dunster and Bartel in a state of shock and some bewilderment.

Was the neo-age about to collapse or transition to something darker and sinister?

They v-talked about it as though they shouldn't use t-speech – and discovered they were whispering to each other.

"Can I let Andrew know?" Bartel v-asked.

"To be honest, I don't know the answer to that," Dunster v-replied. "I think you shouldn't because we don't know what it means. But I'm not the arbiter on this. If Serena were here it would be a good deal better for her to answer you."

"I don't know what to do in that case," Bartel v-replied. "I'll think about it. I suppose we don't know what this means and we'd just be alerting him to something that is at best vague in our minds and more alarming partly because we don't know what it means."

"Let me engage with some of my colleagues in the neotiquette team and see what they know," Dunster v-said.

Bartel was left in silence and found it strange that there was so much going on between Dunster and the team but that she could only guess what was being said. It took a while before Dunster had finished, and Bartel found herself becoming more and more anxious.

"And?" Bartel v-asked.

"Lots of confusion, I think," Dunster v-replied. "The first they knew about it was when thought shutters – that I don't think any of us actually knew existed although there were always rumours that they could be applied – came down and limited engagement between people. This was so unprecedented the team immediately started to be concerned. One additional worry, apparently, was that they couldn't get hold of me. I'm not sure exactly why they couldn't engage me. Perhaps it was down to the thought shutters.

"Anyway a bit later news started to trickle through – not on the weeds strangely enough, and there is so much that is strange at the moment – that there was a major crisis developing. At first none of them were aware what that might mean, but then confirmation came through that Jessie Dressus was making some sort of play for total control. You can imagine this caused a bit of – if I say consternation you will know I mean a lot more than that – concern, then, especially as some of the core elements of the neo-age, and I take neotiquette as not being totally core but one of the building blocks of the neo-age, are direct reports to TCentral and not to one of the individual Trills, although people like Elora take a much greater interest in what we do than some others.

"People immediately started to worry about their roles – which you might find difficult to understand. Nobody has to have a job or even take on a role, but being part of the apparatus of TCentral does give each of us who work in this central area quite a big status and a real feeling that we're doing something positive with our lives and our activities. So did we have a future? Especially as Dressus has always been seen as the one Trill who could be dangerous and unpleasant. At the very least she has a reputation for peremptory behaviour with people in her immediate circle – and that is unacceptable."

"And then what happened?" Bartel v-asked, getting impatient with Dunster's excursions into what Bartel saw as irrelevancies.

"Messages came through that . . . " Dunster was interrupted as two andros came into the room. "What do you want?" He v-asked.

"You are to come with us." The andros had stun weapons and menacingly pointed them at Dunster and Bartel.

Both were immediately in a state of shock – which precluded speaking – and they were motioned out of the room and into the hall where they were handcuffed. Nothing was said and they were guided out to a waiting autonom and locked in. The autonom immediately drove off and they were taken to a very large building some way off from TCentral.

Neither v-said or t-said anything.

They were guided through the entrance and deposited in a holding area of some kind. At last Dunster t-spoke: "I don't understand." Bartel felt it prudent to remain completely silent. But it had been comforting that Dunster had communicated to her.

Andros were everywhere – moving quickly and apparently purposefully but without any pattern or perceptible rationale for what they were doing.

Velasquez t-engaged them both. "Remain calm. No-one is sure what is happening. I'm with Elora and we are safe but Dressus is obviously well prepared and has subverted TCentral as far as we can see. She appears to have no allies amongst the other Trills and this is a pretty desperate throw of the dice for her. At the moment we are trying to engage with all the other Trills – starting with Jerry and Alexandr."

"So that is Kalo, Elura and Gyro working together?" Bartel t-asked.

"I can't say that it is as formal as that – not yet at least," Velasquez t-answered. "We're also trying hard to contact Sousousa, Trarieux and Smith. It's proving very difficult – and if you think of the power of sswipe, we probably don't have much of a window before selective memory wiping makes it difficult for everyone other than Dressus."

"What should we do?" Bartel t-asked – though she felt that she almost shouldn't interject anything. She knew so little and was so unaware of the internal politics, whatever she said would be useless. But the thoughts kept bubbling into her head.

"I'm trying to establish contact with Elora's teams – andros and liveware, as Dressus so nastily refers to human beings sometimes," Velasquez t-replied. "At no point should you show any resistance – at least not yet."

"Should I engage Andrew?" Bartel t-asked.

"Let me think about that," Velasquez t-responded. "Yes. I don't see why not. I think what we're witnessing is exactly the danger that Andrew and the rest of us have been concerned about – and warning about for quite some time. At the moment there are absolutely no reports of any of this on the weeds and while it won't shock him, it will galvanise him. I don't know what he'll do – and he probably doesn't have many options, but it will be good to get some information out there, especially if Dressus deploys sswipe and blocks t-conversations."

"Is she likely to do that?" Bartel t-asked.

"Almost definitely," Dunster t-replied, cutting through. "I think I need to make contact with the rest of the team. Are we under arrest do you think, Serena? I can't see any other way of describing being hauled off and handcuffed."

"I guess so," Velasquez t-replied. "I don't quite know what that means. I haven't yet been able to make contact with anyone else in your team – but do try yourself. I'm not sure how this works – and whether any form of the rule of law applies. Probably not, if I know Jessie Dressus."

"Ok," Dunster t-replied. "It's tricky then. Sorry – that's obviously an understatement. Are there any contingency plans for this sort of – what should I call it? – subversion?"

"Curiously enough in view of what we were trying to do, there were no plans of that kind," Velasquez t-said. "It was felt that the chances of anyone being successful against TCentral and the GLEAKES was so minimal that we – that is the Trills – didn't need any such plans. Ironically enough it was felt that there was no threat from amongst the Trills and, worse than that, to suspect any of the Trills was to show bad faith and indicate how that particular Trill, himself or herself, was thinking rather than a sensible precaution."

"So the Trills were laying themselves open to just such an approach to gaining all the power as Jessie Dressus was able to plan in secret?" Bartel was taken aback with what she was t-saying as she said it.

"True enough," Velasquez t-said. "So we're scrambling a bit now to regain some upper ground, but Dressus and Latitude have the upper hand."

"It just can't be this simple," Dunster t-said, in disbelief. "I mean – what on earth can Dressus achieve that she hasn't got already – and worse than that, how is it so easy for her to grab all the power levers?"

"Think of it this way – do you know how this society is actually managed?" Velasquez t-asked. "There are no manuals and no constitution. It was never felt amongst the Trills that they needed anything like that. The Guiding Principles were felt to be more than sufficient – and they always have been up till now. It was just felt to be too remote a fact that one of the Trills would try to overturn TCentral and the rules we work by – those same Guiding Principles."

"Pretty naïve, in my opinion and that's coming from me," Bartel t-said thoughtfully. "But what are you actually doing now, Serena?"

"Establishing the facts," Velasquez t-replied. "Trying to work out where the immediate danger is and seeing what mitigation or restoration we can achieve."

"One thing I have to ask, is why is Dressus allowing us to have this t-conversation?" Bartel was genuinely mystified. "It seems to me that if she had worked all this out in detail she would have been able to plan to stop any counter-moves."

"I suspect – and it is only that I suspect because I don't know – that she was triggered into taking this action somewhat earlier than she anticipated and hadn't got all the pieces in place," Velasquez t-said. "This looks cobbled together as much as planned – and I suspect that there were too many moving parts for her to be on top of everything. Just my surmise – but otherwise I can't imagine what this means."

"Is that because of what we saw at the TCentral meeting?" Bartel t-asked.

"I think so," Velasquez t-said. "We know that she was mightily put out by the restrictions that might have been put on her – and sswipe for that matter – and perhaps she felt she had to move quickly to avoid being outmanoeuvred."

"Sounds plausible," Dunster t-agreed. "But where does that leave us?"

"I think I must get back to Elora and work with her," Velasquez t-said. "I think you two ought to engage with Andrew and anyone else. Then your team, Wilfred. I know you can't organise anything – how could you – but try and keep an eye out for what is unfolding that is likely to make Dressus vulnerable."

"I do have one thought before you go, however," Bartel t-said. "Isn't this exactly what you and people like you, including Andrew, were looking and waiting for? The division between the Trills makes them vulnerable and now would be the ideal time to take over and remove the Trills from their omnipotent position, as they are undermining their own strength. Isn't that what you've been waiting for – perhaps even planning for?"

"It's an interesting dilemma, of course," Velasquez t-said. "Do we try to strike now – or do we support the other Trills against Dressus? I think the answer is obvious. We have to stand with the Trills against Dressus."

"That may solve the issue of Dressus, but it will inevitably strengthen the Trills who remain – if they beat Dressus," Bartel t-said. "Is that what you want?"

"What's the alternative?" Velasquez t-asked. "If we strike against the neo-age – which we would find difficult anyway – what happens if we win? The whole point of our opposition is not to destroy the positive elements in the neo-age but to make sure that we change the whole structure so that the insanely powerful cannot dictate what we think, what we do, and how we fulfil our lives. You have to remember that the term gramscian was originally – until the Trills made it into some sort of orthodoxy – a revolutionary ideology explaining how the rich and powerful in the twentieth controlled society while appearing to be democratic and neutral. We are working towards something valuable and, at heart, very human because it respects the individual."

"That's plainly daft," Bartel t-replied. "I know you are putting me in the dangerous position of being the radical against your cautious pragmatism, as you might call it – sort of reversing what things are really like comparing you two and me – but if you were serious about the enervating effects of the neo-age this is an ideal opportunity for you. I'm not saying you should, I'm only saying that if you are right in what you think – and I'm not saying you are or you aren't – then you should follow the real logic. You won't have a better chance."

"That's sort of academic at the moment," Dunster t-said, firmly and quietly. "The truth is that we are not ready to take any action as far as I know. How would we even attempt to take on the Trills divided or not?"

"I think that's been my point," Bartel t-said. "Aren't you just a sort of dilettante organisation – if you even are an organisation – without any capabilities and without a plan."

"That is actually unfair," Velasquez t-said. "It's true we aren't in any sense that you'd recognise an organisation. Just a moment, Elora is trying to engage."

Dunster and Bartel were left for a few minutes just looking at each other. Bartel felt very uncomfortable and was anxious about her position and what she was saying. Obviously things were better if the status quo were maintained – as much as possible – but then she caught herself. The indecision and apparent lack of any cohesion in Dunster and Velasquez's position made her feel that she had to do something – but that was the last thing she wanted.

"I'm going to engage Richard, while Serena is engaged with Elora," Bartel t-said.

"Can I engage with him too?" Dunster t-asked.

"Do you know him?"

"Well – no – but I've been on calls where he was involved, well, not so much involved as mentioned," Dunster t-replied.

"Let me start and then I'll call you in, if that's ok," Bartel t-said.

"Ok – while you're doing that I'll try to engage with any member of the neotiquette team."

She blocked Dunster and engaged Pennington who responded quickly.

"What's going on, Emma?"

"I'm not entirely sure," Bartel t-said. "I think there's a rather catastrophic breakdown within TCentral and it is really confused. What do you know?"

"I know very little," Pennington t-replied. "It seems there is a news blackout of some kind on the weeds so that there is a great deal of speculation. What do you know?"

"Not much more than you, I think. Perhaps a bit more. Jessie Dressus of Latitude has a serious dispute with Kalo, Elura and Gyro – over the deployment of a new, advanced memory technology."

"Is that sswipe?"

"You've heard of that?" Bartel t-asked.

"Yes – but I don't know what the flash point is."

"It's because it has this selective memory wipe, the other Trills – well at least Elora Ghose, Jerry Fernandes and Alexandr Dermatov – see this as a threat to their positions," Bartel t-said. "It's not certain yet that Ghose, Fernandes and Dermatov are ranged against Dressus – but that looks like the pattern that is emerging."

"What about Smith, Trarieux and Sousousa?"

"They were unconvinced when I saw them, or probably their holos, at TCentral whether there was a problem," Bartel t-said. "Don't know what's going on. Presumably Dressus is isolating each of the other Trills so that he can divide and rule – or at least eliminate them as threats one by one."

"Why do you think that?"

"I'm guessing," Bartel t-said. "It's pretty scary."

"What does that mean?"

"Wilfred Dunster and I were – I think the only word must be *arrested* – and brought somewhere – presumably a Latitude safe house or prison of some kind. It is pretty serious," Bartel t-said. "I didn't know whether to engage you but Serena Velasquez thought I should. She said we need to get the information out there."

"That's good," Pennington t-replied, thoughtfully. "Are you in danger?"

"I don't know," Bartel t-responded. "But Andrew you are missing the point."

"Which is?"

"Isn't this just what you've been talking to me – and trying to interest me in – for the last months – if not years? Isn't this your opportunity?"

"It is and it isn't," Pennington t-replied. "What I – and I can say *we* at this point – was worried about is precisely what would happen if a Dressus decided to make a power play of the type that I think is happening. Yes – we were worried that the world had become smaller and smaller around most people, by which I mean that the possibilities were becoming more and more confined for people to be themselves and for creativity. You know – what I call amblytopia. And I think that was – and is, I might stress – a real threat to humanity and humans. Perhaps as big a threat as the initial fumbling with AI was – artificial intelligence."

"I know that."

"Sorry – just used to thinking about this on my own," Pennington t-said. "So I felt that it was just dumbing down of the whole population for the benefit of a minority. A sort of repeat of the early twenty first when politics became so corrupt and everything was hidden behind slogans. But in another sense, this wasn't the biggest threat we faced, and we needed to do something about it."

"So what was the real threat – although it's strange you never mentioned it, as far as I can remember?"

"I did," Pennington t-stated, "but I guess that it got lost in the usual argument we had. Actually I don't think it ever was an argument between us because you just shut down about anything I said involving resistance to the Trills."

"Not entirely fair – but leave that. What is this threat?"

"Let me start with something else," Pennington t-said. "You know that we know virtually nothing about the Trills and TCentral and any of the political apparatus that is in place globally now."

"Not true," Bartel t-replied. "We know a lot about the individuals and their lives."

"We don't," Pennington t-said, firmly. "What we *know* is what we are allowed to read in the weeds and other media. It is all carefully homogenised and packaged – so we learn of minor spats between various Trills that amazingly enough get resolved amicably after a few episodes, just like a twentieth soap. We know about various relationships each of them have, and we learn about their achievements – and, occasionally, for some sort of sense of balance but to give them impression that the weeds are actually holding the Trills to account, we hear of failures or of real difficulties that one of the Trills has, although it's usually depersonalised and becomes a failure of one of the GLEAKES. So we know next to nothing about any of the developments that may or may not happen between the Trills who are supra-national and answerable, actually, to no-one. That may not be true – they are answerable to each other, I guess.

"What we were concerned about is what happens if one – or more – of the Trills decides that he or she wishes to take over completely and to ditch the whole of the neo-age? We just have no knowledge of their real personalities, their real political leanings and how authoritarian they are. I – and we for that matter – suspect that they are hugely authoritarian but have learnt from the late twentieth, the twenties and the thirties that this is a double-edged sword and what they have to do is control the political process like they did in the sixties, seventies, and eighties of the twentieth by apparently not being in control of the Overton window, but in fact directing it very precisely. That way they will win much more effectively than by repressing people. So they control everything in an apparently subtle way. But what happens if one or more of them decides to forget that lesson – and, for whatever reason, and it might be that absolute power corrupts absolutely as they used to say, they impose a draconian rule?"

"But you said the Trills have learnt that lesson so that's very unlikely," Bartel t-protested.

"People forget – and people take advantage of opportunities," Pennington t-said, bleakly. "And what I was worried about was exactly what you are suggesting Dressus is doing."

"But why would she think that she can upset the apple cart in this way and forget the bitter lessons of the twenties and thirties in the twenty first? She's not daft – obviously not."

"But what has happened is something that I tried to talk to you about," Pennington t-said. "You didn't want to hear any political analysis and I have to respect that. Especially since your whole education was around the concept that history is dead and that the world will just go on as it is now. I said to you that the neo-age is remarkably stable because most issues of supply and demand have been dealt with. We don't have hunger, we don't have homeless people – we don't have stress, we don't have pandemics and disease like we did, we don't have crime like we used to – and what crime we do have is immediately solved if it is in the best interests of the Trills to solve the case. But what can destabilise the neo-age is exactly what I predicted – a technological advance that is so fundamental it can destroy humanity – that is both people and our humanity.

"You probably weren't taught this, but like the black death destroyed feudalism and paved the way for capitalism in the fourteenth and fifteenth centuries, and AI almost finished off capitalism, not to say all humans, in the twenties and thirties, I was concerned that some probably unimaginable technological advance – and it would be technological because that is what drives and underpins the neo-age – would be the trigger to destroy the neo-age. The revolution devouring its children as it always does – or used to do." Pennington paused and Bartel could feel him fighting for ways to explain what was going on not only to Bartel but to himself as well.

"That sounds very bleak, Andrew."

"So sswipe – not just creating amnesia but being able to selectively wipe out all memory – may be just that technological advance that does this," Pennington t-said. "Do you see this, Emma?"

"I see what you are saying – and I see that this could be true," Bartel t-said. "But is sswipe so revolutionary that it has the power to trigger the death of the neo-age?"

"I think so," Pennington t-said. "And in the hands of an unscrupulous person it would definitely be my weapon of choice to create the platform for an authoritarian – I mean overtly authoritarian – regime. Because don't forget that the neo-age is already authoritarian but with some sensible checks that make it palatable to most people. Can you see why I was worried – and why the people in the group were worried?"

"I guess so," Bartel said. "And it is a group?"

"Not in the sense that you might associate with that word," Pennington t-said. "We're not terrorists or anarchists. We want proper scrutiny of the Trills – and we want proper responsibility in our political system. But we're very independent and, as I said, operate in cells and don't necessarily co-ordinate anything across the movement. At the moment could you tell me whether any of the Trills are decent people not corrupted by power? Is Dressus an anomaly or is this her real character? Who will win?"

"I have no idea and you know that being caught up in all this is complete anathema to me," Bartel t-replied, "which is one reason why I feel so concerned and so anxious – but also so disappointed in you."

"Why is that?"

"I think this is the opportunity that you have been waiting for," Bartel t-said. "With the Trills at each others' throats, you have an opportunity to take them on and remove all the opacity. Isn't that true?"

"You disappoint me, Emma," Pennington t-said. "We don't have a plan at this moment. We weren't anticipating this so quickly – clearly it's our fault and mistake – but that is true. So what do you think we should do now?"

"That's not for me to say," Bartel t-said. "I'm not a member of your group – whatever that is. I've stayed a long way away from it. But now I am seriously worried and apparently there is no way we can intervene and ensure that Dressus doesn't succeed in whatever she's trying to do."

"That's not true either," Pennington t-said. "There is always a way."

"But at the moment you are just going to support the neo-age – which you say is anti-human and an amblytopia – and hope that Dressus fails?"

"I don't know what else to do," Pennington t-said. "But feed any information you have to me as soon as you can, because this is a developing situation. I've just seen that one of the weeds is reporting a disturbance in TCentral – which must mean that information is getting out and this is serious. Stay in touch, Emma. Let me know anything and everything you can. I'm not doing nothing – but this isn't the moment for taking on the Trills in general."

With that, Pennington disengaged. And Bartel was left in an even more anxious state.

"Any good with Andrew Pennington?" Dunster t-asked, breaking into Bartel's thoughts.

"Yes and no," Bartel t-responded honestly. "On the one hand he sees the danger in what Dressus is doing. On the other he doesn't have any ideas about exploiting the situation to ensure that his group – as he has admitted it is – can take advantage of this moment. We'll see. Would you count yourself as part of his group – and or Serena? And what does that mean?"

"Nothing so formal," Dunster t-said. "I suppose I am what you'd call a sort of fellow traveller. I share the concerns and I do want to do something about it – and I am aware, not so much about Andrew but about the people who are associated with him, and I know it is a loose alliance. Actually I don't know that – I just assumed that was what it was, as there is never any hierarchy of organised responses as far as I am aware. Perhaps if Andrew calls it a group it is more defined than I thought.

"Serena, as strange as it may seem noting her closeness to Elora Ghose, is, as you know an activist – although, again, I'm not entirely sure what that means. Certainly we have talked about the issues together. Is it a group? I don't know. I doubt it. But I think you are being very purist about all of this. On the one hand it doesn't matter if it is a group or more formal than I think – it matters that there is a resistance to the Trills that the Trills know about and understand and I guess tolerate. Odd though that may seem, since any such grouping would be aiming to reduce the power of the Trills if not eliminate it completely, but I think the attitude of the Trills is that they would much rather it was completely out in the open rather than hidden. They are nothing if not sophisticated in the way they handle opposition – they learnt a lot from the oppression of the twenties and thirties as we've discussed. On the other hand, you cannot expect even the most tightly knit group – which I sincerely doubt this is – would be able to do too much to exploit any divisions between the Trills. I know you see it as a weakness and a capitulation to what the Trills do, but I don't think you understand just how powerful they are and what control the actually exercise. Don't judge either Serena or Andrew by an unrealistic yardstick is what I'm saying."

"Let's disagree about that – or let me think it through more seriously. What about your team – any joy?"

"The neotiquette team – which isn't my team by any stretch of the imagination but the team that I belong to – is pretty much under lock and key – well, as much as we are," Dunster t-said. "They don't know what is going on and are feeding on rumours."

"One thing I wanted to ask you was why the team exists at all," Bartel t-asked. "It seems to me this is an area that could easily be done in the normal way – by AI systems rather than using humans. Why did it come into being and why does it exist?"

"The answer is that there was always a team involved from the beginning of the neo-age proper," Dunster t-said. "Remember when t-comms were first invented the systems that could do what we do now weren't anywhere near as sophisticated. As I understand it, they were sophisticated enough by the mid-thirties, but no-one really trusted them to do this highly sensitive and highly human-oriented work. It was almost the last really defined work group. So it wasn't brought into being but lingered on – and then it was felt that giving it a human face – I know how ridiculous that sounds – was probably a good idea in order to keep public acceptance of the role – but more importantly the new etiquette rules – at a high level. We do rely heavily on systems of course – but our most important function is that we argue and always look for weaknesses in whatever is produced. And I also think that some of the Trills – and especially Elora, likes the idea of having a team around her of living beings. Pretty old-fashioned to say that – but there is a sense in which warm bodies – what I think some twentieths called *liveware* – are re-assuring."

"But if you think of how much has been taken away from any human interaction, it seems a little odd," Bartel t-said. Then she caught herself. "I'm sorry Wilfred. I think I'm trying to take my mind off what is happening – I know this is irrelevant and I know I don't need any sort of answers. I just suddenly feel very frightened."

"I do feel frightened too," Dunster t-admitted. "I've been trying not to show it – but I just don't think we know enough about Jessie Dressus or what's actually going on not to be really frightened – terrified, perhaps."

"Any ideas about what might happen?"

"I don't think I've a clue," Dunster t-said. "I wondered if I should keep putting on a brave face but I think it's best that we're realistic with each other. The team was at best jittery. They'd actually seen nothing but knew they were under – what's the word – outside control. The one thing I guess we should hold onto at this point is that I don't think we're under physical threat – and I don't think our lives are at risk."

"Why not?"

"I think – well, I've been trying to think this through – that at least in the short term Dressus needs to present this all as business as normal – even though everyone can imagine that it isn't. If you think that the major strength of the GLEAKES, the Trills and TCentral has been stability, emphasised by replacing all those early century riots and civil unrest, all those global war zones, with some form of peaceful co-existence after the threats of pestilence, nuclear war, and climate catastrophes, then Dressus will have to present what she's doing as continuity, absolutely continuing that stability otherwise whatever position she can create for herself will be continuously threatened."

"By whom?"

"By the other Trills of course," Dunster t-said, thinking this through as he was saying it, "and don't forget that however powerful and strong the Trills are together, once they are perceived as potentially at each other's throats, there are still deep rooted opponents to their regime who might be able to take advantage of instability."

"Do you mean Andrew and his grouping – and people like you?"

"No, I didn't. Essentially, as you have put your finger on it in no uncertain terms, Andrew and people like Serena – and possibly me, if you don't mind the self-aggrandisement, however limited it is – want to overthrow the Trills but do want to keep the positives of the neo-age. It's always been recognised by them, that is people like Serena and Andrew, that this is a difficult balancing act. Essentially they have no plan that they can put into place that has any chance of success at this point – you've seen that. And the Trills have known that, which is another reason why they have tolerated this overt opposition.

"But there must be organisations out there – despite all the surveillance, all the thought control and thought awareness – that are looking for just this type of instability to achieve whatever their ends are. They might just want to supplant the current generation of Trills or they might want to destroy the neo-age completely. Although we have exposed thoughts, we haven't necessarily removed people with evil intentions from ever achieving their ends – whatever they are."

"I thought we had virtually eliminated, say, fascism from all discourse and therefore it wasn't a threat," Bartel t-said.

"And there are lots of reasons why that is true – but you cannot eliminate ideas however evil."

"So I should be even more frightened now?"

"Not necessarily – because I was explaining why Dressus, whatever her plans, knows that achieving total power can't be done by destroying the stability that the Trills and TCentral have brought. That's why she cannot bring in a reign of terror for example – such as happens after any revolution up to now. That would unleash forces that will destroy the neo-age."

"But this is a sort of despair, then," Bartel t-said. "So all Andrew's – what should I call it? – plotting? – was just purely academic with no substance, no function, just a token way of sitting in the dark and whistling."

"I don't know where you quite get that from, Emma," Dunster t-said. "Andrew's opposition to the Trills was, as you know, based on the dehumanising forces in the neo-age and what he – and others of course – wanted to achieve was to put back ambition, struggle – not in the sense of a struggle to survive but a struggle to understand – and individuality. He – we for that matter – see that a human life isn't just a way of existing, but it has to have achievements. And what does the neo-age offer? Everything is on a plate – whether it is food, drink, comfort, sex, health. That's all good in its way. And after the despicable political games of the rich and powerful at the beginning of the twenty first – a relief. But our belief is that there is more to life than that."

"So what Andrew wants is to understand?"

"Yes – and no," Dunster t-said. "He wants that to be a goal for everyone. I know it sounds weak and unobtainable."

"No it doesn't," Bartel t-said. "I don't see why ensuring people have the ability to understand themselves is unobtainable."

"Ok," Dunster t-agreed. "I got that wrong. But Emma – we're arguing or discussing nothing that isn't obvious. I want to be able to do something now."

"And you think we can't?"

"What do you think we can do?"

"I've no idea and I didn't ever want to be in the position where I'd have to do anything or something about the world and the neo-age," Bartel t-said. "It's you and Andrew – and Serena – who should be capable of answering that. I was content with the neo-age – it gave me opportunities that would have been denied to previous generations. I want to preserve that."

"At the risk of creating what Andrew calls amblytopia?"

"Yes," Bartel t-declared, firmly. "Well – no. I don't want to think like this. I was happy as I was. I had my daughters, I had my role and as much creativity as I wanted. I had a creativity partner whom I was training – and that felt good. I had relationships and I had no underlying worries. Why would I have wanted to change that?"

"I know," Dunster t-said. He went very quiet.

Bartel reached out and held his hand. She had tears in her eyes and wasn't quite sure what was the cause. It was just all too much. Should she have listened more to Pennington? Was she too self-obsessed. Suddenly it was all too bleak.

Dunster put his arm round her shoulder and t-said nothing, letting her live in her mind.

Chapter 33

They sat in silence for a long time – with the minutes dragging past. Three was so much to say but it felt odd to talk or communicate in any way. Bartel felt very weak as a person and struggled with herself but kept bringing her mind back to the situation and was grateful for Dunster's arm around her shoulder in a way that normally would have embarrassed her to need.

Clearly something was happening somewhere but how would they know?

"Do you think we can leave?" Bartel eventually asked Dunster.

"A good question, Emma. I guess we could try it – but where would we go and what would we do? I've never been in a situation remotely like this. It's as though we are cut off – although that's not right as we still can communicate outside of this room." Dunster was quite reflective and obviously thinking it through out loud.

Velasquez then engaged them. It was a relief she still could. "How are you two?" Dunster t-said they were all right but concerned.

"Not surprisingly," Velasquez t-said. "It still isn't very clear."

"Are you with Elora Ghose still?" Dunster t-asked.

"Yes," Velasquez t-replied. "It's all rather at sixes and sevens here – but is becoming clearer."

"How?" Bartel t-asked, unable to wait for Velasquez to explain herself.

"It's certainly a power grab of some sort," Velasquez t-replied. "It is focused, as I suspected, on sswipe – and Dressus is trying to deploy it as widely as she can. She is having some issues with that as it is not clear how it works in a stand-alone position – I mean, if you come out of Sofari as people do when they've exited Dread-Demotic for example, it is automatically triggered and rather carefully honed to that experience. What we don't understand at the moment is whether Dressus can trigger it independently – so that any of us could have our memories selectively wiped at the drop of a hat. We think she must be able to do that otherwise she wouldn't have got into this position – because we think that it's only with sswipe that she can succeed."

"So that means you – that is Elora and her two fellow resisters – were right to see sswipe as a major threat?" Bartel t-asked.

"Yes – that's the current view," Velasquez t-replied. "It looks like sswipe was as big a threat as we anticipated."

"Have you been affected by it yet?" Dunster sensibly t-asked.

"We don't actually know," Velasquez t-said, very worryingly. "We believe not – but since it can wipe memory selectively – we don't know how sensitively – perhaps it already has been deployed. We have to control it or find a way to control it – but unfortunately Dressus has taken advantage of the way TCentral operates to ambush TCentral and is now apparently in control."

"What does that mean?" Dunster t-asked.

"We think it means that the whole andro secretariat is under his control. The weeds appear to be totally under Dressus's personal control and now direction – Latitude does own and control most of them anyway but now it's clear that the messages being broadcast are in support of what's she's doing, at first they were ignoring the events but now they are suggesting that JD is having to work to preserve the neo-age," Velasquez t-replied. "Of course we've got Jerry – Fernandes, so that's Gyro – and Alexandr – Dermatov, so that's Elura, all opposed to Dressus, but Dressus is still able to utilise all the services and activities of each of the GLEAKES because that was fundamental to TCentral."

"So are you saying that even if Dressus is directly attacking and subverting TCentral there is nothing that the members of TCentral can do, because of the constitution of TCentral? That's plainly daft," Bartel t-said in disbelief.

"You can't be too purist about this, Emma," Velasquez t-said. "If we lose TCentral then we lose so much that is positive about the neo-age. But I am sure that we can marshal our resources in such a way that we can head off what Dressus is doing."

"Is that Elora's position too?" Dunster t-asked.

"Yes – and she is actively seeking a meeting with everyone else," Velasquez t-said.

"Can you answer me one question, Serena – well, it might be complex and more than one question?" Bartel t-asked.

"If I can."

"How has Dressus got herself into this dominant position?" Bartel t-asked. "And let me explain my reasoning. Number one – why is Latitude so important? Yes it has Sofari – and that's valuable to me, and it has the weeds, and now sswipe. But it doesn't have much else."

"Don't forget how important Sofari is to people – it is the main entertainment structure – it's not just a scenario builder is it? You think how important entertainment and experiences are in the neo-age – and you will see that while it started out quite a minor player in the neo-age, Dressus was able to exploit its contact with every citizen to create the biggest and most integrated database of people in the world. Yes, there is overlap with most of the other GLEAKES, and inter-dependencies – Elura for finance for example – but rather impressively Dressus has built Latitude into the most important and perhaps dominant of the GLEAKES in most people's every day lives. You might think that something like gSynth would be higher in most people's consciousness, but once you know food is secure and available, it tends to get forgotten about, and that's true of so much else that supports the functioning of the neo-age."

"That's helpful, Serena – and you especially know that I am late to this and my understanding is very flawed," Bartel t-replied. "But let me go on. I know what you say is right, but without Kalo, and Gyro – for example – without socio, persono and gSynth that is – Latitude would be nothing."

"Not entirely right," Velasquez t-replied. "It would still be something but as I think we've explained, the Trills set up TCentral in order to ensure that each of the GLEAKES would be interdependent, and while there would be limits to the overlap between them, there should be no cartels."

"But how is that relevant?" Bartel t-asked, genuinely not understanding.

"The key," Velasquez t-answered, "is the word *interdependent*. Not one of the GLEAKES is able to function properly in the neo-age without working with each of the others. This was thought to guarantee the stability and security of TCentral."

"And what it has done is actually destabilise TCentral?" Bartel t-asked.

"In a way, yes," Velasquez t-agreed. "You might remember in the twentieth and in the early twenty first, it was said that some organisations were too big to fail – and that justified giving, for example, the global banks huge amounts of government money when the banks had risked everything and almost destroyed themselves. Naturally the banks and their senior executives didn't pay any penalty – so they could go on taking ever more risky adventures, rewarding themselves – because they bribed the political parties. As I seem to remember it was called *making donations*. I don't know if the analogy holds up – it did when I started this line of thought – but Latitude is too big and important to fail – or in this case be destroyed or taken over. I did think that it would be vulnerable to a take over if the other Trills banded together, but Elora thinks that is wishful thinking. I'm not entirely clear yet why that is so, but it is something to do with the public perception of the GLEAKES as a unified force. So we are stuck with a quandary. How do we resist Latitude and Dressus without destroying TCentral and the overall power of the GLEAKES."

"But I thought you personally wanted to destroy the power of the GLEAKES and the Trills," Bartel t-said, feeling they were going round in circles. "Let me go back to my question – my questions, I think. What I am trying to understand is why those Trills that are neutral or unconcerned are like that – and then why Elora, Alexandr and Jerry are taking on Jessie Dressus."

"According to Elora she, Alexandr and Jerry believe that there is more danger in letting Dressus get away with what is patently a coup attempt than in standing up to her and defeating her," Velasquez t-said. "In deference to the others, that is Uhuru and Derek, Elora sees their point of view, mainly around the dangers to TCentral if they take her on."

"That leaves Sarah Trarieux," Bartel t-said.

"Sarah hasn't declared one way or the other – so it's a bit of a stand off at this point, not that this is a question of numbers and votes," Velasquez t-said. "This is purely about power. And it looks like Dressus has far more power than she should have been able to gain if you look at what resources Latitude has – and this is just because she has the weeds and the propaganda mills that they imply. And information dissemination – whether it is accurate or not – is the most powerful weapon, as the Bills tabloid press of the twentieth and early twenty first demonstrated. Does that answer your questions?"

"Sort of," Bartel t-admitted. "The problem, Serena, is that I just don't understand why anyone in Dressus's position would take such a chance. And aren't there also potential Trills waiting for just this opportunity? I mean to say that whatever Andrew has been planning – with or without you – in order to undermine TCentral and the power of the Trills seems to me to be hopeless and always has seemed to be hopeless, but as the history of the successive generations of Trills, and the Bills before that for that matter, demonstrates, there has always been room for newcomers usurping the last group. So what is being done about any potential threats from that sort of source?"

"I doubt very much is being done at this moment as there are more important and immediate threats – though of course the ability to carry out surveillance is extremely important and no doubt there are people in ImCirc who have a role assessing the threat from any newcomer even now. They may not be able to stop a newcomer but they will probably know about him or her or them." Velasquez t-spoke but didn't seem comfortable. She t-continued: "But don't write off what Andrew and the group could achieve – it's just at the moment we need the stability of the neo-age in order to make the kind of redistribution of wealth and power that we believe in and give back to people some sort of sense of worth."

"So what are you doing?" Bartel t-asked. It was becoming very repetitive and frustrating.

"Well – and this will sound weak because it is weak – we are assessing what we can do and also what Dressus is likely to do next," Velasquez t-said. "She's taken over most of TCentral's functions as far as we can see and is using that power base to take over key functions so that she can deploy sswipe as soon as she feels safe to do so. As I said, she may well have done so already but we doubt that."

"But why?" Dunster t-asked, as though coming out of a stupor. "Why was it allowed to get this far when you were all aware of the danger of sswipe – which could undermine every element of TCentral and ImCirc too."

"A good question," Velasquez t-said. "And there will be time to answer it later."

At that moment the door to the room that Bartel and Dunster were in was flung open so hard it hit the wall and rebounded. Two andros dressed in combat gear and holding some sort of gun told them to stand up and follow them. "Keep calm," Velasquez t-said to them as Bartel and Dunster obediently followed the two andros. "We don't know what this is but it is going on across the whole of TCentral at the moment."

"Where are you?" Bartel t-asked.

"Safe," Velasquez t-answered.

"What are you actually doing – I mean what are you doing about the Dressus coup – if I can call it that?" Dunster t-asked.

"It's best that I don't communicate too much but there are moves afoot," Velasquez t-replied. "And I don't think it's helpful to go further than that. Do you understand?"

"Of course," Bartel t-responded. "But what does this mean for what we were talking about before? What Andrew was thinking about?" Bartel tried to make her question as opaque as possible.

"It means nothing at all for that," Velasquez t-said bleakly. "I will tell you more when I get the chance."

"Can you say why Dressus hasn't blocked all t-communications?" Dunster t-asked.

"I think she has attempted to but Elora has control over socio and persono of course and so I think Elora has successfully resisted all JD's attempts to shut down t-comms," Velasquez t-said. "Obviously we don't know for how long – but it's looking pretty foolproof at the moment. Can I reiterate that you should do nothing yourselves but continue to observe whatever you're told to do and I'll be in touch as soon as possible with an update."

With that Velasquez blanked and Bartel felt very alone and reached out for Dunster's hand. "Don't worry too much," Dunster t-said to her. "I've been thinking again whether JD, as Serena usually calls her, can achieve what she's apparently aiming to do. I believe I've not been thinking straight. One of the key elements in TCentral is the fact that the Trills deliberately ensured that there was interdependence between the seven organisations. That I think is the ultimate safeguard. Dressus cannot possibly manage to take over the whole of TCentral just like that."

"But I think she has," Bartel t-said. "Serena didn't sound too confident and she could just be whistling in the dark and trying to keep our spirits up."

"True."

"But let's hope you're right," Bartel t-said.

They were guided along a corridor and there was no aggression towards them but just an overall sense of menace. They then found themselves in what seemed just like another holding area.

"Do you think they don't know what they're doing with us?" Dunster t-asked.

"Who can tell."

They were told to take seats in a small room which had penetrating light in it – unusual for the neo-age when the light was subtly adjusted at all times to reflect the needs of people it was illuminating. Neither Dunster nor Bartel were able to feel comfortable and the light played a small part in that.

"Now what?" Bartel t-asked.

"Goodness knows," Dunster t-replied. "I guess we do as Serena suggested."

Chapter 34

Bartel felt very alone despite having Dunster there with her. She also felt once again a real frustration. It was partly with herself and that made it all the more difficult. What she couldn't quite deal with in herself is that she hadn't taken anything that Pennington had been trying to interest her in seriously or at least felt that it was important, and yet now that there was a chance to achieve whatever Pennington had wanted, he and his fellow – what were they *conspirators*? – were paralysed and unable to make any moves. Whatever else Bartel knew, she understood that when an opportunity presented itself, it should be grasped. And although she didn't feel that what they wanted was going to solve anything or do any good, it was important, if you believed in something, to get on with it.

And if the Trills were divided amongst themselves in what seemed like a very serious way, then what better time would there be to disrupt the Trills and TCentral?

Why couldn't Pennington of all people see that?

What was she missing?

Bartel moved closer to Dunster and he put his arm round her again – so strange that there was this comfort from that simple action – from someone that she hadn't known just a few days ago.

"I'm sorry to go on, Wilfred," Bartel t-began, "but I really don't understand any more why this isn't a great time to take on the Trills."

"I can understand that," Dunster t-replied. "The point is that nothing we had in mind had been planned. We wouldn't know what to do if we could do anything – and at the moment, I'm not sure we can do anything anyway."

"Is this going to get violent?"

"I would imagine so," Dunster t-said, soberly. "I don't know of any coup or revolution or whatever that ever stayed peaceful. I'm not sure what this is, and how successful it is or isn't, but my guess is that this is quite a seismic shock to the neo-age."

Dunster suddenly stopped talking. "Serena is trying to engage."

"Is there a problem?" Bartel t-asked.

"I think Dressus has probably managed to block t-comms at least to some extent," Dunster t-said. "That's worrying. I did just catch something – Serena t-said that they were working on how to engage – so I think there's a chance that Dressus won't be successful. She also did manage to say that she hadn't been able to t-engage with you. I'm not sure whether that's because we have a more sophisticated infrastructure – even at the personal level – in ImCirc – or whether that was just unlucky."

"That sounds serious," Bartel t-replied. "It could mean that co-ordinated responses to whatever Dressus is up to, will be difficult, if not impossible if t-comms are restricted."

"It is," Dunster t-agreed. "I wonder whether it's possible to get through to any of the neotiquette team still. Let me try."

Dunster concentrated and Bartel waited. Without t-comms it was going to be a whole different world. It reminded her of a novel she had read that was written in the thirties and there was a discussion between some teenagers who couldn't quite believe that there had been a world before hand phones. Although Bartel had spent nearly twenty years in a world without t-comms, it was still difficult for her to imagine what it had been like – and what it would be like now if t-comms didn't work.

"But we're using t-comms," Bartel t-said, more as a sudden realisation rather than a conscious thought worked out through logic.

"Perhaps it's possible to use t-comms close up."

"I hope so," Bartel t-said. "On the other hand, t-comms is most useful over distance – so that's a bit of a false hope."

"Just a minute," Dunster said, rather excitedly, "I'm being engaged by a couple on the team. Let me focus on that and see where we get."

He was silent and looking at the floor, nodding his head now and again. He then looked up at Bartel.

"Well?" she t-asked.

"There's no fighting, but all sorts of aspects of life are closing down at the moment," Dunster t-said, eventually. "Somehow or other and we don't know at whose hand, gSynth has stopped functioning."

"That's serious," Bartel t-said. "Without a steady and stable food supply what can happen?"

"And what's more we don't know if that is because Gyro and Jerry Fernandes have shut it down, or whether this is something that Dressus has done," Dunster t-said. "The team's bet is that it isn't Dressus but a counter-measure by Fernandes."

"But none of this is confirmed, is it?"

"None, I think," Dunster t-replied. "But something serious must be going on for anything to interrupt what gSynth does."

"Is the neotiquette team ok though?" Bartel t-asked.

"They tell me that there has been no violence yet," Dunster t-said.

They lapsed into silence at that word as it was once again a sober reminder that the current position was so fraught with danger for everyone.

Immediately on thinking that, Bartel decided that she had probably been too self-righteous about her criticisms of Pennington and Velasquez and whoever else was in the opposition to the Trills. Perhaps they really did have a point – and perhaps the good things about the neo-age were too important to jeopardise.

She felt completely at sea.

"Is anything further happening that you know about?" Bartel t-asked, eventually.

"From the limited bits of information that are trickling through to the team – and one or two words that Serena managed to convey – I think there are moves to isolate Dressus and also to undermine her business because it is so dependent upon the infrastructure that the rest of the Trills provide – but I think we've already said that," Dunster t-said. All the worries were making him feel disorientated – because this was nothing like life in the neo-age that he was used to, and especially nothing like life in ImCirc.

"So no real new news?" Bartel t-asked.

"One thing, I think," Dunster t-replied. "There is some global disquiet apparently."

"Why?"

"Because," Dunster t-began and then paused to gather his thoughts, "and I don't know this for sure, it's because the weeds and all media – all media – are reporting that there is a major disruption at TCentral. And I would have thought that if gSynth isn't working properly, that would cause alarm. I am surprised at that, as I would have thought that Dressus would move heaven and earth to ensure that gSynth was functioning in order to pretend, at least, that nothing was happening that was untoward."

"But couldn't that mean just anything – from a technical issue to some sort of personal rivalry between the Trills of the kind the gossip weeds love to portray?"

"Exactly," Dunster t-said, "which is why I'm hesitant to say too much. On the other hand, I think any reports of disruption probably mean that Dressus hasn't yet got full control."

"So what do you think . . .?"

"Just a moment, Emma," Dunster t-interrupted. "Serena is trying to engage. Give me a moment."

"But I thought you said that Dressus had ways of blocking t-comms." Dunster said nothing but waved his arm at Bartel to try to get her to be quiet. "She wants to engage with both of us – and they have found a way to break through the barrier to t-comms, although Serena doesn't know how stable this will be. Stand by, Emma."

There was nothing at all and it was impossible to suggest that Velasquez was trying to engage – so they sat in silence waiting, then suddenly Velasquez broke through and t-began: "I'll make this short because we don't know how long we can hold this engagement – but we're working on it. Elora has her best brains on this – and they are working on several strands. But first of all – I want you to take notice, Emma. Especially take notice of this. I am so angry."

"With me?" Bartel was dumbfounded.

"Yes," Velasquez t-replied. "With you. We are in an absolute crisis – a crisis about the whole structure of the neo-age, and we don't need to go once again through the benefits that it has brought. And you see this as a moment to criticise the people who have shown the only opposition to it for not taking advantage of this moment to overturn the whole neo-age – when that was something we – and I say *we* decidedly – we didn't want. We wanted to remove the power of the Trills and not destroy the neo-age, but to give people back some sort of purpose in their lives. So you are diverting energy and focus from the main task which is to nullify Dressus – and turning it into some kind of vendetta against Andrew Pennington and the people who are part of the resistance to the petrifying factors in the neo-age.

"I don't think that's at all fair, Serena," Bartel t-responded. "What do you think, Wilfred?"

"It's taken me completely by surprise but I guess there's a grain of truth in what Serena is saying," Dunster t-said, rather hesitantly.

"Ok – I understand," Bartel t-replied, feeling very defensive and not a little hurt.

"The reason I said this was not to get at you, Emma," Velasquez t-replied. "It was because I think you are making a big mistake. And that's why I am angry – not so much with you, although that's how it feels I should express my anger, but with anything that allows Dressus free range."

"Wouldn't you be better off being angry with those Trills who are sitting on the fence or are however passively supporting Dressus?" Bartel t-asked.

"In some ways the answer to that is obviously yes," Velasquez t-agreed, "but the point is that we need to be united to defeat this gross attack on our principles and the neo-age. I know that's asking a lot – to distinguish between what the Trills have created positively and what the Trills have done to virtually enslave people into a dull and pointless existence."

"But I'm not the one saying that – you are," Bartel t-said. "So I have only been asking you to follow your logic."

"Ok," Velasquez t-said. "Don't forget what I said. But let's focus on what we've got to do."

"What do you think is motivating Dressus to strike like this at this point?" Dunster very sensibly t-asked.

"You know that some people say it is hard to attribute motives to people when you only see what they're doing," Velasquez t-said. "But I think it is all too easy to do so. I guess what I'd say is that none of us knows what her motive is – or probably motives are. I doubt she has just one aim at this moment. But certainly she has become increasingly frustrated with TCentral and the requirement that everything is unanimous. So that may be one motive. Secondly she is increasingly concerned that the interdependence that is at the heart of TCentral means that she is denied what pre-eminence she feels is her due because of the importance of Sofari and its additional functions and the essential nature of the weeds. Thirdly? I just don't know."

"Could it be that she resented the First Amendment to the Guiding Principles?" Dunster t-asked.

"Which is? Do remind me," Bartel t-asked wondering how arcane and abstract this discussion could become.

"The one that Elora brought in," Velasquez t-replied. "It was passed unanimously – eventually after Dressus raised all sorts of objections. It's the one Principle that really enshrined what we mentioned before – the interdependence of the Trills so that no one Trill could take on the others, just in the way that Dressus is doing at this moment. *Competition, co-opitition and co-operation.* And I think you may have a good point there, Wilfred."

"I never really considered what that meant – but I guess I do now," Bartel t-replied. "I don't think I ever saw how cleverly those three words are put together. And it's interesting that the middle word combines the two outer words. Clever, as I say."

"But this is arguing over trivialities," Velasquez t-said, impatiently. "There will be a time and place for this sort of discussion, but what we've got to do now is focus on isolating Dressus and restoring some sort of order to TCentral."

"So what are you doing about that?" Bartel t-asked, not surprisingly.

"The first thing is understanding what is going on," Velasquez t-said.

"And do you know enough to say with any certainty that you've got that nailed down?" Bartel t-asked.

"Yes and no," Velasquez t-said. "We have to guess, but I think we're on sufficiently good grounds to move forward."

"And so?" Bartel t-asked. She noticed how Dunster was saying nothing but obviously thinking hard. Did that matter? Hardly.

"The second action is getting the wavering or neutral Trills on side – and Elora is working on that," Velasquez t-said. "I guess you can see why it is so annoying – to say the least – to have you, Emma sniping away on the sidelines, especially when we know that you don't actually support the opposition to the Trills."

"It's not that," Bartel t-protested, "it's that I am confused. Look I don't want to make the situation any more difficult than it is."

"I don't think you can – and what you're doing is a blip of course. But it's a blip we can do without, so I want you to forget about that at the moment," Velasquez t-said quite determinedly. "And the third element is slightly tricky we think, but we're working on it."

"And that is?" Dunster t-said unexpectedly.

"Well, actually," Velasquez t-began, "it's two things – or maybe it's two different things and should be actions three and four." This didn't sound very encouraging, as though Velasquez was making things up as she was going along. "Right – the third thing is getting all our people together – which means identifying where our groups of people like you two are and bringing them out of whatever situation they are in. It is a priority, I can assure you of that, but we have other issues of course and that is the fourth action. In terms of t-comms we have to stay ahead of whatever blocking and neutralising Dressus has – because without t-comms we probably can't win against her."

"Does that mean that part of her planning for this coup – or whatever it is – has involved creating an arsenal of anti-t-comms technologies?" Dunster t-asked.

"Yes." Laconic and rather chilling but Velasquez didn't appear to be too concerned, but that was perhaps putting a brave face on things.

"So you are in a sort of arms race with Dressus over t-comms?" Bartel t-asked.

"Yes. Fortunately we have all the resources behind socio and persono within Elora's Kalo, we have the financial stuff with Elura, and all of Gyro's capabilities," Velasquez t-said.

"I don't think food and drink and financial products are going to help us much, though obviously persono and socio are based on t-comms – or use them extensively – so that's an advantage," Bartel t-said. "But without Sapiens and all the AI stuff we are at a disadvantage, surely?"

"At the moment Sarah Trarieux is fortunately or unfortunately neutral – and we're working on her – because you're absolutely right," Velasquez t-said. "We need Sapiens."

"But one question, Serena?" Dunster t-asked.

"Yes?"

"Aren't we too insignificant to worry about? I can't understand why you are dealing with us – a member of the neotiquette team and an imagineer. We have no strategic value – surely?" Dunster had put his finger on something that had been just below the surface of Bartel's consciousness.

"You don't understand," Velasquez t-replied. "Look – this is a battle essentially of ideas as all twenty firsts are. Yes – in the scheme of things, put like that, a neotiquette team member and an imagineer are hardly front line people. But that's to misunderstand how this will play out. You think how important neotiquette has become in most people's lives now. And Dread-Demotic has been and is the biggest experience ever, so we will need to use Emma perhaps to front some of the messaging we will put out on the weeds. Not strategic, as you say, Wilfred, but highly influential and significant."

"How do you know I want to be part of that?" Bartel t-asked, rather worried that she was becoming involved in something beyond her thoughts and possibly far more dangerous than what had been happening.

"To be brutal," Velasquez t-said, "we can obviously use holos of you two if we need to, but even now, even with the most sophisticated technology behind us, it can be possible to distinguish between a holo and the real thing. Not by most people, but by enough. So we want you two actually on side – and there is enough at stake that I wonder that you even question which side you are on. And you, Emma – you are one of the biggest supporters of the neo-age so why wouldn't you do everything to sustain it and restore stability?"

"Ok," Bartel t-said, somewhat shamefaced. She knew that she was not thinking straight and had all sorts of conflicting emotions and ideas. "Just take it from me, Serena, that I am out of my depth."

"Not at all," Velasquez t-replied. "You may think that, but I do know from your history – and more importantly from probing you – that you are well within your capabilities to be a strong force for good here." It was probably just flattery, Bartel thought. But it made sense.

"So where are you in the arms race over t-comms?" Dunster t-asked.

"Just ahead – but it's changing by the hour," Velasquez t-said. "Which is why were unable to engage earlier. We may well not be able to engage at various times over the next few hours, but we will do our best."

"So are you going to rescue us?" Bartel t-asked.

"As soon as we can find out where you are and can effect a rescue – because that is what it will be, and you are correct to say that – we will," Velasquez t-said. "Up until we do, keep positive and look after each other. And be ready. We can get to you at any moment. And we will try to keep you up to date until you are here with us."

"What's happening with gSynth – because I would have thought that if food isn't available it's going to cause inordinate resentments and probably riots and disruption?" Dunster t-asked.

"That was Jerry's idea – but we have convinced him that gSynth must be re-activated – and it will be," Velasquez t-replied. "He thought it would be a good idea to show JD that she's not able to control the neo-age, but on reflection – serious reflection between Elora, Alexandr and Jerry – Jerry realised that destabilising the neo-age plays into JD's hands rather than thwarts her."

Velasquez disengaged and in that moment Bartel and Dunster again felt very alone and vulnerable.

Chapter 35

In the glaring light both Bartel and Dunster felt uncomfortable and apprehensive. They v-talked for a while but then remained quiet, having exchanged concern over the use of the word *rescue* even though Bartel had used the word first. When she had t-said it, it was just a way of talking. When Velasquez repeated it to her, it took on a sinister edge.

The minutes dragged on – and as there was no concept of a time when this would be over, every minute stretched out until they felt abandoned. The weeds had gone into a sort of circular pattern, with the same information being sprayed out in a different order but essentially saying that they should await further news as there appeared to be a confrontation or disagreement – both words were used – within TCentral. The weeds also suggested that Dressus was alone in fighting for the best outcome for everybody – so the propaganda was starting to become overt.

They tried t-comms with each other again, although v-comms was much more comforting for some reason, and they discovered that it was at least partially blocked. They didn't feel confident enough to convey too much about their feelings. It was enough to hold hands and wonder what was happening.

To Bartel it was strange to be in such a position with someone she had not known 48 hours before. Strange because it felt as good as it might be. Strange because it was being isolated with someone who might not be a perfect stranger, but who was so new to her. As a person, Bartel liked to engage and encounter new people – and was good at it – and people usually got the wrong impression of her because she seemed so immediately at ease with anyone else, whereas Bartel was so well aware that this was, even in the neo-age of persono and socio, a mask that she created to hide her real self.

Dunster engaged her with t-comms, so Kalo must have gained an advantage in the technology war and managed to defeat the block to t-comms once again.

"Have you any idea what is happening now – or insights from your neotiquette team?" Bartel t-asked Dunster.

"None at all. I'm completely unprepared for this type of thing, Emma, and I am frightened, although I almost don't know what I am frightened of," Dunster t-said. "Emma." He paused. "Would you have any interest in making this relationship between you and me have a bit more permanence?"

"That's such a weird question, Wilfred. I just wouldn't know how to answer that. Is it something that is bothering you?"

"Not really bothering me, but I needed a way to focus on tangibles and reality, and asking a question like that seems to take my mind off whatever's happening in the world at this moment."

"I think you must be 10 or 15 years younger than me, Wilfred. I know that's not a meaningful contribution to this discussion, but it is a point."

At that moment there was a huge commotion outside the room they were in and the door was battered open and two andros came in and showed them their Kalo badges – and the first v-said: "We're to take you to TCentral where there's a meeting. We're not sure how safe the passage there will be, so we need you to remain both v-comms and t-comms silent and to do exactly as we suggest."

One andro led the way and Bartel and Dunster followed in single file, with the second andro following up. It was unusual for andros not to introduce themselves, as that was part of the neotiquette that had been developed, but the situation was too tense to worry about that. All sorts of questions were going through Bartel's mind but she obeyed the instruction to remain silent and followed through what seemed a labyrinth of passages into a Kautonom which whisked them without the andros back to TCentral. They didn't know whether they should remain silent, and so did. As the autonom came to a halt outside the building which Bartel recognised with some relief, an andro came up to them and asked them to follow. They were led through the building which seemed familiar and comforting even though Bartel had only been in it that once. After using an elevator to go up what seemed a large number of floors, the doors opened and the two of them followed the andro, who opened the door for them and showed them into a peacefully quiet room, with lighting that was normal. Bartel realised she had been holding her breath as much as possible, but she was now able to relax and breathe normally. "Please take a seat." It was a quietly authoritative command and they both did. The andro then left.

"I guess we can talk now," Bartel v-said, thinking that voice was less likely to be interfered with.

"I'm sure of that."

"What do you make of all this, Wilfred?"

"I'm just relieved – to be honest, Emma," Dunster v-said. "And I think you're right to use v-comms. And I guess we just wait again. That was such a dramatic rescue. Do you have any idea where Dressus was keeping us?"

"It's more likely you would know than me," Bartel v-replied. "I know nothing about where TCentral is and what's around it. I'm just pleased we were – and I think it is the right word - *rescued*."

"I agree," Dunster v-said. "I've so many questions."

"Me too."

"I just think we must be lucky to be here unscathed," Dunster v-said.

The door they had come through opened and Velasquez came in. They were so pleased to see her – but she was grim faced and hardly friendly. "Listen to me," she immediately v-said. "There's going to be an emergency meeting of TCentral in a little while."

"Will Dressus be there?" Dunster v-asked immediately.

"We don't know - but I doubt it," Velasquez v-said. "The point is that we need to ensure that the Trills are united against her – and that isn't the case at the moment. There's going to be a debate of sorts – but I don't think that JD can afford to be there – and yet she can't afford not to be there. I know that's a paradox but I think we – that is Kalo, Gyro and Elura – have the upper hand, but we've got to ensure that Sapiens is brought over – and we have to convince Ambience and Eclectic that this is a major threat to them."

"What do you think are the chances," Dunster v-asked. Bartel was feeling rather detached and it didn't seem to be the right way of going about things – although she couldn't think what might be the right way.

She was still confused about what the role of Pennington and, for example, Velasquez should be – so she just wanted to stand back. She knew that the last thing she should do would be to raise her point again about this being the time to take on the Trills.

"I think we're in a strong position," Velasquez v-said. "On the one hand it is clear to them that this isn't a threat necessarily to them individually – what we have to do is convince them that it is a threat to the GLEAKES – that is all of them – and in turn that threatens the neo-age and all of what they have individually and collectively."

"So what arguments can you use?" Dunster v-asked. "It seems to me that Dressus must have been planning this for some time and will have organised her position and will have been using her arguments with Sapiens, Ambience and Eclectic. So how powerful can what you say be? It seems to me that it could be touch and go."

"We do have a major argument which I'm not going to go into now," Velasquez v-said, very firmly and both Bartel and Dunster could see that this wasn't going to come out into the open now, probably for good reason. "The point is that the sort of arguments that Emma was using are irrelevant at this point. I think you agree with that. Don't you, Emma?"

"Up to a point," Bartel v-said. "No. You are right. I won't think about them again until this is over."

"I'll take that," Velasquez v-said. "Just don't go communicating it whatever you feel. The point is that this is a major crisis and we have to deal with it first. Later we can sort out other things. Now – to be practical. Wilfred – your team is close by and I suggest you join them. There are some fast moving things here and I think that the neotiquette team should be looking at all of the elements of this."

"What for example?" Dunster v-asked.

"For example, how is this communicated in such a way that people understand the fact that this is a serious attempt at destabilising the GLEAKES, without them losing either belief in the neo-age or confidence in it," Velasquez v-said.

"Isn't that nothing to do with neotiquette and everything to do with the weeds?" Dunster v-asked.

"You have a point, of course, Wilfred," Velasquez v-said. "It's not as simple as that. We have to show people how they should react and what they should do, not just what they should believe. Do you see the difference?"

"I suppose so," Dunster v-replied, doubtfully.

"You need to give people the way they should be behaving," Velasquez v-said. It was a pure command now. "And, of course, we need to ensure that we control the weeds somehow. We're working on that."

"And me?" Emma v-asked.

"You will come with me," Velasquez v-said. "I'm not sure that it would be appropriate if you hadn't been seconded here."

"Seconded?"

"Well – whatever term you need, Emma," Velasquez v-said. "You are here – and you have a brilliant imagination. We need to create a new, convincing scenario – but this time a reality – not just an experience."

"I'm not sure I understand," Bartel v-said.

"You will," Velasquez v-said, very brusquely. She paused, then added: "Look – I'm sorry if I'm being very abrupt and difficult. But I don't feel as though I can waste any time. And that's partly the reason why I am on at you, Emma. I'm concerned that you don't understand the seriousness of this – not for TCentral and not for the GLEAKES, but for our existence. Yes – we are opposed to the Trills and the way that they have complete authority – more authority than the old country states, more power, more focus and a complete lack of understanding of what they are doing to humanity in order to preserve their power and position. But we cannot throw out the benefits of the neo-age and that's what is under threat now. Yes – it makes them vulnerable, but it also makes this neo-age completely vulnerable."

"Are you absolutely convinced of that?" Bartel v-asked.

"Yes," Velasquez curtly v-said. "And I know why – and how. Look you two – although I don't think you are as distant from this as Emma is, Wilfred – you have to understand that although there is now no real democracy, not that there was that much in the twentieth or the twenty first, human conditions are so much better than they have ever been. We know there is a cost – which we regard as unacceptable – in terms of fulfilment that people can achieve and in terms of struggle, which all humans need something of. And that is serious. But the elimination of hunger, need, security is something very valuable too.

"I know I've given you history lessons before but I think it's worth repeating and let's look at the twentieth and you'll see what I mean. I know you learnt about the Second World War – but I don't think you learnt about the settlement that ensued – when ordinary people were essentially bought off with a promise that life would get better and better, and health care, education and social support were bundled into something called the welfare state. In addition, real measures were taken to break down country states and create pan-continent political bodies. People who had achieved that mid twentieth thought that they had created a lasting and inviolable foundation – only to see how the rich by the early twenty first had completely taken over all forms of information – broadcast and media, as they called it, newspapers and magazines – and completely moved the Overton window to the point where the Bills effectively controlled thought and impoverished people. The Bills did it so easily – just by controlling information – what we now call the gramscian approach. Within twenty years the Bills – and the useful idiots they bought off by the Bills giving them a bit more privilege and some insulation from the worst effects of the dismantling of that welfare state – had reduced most people to a level of poverty and ill health that harked back to the nineteenth. It happened so easily – so you had people voting against their own best interests where they were allowed to vote at all.

"And the obscenity of the poverty versus the wealth of the Bills was completely hidden by the usual trick of gaslighting and diversion – usually using a minority ethnic group as scapegoats. Hence what we talked about before when enough people began to realise the huge fraud that had been perpetrated on them. That's when the riots started and the Bills started to take fright. I don't need to say any more – but just remember over the next few hours – days even – how fragile a society can be against ruthless people."

"And Dressus is a ruthless person," Bartel v-said, unwilling to back down completely even though she had been admonished.

"That is true – and the Trills are all ruthless in their own ways," Velasquez v-said. "No – I'm not defending them – but remember I was allowed to hold my views and be known for how I thought and felt."

"Because they felt they were invincible," Bartel v-replied.

"I told you it's not quite like that as the Trills as a group are quite paranoid," Velasquez v-said very quickly. "But what they also remember is the riots and the civil disorder that helped destroy the first and second generation Bills who had forgotten the lessons of the first third of this century. Wilfred – you should be off – the andro outside the door will take you to the team. Emma – will you come with me?"

It wasn't really a question and Bartel nodded.

Velasquez had done a good job of convincing her that whatever she felt, she didn't know enough to stand up for what Pennington and others believed in, especially as she had been the one opposed to what they were saying and aiming to do – or if not opposed, then at least indifferent.

Bartel did feel confused with everything – and with herself and how strongly she had started to feel about the opposition to the Trills.

Velasquez guided her out to a long corridor and they walked briskly and apparently purposefully towards a place where corridors crossed.

"Come on, Emma," Velasquez v-said, "I want you to be part of the next meeting – and it's with Elora and her chief advisers."

"Does that include you?"

"Yes," Velasquez v-said.

"But why me? I can't bring anything to this crisis – and I don't know enough to be part of this, even if I wanted to be," Bartel v-replied.

"You underestimate your value to us, especially at this moment of crisis. I told you why you were brought to TCentral and introduced – if not yet inducted – into ImCirc because of what you had achieved with Dread-Demotic but there was more to it than that. One of the things that is almost a secret to the Trills' power is that they understand how knowledge – and control of knowledge more particularly – is the most important factor in the neo-age and its stability. It isn't a secret but is hidden in plain sight with all the gramscian overtones.

"What I need you to do as we are sitting there observing TCentral in action is to create a scenario or scenarios in your head that we will be able to use to ensure that there isn't panic throughout the neo-age. Is that ok?"

"Yes," Bartel v-responded. It was interesting that it had taken the insurrection and its ensuing crisis to reveal the real reason she had been brought into this strange, rarified world. She could feel a slow anger building inside her that she had been, in essence, manipulated. The edge of anger and frustration was all the more real because she knew only too well how the Trills operated because although she had never listened with any real interest to what Pennington tried to talk to her about, she knew there was an underlying truth in what he believed. That it was too uncomfortable for her to embrace his world view and his opposition to the Trills didn't mean that she was actually prevented from understanding how the neo-age was built on the most subtle coercion. "I'm not sure I am up to that task – but I understand now much more why I am here."

"We weren't anticipating this JD action, Emma," Velasquez t-assured her. "None of us believed that there would be a threat that couldn't be controlled from within the GLEAKES. But I wasn't entirely disingenuous when I was telling you that you were the type of person who was important and that was why you were brought to TCentral. What both generations of the Bills and the first generation Trills underestimated – or really didn't care to think about as they believed they had so much power – was the intense need for a shared or promulgated world view that cemented their position in society.

"The current Trills may be many things but they are adamantly committed to creating and sustaining a particular type of consciousness about the neo-age because they see that is vital to maintain their position. In the days of monarchy, this was understood only too well by the royals and they survived far longer than anyone might have imagined. As you know that was until the current Trills dealt with them. First of all they made them irrelevant by never reporting anything about them and then they apparently forgot about them. And they disappeared almost without trace.

"So if you think about it, JD is far more dangerous than you might suppose because she has Latitude and of course Latitude has Sofari – the creator of dreams, as the strap-line has it. And we need someone as skilled as you to get the best out of it."

"But I thought some of the new imagineer programmes have eclipsed the sort of – what would you call it? – stereotypical experiences that I and my fellow imagineers have produced," Bartel v-said.

"Again it's yes and no, Emma. Think what you did with Dread-Demotic and how that transformed a whole experience into something addictive and unique. I guess the new imagineer programmes can do that – but we – Elora and I – didn't want to take a chance," Velasquez v-said.

"So what happens now?" Bartel v-asked.

"We go to the meeting of TCentral and see what is happening – I thought I'd said that," Velasquez v-said, again showing a flash of anger. It was clear that the tension in the situation was having quite an effect on Velasquez who was utterly different from how she had been when Bartel was first introduced to her. Even a bit frightening. She added: "I think everything will be conducted in v-comms – but be aware that we might be able to use t-comms. I guess it doesn't matter but what you will be aware is that this will be the Trills who are there actually there – no holos not even singularities. That just shows you how serious this is."

"Will we know what Wilfred and the neotiquette team are up to and how they're getting on?" Bartel v-asked.

"I see that's important to you," Velasquez v-said.

"I wouldn't exaggerate that," Bartel v-said, suddenly and was for the first time in probably years really deeply embarrassed, although there was no reason to be. "Yes – in the short time we've known each other we've shared a lot. There's nothing like an uncertain danger to bring people together."

"Yes – we'll keep in touch with him and you'll know what is being decided, if anything, within that team,"

For a moment Bartel wanted to get away from the pressure that was building up, and thought to herself that she wished she knew nothing of what was going on. But that thought – so much the old Bartel – more or

398

less immediately passed, because she realised that being at the centre of things was important to her, now that she had been brought into it. And despite Velasquez's anger and dismissal of what she had begun to think, she realised that she did have a different perspective. Then she realised that Velasquez's anger had actually been the catalyst that had woken something in her – something that months of prodding by Pennington hadn't managed to get under her skin.

It had been absolutely logical for her to say that Pennington and whoever should seize the moment when the Trills were distracted to try to usurp the power of the Trills and the central role of the GLEAKES in everybody's life. It hadn't been a political statement or anything more than seeing the most obvious truth. Pennington's caution and – to Bartel – pusillanimity had irritated her but not actually altered her view that she wanted nothing to do with destabilising the Trills. It was only when Velasquez turned on her that she started to believe that something had to be done about amblytopia and the Trills, and the moment should be seized with both hands – actually all available hands.

Bartel wondered to herself whether she was just showboating and was actually being carried away by the moment with its dangers and its possibilities, but she knew at that moment that she wanted to do something to make the neo-age more fulfilling. The realisation was quite a surprise to her and she recognised that and laughed at herself to think that the new Bartel was only two days or so in being. Then she realised even that wasn't true. The new Bartel was hours old – and it was quite a sobering thought.

Bartel knew she wasn't a revolutionary leader – but at that moment she knew she couldn't let this moment go by – whatever that meant.

Chapter 36

Bartel didn't know whether Velasquez had picked up any of what she had been thinking – and it wasn't important if she had because it would make no difference at the moment.

Nevertheless, she probably had.

They made their way to the council chamber. As they walked Dunster engaged Bartel just to pass on that he was fine and hoped that she was able to cope with what was going on. Bartel, beginning to feel that she had more strength than she was being credited with, reacted quite strongly to what he was saying but did also see that he was only trying to be concerned, so she didn't show any signs of her annoyance.

Why shouldn't she be fine?

But then she supposed she had gone out of her way earlier with him to show that she wanted nothing to do with the resistance to the Trills and had also appeared to be quite weak when she needed his physical touch.

She t-replied: "I'm fine, Wilfred. Do keep in touch and let me know what you and the team are doing." At that moment t-comms was interrupted presumably by the escalating technological war between Latitude and its opponents, but she hoped the whole message had gone across to him. Clearly all was not right with the world.

Velasquez was silent. This was hard for Bartle who wanted to talk more about what was going on inside her and to express her changing feelings and thoughts. It was curious to her that at the very moment she was approaching what Pennington – and whoever else – wanted and were aiming to do, she was becoming more isolated from them. Her frustration was getting more insistent, but she was always a disciplined person – perfectly capable of submerging her feelings and thoughts to achieve what she knew had to be done – so she suppressed her words and remained silent too.

"I know the pent up feelings and thoughts you have, Emma," Velasquez did eventually v-say. "We disagree. You know that. I can't say you're wrong. I wouldn't make that judgment. But I do believe that we have to focus on removing the threat that JD poses. No. I won't rehearse any more of that. You know it. Just hold on to what you believe – no problem with that – but go with our flow for the moment. Can you do that?"

"I don't know."

"At least that's honest," Velasquez v-replied. "I never expected this of you, Emma. Andrew had informed everyone that you were really unwilling to confront what you knew to be true about the neo-age and that you preferred your comfortable position and actually preferred amblytopia – but only because you weren't awake properly to what was going on. I know that he always felt you would be one of us – but you weren't the sort of person who would make the right commitment. I think he was so wrong."

"Not necessarily," Bartel v-replied. "You mustn't take my statements as a firm indication of what I will do. I am as surprised at myself as you are. But I do feel that the disappointment I felt in what you and Andrew were saying about maintaining the current status of the Trills for your own ends radicalised me in a most unexpected way. It got under my skin in a way that I would never have expected."

"I think I understand," Velasquez v-said. "Can you just let things develop in front of you now – with the promise from me that I take your view seriously?"

"I'll try," Bartel v-said.

"And can you think seriously about the experience that you might be able to develop to counter any impressions that are created by any of the weeds reporting any of this?"

"I find that hard to even think about," Bartel v-replied. "But I promise I shall watch the proceedings with that at the forefront of my mind. Just be aware that part of any experience that I create will also have to be subversive of the power and control of the Trills."

"I don't know how that will work out – but as a starting point that's fine."

They carried on in silence, and then approached the council chamber and they were able to get into the place where Bartel had first seen the workings of TCentral. The only person in the speaking chamber was Sousousa who was, apparently anxious as she wasn't doing anything completely but flitting around between the podium and the desks, trying to prepare for what could be the most momentous meeting of TCentral ever. It might just have been in Bartel's mind, but there was an intense foreboding in the air.

"Do you think Dressus will appear?" Bartel v-asked.

"Goodness knows. She should but she is probably consolidating her position outside TCentral in whatever way she can, so it seems a long shot."

"So what can TCentral do to stop her?"

"That's where the interdependence comes in," Velasquez v-said. "What can she achieve on her own? Well – she'd lose persono and socio, and gSynth. But maybe she has a way round that. Let's see. I know Elora is about to enter the chamber and both Jerry and Alexandr are close behind. They will make a strong case. As you know they have to persuade Sarah, Uhuru and Derek to oppose her. That would mean that all the AI tools, all the infrastructure behind t-comms and for that matter v-comms, and the whole financial system will be opposed if she can achieve that. With Derek's raw materials and services businesses on side that would be a substantial hill for JD to climb."

"But isn't Derek – what did you call his position? – unconcerned?"

"Apparently," Velasquez v-said. "That's what we have to change. Then there's Uhuru's health systems and legal structures. If we can change her from unconcerned to opposition, we have a winning hand. But I guess if we don't get Sarah and her AI resources on board, JD still has a chance."

Elora Ghose entered, and Jerry Fernandes and Alexandr Dermatov followed her closely. Uhuru Sousousa called the meeting to order even though Sarah Trarieux and Derek Smith were not present yet. There was also no sign of Jessie Dressus.

"I've called the meeting to order," Sousousa v-said. "You know we have to use v-comms. There is a quorum of seven for any meeting of TCentral, so there is no way we can conduct this meeting without the other Trills. I am willing to wait a further five minutes then I will have to call the meeting closed."

"Not entirely true, chair," Ghose v-said. "in an emergency we can have a quorum of 6 – and you may remember that was introduced precisely because of a circumstance like this."

"Why is it an emergency?" Sousousa v-asked. She clearly didn't want the meeting to go ahead and as chair had that power, in her own mind at least.

"It's an emergency because Jessie Dressus has attacked the very foundation of TCentral and all that that means for the neo-age," Ghose v-replied. "I know that at the moment you are unconcerned, Uhuru, but I think we need to explore the issues and we can only do that if you rule that this is an emergency. Otherwise Jessie has a veto over any actions we might wish to take even if one of the Trills attempts a coup or revolution."

"But we haven't got a quorum of even 6," Sousousa v-replied. "I'm willing to see whether the other two are on their way. Clerk – find out where Sarah and Derek are and if they are intending to attend." There was a brief pause. "Thank you – I can tell everyone that they are on their way."

Another pause. "Does anyone know whether Jessie is coming?" Silence. "She's not made up her mind yet apparently. It depends how the debate goes. Fair enough. No doubt she is tuned into this meeting of TCentral and will know precisely what is going on. I understand that she is within physical access distance." More silence. "How do people want this debate – discussion – or whatever to proceed? As chair, I don't want to dictate – and as you know I don't know why everyone has got into the state they have. We've had the next technology as a threat so many times in the past – technology that we were assured would alter the balance of power within TCentral – and it never has. I don't like to say this to my fellow Trills but I do believe we have to keep a sense of proportion and understand that the interdependence of all of us at the head of the GLEAKES ensures that we maintain stability at all costs. So who wants to speak?" Another pause. "I recognise Elora Ghose and you have the floor."

"I want to start by insisting that this is probably the most serious meeting of TCentral that we have ever had, even going back to the original meeting that set up TCentral and formalised the position of the second generation Trills and all that that means," Ghose v-said. "And, Uhuru, you are right that we have had many new technological advances in the past that have seemed to be threatening to the neo-age as we know it, and we have absorbed all of them without a ripple when it actually came down to it."

"I'm glad you acknowledge that," Sousousa v-responded.

"That has helped me immensely in understanding your position, Uhuru – and possibly that goes for you too, Derek – though I don't want to put words into your mouth," Ghose v-added. She looked around directly at Smith. "I can see, Derek, that you do think the same as Uhuru – and I am glad to understand your position. I must say that neither I, nor Jerry and Alexandr, actually think that the advent of sswipe is in any way comparable to, say, the introduction of gSynth, the vastly improved socio and persono – nor the financial environment that was created by Elura, out of the remnants of the old fiat monetary systems. And I will go on to explain why that is the case.

"First, however, I want to address the concerns – or actually lack of concerns – that you, Sarah, have about the introduction of sswipe. Whether you agree with me, Jerry and Alexandr that sswipe is a direct threat to TCentral, the neo-age and what we have jointly established, or whether you agree with Uhuru and Derek that this is nothing more than the introduction of a new and unthreatening technology, I don't see why you regard this matter as trivial and not worthy of taking sides over. Not being concerned because you don't believe it is a threat, as Uhuru and Derek believe, is very different from being neutral and not taking sides. Can I ask you why you don't want to get involved in this dispute with Jessie over sswipe."

"You can ask but whether I want to dignify this storm in a teacup with an actual response is not actually something I want to discuss," Trarieux v-replied. "My business and my power and what I do with my life and how I value and regard the neo-age is really irrelevant. I am effectively a generic supplier. None of you can actually function without the services that my intelligence creates and sustains. And that includes Jessie. Without my AI, her Sofari and her sswipe are merely playthings. They have no value without all the insights and capabilities that Sapiens provides. So I am indifferent to whatever is going on. And I know that the existence of TCentral and the neo-age and their value is well recognised by Jessie – and she can hardly jeopardise what we have now. So I believe you are over-reacting."

"Thank you for that insight, Sarah," Ghose v-replied. "I was struggling to understand your indifference to what Jessie is doing. But you have made that clear. I expect you understand that I have not made a prepared speech – no time for that though I obviously have called on all the tools that Sapiens has provided to create what I can. I doubt that I can persuade you directly using any arguments that I can muster. I would talk about the effects that selective memory wipe can have on all of us – but you understand that. It's not for nothing that there is an old adage that if you control the past you control the future. We, as Trills, know that better than most. But leave that aside.

"What I want you to consider is not whether the technology is a threat to TCentral and the neo-age – which we believe it is – but look at the actions that Jessie has taken. I can't see how isolating people, threatening people in the way she has, and virtually imprisoning them are the actions of a person who has the best intentions."

"When has she done that?" Trarieux v-asked.

"Today – and you know Emma Bartel – she was one of her victims, alongside Wilfred Dunster one of the neotiquette team that I know for sure were rounded up by andros at Jessie's command," Ghose v-said. "And that's just the tip of the iceberg – but I wanted to give you actual examples."

"Are you sure this wasn't just a misunderstanding?" Trarieux v-asked. "It seems to me that any action like that wouldn't have focused on an imagineer, however famous now, and a neotiquette team member. If I were going to do something like that I wouldn't have gone to detain such people. To be frank, Elora, I would think that you are creating issues where there are none."

"I understand, Sarah," Ghose v-replied. "But think about it. If she is willing to employ strong arm tactics on such people – such, as you suggest, trivial people – what might she do if she were to get the opportunity? Look – you are right to stress our interdependence, but sswipe is a threat to that – and a threat to TCentral. Can I persuade you at all?"

"Not like this," Trarieux v-replied.

"Let me try something else before I let Alexandr or Jerry have a say," Ghose v-said. She was clearly, even to Bartel, exasperated but it didn't seem to make any difference to Trarieux. "You know how important the weeds are to our power and position. I don't have to rehearse any gramscian statements to you."

"Certainly not – and don't," Trarieux v-replied, probably too quickly, which might suggest that she was not entirely comfortable with her position. That felt like a chink of light to Bartel.

"Then," Ghose v-said, pausing for effect, "remember that Latitude controls all the weeds – all the messages that we give out. I know that the experience engines that Latitude has, especially Sofari, are important but far more important is how we control the Overton window."

"Look – I told you I don't need to be told about gramscian issues," Trarieux v-said very abruptly and apparently angrily.

"I'm not, Sarah, teaching you about that just mentioning it," Ghose v-said quickly and emolliently. "I just want you to consider how control of the weeds – all the web feeds – makes Jessie quite powerful. If you combine the effects of the weeds with sswipe – just think for a moment what Jessie could do. If people cannot remember – have no way of remembering – what has happened – and the weeds tell a story that is false or only half-credible at the moment, just think what the effect would be. She could undermine trust in us, trust in TCentral and the GLEAKES – and at that point we know there are enough forces out there that could overturn all that we have achieved."

"Ok," Trarieux v-said. "I take your point."

"And?"

"And nothing," Trarieux v-said. "What do you want me to do?"

"I want you to oppose Jessie and ensure that she at least backs down," Ghose v-said. "In my view, however, that won't be enough. She has revealed her hand and her objective – which seems to me to be totally obvious. She wishes to abolish TCentral and replace it with her own rule and power. And we have already seen that she is not in any way a benign person. She is breaking the very foundation of the neo-age. Come with us and let's put this to an end."

"Do you mean to take over Latitude?" Ghose v-asked.

"I don't see any alternative," Ghose v-replied. "Do you?"

"Let me think about it," Trarieux v-said.

"While you're doing that, perhaps Alexandr or Jerry want to add something?" Ghose v-asked.

"To my mind – and it's all I want to say – this move by Jessie is an existential threat and we must oppose her as hard as we can," Fernandes v-said. He was quietly spoken and he almost had a drawl which contrasted well with the seriousness of what he was saying. "I think she has created the end of the current TCentral and spelt out the end of the GLEAKES – and we must remove her from any position of power and take over Latitude."

"Alexandr?" Ghose v-asked.

"I agree with Jerry and with Elora," Dermatov v-said. A burly figure who rather spat out his words. "This is an existential threat. And Sarah – listen to this please – I think you need to understand that we either find a way of lessening her position at the very least or we, preferably, take her out of the equation. I don't mean any violence, but she should be nowhere near the levers of our power."

"This is highly inflammatory stuff, Alexandr, Elora and Jerry," Sousousa v-intervened. "I have heard what you say but speaking for myself, I don't see anything that is going on as a threat to me or my position. TCentral is not essential. We can maintain our power, prestige and position without it. But let me ask Derek first what he thinks at the moment and whether he is convinced by what you, Elora, Jerry and Alexandr have said. Derek?"

"Storm in a tea cup," Smith v-began. "Alarmist nonsense. What can Jessie do without us? I'm with you, Uhuru, in thinking that we are wasting time even considering this. What can she do without us? Answer me that."

"Let me speak first in response to you," Dermatov v-said. "I know that you and I, Derek, have rarely seen eye to eye over anything. But we work together because we recognise the interdependence that has kept us together in power and influence for these past years. Your services underpin nearly everything we do at a physical level. Where would we be without the raw materials that Eclectic supplies and the andros and the autonoms. The very tools that Jessie has brought to bear to gain ascendency. My financial systems in Elura create the wherewithal so you can function effectively in our neo-age – and we are the best example of how interdependence actually creates stability. What Jessie is attempting to do is completely disrupt the interdependence. She wants to appropriate your andros and autonoms – and your services entirely. Do you think there will be any room for you if she manages to do that? What use would you be?"

"You haven't answered my question at all, Alexandr," Smith v-replied. "Better than that – you have actually confirmed my point – that Jessie can't do anything without the rest of us because of the interdependence that is at the heart of TCentral."

"In that case, Derek," Dermatov v-began, "it seems to me that you are not aware of what Jessie has done to upset the equilibrium that we have maintained. That is fundamental to the function of TCentral."

"You don't know that, Alexandr," Smith immediately v-replied. "As far as I can see, all she has done is upset you, Elora and Jerry in some way. I think you should understand that upsetting you three isn't something that particularly concerns me at all. Remember the Guiding Principles – there should be no cartels and no restrictions on what business any of us do."

"Perfectly true as far as it goes," Dermatov v-replied. "But there is more than you realise going on. This morning, for example, the neotiquette team were forcibly removed from their work place and those not there were rounded up and to some extent terrorised. We've managed to release them but – and note that word *release* – they should not have been detained in the first place. Jessie is taking dangerous steps forward. It's not a question of her antagonising Elora, Jerry and me. It's a question of all of our safety. If she's willing to go to those lengths with a team that is hardly at the forefront of her battle for supremacy, what will she do, if given a free rein?"

"I don't think that's worth worrying about," Smith v-said.

"Two more things then," Dermatov came back to him with. He was a thin wiry man and while he was speaking he seemed to push himself forward. It was an illusion as he didn't move, but there was a determination about him that occasionally felt threatening, which was curious to Bartel. "The first is that you know full well that there is a tension – deliberate and unreconciled – between the Guiding Principle that rules out cartels and the vital element that keeps all of the Trills safe from each other, which is, of course, the interdependence that we've already been discussing. Only interdependence safeguards TCentral and the position of each individual Trill. I know you understand that as well as I do."

"Of course I do," Smith v-said. The contrast between the two men – Smith, round, chubby, balding and yet very sharp-eyed and Dermatov's long, very thin body – made the discussion almost comical. "I think I was the one who first established the paradox and explained how important it was to all of us. For heaven's sake, it's not an issue."

"But there is an issue over the cause of the initial dispute that we had in TCentral just before," Dermatov v-said.

"And that is?" Smith v-spoke but was acting as though he was scarcely interested.

"How serious sswipe is," Dermatov v-said, almost spitting out the words, and letting his waspish nature show too much if he really wanted to get Smith on side.

"It's just a new technology," Smith v-said.

"Not in my opinion – and not in Elora and Jerry's opinion," Dermatov v-said. "If all memory can be selectively wiped what on earth do we have that will provide stability and continuity."

"Don't be alarmist, Alexandr," Smith-v-replied. "We have databases that stretch back years and years – they provide a collective memory. We can rely on that. You – I mean anyone – would find it difficult to erase all of those and to ensure that none of the Trills and none of ImCirc would be able to retrieve any information. I'm afraid it's what I said at first. Alarmist nonsense. Don't you agree, Uhuru?"

"I do," Sousousa v-said. "It's difficult enough keeping TCentral working properly without imagining the worst every time there is something that you think is a danger to it."

"Can I come in here – and thank you Alexandr for all that you've said," Fernandes unexpectedly v-intervened. "Let's set aside the actual violence that we've seen these last few hours from Jessie. I don't say forget – and I'm not sure we should ever forgive. But there is an important point here that you, Derek, and you, Uhuru, are missing. Yes – you are right that the databases contain everything and sswipe cannot remove that collective memory. But if Jessie can remove our individual memories – selectively wipe them, remember – then how do we know what we have forgotten. If we don't know the databases, for example, exist, how can we access them?"

"You're playing games now, Jerry," Smith v-said, contemptuously. "Who cares?"

"You should," Fernandes immediately v-retorted. "This isn't mind games or semantics but real. If you have no memory of something how do you know what it is that you need to remember? And if you have no memory of it at all, how would it occur to you to go and find the missing memory?"

Chapter 37

Bartel felt the change in atmosphere within TCentral rather than understood what it was. Both Smith and Sousousa went very quiet. Was it really as game changing as it appeared to be – what had seemed just another line in an argument rather than a decisive thrust?

There were more exchanges but neither Sousousa nor Smith had any ebullience in their manner now. Bartel looked at Trarieux to see if she was affected by the exchanges at all – and Bartel could see that she too was puzzling over this statement.

At that point there was a disturbance and Dressus came into the main chamber of TCentral. Sousousa called her to order as she was at best menacing. It appeared to Bartel that if that didn't convince Smith, Sousousa and Trarieux nothing would.

"What on earth is going on?" Dressus immediately v-demanded. "You call an emergency meeting of TCentral and then debate without me being here. I don't understand you. Yes. We have a disagreement – over sswipe – but that shouldn't be enough to disrupt the whole of what we have."

This seemed completely odd to Bartel and she v-asked Velasquez whether this was as bizarre as she thought it was. According to Velasquez this was about typical of Dressus – who was always the most extreme of the Trills and also one whose understanding of herself and others was at best minimal.

"Do you want to make a formal complaint?" Sousousa not unreasonably v-asked.

"I certainly do," Dressus v-said, almost shouting. "You see me as a threat. To what? I am just establishing my own value and my own power. It doesn't take anything away from any of you? And if you think it does, tell me how."

"Let me try to answer you," Ghose v-replied, quietly and yet insistently. She wasn't going to take no for an answer nor be bullied by Dressus. "As you know, we see sswipe as a direct threat to TCentral and to the control that we Trills exercise over the planet and everyone on it.

411

Yes – we do have a democracy in the world. People other than Trills get to vote and we don't interfere in any of that, no more than the ruling elite interfered in the twentieth and the early part of this century. We control the weeds and the parameters of discussion – so we are well protected and nothing happens that we don't want. And we can vilify and nullify any threats to us – and that control works really well.

"There is some opposition to us but effectively we control that easily. In fact we are extremely relaxed about that opposition – and we let it exist in full sight. But Jessie – think of this. If your sswipe gets into the wrong hands, think what it could do to the managed democracy that we have instituted in the world. With no memory, for example, of what life was like before the neo-age, then why would people appreciate the value of the neo-age that we have ushered in?"

Bartel was expecting her to continue, but she stopped abruptly. It was strange that she had veered away from the arguments that had been used before Dressus arrived. Would that have an effect on Trarieux, Smith and Sousousa?

"That is ridiculous, Elora," Dressus v-replied. "How can it get into the wrong hands. And anyway I didn't think that that was your argument at all. I've been listening in and you and Jerry and Alexandr were talking about a completely different scenario. Are you just making this up as you go along in order to destroy TCentral and the power of the Trills?"

It was very neat the way Dressus was subverting the argument and turning the tables on her opponents by using their arguments and concerns.

"Not at all," Ghose v-replied. "I had thought that this argument – about sswipe getting in the wrong hands – would be far more potent an argument for you. When we were discussing this with Sarah, Derek and Uhuru, we had to understand what it was that was preventing them from seeing the danger that your sswipe posed to us. And we did that. Clearly that wasn't an argument that you would find potent because you apparently feel that sswipe is yours and totally securely yours – and you haven't considered what would happen if it got into the wrong hands."

"Of course I have," Dressus v-responded. "What do you take me for? I know that our position and power is not guaranteed and that it could be taken over by forces that are malign towards us. Which is why we built in so much protection for the application. We are very secure and we know sswipe is very secure."

"Nothing is totally secure," Ghose v-responded. "You know that. If our opposition – feeble though it is – and pusillanimous too – suddenly became capable, there is no way safeguards would prevent them – whoever they are – from deploying sswipe and using it against us. We are at a crossroads here, as you well know, Jessie."

"Hardly," Dressus v-said.

"You have effectively made a bid for total power," Ghose v-continued. "No – don't protest. We know that's what you have done. You can deny it and I know you will, but we know the truth. You have attacked the very foundation of our continuing power and position, Jessie. You know that and we know that. TCentral is vital – and you are trying to bypass it. The Guiding Principles are vital too – and you are attacking them. Without the veneer of legitimacy that they give us, we are likely to find our uncontested power and position under threat and attack – and not just from the idealists who think that we have completely subverted human aspirations and human nature by creating the neo-age, but from really effective people who wish to overthrow us, not to create a better world, but in order to give themselves our power, privileges and position. We keep those forces under control – our gramscian programmes ensure that – but once you open the floodgates of opposition and give whoever is in a strong enough position to take us on, and they will be malign, an opportunity, we will be on the back foot. You recognise implicitly that you are undermining TCentral and what we stand for. You are doing that deliberately. But we can't let you do that."

"How are you going to stop me?" Suddenly Dressus introduced a completely different tone into the argument.

"I can't tell you that," Ghose v-replied. "What I can tell you is that we will use everything in our power to stop you because what you are doing is throwing open the world to anarchy – an anarchy that will sweep not only TCentral away but also you and all of us."

"You can't stop me," Dressus v-said. "I now control pretty much everything. It is naïve of you, Elora, to imagine that I started this without a plan and without the preparations that would be required. My people and my andros control the levers of power now. You think that interdependence is the safeguard to the rule of the Trills and to the position of TCentral. What you have is actually nothing. The interdependence that you imagined meant that I couldn't take full power, has actually worked in my favour. None of you can do anything without each other – and you are essentially weak. You are, not to mince my words, trapped here in TCentral – and I have the levers of power. If you resist me, then you know that TCentral is at an end and the Trills are effectively no more. This whole campus – not just this building – is under my control and you either do what I ask, or I will bring the whole edifice tumbling down."

Bartel watched the faces of Sousousa, Trarieux and Smith as they realised that they had been wrong not to oppose Dressus.

"What are you going to do, Jessie? Kill us?" Ghose v-asked.

"That shouldn't be necessary," Dressus v-responded. "I'm sure you will see that you have no alternative to accepting my terms. So you have half an hour to consider what I've said. Remember that TCentral as it is currently – is dead. It will continue of course, as we have to maintain the illusions that we created and now that I control everything, I will do whatever is necessary to consolidate my position. I'm very happy for the GLEAKES to appear to carry on, but I am prepared to make changes to consolidate my position. So get considering."

Dressus left the chamber.

"Let me say first of all that I got this entirely wrong," Sousousa immediately v-said. "I never believed that Jessie would ever attempt such a thing. I guess that goes for you, Derek?"

"Yes," Smith v-said, very shaken. "What has just happened?"

"What we warned you was happening," Ghose v-said. "Sarah – I expect you are as shaken as the rest of us. Is that true?"

"Shaken?" Trarieux v-asked. "I never believed it would come to this. I thought our interdependence meant that we were all protected and that TCentral was sacrosanct. Did you know anything about this – Jerry, Elora, Alexandr?"

"No – we weren't expecting this, although the strong arm tactics with, of all people, the neotiquette team did suggest to me, at least, that there was more afoot," Fernandes quickly v-interjected.

"So what do we do?" Ghose v-asked. "Let's not waste time imagining what we got wrong or how we got it wrong. This is the end of the GLEAKES as we have known it. We always thought that there would be an external threat, which is why we were so good at surveillance and why we maintained what seemed to be a total openness to the various groups who were opposed to us and the power of TCentral. I don't think any of our defences will work against an internal threat such as Jessie now poses. In a real sense all our internal controls work now to her advantage."

"I think that's true," Fernandes immediately v-said. "What indeed is to be done?"

"Let's be serious. First of all we need to question whether it is possible that she is in total control. What do you think?" Ghose v-asked. "To answer my own question, I would have thought that whatever control she is exercising is inadequate and that the populations of the countries will immediately know something is up and, as we have always agreed, the impression of stability is as important as stability itself. If that goes – and presumably it well might – then the stability of the neo-age will be under threat. No amount of re-assuring information through the weeds can actually deny reality for very long. It will work for a short period, obviously, but not in the longer term."

"Not entirely true," Dermatov v-said quickly. "Just remember how much we initially had to propagandise in order to establish the neo-age – and most of that was not actually perceivable until say twelve months after we initiated the neo-age."

"And remember the experience in the twentieth and the first two or three decades of the twenty first – when the Bills and then the first generation Trills bought the politics of most of the countries round the world and most of that was based on falsehoods," Fernandes v-said, ruefully.

"With the added bonus that several of them muddied the whole thing by claiming that what was said in what passed for weeds in those days – I think it was called the media and social media – was so-called *fake news*,"

Dermatov v-added. "In the end no-one believed a word of anything in a complete justification of the arendtian thesis. This then meant that the Bills and then those Trills who usurped them could virtually do anything."

"But we cleaned that up," Ghose v-said. "When we took over, we instituted the Guiding Principles. Do you think people are that gullible that Jessie can just over-ride whatever it is that people see – even with, say, shortages of food?"

"Remember sado-populism," Fernandes v-said. "They got people to accept worsening conditions for themselves – and even more bizarrely, worsening conditions from those for their children, by pretending that although things were bad, it was worse for another group in society – and that divide and discriminate process worked. Remember people were allowed to vote in those days too – and the Bills and first generation Trills controlled what they could vote for by demonising anyone who challenged them. And having taken over all the forms of information they could – and having bought the so-called politicians, for very little as it happens, and they called it making donations when it was clearly bribes – their rule was secure."

"Until they went too far," Ghose v-said, soberly. "Remember that – there was that point when the rioting and the civil disobedience started and then came the initial crack downs and then more and more abusive controls were brought in, until the whole thing broke. You can distort reality only so much."

"But that went on for years before the system collapsed as the Bills, then the first generation Trills struggled and couldn't understand why their power was edging away," Fernandes v-said. "We haven't got years. I think we're wasting time and we've got about ten minutes."

"So what do we do?" Sousousa asked.

"What can we do is a better question," Ghose v-said.

"We can pretend to go along with what Jessie wants," Smith v-said.

"That will last about five minutes," Ghose v-said, quickly. "No. we need an immediate plan. Can we sabotage gSynth again, Jerry?"

"Be difficult and, as you pointed out when I did that, self-defeating," Fernandes v-replied. "We need to ask for an extension as we can't work out our plan in the few minutes remaining. Can you contact her Elora?"

"Ok," Ghose v-said. She tried to engage Dressus. There was no response. Then suddenly there was a question from Dressus. "We need more time," Ghose t-said, including the other Trills in her t-comms. "We realise the position we are in and we recognise that you hold most – not all – of the cards. We therefore need a little while to understand what we think we can do and how we can do it to meet your demands."

"So you understand that I am in total control?" Dressus t-asked.

"We don't know that," Ghose t-said. "We imagine that is the case. But Jessie – we have worked together long enough to know what you are capable of. So we are not thinking we can do anything except accommodate you. At the moment we need time to work out what that means. For example, we want to come up with questions for you."

"Such as?"

"Such as," Ghose t-said, rapidly trying to bring up appropriate questions, "what role you envisage for each of us – if you do, that is."

"That's valid," Dressus t-said. "I'll give you an hour more. But that's it. Anything more and I know you will be working out how to sidestep me – and that's a waste of time. A waste of my time – and yours because you cannot find a way to block me. Now – an hour." She cut off the engagement.

To Bartel it looked as though the six Trills were paralysed, which was something of a shock as all the weeds and all the indications emphasised the view that they were indefatigable and resourceful. It was fascinating and at the same time Bartel was amazed that she would be able to see this with her own eyes. Clearly none of this would be reported and even if the six Trills were eliminated by Dressus in whatever way she might be able to do that, they would still continue to exist as holos at the very least. That was a worrying and scary thought on top of everything else.

Bartel was expecting that Ghose would take the lead again – although she wasn't sure why that should be so, but Ghose looked just as beaten as the other ones.

"Do we have a choice now?" Fernandes eventually v-asked.

"We must have," Ghose v-replied. "I'm not sure what it is. I think first of all we have to work out what the current position is. What levers and tools does Jessie have and what have we got to withstand her? It seems to me to be absurd that the Trill who has really only got experience engines can dominate the rest of us so easily."

"Remember she also controls pretty much all of the weeds and the other media and that does give her tremendous power," Fernandes v-responded.

"True and in the neo-age – much like the twentieth and early twenty first – that is an enormous advantage," Ghose v-agreed. "But we still have interdependence. She doesn't have resources, raw materials. She doesn't control gSynth as we said. She hasn't got persono and socio. We still control all of that, plus the health systems, the legal systems, financial systems however virtual all of them are, and raw materials. How has she managed to gain control over us when we have all of those at our disposal? Derek – all your services and all your andros. How has she taken control of those without you knowing? Or has she?"

"I can't get hold of my management team," Smith v-said. "My supposition is that she has neutralised them somehow or other and has taken control of all the services. I guess that my indifference to what she was doing allowed her to take over control without me realising."

"No time to tell you we told you so," Ghose v-said. "But we did. Ok. Water under the bridge. We have to be able to fight back."

"What about persono and socio – your responsibility, Elora?" Sousousa asked.

"They are essential to neo-age life, of course they are," Ghose v-agreed, "but you see Jessie is using them in a quite canny way. I could obviously – well, I hope I still could – turn them off. But you know what the problem is. If we were to do so, then everybody in the world will know that there is anarchy in TCentral and the position of the GLEAKES will be compromised and it would cause an immediate loss of confidence in us – in the Trills – and without that confidence, who knows what might happen to TCentral and our power. You see? That's why she is being so clever. We can't actually admit that there is dissension in TCentral without it meaning that TCentral and the power of the Trills will be questioned. And then stability – the stability we've fought tooth and nail to create – will be lost. If people don't believe that we are acting in their best interests, then we are finished. You know that. That might sound too dramatic – but at the very least that is the calculation that Jessie is working to, and she expects us to realise that, and accept the fait accompli that she has managed to deliver."

"Isn't that too defeatist, Elora?" Dermatov v-said. "What resources do we have? That's where we should start. Come on – we're wasting time. We've lost the initiative as we weren't united against Jessie – but let's regain some semblance of our confidence in ourselves and focus on what we can do and can do now."

"All right, Jerry," Ghose v-replied. "I just don't know what. Do we give in – and let her win or do we have any way of resisting what she's doing? It seems crazy to me that the whole edifice of the neo-age can crumble with just this assault – from a person who doesn't even control the main levers of power – the interpersonal systems, the food supplies, the supplies."

"We have one immediate weapon," Smith v-said.

"And that is?" Sousousa v-asked sceptically.

"She doesn't expect us to resist," Smith v-replied. "It's clear that she believes this is a fait accompli and we can do nothing."

"Not much of a weapon," Ghose v-said.

"But we can cut off all supplies, we can ensure that, for example, gSynth doesn't work and we can make sure that Eclectic doesn't provide the raw materials and services," Smith v-said. "That, at least, is in my gift."

"But that's precisely the point," Ghose v-said. "In effect you are saying that to resist her and her destruction of our collective power as Trills we have to demonstrate to everyone else that the neo-age isn't working. It may be the right thing to do, but it will have hideous consequences. The stability that we've all fought for and established after the neo-liberalism and sado-populism of the early twenty first will be threatened. In effect TCentral will be over."

"But I think that what Jessie has demonstrated is that TCentral was built on a concept that hasn't worked," Smith v-replied. "We all thought that interdependence between the seven of us meant that we would be stable. Yes – of course we said that there were no cartels, but that's what we said. We knew it wasn't true – and you don't have to have a gramscian thought to know that's true."

"But that will open up a can of worms – I mean that will unleash a catastrophe," Ghose v-replied. "If we show that the neo-age is unstable, then every potential Trill who wants to replace us or, perhaps, join us, will spot an opportunity to overthrow us, anyway. And we know that the opposition groups will use the opportunity to destabilise the neo-age for their own ends. They may at this moment appear to be altruistic – you know, all those high-minded statements about the neo-age being amblytopia and they want to re-establish aspiration and achievement because we have taken away any necessity for struggle in people's lives – but who doubts that within a short period of time, individual ambition and individual interests will mean that this opposition will become corrupt."

"The one thing you can say about us," Fernandes v-added, "is that we're not corrupt."

"That's a very narrow definition of not being corrupt, if I may say so," Ghose v-replied. "To the outside world we may say that and we may mean it. But if you define corruption – as I am at the moment – as bending everything to our personal ends, to creating truths that are at best half truths – no matter that we think it is to a good end – then we are corrupt. The only thing you can say about us not being corrupt is that since we have almost total power – despite the much vaunted claims of democracy throughout the world – we haven't needed to get more power and wealth, and we have recognised that to preserve our position we have to create the neo-age, where we have bought off all opposition, just like the ruling classes did after the Second World War."

"Ok," Fernandes v-conceded, "you are right, of course, Elora. But we are becoming just theoretical. What is there to be done?"

"If I may say something," Dermatov v-began, having been silent and just listening, looking as though he was unconcerned, "there's a way that we can thwart Jessie without exposing ourselves to attacks."

"And that is, Alexandr?" Ghose v-asked sceptically.

"My control of the financial system is part of the answer, as I see it," Dermatov v-said. His thin, wiry body which was usually apparently relaxed, seemed to be quivering with power. "Jessie obviously doesn't need money in any sense – certainly not in the sense that we use money in the neo-age – except one. Money as such has no value in the neo-age. It acts only as a constraint on excess – and we regulate it well enough. What if we flood the world with money?"

"Won't that just destabilise the neo-age in itself," Ghose v-asked. She seemed to be the one who was playing the part of devil's advocate.

"It may well," Dermatov v-agreed. "The point is that if we manage to get the news out about her attempted – or actual, I should say – coup and then people find that what they understand about their financial position is in fact untrue, we will create a general opposition to her. If money means nothing – and we know it basically does mean nothing in our post twentieth world – as opposed to the structures of thought that we so busily use to suggest otherwise, then we have a weapon that we could direct against Jessie."

"As the Spartans so rightly said when threatened by the Athenians, who said that *if we win against you, we will murder all your children, rape all your women, enslave every male and eradicate your rule for ever*, just one word *if*," Ghose v-replied. "You said *if we manage to get the word out* – and remember that Jessie controls all the weeds apart from Tryptic – and she may have that under control now – and every other means of communication."

"Not so – even though that is a powerful argument against me," Dermatov v-replied. "You, Elora control persono and socio. And you may still have Tryptic. We can use that. If I put in place the mechanism to effectively destroy the so-called value of all the currencies, which I can do quickly by distributing as much money as we think it will take, and you immediately launch a socio assault on people's consciousness tying this into an attack by Jessie on TCentral and the Trills, we have a chance to undermine her position, perhaps threaten a general uprising against her, and thwart her ambitions."

"Seems a long shot to me," Ghose v-replied. "What do other people think?"

"It has the merit of doing something and not just rolling over in the face of such a severe threat to all of us and the neo-age," Fernandes v-said. "You may, however, be right, Elora, that doing that will destroy the credibility of the neo-age and we may lose because of that. But what's the alternative."

"I wouldn't want it to come to this," Trarieux v-said. "From my point of view, I would have thought that our AI systems should have warned us about all of this – but since they haven't, I don't know what else we can do. I'm in with Alexandr's approach. Everything that I have fought for over the years, from when I developed Sapiens, has been focused on *what ifs* and creating mitigation plans, but this has exposed a serious weakness in what I have been doing. I don't feel proud of that nor about my passivity initially when Jessie created her coup. We have to resist – and if we lose the neo-age in the process, I can't see we have an alternative."

"Uhuru?" Ghose v-asked.

"There is no alternative," Sousousa v-replied.

"There is always an alternative," Ghose v-said, quite angrily. "It's defeatist to say that and I've fought against that all my life. There is always an alternative and it's never a good reason to stick to something because you think there's no other way."

"Does that mean you are opposed?" Smith v-asked.

"No," Ghose v-replied, with a defeated look on her face.

"Let's do it," Smith v-said. "Elora – get your people and andros focused now on this. Use the neotiquette team to craft the outgoing messages."

"Why them?" Ghose v-asked.

"They understand how people think – that's their job or role, should I say," Smith v-replied. "I will instruct my andros and management team now. Let's do it."

Bartel had watched and listened in astonishment, partly because it emphasised how significant Dressus's actions had been, and how effective they had been, partly because it revealed something she had begun to suspect, that the Trills were more vulnerable than she had imagined, partly because the Trills collectively had scarcely risen immediately to the challenge and partly because she realised that Pennington and his opposition wasn't as nugatory as she had imagined. TCentral was there for the taking, it seemed to her, so no matter what transpired now and whether she thought Pennington was right or not – and she still didn't know – she knew that something had changed completely.

Characters

Bartel, Emma	Imagineer of experiences
Bartel, Roseanne	Emma Bartel's elder daughter
Bartel, Alice	Emma Bartel's second daughter
Dermatov, Alexandr	CEO Elura
Dressus, Jessie	aka JD – CEO Latitude
Dunster, Wilfred	Bartel's lover in TCentral and member of the neotiquette team
Fernandes, Jerry	CEO Gyro
Ghose, Elora	C EO Kalo
Pennington, Andrew	Emma Bartel's friend – sometimes with benefits
Savery, Jonas	Works with Bartel
Smith, Derek	CEO Eclectic
Sousousa, Uhuru	CEO Ambience
Tomlinson, Jeannette	Elora Ghose's close friend and confidante and Bartel's client
Tomlinson, Reginald	Elora Ghose's close friend and confidant and Bartel's client
Trarieux, Sarah	CEO Sapiens
Velasquez, Serena	Director General, New Initiatives Kalo
Worrell, Dave	Lives with Cheryl

Glossary

Accel	Accelerated learning
AI	Artificial intelligence – sometimes called artificial ignorance by wits
Amblytopia	Greyness and dull – not a dystopia nor a utopia.
Andro	Android made by Eclectic
Arendtian	The ideas of Hannah Arendt
Aspirations	Shortages
Autonom	Autonomous vehicle – car by Eclectic
Bezo	(Verb) To create the separate world of the Trills
Brainsharing	Brainstorming with thoughts
Bubonic	Viral
Deflection	Politics as we understand it.
Diffusing	Sharing via socio
Dread-Demotic	Bartel's ground breaking experience
Edu-world	Universal curriculum
El-icopter	Electric helicopter
El-ipad	Electric helicopter helipad
Encounter	Physical meeting
Engagement	Virtual meeting
Enquire	T-ask
Equilibrium	Balancing doing things against just being indolent
Exo-sim	Virtual reality physical suit
Experience	A virtual world of challenge – c/f a video game

Eye-display	Smart glasses
Eye-screen	Enhanced reality screen below the eye
Feedcaster	Journalists for feeds
Gramscian	Using Antonio Gramsci's ideas – essentially creating hegemonic control through media
Grooming	Preparing people to be part of the Trills' outer circle
gSynth	Synthesised food and the synthesised food preparer
Guardians	The surveillance teams
Handro	Hologram andro
Hedo	Hedonist
Holo	Hologram
ImCirc	Immediate circle of the Trills
Incise	To question using thoughts
Inconsistencies	Where the technology really doesn't provide the full scale environment for human life – some human medical interventions for example
INsighto	Artificial intelligence in inanimate objects – underpins all – Apple
Intrusion	Presence of a third party in your persono or socio
Kautonom	A Kalo version of the autonom
Medi-Assist	Diagnostic medical tool
Medi-stat	Medical status
Mephi	Mephistopheles or sort of spirit guide – here it is Velasquez
Murdoch	(Verb) To be mean or economical or to be penny-pinching.

Neo-age	The culture of the age of the Trills
Neotiquette	Post socio and persono neo-age sexual and personal etiquette
Paleo-age	Pre turning point, pre-Trills' neo-age
Persono	The parallel system to brain memory which holds all your own personal details and which has controls so you can let people in to part of it, all of it or none of it.
	Contains diary, agenda, access to internet, and is the tool that socio runs on; embedded chip
	Equivalent to a smart phone with three internal levels:
	Lock
	Open
	Clarity
	Filters:
	Closeness
	Significance
	Appropriateness
	Unknown
	Random
Plastic	Having form and substance
Probe	Interrogating another's database of personal information
Project	Reply in thoughts
R button	Recharge button for socio implant
Scenario	The environment created by Sofari from an experience imagined
Sensitive	Virtual

Sensuo-Contacta	Bartel's scenario where she improvised sexual experiences
Serene	Between Hedo and Spartan
Setiquette	Socio etiquette – the original concept behind neotiquette
Singularity	A fully personally controlled holo
Soapy	Shorthand for rather complex and contradictory relationships
Socio	It allows transmission of thoughts – again with controls:
	Lock – *as private as possible*
	Bland – first level access for other people: they can receive your thoughts but only the ones you direct at them
	Acquaintance – second level, allowing thoughts to be transmitted or probed that are consciously allowed
	Friend – third level access, allowing people to have access to unguarded thoughts
	Relaxed – total access within the limits of the technology
Sofari	The equivalent of *paint* but in 3D, with physical sensations and complex interpersonal reactions – a video virtual environment brought to life with the Eye-Screen and other features.
Spartan	Ascetic
sswipe	Selective memory wiping – lower case sswipe

Surfeit	When a person is overwhelmed by the opportunities that are presented
T-	Thought
T-call	Thought call
TCentral	The Trills' quasi parliament – more a mediation service and law enforcement service
T-comms	Thought communications
Thought-trans	ESP
Treaty of Delphi	The historic treaty which entrenched the power of the second generation Trills and delineated their spheres of influence – so *no cartels* **but** also interdependence as a safeguard against one of them becoming too powerful
T-reply	Thought reply
Trills	Trillionaires
Tryptico	24 hour news, current affairs and tech developments. From Latitude – a small rival to Veritable
T-searching	Rummaging through someone's thoughts
Turing	The standard for androids and holograms
Turning point	The moment the second generation Trills became all powerful
Twentieth	20th century
Twenty first	21st century
V-	Voice

Value	The equivalent of money
V-call	Voice call
V-comms	Voice communications
Verisimilitude	How accurately an andro resembles a human
Veritable	News organisation controlled by Latitude
VR	Virtual reality
V-reply	Voice reply
Weeds	Web feeds
Weinsteining	Taking advantage of someone – usually younger – from a position of greater power and influence

GLEAKES and Products

GLEAKES	Ambience, Kalo, Gyro, Eclectic, Sapiens, Elura, Latitude
Ambience	The health and legal system.
	All products have Care in the name – hospcare; homecare; seniorcare, judicialcare
Eclectic	Service provider and manufacturer and source of raw materials.
	All products have a hyphen and capital letters and usually *assist*– Medi-Assist; Home-Assist; Office-Assist; Make-Assist; Materials-Assist; Indi-assist; Mobility-Assist – the real name for autonoms; Rest-Assist
Elura	Finance system based on blockchain and virtual currencies: all products begin with El – El-balance, El-card, El-pay
Gyroscope	Food, drugs and consumables. All applications have a *g* at the beginning – gSynth.
Kaleidoscope	Socio – thought communications; Persono – personal assistant and personal database
Latitude	The environment that Bartel and Savery work in – utilising Sapiens, particularly Exo-Sim, and Kalo infrastructure including INsighto. Main product is Sofari: *sofa; so far; safari*; uses Sapiens; also owns or controls all the weeds – web feeds, excluding Tryptico. Veritable is the news provider for example

Sapiens   The artificial intelligence provider –
               developed from search. INsighto the
               major product. First two letters
               capitalised.

Guiding Principles

Owner	Principle	Comments
Kalo	No cartels – free competition	But total surveillance and subject to First Amendment
Eclectic	Nothing should interfere with innovation	Innovation by the Trills
Sapiens	No coercion and, at the same time, no tolerance of hate crimes – and a focus on the surface meaning – and an absolute respect at all times for the rule of law	Laws of course belong to the Trills
Gyroscope	As little interference in free will as is possible – where it doesn't impinge on someone else. So no restrictions on drugs, sexual orientation or sex, religious activism, political activism	Ambience also responsible for policing this – with its justice andros

Owner	Principle	Comments
Latitude	Freedom of thought – religion, political beliefs, methods of association, criticism of any political system or statements	Provisos around causing mental or physical harm to anyone which must be prevented
Ambience	Total health care – including preventative medicine – and full legal protection	A background service
Elura	Freedom from financial worries for all	Ability to afford inessential items strictly controlled
GLEAKES	Everything should be transparent and open to analysis and examination	But reveal as little about the real world of the Trills
GLEAKES	**First amendment:** Competition, co-opitition and co-operation	Making interdependence a vital element of TCentral